Unknown Variable

J.W. Clay

Picture City Press, LLC, Virginia, 23510

Published 2024

Printed in the United States of America

ISBN-13: 978-1-950342-13-6 (softcover)

ISBN-13: 978-1-950342-12-9 (ebook)

Editing services provided by: John Paine

Editing services provided by: Jenna Love-Schrader

Proof Reading services provided by: Katherine Stevens

Cover design provided by: Dissect Designs

One

Mexico City, Mexico

Flashlight beams glide across a row of chemical tanks suspended on a storage rack that rises forty feet in the air. Green, white, orange—the colors correspond to the chemical contents in each. Some are for industrial use. Others medical. More for laboratories. A select few have extremely dangerous chemicals hidden inside.

Terrance Kline is walking between the racks, searching. The warehouse is owned and operated by one of Mexico's largest chemical distributors: World Chem. It's pitch black, save the flashlight beam. It's also past midnight, and employees are home in bed, giving him free rein to conduct his investigation.

Terrance freezes as his flashlight beam finds a row of white tanks on the rack's second level. They're large. Five feet tall. Likely over a hundred and fifty pounds. The white paint is a warning; explosive propane gasses are inside. He glances toward his partner, nods.

"I'm carrying all of the heavy stuff," Robert "Bobby" Hollice says, who is a member of the U.S. Army's elite counter-terrorism unit known as the Combat Applications Group, or Delta Force.

Terrance appraises the man across from him, who is wearing a lightweight assaulter's kit accompanied by a suppressed H&K MP7 submachine gun. A week's worth of brown scruff covers his rugged, probing face, which is rounded out by a prize-winning tan from a recent holiday in Syria. His six-foot frame packs two hundred pounds of muscle. Easy climb, despite the gear. "Weight is a subjective term. What may be heavy to you may not—"

"Nope," Bobby interrupts with a smirk. "I'm pulling security, remember? Don't worry . . . I'll catch you if you fall."

Terrance sighs. "Don't remember the last time I climbed anything. Probably never."

It's true. Terrance is a buck twenty, and that's soaking wet. Physical fitness isn't his gift. He's a genius, having earned a PhD in computer science by the time he was twenty-two. The first African American to achieve the feat in Harvard's history.

Terrance approaches the rack, planting a foot on a crossbar. He places his hand on a rusty piece of metal, gives it a tug. Solid. He manages a couple of big heaves and reaches the second level. Easier than expected. Proud of himself, he begins traversing the rack. Maybe he's more suited for field work than he thought.

"Aren't you glad we wouldn't give you a gun?" Bobby asks, amused as Terrance struggles between pallets full of tanks.

Terrance momentarily loses focus, glares down at Bobby. "No."

He continues, hands latched onto the overhead shelving. He reaches the white propane tanks, studies them. Nothing special, at least not to the untrained eye. Warning labels. Serial numbers. A barcode, which Terrance photographs with his phone.

Placing the phone back in his pocket, he pulls a gas mask off of his belt. Before securing it over his face, he says, "Mask up! Unless you wanna take the ride of your life."

"Hate to pass up a good time," Bobby replies.

While his companion dons protective gear, Terrance unscrews the nearest tank's protective cap, revealing a valve. He extracts a drug testing kit from his pocket and dons latex gloves to protect his hands from the kit's acid. Next, he removes a cotton swab, hovering it over the tank's nozzle. Turning the valve unleashes a bolt of white vapor. It wafts upward into the atmosphere before dispersing.

Terrance tears open the test pack and dips the swab into the liquid. It flushes blue in seconds. Confirmation. The tank is full of superheated liquid cocaine, around twenty-five kilos' worth. Estimated value of a single tank? Hundreds of thousands of dollars.

It's a perfect ruse to smuggle drugs into the United States of America. Propane tanks use high-quality valves and gaskets that won't leak, a requirement to transport combustible liquids. It also enables them to defeat drug-sniffing K9s. X-rays show a belly full of liquid, just like the hundreds of other chemical tanks that pass into the United States every day. The men who run this warehouse have smuggled millions of dollars' worth of cocaine directly past U.S. customs agents.

"How's it lookin'?" Bobby asks.

Terrance tosses the baggie to him. "Got 'em." He climbs down while Bobby examines the kit. Reaching ground level, he says, "Let's find the computers. We have to figure out where they get this stuff."

Newspaper, yellow and stale from the sun, is taped over a glass window. Rocco Gutierrez reaches up, pinches an ear, and begins tearing downward. The open sliver gives him a decent view of World Chem, the warehouse just across the street from his own.

It's a building he's accustomed to seeing. For twelve straight days he's been living in the same office. No running water. No electricity. No security cameras or computers to make surveillance easier. His boss, Alex Varga, had been adamant about the last part. No technology—not even a cell phone. The only device he has in his possession is a battery-operated analog radio scanner. Capable of intercepting his "go" orders from several miles away—and little else.

"Rocco."

The whisper was barely audible.

Rocco turns to find a trusted subordinate standing in the doorway. The man's frame is large, matching that of Rocco's. Aztec tattoos turn the silhouette a shade darker. While Rocco can't see it, his subordinate has a piercing in his bottom lip, mirroring that of an Aztec warrior.

Always there, like his own. They were gifts bestowed on them both after proving their loyalty to Alex Varga, Mexico's most ruthless cartel boss.

"The Americans are here."

Rocco heads toward a desk, abandoned when the previous tenant vacated the premises. Weeks' worth of food wrappers are piled on the surface. Mounds of empty water bottles are tall enough to hit the ceiling tiles. He looks over to the bucket in the corner. Hasn't gotten used to the stench, but he won't have to tolerate it after tonight.

After grabbing the analog radio scanner off the desk, Rocco starts for the office door. Senses guide the way, along with a few errant rays of moonlight. "Won't be long," he whispers, reaching his man.

The subordinate gently taps the receiver of his AK-47. "We're ready."

Two

Bobby stops in front of a thick wooden door, settles the visible laser of his MP7 on the glass nameplate. The red beam bursts and splinters as it crosses the CEO's name. Their primary objective is waiting inside. He tries the knob, and it turns. "Was hopin' for some fun . . ."

Terrance gives Bobby a pained look. "Your knees will thank you in a few years. Mine already hurt from the climb."

Bobby chuckles. "How have you managed to live this long?"

Terrance doesn't reply. He is focused on the next target: two computers sitting on the desk of the CEO. He sits in the office chair and appraises both. One is hooked into a broader network used by the company's employees. The second is offline and air-gapped, meaning it has never been exposed to the internet.

He extracts his laptop, hooking it to the air-gapped computer. Once everything is plugged in, he turns on both computers. They finish booting, and he opens a command application on his personal device. He types a command: *Anne, run a vulnerability analysis.*

"Initiating, Mr. Kline," Anne replies via the laptop's speakers. *Anne* is short for Advanced NeuroNet Engine. It's a quantum computer system engineered by Andrew Xiao during his tenure at the Massachusetts Institute of Technology. When it comes to hacking and digital security, the technology is revolutionary. Nothing is capable of withstanding the assault of a quantum computer.

The analysis indicates that the target computer is running an outdated version of Windows XP. Multiple known vulnerabilities exist.

"Let's insert a payload . . ." Terrance whispers. He begins scrolling through a list of malware inside a purpose-built hacking system and lands on *Broken Glass*, which is what happens when a stone hits a window pane, or in this case, his malware hits a vulnerable version of Windows XP.

Run my selection, Anne.

"Initiating intrusion."

Anne works quickly. The payload is injected into the target computer, exploiting a vulnerability in the login screen, allowing Terrance to bypass it. The home screen becomes visible, along with dozens of files.

The next task is an easy one: exposing the computer to the internet. He selects the *World Chem* SSID from the network menu and joins. He beats the password prompt by pressing the button on the router neatly placed on the CEO's desk. Hacking made easy.

Anne, begin uploading local contents to the tactical operations center.

The process starts from the target laptop, allowing him to disconnect his personal device and stow it. Every piece of sensitive information about World Chem's operation is being stolen. Customers. Transport routes into the United States. Shipment volumes and revenue.

Gabriella Martinez's voice sounds through Terrance's radio. She's the CIA officer in charge, and ordered the night's intrusion. "We're receiving, Medusa Three," she says, using Terrance's call sign. "Four minutes and you're home free."

Ten men are clustered inside a semi-trailer parked in World Chem's back lot. It's a sauna; blankets with lead cores have been screwed to the ceiling and walls. More have been laid down on the floor in an effort to defeat the thermal-imaging equipment attached to an American surveillance drone thousands of feet overhead.

Alejandro wipes sweat off his brow. Keeps it from stinging his eyes and clouding his vision. Other than that, the effort is pointless. Everything from his shirt to his socks are soaked. Nearby water bottles are brimming with electrolytes. Only seven hours into a twelve-hour shift, and he reminds himself to ration the water, no matter how bad the dehydration feels.

The only light source inside the trailer is an orange LED screen on his analog radio scanner. He double-checks it. Finds it set to the correct frequency. The glow provides enough light to survey his men—his soldiers.

No way to see their eyes, but their backs are not slumping. Small air vents cut into the trailer's floor keeps their oxygen supply steady. Rifles are pointed upward, under control. *Warriors,* he reminds himself. They've earned the title directly from Varga. Despite the scanner's silence, he's certain they'll be putting their skills to work shortly.

A vehicle is idling just feet away from the trailer. The V-8 engine sounds old. Steady knocking vibrates through the trailer's metal walls. Alejandro has been rotating in and out of this trailer for almost two straight weeks. Never once heard a noise like that at this hour.

A call comes through the scanner. The voice is scrambled, machine-like. "Warehouse is *go.*"

Without a word, Alejandro and his men begin stacking up on the trailer's doors. Silent footsteps on the lead blankets. Rifles kept away from anything that'll knock. Five men on the side door, facing the rumbling V-8. Another five on the back door, ready to stream into the warehouse. But their hands stay frozen on the latches.

Those orders weren't for Alejandro. Theirs will be coming shortly, when the time is just right.

Martinez's voice comes through Bobby's radio. "We've got movement inbound on your position—twenty hostiles and climbing. ETA, one minute. Get out now."

Bobby instantly generates a tactical assessment. The enemy is directly on top of his position; it didn't happen by accident. They were prepared. "Copy your last, TOC. Moving to exit now."

Terrance continues hammering on the air-gapped computer's keyboard, concerned that his hacking tools will fall into an adversary's hands. With a final few jabs he deletes the malware. Before he is fully closed out, Bobby rips him out of the office chair.

Shadows begin creeping in through the office windows. Dozens, jerking violently, propelled forward by orange streetlights. They bob and weave and climb the walls until their owners arrive, accompanied by the sound of stomping boots, falling safeties, and bolts shoveling ammunition out of fresh magazines.

Bobby pushes Terrance out of the office as the breach starts. Orange muzzle flashes leap out, painting their faces as they pass not ten feet from World Chem's front entrance. Bullets eviscerate the glass doors. Shards of glass blanket the floor.

With one hand driving Terrance forward, Bobby twists and flips the safety on his MP7 to sustained fire. Keeping the weapon's stock locked under his armpit, he begins punishing the cartel gunmen as they try to make entry. The fatal funnel—the riskiest portion of any breach. Nowhere to hide, only one pathway for bullets to travel.

Bobby depresses the trigger and doesn't stop until he feels the bolt lock rearward. Audible cracks and crunches and snaps fill the lobby—bullets finding bone or metal or soft tissue. Four wounded or dead cartel members are left in his wake as he pushes Terrance down the final stretch of hallway leading to the warehouse floor.

Shocked cartel gunmen are forced to duck for cover. They angle their rifle muzzles past stalactites of shattered glass and blindly fire into the lobby. Muzzle blasts dislodge chunks of glass in the door. Bullets pepper the walls. Chunks of wood explode off of desks. More tear through ceiling tiles. Polystyrene drifts in the air like a winter blizzard.

Bobby guides Terrance into the maze of tanks as bullets snap at their backs. The cartel gunmen are too rattled to deliver accurate fire, but they're bloodthirsty. Sharp metal thwacks echo in the warehouse as rounds pierce chemical tanks suspended on racks. Gas hisses and vapor clouds form.

A nearby rack full of tanks is ideal cover, and Bobby shoves Terrance into safety. He forces Terrance down and maintains physical contact with the man he's protecting—losing sight of him in a situation like this would be a catastrophe.

"Masks up!" Bobby yells.

Both men rush to don their masks, already tasting chemicals on their tongues. What they're inhaling could be deadly.

Bobby gets his mask on quickly, then begins to help Terrance. The hacker's hands are shaking badly, and he's struggling. Once the straps are tight, he shouts, "You got a good seal?"

Terrance takes in several deep breaths. The mask sucks against his cheeks. "Yeah! Thanks!"

Bobby performs a quick reload and begins preparing to dust the cartel thugs ruining his evening. Two smoke grenades are extracted from his kit. Safety rubber bands are uncoiled from around the spoons, and he pulls the pins, tossing them into the racks. "TOC, talk to me! What's going on?"

"Keep moving to the rear exit, Medusa One," Martinez replies. "Your egress is clear from the back of the warehouse."

"Don't think it's a good idea to hang around here much longer!" Bobby shouts, then grabs Terrance by the arm. They begin snaking through the racks as the gunmen fire blindly into the smoke. They're held up by a mixture of blindness and fear. The gas could be deadly, not unlike the submachine gun of a Delta Force member.

Breathing is restricted and labored as they run. The lenses on their masks fog. Still, Bobby can see the exit up ahead. Twenty yards away. World Chem's warehouse door is sandwiched between larger doors for trailers. It leads directly to the rear parking lot. Cameron Vinke, another Delta operator, is waiting behind the wheel of their vehicle, ready to whisk them out of this hell storm.

Bobby activates his mic. "Medusa Two, this is One. We're thirty seconds out. Be ready."

Cam's reply is instant. "Two copies. All quiet out here."

Gunfire is dying behind Bobby and Terrance. Cartel members realizing they're the only ones doing the shooting. Bobby's hand grips Terrance's shoulder a little tighter, and their legs kick a little faster. The time to get out of this warehouse is now, before the cartel members grow testicles large enough to walk through the gas clouds.

Ten yards to the rear exit. Ten heaving footsteps. Metal clicks into place. Not once but twice. Bobby can't place the sounds. Not the sound of a rifle's bolt working or a deadbolt turning. *Latches.*

Two trailer doors are thrown open. One to Bobby's left, one to his right. Cartel gunmen pour out of the trailers. Close to a dozen rifle muzzles are now pointed directly at him and Terrance. The gunmen order him to drop his weapon and surrender. Despite their superior numbers, he's not convinced.

Bobby rams Terrance facedown into the ground and shields him with his own body. The laser beam of his MP7 lands on a cartel member's chest and guides a bullet into place. Rounds are dispensed in short bursts—*double triple double double*—and for a brief, almost magical second, the warrior inside Bobby feels like he's winning.

The cartel members are dropping. Numbers thinning into a manageable prospect. But they keep coming. Demons from a nightmare. Faster and faster, refusing to drop, until one careens into Bobby at full speed, tackling him off Terrance.

Mob rules take over, and the cartel thugs swarm Bobby. Stomping and kicking. Savaging gear from his kit. The mob's largest steps into the center, holding his AK-47 overhead like a battle axe. The butt stock crashes down on the back of Bobby's head, rendering him unconscious.

"Terrance, tell me what you're seeing. Describe faces. Names you hear. People you recognize."

The words come through Terrance's radio as he's ripped off the ground. Feels like a roller-coaster ride. Up slow, just long enough to hang in the air. Then *whoosh*. Both knees crack into the ground. His hands are quickly bound with zip ties.

"We're with you. Just talk to us."

Sloane's words. His best friend, and she forces him to react. He surveys the situation. Over a dozen men surround him now. Cartel thugs, each one twice his size and heavily armed. They're choking on chemicals, but that's not stopping them from hovering over him, proud of their trophy.

Bobby is lying beside him, blood dripping from the side of his head and across his face. Cameron's unconscious body is dragged into the warehouse through the back door. Unenviable position: last man standing, with a high likelihood that he's going to witness two executions before experiencing his own.

A man who appears to be in control breaks out of the crowd toward Cameron as he's dropped onto the ground. The Delta operator's hands and feet are zip-tied. A nylon bag is placed over his head. That same man repeats the process for Bobby.

Terrance had been at a loss for words, but now he's got something incredibly important to say. "I think Bobby and Cam are alive—"

The transmission is cut short. His gas mask is torn away, and his radio is ripped off his kit. Chemicals singe his tongue. He sucks and wheezes, each breath straining against the last. Finally, the man with the bag approaches, and his chest constricts. *It's over.* Black nylon is thrust over his head, and the world he once knew disappears.

Victor Orlov is the man with the radio. He used it to spring World Chem's trap from inside a surveillance van, parked miles away. All three members of Gabriella Martinez's team have been captured, including one of her superstars: Terrance Kline. Each will be leverage held over Martinez's head—forcing her to capitulate to cartel demands, allowing her to see Mexico clearly, the way the cartel does—the only way. American intervention will not be tolerated.

While Terrance hacked World Chem, he watched from inside the target network, notating what Martinez took. Every item the Americans stole is documented on a set of computer screens. Commands appear as lines of code. Lists of folders and files are neatly organized. The attack happened too quickly to observe in real time. It'll take days to fully account for the damage the Americans have caused, but it can be remedied.

That remedy is the reason he was sent to Mexico City. He knew

Martinez would be coming, and he knew she was going to access critical information. She was successful, but he'll counter it. Cartel smuggling routes will change. Customers will change. The trail Martinez is following will vanish, like her people.

Victor's files are backed up and secure. Job complete. He switches off his radio. Same with the van's computers. If the American drone overhead hasn't already locked onto his signal, it soon will. Time to move before Martinez can order reinforcements into the area.

He settles into the driver's seat and keys the ignition. Onto the next rendezvous location. He wants a personal look at Terrance Kline before he disappears into the narco underbelly of Mexico City.

Three

United States Embassy, Mexico City

Gabriella Martinez is living a nightmare. She's watching it unfold live inside the embassy's secure conference room. It's serving as a makeshift tactical operations center and is almost a complete match to the White House Situation Room. Large conference table at the center. A dozen television screens flickering. A State Department seal hovering proudly on the wall. Secure communication lines linked to Langley. The space is chock full of resources—few of which will do her any good to combat the unfolding situation.

Industrial buildings whiz by on the Intelligence, Surveillance, and Reconnaissance feed as the three vehicles race away from World Chem. Men she ordered into harm's way are inside the convoy's center vehicle, and this could be her final chance to save them.

"ISR is struggling to track the target vehicle," Sloane Hamilton shouts. She's responsible for communicating with the pilot of the ISR drone. She's also a Southern Belle from Georgia—and a skilled hacker.

"Rate of speed?" Martinez asks, arms crossed over her tall, slender frame as she observes the vehicles. They're slipping from the viewfinder's grasp.

"Ninety, no, one hundred miles an hour."

Martinez is running out of time to solve the problem. The cartel was prepared. Instinct tells her she's witnessing the finale of a well-designed plan. "Mr. Xiao?"

"Radio traffic has stopped. Our drone's onboard stingray isn't detecting any local cellular signals," Andrew Xiao, the engineer who designed Anne, replies. At present, he is working to map equipment the cartel may be using to communicate.

"Hold off—" Martinez feels a hand on her shoulder. It's Major Trey Bingham, the Delta Force troop commander assigned to manage the operation's tactical elements.

Bingham is one of the Unit's most decorated and respected officers. He lost his right leg above the knee to an IED during his fifth deployment. He recovered, then came back for two more rounds in the sandbox before becoming an officer.

"Locals?" Martinez asks.

Major Bingham nods, replies with his hand covering a radio's handset. "Mexican National Guard is six minutes out."

"Ma'am! I think we're about to lose visual contact."

Martinez returns focus to the center screen at Sloane's warning. The three vehicles are slowing, preparing to enter a multistory parking garage. "Order the drone to drop its target lock and switch to a wide-area visual."

"Yes, ma'am."

The ISR feed shifts away from the vehicles as they enter the garage and disappear. The screen blinks. Multiple city blocks engulf the screen when it repopulates. An industrial area. Still desolate. Large warehouses or office complexes. Streetlight bulbs are burned out or flicker to strange rhythms. Shreds of plastic and paper refuse twist in the breeze like modern-day tumbleweeds.

"ETA on the National Guard?" Martinez asks.

Major Bingham relays Martinez's inquiry over the radio and delivers her an answer. "Four minutes."

Not enough time. Headlights split the garage's exit. A car speeds out. Another vehicle exits, moving in the opposite direction of the first. Then another, then another, until over a dozen vehicles exit the garage, each one traveling in a separate direction. No way to track them all.

"Ms. Hamilton, switch the ISR feed to thermal. Begin searching for vehicles with multiple occupants," Martinez orders.

Sloane relays the order, and the drone operator begins a rapid search. Looks like a photographer snapping photos before changing targets. Plain view, night vision, thermal—rapid shift to the next target.

The first two vehicles have only one occupant. Finally, it lands on a four-door sedan. Two white-hot bodies glow through the windshield. That's their target, found in the nick of time. As the drone locks on, the other vehicles disappear across Mexico City.

Major Bingham rattles off descriptions of the disappearing vehicles to the Mexican National Guard, along with directions of travel.

Martinez waits for a break before saying, "Request an interdiction of our target vehicle."

Bingham's brows knit together beneath his glasses. They're throwbacks to the oversized frames of the '70s. Always the shooter, he had trauma-resistant lenses installed. "It'll be high risk, ma'am. Varga's men have standing orders not to surrender to Mexican law enforcement."

"Put in the request."

The major does as ordered. "They're sympathetic. Expect a vehicle interdiction in the next two minutes."

"Guide them in," Martinez says.

The room falls silent, save the intermittent directions offered by Major Bingham. Last chance, and it comes with long odds and desperate prayers. Recipe for heartache.

Flashing lights overtake the sedan. Three National Guard pickups, their beds packed with armed soldiers and mounted belt-fed machine guns. The sedan yields to the siren and Martinez's heart drops. If they had a hostage, they'd likely evade. Or they're going to harm the person they have in custody. *No one screws with the Varga cartel.*

The National Guard members dismount and begin fanning out, taking cover behind their pickups. They're shouting orders: "Kill the ignition! Throw away the keys! Hands out the window!" The men in the sedan refuse to comply and instead chat frantically back and forth. Flurries of hand gestures flash white on the thermal ISR feed.

Both of the sedan's doors open in unison. The two occupants fly out, pistols in hand. They point their guns at the National Guard units. White-hot muzzle flashes. Glowing shell casings arc through the air.

The two cartel gunmen manage only several paces across the asphalt before they're gunned down. Hunks of white explode from their heads and torsos. Bodies are splayed against the asphalt, more white oozing into nearby gutters.

A team of guardsmen stack up behind a pickup before approaching the sedan via an offset angle, allowing their teammates to provide cover. Martinez holds her breath as they reach the sedan and clear the cabin. Nothing.

A guardsman reaches into the vehicle. The trunk swings open. A black void on the thermal feed—no hostage present.

Martinez takes a deep breath, trying her best to keep her emotions in check. Three people under her command are officially lost. Blame rests squarely on her shoulders. Adrenaline is waning, bringing with it a whirlwind of questions about where she could have gone wrong or what could have been missed.

No different from the others in the room. They've all lost close friends tonight, and the room is suddenly quiet, withdrawn.

But Martinez refuses to let the loss become the night's defining moment. Emotions will be put to the side, and they'll fight onward. It's the only way to bring their missing people home. "Ms. Hamilton, terminate the ISR feed and get started on what Mr. Kline retrieved in World Chem's computer system. Mr. Xiao, run me through the cartel's intercepted radio traffic. I'm looking to start a new hit list."

Four

West Texas

"Shooter ready. Stand by . . ."

Beep!

Jen Yates grabs her 2011 pistol off a table, rams a magazine into the mag well, and racks the slide. Driving the pistol straight out, she addresses three pepper poppers down range at twenty-five yards. The first shot hits, rings the steel silhouette, and it falls. The sights land on the second steel target, followed by a smooth trigger pull. Another hit, another satisfying ring.

Jen rushes into the third popper and breaks the shot too quickly. It's a miss, poorly timed. She'd gotten ahead of herself and started to move off the shooting station before striking the target. She returns to the station and reengages—a costly waste of time.

The men behind her exchange glances as the third pepper popper falls. It's a chorus of bobbing heads. Pre-match bets have been made, and Jen is vying for the number-one position at her local IPSC match. Today, fortunes will be made and reputations lost.

Next on Jen's hit list is an array of four targets moving left to right along the stage. The people who put on the match decided to make them difficult. They're cardboard silhouette targets, the typical fare at IPSC matches, resting five yards away. The distance isn't a challenge, but they're hostage targets. Two of them are covered to their torsos, and two of them are covered to their heads. They also alternate from torso to head to torso.

Jen decides to take them on the move. With smooth footwork, she walks perpendicular with the targets, putting double taps on each. Keeping a laser focus on her front sight, she sweeps the array, landing clean hits on each.

Time to move to the second phase of the stage. Jen flicks the butt of the pistol as she depresses the mag release, and a silver magazine slips from the bottom. In seconds it's replaced with a fresh twenty-round magazine. Jen's shooting a custom Staccato XL 2011 pistol, made in her home state of Texas. It's chambered in .40 caliber, has a flared mag well for fast reloads, and a custom trigger. A race gun if there ever was one.

Jen steps into a chute that heads straight back toward the range's berm. The walls on each side are created with two-by-fours and orange mesh fencing material. Two windows have been cut intermittently into the mesh to serve as firing stations, and the chute terminates at a third shooting station.

Leading with the muzzle of her raised pistol, Jen reaches the first station. Two paper targets greet her. In front of those are two round steel targets, each eight inches in diameter. The rules here are clear: the small pieces of steel must be engaged first, and if a miss strikes the paper target behind them, she draws a penalty.

It calls for a drop in her shooting speed. Jen rests her sights on the first piece of steel and carefully breaks the shot. The steel rings and tumbles off its stand. She repeats the process on the second piece of steel, hitting the target clean. Before she engages the two pieces of paper, she makes sure the final piece of steel released a trip wire connected to targets at the final shooting station. Satisfied, she puts double taps on the two pieces of paper and moves on.

Jen reaches the second window and finds a repeat of the array she just engaged. Feeling confident from her performance at the last array, she feels an urge to rush, making up for the lost time at the beginning.

She forces herself to slow once more and land clean shots on the two pieces of steel.

Exhaling some tension, she finds a clean sight picture on the first piece of steel and tags it. The success is repeated on the second piece of steel, and the trip wire releases. She puts double taps on each piece of paper and rushes to the final shooting station.

Two paper targets are swinging left and right as she moves in. Each of these was triggered earlier because their wires were connected to the steel target plates. They'd been set behind cover: meaning, if a shooter couldn't hit the plates, they'd reach the final shooting station unable to engage the targets, resulting in big penalties.

They're moving fast. It forces inexperienced shooters into chasing them, guaranteeing misses. Jen levels her pistol at the first one, trying to find the center point in its movement—a place that no matter how fast the target moves, part of it is always present. Usually, it's toward the middle of the target's swing. She breaks two shots on the target, then adds a third for safety. It's moving too fast for her to check the hits, and despite her insecurity, she moves to the second swinger.

It's moving slower than the first. Springs losing their tension. Finding the center ground again, she puts two shots on the target, confident that they've landed. All that's left is to dust three pepper poppers set between the swingers. They're close, only ten yards out, and Jen nails each one cleanly.

As the final piece of steel clangs to the ground, the range officer, who'd been following her the entire stage with a shot timer, says, "If you're finished, unload and show clear."

Jen drops her magazine and places it in her belt. Next, she unloads the gun and shows the RO the empty chamber. Getting a nod from him, she drops the slide, then the hammer, and holsters the gun. "What's the time?" she asks with a smooth Texas drawl.

The RO looks at this shot timer. "Twenty-two point three-seven seconds. You stickin' around while I call out your hits?"

Jen smirks and shakes her head. "Got business."

The RO gives her an eye roll. "Uh-huh."

Jen begins walking to the front of the range, picking up her dropped magazine on the way. Blowing off a layer of fine Texas dust, she tucks it back into her belt. As she reaches a group of shooters, who are all staring at her with their arms crossed, she says, “Y’all better start reaching for your wallets.”

They sigh. All five of them reach into their back pockets and extract five-dollar bills. Jen collects them, one by one. They’d been betting on time, with disqualifications for penalties. Jen had the fastest time for the stage and no penalty shots. But the match’s overall winner has yet to be declared, and there’s a larger bet riding on that outcome.

Mel, one of the local masters, watches Jen tuck the money into her range bag. “Better mark my initial on that five, ’cause I want her back.”

“I’m the tax collector,” Jen says. “Once I got your cash, you don’t get it back.”

Mel laughs. “You’re full of it, Yates. Either way, you’re payin’ up next stage.”

As the shooters gather their range bags to progress to the next stage, they see a trio of black Suburbans rumbling down the dirt road. Everyone stops and looks at Jen, whose shoulders have begun to sag. Those vehicles are coming for her.

It’s an ominous sign. Short notice means something serious has happened. Jen immediately worries for her friends who are in harm’s way. Herself too. She hasn’t been in the fight since Beijing. That punishing ordeal was a year ago, and she’s not sure she’s ready to return.

Jen drops her bag on the ground, extracting the day’s winnings. She’s going to lose her main bet after all. Failing to complete even one stage will guarantee a loss. She smirks. “Before I hand this damn money back, y’all need to know this loss is a one-time thing.”

Mel returns to Jen. “As I said, Yates: full of it.”

Another one of the shooters returns as well. His name is Cotton. He’s got white hair under his bucket hat. Tanned skin like leather, criss-crossed with wrinkles. “Way I see it, you oughta hang on to that cash. Seems you’ll have a good use for it comin’ up.”

“Come again?” Jen asks.

“I think you should buy a box o’ bullets on me. Put ’em to good use wherever it is you’re headed.”

The other shooters nod—a consensus has been formed.

"Besides," Mel adds, "we wanna beat you fair and square. Losin' a match 'cause you didn't finish doesn't count for much."

Jen folds the wad back up, returning it to the bag. "Guess it'll go to good use after all."

The SUVs slide to a stop on the gravel. A black-suited officer steps out of the lead vehicle and shouts, "Ms. Yates! A word!"

"Be safe where you're goin', ya hear?" Mel says.

Jen nods. "Don't worry. I'll be back to claim my spot on the podium."

She picks her range bag up out of the dust and rushes toward the SUVs. The doors remain closed, a disappointment; she'd expected to see Martinez step out. Her absence is a worrying sign, and by the time Jen climbs into the middle vehicle, she's certain that somewhere in the world, the people she cares for are in trouble.

Five

Barbed wire coils around wooden fence posts, straining to contain endless stretches of Texas brushland. Plots of land so vast, they reach to the horizon and fall into oblivion. Cattle spend their lives here and never graze the same pasture twice. This is Jen's home, and she's being asked to leave it once again.

The Suburban glides past signs that point to I-10 South, en route to San Antonio International Airport. Soon, these cherished lands will be replaced by apartments and strip malls and throngs of traffic. Almost motivation to turn around, go back the way she came.

Almost.

Her unease grows, despite how familiar it feels. She's answering the call to serve, which she's done countless times in the past. It never seems to get easier. In fact, it's the opposite.

Her body constantly reminds her of the sacrifices she's made while serving the United States. Pins in her left wrist and a scar that snakes halfway down the underside of her forearm. A hairline surgical scar on her left cheek bone. Knuckles that snap and pop—she's not sure if that's from all of the typing she's done or the punches she's thrown. Probably both.

Yet the physical injuries can't compare to the mental ones. Jen's most recent deployment to Beijing was the toughest she's ever endured. Had things gone a touch differently, she'd be rotting in a Ministry of State Security detention center until her final breath.

Strangely, China's detention centers don't seem all that daunting. For Jen, the true hardship comes from those she lost along the way—friends that felt more like family. People she'd have given her own life for, if only she'd had the opportunity.

That's what forced her into the Suburban today. Something happened. She needs to know if it involves the people she cares for. It's the only way to loosen the knot in her chest.

Jen takes off her ball cap, letting her blonde hair drop past her shoulders. Her shooting glasses are placed on the seat, and the sun splashes into her green eyes. She's a hundred-and-ten-pound Texas firestorm, hardened by the years of violence she's endured. Her powerful intellect pairs nicely with her scars, producing a rugged yet refined poise.

Files are stacked next to her on the seat. She grabs the first, marked with the Central Intelligence Agency seal. Langley isn't where she started her career in espionage. The NSA's Tailored Access Operations gave her the opportunity to work with the best hackers in the world. She spent eight years in the NSA, and that experience rubbed off. When she retired, she was one of the NSA's top cyber espionage specialists.

Retirement didn't mean cocktails and white, sandy beaches. Jen formed her own Technical Access Group—a term used to describe elite, compartmentalized teams of hackers—and embedded it in Montana's remote back country. That Group specialized in cyber-kinetic warfare—hacking with the intent to cause death or physical destruction to both military and civilian targets. They initiated a campaign against one of China's most important leaders. Jen's Group was effective. They also suffered disastrous consequences.

In the wake of that tragedy appeared Martinez and the Central Intelligence Agency. During Jen's time at the Special Activities Center, Martinez became less of a superior officer and more of a sister. In Jen's eyes, Martinez defines what it means to be an excellent leader—one who would fall on her own sword to save her subordinates.

Jen flips the file open. Alex Varga's mugshot greets her. Someone she's known from the news and her work in the intelligence community.

Before reading further into the file, she studies Varga's picture. His eyes seemingly engulf the photo. Wide and penetrating with a cruel type of intelligence working behind them. They dominate his overly square face, which is accented with a thick, black mustache.

She continues through the workup. Varga's cartel has long been a source of mystery in the intelligence world. It's Mexico's most powerful, yet little is known about its inner workings. Occultism surrounds the organization. Entry into the cartel's highest levels is granted exclusively to Varga's handpicked soldiers, and those men pay a steep price for admission.

Varga considers himself an Aztec priest; Santa Muerte and the other dark gods of Mexico's underworld are pale offshoots in Varga's fiefdom. Ritual sacrifices are said to take place at his home. Crime scene photos inserted into the file depict victims with their heads and hearts removed. Aztec priests would have sacrificed these to the sun god, Huitzilopochtli.

While he's considered a priest, his disciples are considered Aztec warriors. They're adorned with burns, tattoos, and piercings that would have marked some of antiquity's most terrifying soldiers. As indicated in Jen's file, these marks aren't for show; they're paid for in blood.

Varga is no doubt a menace, but it doesn't stop Jen from wondering why Martinez is chasing him. An intelligence officer of her caliber is built for different assignments. Countries like Iran are careening toward functional nuclear programs—a problem Martinez's Technical Access Group has plenty of experience with. Russia's aggression in Eastern Europe is virtually unchecked, and Martinez would be ideally suited to a challenge like that.

Instead, she's in Mexico City, chasing a religious whack job.

Answers are provided in the workup's final pages. Chemical tanks were intercepted by U.S. Customs and Border Protection at the Nogales border crossing. Their bellies were full of superheated, liquid cocaine. But there was a hitch.

Something tripped a highly tuned piece of equipment on the U.S. border: gamma radiation. One of the chemical tanks was laden with the substance, and it led to the capture of a World Chem box truck filled with narcotics.

Preliminary tests conducted by Langley indicated that the chemical tank would have produced about twenty-five kilos of radiated cocaine. Enough to injure or kill thousands of Americans. A mass casualty terror event sneaking into the United States via its own backyard.

Martinez was dispatched to Mexico on the heels of an intense pressure campaign that originated at the highest levels of the U.S. government. Mexico was caught by surprise, both by the failed attack and the ultimatum that the Oval Office issued: *You are either complicit in narco-terrorism, or you are part of the solution that eradicates it.*

For Mexico, the choice was obvious.

A Joint Forces Tasking Agreement allowed Martinez and the Central Intelligence Agency to embed U.S. soldiers in Mexico City. A troop of Delta Force soldiers were deployed to Campo Militar 1—Mexico City's largest military installation—to assist Martinez with the investigation into Varga and conduct raids against targets associated with the terror event on the border.

Jen closes the file as the SUV exits the freeway, nearing San Antonio International Airport. She idly runs her finger along the file's edge, digesting everything she's just read. Even for an experienced intelligence officer, it's shocking. Nogales isn't but a stone's throw from West Texas—her home. Terror has a nasty habit of striking at the heart of what's precious.

The SUV passes the airport's security checkpoint and approaches a small hangar. A private jet waits on the tarmac. Martinez is out front, pacing—more like wearing grooves into the tarmac. Distance can't hide her exhaustion. Wrinkles fan out across a days-old suit. Long black hair is pulled into a tight, efficient bun.

Jen's hand is resting on the door handle as the SUVs come to a stop. She exits and rushes to her best friend. Up close, Martinez looks worse than Jen expected. She has a face that could grace magazine covers, but there are bags under her bloodshot eyes. As they embrace, Martinez's muscles feel like reservoirs of tension. "What's going on, Gabby?"

"Terrance and two others were taken. C'mon, we'll talk more on the jet."

Six

Jen steps into the aircraft and finds the cabin a disaster. Stacks of files are piled on empty seats. Photos are pasted to headrests and bulkheads. Multiple computers are open on the tables.

The information begins telling Jen a story. One of a well-planned kidnapping, executed with ruthless efficiency. And while the evidence is composed of grainy ISR photographs and dryly written Agency documents, the full picture is devastating.

Terrance Kline isn't just a Group member; he's a brother. He was willing to throw his career—and possibly his freedom—away for Jen when things went badly in Beijing. She's never met a more honorable man.

Jen has never met the two men captured by Terrance's side, but she already considers them part of her responsibility. They fought selflessly to protect Terrance, and in this business, there's no higher standard.

Jen stops at the edge of a seat, waiting while Martinez transfers a stack of files. Once it's clear, she drops into the seat, asking the day's most significant question: "Do we have proof of life yet?"

Martinez wedges into the cluttered space and takes several swigs from a thermos of coffee. "No contact yet."

"Doubt they're the type to stay quiet for long."

"The cartel has a playbook for situations like this, and they're gonna run it. I'm confident we'll have something within twenty-four hours," Martinez replies.

A stopwatch is sitting at Jen's right hand. Digital. Bright-red numbers ticking away. Twelve hours and twenty-six minutes. Time elapsed since the kidnapping. Every additional second notches her anger higher. Too much time has already passed waiting for contact. "Walk me through it."

"Did you make it through the files in the Suburban?" Martinez asks, attempting to gauge where to begin.

"Every one of 'em," Jen replies, sensing trepidation in her superior officer. She's about to come out of retirement. Rescuing a close friend isn't a dive into the kiddie pool. It'll be taxing, mentally and physically. This spot in the fight isn't given, and she resolves herself to earning it.

Martinez extracts a set of photographs from the stack and passes them over. "Not only did they know we were coming, they had every single one of our moves covered."

Jen flips through the crime scene photos, starting with one that depicts a trailer lined with lead blankets, preventing overhead ISR from detecting its heat signature. Mounds of food wrappers and water bottles litter vacant offices across from World Chem. The final images are the most disturbing—the point where the trail goes cold. Three abandoned vehicles sit inside a parking garage, their doors and trunks left open. Drag marks and blood stains were left behind on the concrete.

Jen tries to control the tremors rocking her hands. Incredible brutality shown to three good men. A favor worth returning. "This took days . . . maybe weeks' worth of planning."

"It started before we initiated surveillance—the only way to pull it off. They knew we'd hit World Chem after their narcotics were intercepted in Nogales."

"Our people were the target," Jen says as she drops the pictures in a pile. "Did Terrance's penetration yield anything solid?"

"They confirmed that narcotics were on site and hacked an air-gapped computer belonging to World Chem's CEO," Martinez replies. "Using intel from the compromised computer, we were able to map cartel shipping lanes inside the U.S."

"Guess the DEA is taking over from there?"

Martinez nods. "It's technically out of our purview. Moreover, it's going to take time to surveil those routes."

"Time we don't have," Jen remarks, returning to one of the photographs. Her mind is stuck on the trailers butted up to World Chem's warehouse. "They weren't protecting this place. They kept World Chem active to make a kidnapping attempt."

"Only thing that makes sense. In one stroke, we went from investigating Alex Varga to working overtime on a hostage rescue. If Varga is hiding something, he's got breathing room to clean it up. We get too close, he's got the leverage to back us off."

"We've got leverage of our own," Jen says, thinking of a hundred different ways to stick a knife between Varga's ribs and twist it. "Is it possible you were compromised before the operation kicked off?"

Martinez already has a file in hand and passes it to Jen. "There's your answer."

"Must be a mind reader," Jen says, almost meaning it. In the intelligence world, Gabriella Martinez is a star. She has a level of foresight that borders on clairvoyance. Langley hasn't seen a better intelligence officer in a generation. "Admiral Mateo Perez?"

"The senior officer at Campo Militar 1, and my counterpart inside the Joint Forces Tasking Agreement. Technically, he has to green-light anything kinetic inside Mexico."

Jen flips through the pages, sucking in Perez's information. The more she reads, the worse his write-up gets. "This guy is the definition of crooked."

"That's why I didn't alert him to the operation—not until the last minute, at least," Martinez replies. She laughs at the thought of her conversation with Perez. "He was pissed that I boxed him in, but I pried the green light out of him."

Jen nods, impressed. Martinez had every angle covered. Despite the best planning, operations go sideways. Just the nature of the business. She keeps reading and lands on an unusual piece of information. "His wife is young enough to be his granddaughter."

Martinez leans forward, pointing to another section of the file. "She comes equipped with a mansion and offshore bank accounts."

"Never met a twenty-two-year-old with so much wealth."

"They're using her identity as a front for the money that Perez collects from Varga . . . and whoever else he works for."

Jen snaps the file shut. "You know he's dirty. Why are you letting it play?"

"Mexican officials have a tendency to balk at our accusations of corruption. Removing him will require political capital I'm not willing to spend."

Jen nods, familiar with Mexico's political theater. They have a history of forcing the United States to return criminals that were arrested north of the border. Much of the Drug Enforcement Administration's work is scoffed at or disregarded. Corruption, floor to ceiling. Trust no one, suspect everything.

"We're also letting Perez slide because he's a known quantity," Martinez continues. "By our standards, he's corrupt. By Mexico's standards, he's more like an ambassador, forwarding messages while preventing a world war from breaking out. Who knows what we'd get if we removed him?"

"Makes sense," Jen agrees.

"If the time comes, I'll use what I've learned as leverage. Threaten to put him in a U.S. prison, take what I need from him." Martinez peers through the cabin window. Asphalt cooking under the Texas sun. Tumbleweeds caught up in the fences bordering the airport. She sighs. "This one's on me, Jen."

"Not the way I see it, Gabby," Jen says, allowing her trademark ruggedness to show through. "These cartel thugs throw a nice sucker punch. Can't blame yourself for catching one on the chin."

Martinez sighs, runs her hands through her hair. "It's my job to see those coming."

"No, it's your job to return the damn favor and get our people home," Jen replies, already sensing a rise in Martinez's spirit. "Now, what's your plan to get our people back?"

Seven

"You're going to target a telecoms network, but there's a catch."

Jen sits back in her chair and chuckles. "What else is new? Lay it on me."

"You'll have to find it first."

Jen stares at Martinez, deadpan. Telecommunication networks are owned and operated by some of the world's largest corporations. Oftentimes, they're more clearly mapped than Route 66. Finding one should be the least of her worries. "Here I was, hoping you'd make things easy on me."

"Easy? No. But I can offer you a head start." Martinez uncovers a data request that was sent to a Mexican telecommunication company, MexTel, Mexico City's largest provider. The request demanded the cell phone records for Alex Varga and his known associates. She passes it off to Jen. "Want to guess at what it turned up?"

"Not a thing," Jen says, thumbing through the document.

Martinez nods. "Varga had been using the network up until five years ago, but at that point traffic suddenly dropped off."

Jen listens intently. These are the types of problems she's built to solve. "You think Varga created his own telecommunication network in Mexico."

"I don't think; I know." Martinez hands Jen a set of ISR photographs. They depict two gigantic cell towers on the outskirts of Mexico City. "Those are MexTel's base stations that serve the entire city. Notice anything odd?"

Jen studies the photographs before nodding. "Looking a little crowded up top."

"There's a parasitic set of cellular transceivers attached to the top of the towers," Martinez observes.

Transceivers send and receive cellular signals. They're an integral part of a cellular network. Without them, an area's service would drop completely.

"Heard a report about this on the news. Did several MexTel service technicians recently disappear?" Jen asks.

Martinez hands Jen another set of photographs. "You won't like these."

Images Jen wishes she could unsee. A man is hanging from a Mexico City overpass. Parts of his MexTel uniform have been torn from his body. A sign around his neck reads: *No more service interruptions.* "So he went to service a tower and killed the power to do his job. It took the cartel's network down in the process."

"Paid with his life, but he went out swinging. Check the next photo."

Jen flips to the next photograph. It was taken inside the cell tower's utilities shed. It focuses on what is called a base station controller—the heart of any cell tower. Base station controllers match cellular frequencies. In doing so, they connect calls between the network's users.

"It took some courage to bring this to light," Jen remarks, sensing the sacrifice made to capture the photo.

"MexTel forwarded it to us, along with a plea for help in managing the cartel's presence in their sites." Martinez finds a surveillance photo of one of Varga's top lieutenants with a cell phone stuck to his ear. "It was incredible because we'd see Varga's people making calls, but we couldn't find the numbers or who was routing the traffic."

Jen's eyes go wide as she begins piecing everything together. "We could be holding the keys to the kingdom here. If they have excess confidence in their network security—"

Martinez's enthusiasm starts to rise with Jen's. "They're not protecting their communications. We could learn a lot from call and SMS message logs. GPS histories. This has the highest probability of showing us where our people are hidden."

"Once we get that information, we plan a raid and hit fast," Jen says, visualizing success. "I take it that was my head start."

Martinez nods. "It was. We're missing the location for an integral part of Alex Varga's network: the mobile switching center. Without it, we don't have the information we need to stitch together the network and find our people."

In a cellular network, the mobile switching center is critical to controlling user information. It's where a service provider can monitor accounts and who can access them. If bills go unpaid, it's where a service provider terminates the service. Most importantly, it's where call, SMS, and GPS records are stored for a service area.

"Something like that might not come easy," Jen says.

"That's why you're going straight to Mexico City. I need you inside both base station controllers by tomorrow morning. From there, we triangulate cellular traffic back to our missing piece—the mobile switching center."

Jen doesn't flinch at the challenge. Two hacks. Use them both to lock onto her final target's location—and smash it. "Let's talk contingencies."

"It's paramount that you avoid detection. Remember, our people are in custody. If the Varga cartel learns they've been attacked, our guys could suffer reprisals."

"What about an unplug?"

"We consider it unlikely that Varga will disconnect his network in the event of detection. It's too integral to cartel operations." Martinez reaches into a nearby seat and hands Jen a messenger bag. "This is a light technical kit for your trip to Mexico City. The computer has a target workup on both cell towers. Travel documents are in the front pocket."

"Guess this is your way of getting rid of me."

Jen snatches up the bag. Texas treated her well. Gave her some space to heal and lick her wounds. But Martinez's target package reminds her just how much she missed her job. This work is who she is. That good people are in trouble only compounds her urgency to act.

Martinez nods at the stopwatch at her left hand. "Clock is ticking."

Eight

Lush roses. Ivy stretching over trellises, shading an outdoor dining table. Magnolias scenting the air. Victor is walking through Varga's garden, wondering if a bullet will enter the back of his head. With some luck, Varga might do him a courtesy and plant him under a rosebush.

He's on his third lap around Varga's estate, touring, while Varga clears his morning calendar. The disrespect grates on Victor, along with his wingtip shoes and his suit, which is stifling. Walking the estate is no small feat. It spans over one-hundred acres and is surrounded by the arid deserts of northern Mexico City.

There are lush gardens and stables full of thoroughbred horses. Olympic-size swimming pools. Ponds with little angels shooting water from their mouths. A narco-billionaire's playpen.

A Mexican villa occupies the heart of the estate. Vines creep from the garden to the villa. They cling to walls while coiling around pillars and intertwine with balcony rails. They bring color and shade and flowers to a home that Victor has long considered a masterpiece.

An oasis found in the desert is usually but one thing: an illusion. Danger has its own dominion here, just like the gardens and stables. At any given time, fifty armed men patrol the compound's high walls. More are waiting in a nearby town, fifteen miles away.

While Victor has never seen a murder take place here, there are rumors circulating like tall tales, detailing Varga's atrocities. But rumors have a strange way of illuminating the men they surround.

Victor can see clearly the nexus from which the rumors originate. A temple erected behind Alex's villa. From the outside, the temple appears relatively normal. It's near identical to its counterpart, only smaller. But that's where the similarities end.

Varga considers it sacred ground—a portal through which he can reach Huitzilopochtli, the Aztec sun god said to bring forth daylight. Offer it prayer and receive its blessings in return. And like the priests of antiquity, Varga is said to engage in human sacrifice within its walls. The whispers started years ago, offering clues to when the cartel leader's behavior began worsening.

Victor can't separate fact from fiction, but he does know that this is an evil place. He's seen a large cross-section of the world's horrors during his time as an intelligence officer, and considers himself a qualified judge.

Following a burst of radio chatter, an armed guard points at the temple. "This way, Mr. Orloff."

Must be finishing morning prayer or preparing my funeral pyre.

Victor isn't one to lose control of his blood pressure, but this morning is going to test his resolve. Murder may well be on Varga's mind, and he's the ideal victim, headed to an ideal location.

His relationship with Varga is deteriorating to dangerous levels, but it didn't begin this way. When they met five years ago, the young narco was talented, and he caught the attention of powerful men.

Victor seduced Varga with the intelligence he needed to protect his fledgling cartel. Once he had Varga's trust, he brought him technology. Powerful tools that could vault him over and above his rivals.

Eventually, Varga learned a painful truth about the technology he'd come to rely on. He had the ability to monitor every phone call, travel route, and safe house inside his organization. But he couldn't control the flow of information. Servers go down. Computers crash. Reams of data need to be properly stored and processed. Varga lacked the ability to manage those problems, and so Victor became a fixture, remedying an endless slew of problems.

The technology and the services it required came at a cost. Victor became the cartel's de facto ruler—more like the controlling partner in a business empire, slowly chipping away at Alex's bottom line, taking more and more for himself. Instead of accepting the partnership, Varga resented it. Hatred swelled, fraying the relationship beyond salvage-ability.

Victor steps onto a stone patio separating the home and the temple. Armed guards circle the area. Butlers are waiting with silver trays full of ice water, pastries, and moistened towels. Nothing is offered to him. The Spanish villa engulfs the temple—but the powerful aura emanating from the temple's ebony doors dwarfs the villa. Fleeing from conflict isn't in Victor's DNA, but this space gives him pause.

The temple's doors swing open and Varga steps out. He is barefoot and shirtless, wearing only blue jeans. A layer of sweat covers his short but muscular body. Long scars cross his hips, laid in by stingray barbs cooked to a glow. Marks of a priest. Scars are molted to his wrists, connecting him to the stars. A circular Aztec calendar is tattooed on his belly.

"Good morning, Mr. Varga."

Varga sizes up Victor with disgust. He's sporting a several thousand-dollar sports coat. Blond. Tall. Well-groomed beard and slicked-back hair. Older than thirty-five but not a day over forty. A primped banker —a thief in disguise. "Here he is! The man with his belly in the gutter, slithering between the shadows. Tell me, Victor, the lies you brought for me today."

Victor lets the jab slide. Varga wants him dead, but he's the one with the power—the control. He stays even, professional. Unwilling to let this powder keg explode. Reaching into his jacket, he withdraws an envelope, handing it to Alex. "Per our agreement, Mr. Varga."

Varga snatches the envelope and tears it open. It's a wire transfer, covering the cost for World Chem's damage. Part of a previous deal. Victor handles the Americans and agrees to indemnify the cartel. The amount satisfies him, and he hands the slip of paper to a subordinate. "You're aware that Gabriella Martinez has left Mexico?"

"I am."

Anger flashes in Alex's eyes, but he speaks with an even tone. With a slow stride he approaches Victor, stopping a foot from his face. "That's not an answer," he hisses.

"I believe she went to retrieve a subordinate," Victor replies, refusing to shrink from Varga. He pulls a photograph from his jacket instead. "I need you to circulate this."

Varga looks over the photo. Finds a blonde-haired woman with bright-green eyes. "This is who she went for?"

"Yes, Mr. Varga. Her name is Jen Yates. There's a strong likelihood that she's currently on her way to Mexico City."

"She doesn't look like a soldier," Alex observes. He steps away and hands the photograph to his subordinate amid the circus of butlers and guards. "Do what he says."

Victor watches, waits for the subordinate to disappear. Snapping a moist towel off a tray, Varga uses it to wipe down his chest, showcasing battle scars from his youth. Fights with box cutters and Saturday night specials, always over trivial amounts of cocaine or drug turf. Each injury seems to have brought Varga to within inches of death, yet here he stands. "That's because she's a talented computer engineer—and a killer."

Varga picks up a glass of water and swishes around the lime floating between ice cubes. He sips, smirking while Victor sweats in the desert heat. "The Americans are sending their killers for me now?"

"She's coming for your technology—although I'm not sure which elements. It's my forte, Mr. Varga, and I'm committed to protecting your organization," Victor says in earnest. He's a computer engineer and a former Spetsnaz soldier. These systems are second nature to him, and he's more acquainted with the cartel's networks than any man alive.

Varga laughs, incredulous. "*You're* committed to protecting me? You can't even protect yourself in Mexico City. My cartel is the one that's exposed. *I'm* exposed, Victor—me! Whoever put radiation—"

"If Jen Yates is coming to Mexico," Victor interrupts, "it means that Gabriella Martinez has already lost this battle." His pulse edges higher, and he's eager to prevent Varga from probing him further about the radiation's source. Varga is right: someone did betray the cartel. It had no part in the radiation detected on the U.S. border. But he doesn't have a culprit for Alex—not yet, at least. "You're safe, so long as you stick to our agreement."

Varga eyes Victor suspiciously before relenting. He nods in agreement. "What would you like me to do with Ms. Yates?"

"Put men on the airport. Find Jen Yates before she gets loose in the city."

"And when they find her?" Varga asks.

"Trail her, but don't harm her. I need to know what she's planning to target."

Varga chuckles, raises a vicious smirk. "Have it your way."

Victor is chilled by Varga's response. Jen Yates is off-limits for multiple reasons. Asking Varga to manage her may have just gotten her killed. He refuses to show his concern for fear of making the matter worse and switches to a more important subject. "Where are the hostages?"

NINE

THE HOSTAGES HAVE BEEN HIDDEN AT THE TOP OF AN apartment building tucked deep inside of the slums in Mexico City. Streetside, the walls are filled with graffiti. Cars are elevated on cinder blocks. Buildings are stitched together via endless strands of extension cords. Inside, there's no elevator or air conditioning. Victor, along with his guard detail, is forced to climb dozens of flights of stairs. Sweat drips down their faces, and they're panting as they climb.

This apartment building is controlled by Varga's cartel. The higher they climb, the more stringent security becomes. They approach a checkpoint, one of several they've encountered. A half dozen guards are assembled in the stairwell. They stand in formation, blocking Victor's ascent. Various weapons hover over their chests: AK-47s, MP5s, UZIs. Backup pistols fill their beltlines.

The guards part, allowing Victor to pass once they see he's friendly. Radio transmissions follow, signaling that he's reached a checkpoint. One of the guards, noticing he's winded, waves a joint in Victor's face. His eyes are wild, with pupils the size of a dime. "This'll take you all the way."

Victor doesn't reply. The joint is called a *martian* in English. It smells like marijuana and gasoline. The gasoline smell comes from *basuco*, a derivative of cocaine manufacturing. When manufacturers make cocaine, they mix it into a paste using gasoline. A cheap byproduct is left behind, *basuco*, and it's considered unsellable in the United States. *Basuco* is toxic but produces an incredible high.

The drug's presence isn't unusual in the building. On the bottom floors, people are shooting up heroin. Drug buyers speed up and down the stairs, eager to cop a fix or ingest it. These enforcers, along with dozens of others, are tasked with protecting those business rackets.

Victor holds his breath against secondhand smoke as he ascends. He reaches a shattered window, barred over despite the height, and takes several deep breaths. He was sent to Mexico City to protect Varga, and he knew it would be miserable. This trek only reinforces the point.

He climbs several more flights, reaching a barricade made of plywood. It is erected on a landing, allowing an armed man to frisk passersby before entry. The wood facade is filled with a hodgepodge of gang graffiti. Aztec symbols painted crudely with spray cans. A belt-fed machine gun barrel pokes out of an aperture in the wood. Victor recognizes the Russian PKM, supplied by his organization.

A guard standing on the trap's exterior waves Victor forward. He's got a radio and a pistol on his belt. His pupils are normal. Eyes are clear. A boss. "Hands up."

Victor complies, receives a pat-down.

"Come through. The other homies need to stay."

Victor looks back to his guard detail and wonders. They're Varga's men too. Why not let them pass? No reason to second-guess the order because he'd never get a straight answer. He steps through the plywood door as it swings open. One more set of stairs between him and the top floor. He takes the stairs two at a time, eager to finish the climb.

He stops at a door: *13.* It's solid metal with a pane of plexiglass wedged in the top half. A bullet has struck the glass, leaving a spiderweb of cracks. Names have been carved into it with knives.

Looking up, he finds a camera hovering above his head. Unplugged. *They're following directions.* A positive first sign that his other directives are being properly carried out. He opens the door and steps into a hallway littered with trash. Smoke, from martians, coils in the air. Hard Mexican rap thumps. Graffiti floor to ceiling.

With a piercing whistle, a tattooed gang member calls him forward. "In here!"

Victor walks past rows of open doors. Dozens of armed men sit in the rooms, watching old Latin television shows. Some smoke and drink beer. Others play with their weapons. Most are packaging drugs for resale, funneling an assortment of powders into plastic bags. Crack cocaine and crystal meth are dropped into vials with tweezers. Enforcers hawk over the packaging process, ensuring product isn't stolen.

Victor reaches the man who waved him forward. He's a hulk with a thick, black mustache and a silver stud in his bottom lip. Customary Aztec tattoos and wrist burns. A rolled-up black bandana crosses his forehead, collecting sweat. Another of Alex's warriors. More importantly, he's sober. Victor figures he's in control of the building.

"I'm Bandito," the man says. "I'll show you around, and you tell me if there's a problem."

Victor catches a steady, hard look in his eye. Appreciates it. "Lead the way."

"Them boys are in here." Bandito takes Victor into one of the apartments. A group of men are inside, dressed as hostages. Only they're not. They're . . . volunteers. Paid by the cartel or unable to pay off their debts. They'll be decoys. Fakes for Martinez to lock onto and waste time chasing through Mexico City.

Tattoos are being applied from pictures taken from Bobby Hollice and Cameron Vinke. Their hair has been buzzed. Facial hair removed entirely. Skin tones are near perfect matches. Baggy black jumpsuits are waiting nearby. They'll further obscure physical features once the tattoos are finished.

"Don't worry about their faces," Bandito assures. "The blindfolds they'll be wearin' will cover everything, top to bottom."

Victor leans in, examining one of the tattoos. It's going on a decoy's hand, resembling Cameron Vinke's. It's part of a sleeve, with a skull terminating on the top of the hand. The tattoo matches the picture perfectly. He turns to Bandito. "I'm impressed."

Bandito nods to the tattoo artist, who's swiveling from the decoy's hand to a wall of Polaroids in rapid succession. "We call him Da Vinci. Best ink in all of Mexico City."

"Where is Terrance Kline's decoy?"

"This way. Didn't have much to do for him." Bandito leads Victor into a bedroom. There's a man sitting on a rotten mattress, trash at his feet. He's skinny as a rail, like Terrance, but his body is racked with tremors. An addict who's in for a nasty surprise once the drugs finally wear off.

Victor checks the corners. Two cameras, both unplugged. Same as the tattoo artist's room. Control is a hallmark of the Varga cartel—the priest sees everything, and it's not through God's power. While Victor didn't install these specific cameras, he connected each one to a data center in Mexico City's downtown area. They're his. He should be able to trust them, but not with Jen Yates in town.

Victor turns his attention back to the decoy. "Doesn't look like Kline."

"Their faces don't match for shit," Banditio agrees, "but we got the hair perfect. Just remember, he'll have a blindfold."

"Did you find any tattoos on him?"

"Not one. Boy was a saint."

Victor shakes his head. "He was no saint—a genius though. I'll give him that."

"What do you think?" Bandito asks, proud of his work.

"I'm satisfied. How many sets do you have?"

"How many do you need?"

"Just one decoy group," Victor replies.

Bandito nods. "Then we'll be finished soon."

"Start moving them around the city. People are coming for them as we speak."

"Heard it was urgent. Rocco's team is on the first group—the originals. He's the best in our organization. Wouldn't want to spend an hour alone with that man though."

"Will Rocco's people handle the hostages carefully?"

Bandito shrugs. "Mr. Varga's orders are followed down to the last detail. You'll have to ask him."

Victor doesn't find Bandito's answer reassuring, but he's forced to accept it. "Thanks. I'll tell Varga how well you've done."

Bandito laughs and throws out his arms. "He already knows. Hell, he knows everything, but I appreciate it."

Victor has seen everything he needs to. He exits the apartment and returns to the stairway. Despite the long climb, he's glad he came. It was reassuring—Varga's people are actually handling something properly. His time in Mexico City is going to be more successful than he expected.

Ten

Jen peels back her sweatshirt's sleeve, checks the face of her well-traveled Rolex Submariner: five p.m. Sixteen hours have passed since Terrance was taken. Too long in her eyes, and it made sitting still on her flight nearly impossible. But she's using her time wisely, making use of the privacy offered by her first-class seat. She's planning tonight's intrusions on the cell towers at Mexico City's periphery.

Photographs are displayed on her laptop, taken via an aerial reconnaissance drone. Multiple viewpoints of the base stations, or cell towers, are neatly depicted. Most cities, even ones the size of Los Angeles, usually only have two or three. Cellular signals are disseminated farther via smaller nodes, which blanket an entire area.

Jen immerses herself in the first tower's details. It's over one hundred feet tall. Large rectangular transceivers are mounted at the tower's peak. Space up top is cramped; a second set of transceivers is bolted against the original equipment. These belong to the Varga cartel.

Wires originating from the cartel's transceivers snake along the exterior of the tower. The engineers didn't have access to the tower during initial construction and were forced to improvise a shoddy solution.

Jen dissects the photographs, searching for gaps in security. She doesn't detect any cartel gunmen present on the site. Telecom employees only show up for scheduled services or when there's a problem. Tire tracks are stale. But the cartel considers the site valuable. Someone is watching, keeping it safe. That's guaranteed.

The utilities shed is the next object of her focus. It contains the base station controllers, her first targets in Varga's cellular network.

The shed looks like a miniature house. Made of brick. Shingle rooftops. Antennas bolted on the roof. The door is made of metal—tough to quietly penetrate if it's locked with a deadbolt. She notes the presence of an alarm system, indicated by a metal panel attached to the exterior.

Cameras hang over the doorway and the gates surrounding the compound. But there's a wrinkle: the camera's cables have been cut, rendering them useless. The station's alarm systems are likely in a similar condition.

Security equipment belonging to the Varga cartel has filled the gap. Red markers hover over the utilities shed and the fence guarding the tower. Each one corresponds to wireless security cameras powered by a local internet source.

The internet source is supplied by a cartel safe house a half mile away, and is marked by a final red orb. Network name, IP addresses, and corresponding MAC addresses are listed in Jen's readout. She saves the addresses on her laptop for later. Those cameras will need to be handled before she makes her access attempt.

First tower down. She starts on the second and finds similar conditions. Limited physical presence at the site. Disabled security features replaced by those belonging to the Varga cartel. A nearby safe house that will enable the cartel to respond rapidly to an intrusion or a disruption in service.

It's going to be a dangerous effort, but Jen is confident. A host of malware will be waiting for her in Mexico City, each strand of it created specifically for telecommunications equipment. The NSA has spent decades executing penetrations on the same type of equipment Jen is targeting, achieving punishing results against America's adversaries. All she'll need to do is conduct the penetrations quietly and slip away, the cartel none the wiser.

The jet banks, and the pilot hops on the intercom. Landing in thirty minutes. Mexico City's periphery appears in the cabin window. On first blush, it's a thriving, modern city—the capital of Mexico. Skyscrapers with enough height to rival New York's. Iconic statues, like the Monumento a la Independencia, dot the city. But the modern accents are camouflage concealing an extremely dangerous cartel. Varga's soldiers will be wedged into the city's deepest, darkest crags, and it'll be her job to confront them.

Won't keep 'em waiting much longer, Jen thinks.

Memories play on repeat as the plane descends. All the way back to a piece of pixel art Terrance had made for her. Godzilla tearing through Beijing. She was meant to be the giant lizard and needed a pick-me-up after a brush with Chinese law enforcement.

The graphic brought a smile to her face.

Only it wasn't so much the graphic; it was the time Terrance had put into it. Their operation was running at a breakneck speed, but he still took the time to create it. She grinds her teeth, livid at her inability to do the same for him.

Final approach. The aircraft is only several hundred feet from touching down, and Jen is eager to begin working in the city. The Godzilla Terrance conjured up is about to be let loose.

She rushes through packing her laptop and augments her dress. She changed before disembarking Martinez's jet. Blue jeans and a hoodie. Nothing that'll attract attention. She extracts a surgical mask from her bag and puts it on. She isn't a germaphobe, but it will obscure her features as she passes through the airport. Wide sunglasses will cover her eyes. She twists her hair into a pile and flips up her hood. If someone is hunting for her, their job will not be an easy one.

Eleven

Benito Juarez International Airport, Mexico City

"Lower your mask, please."

That's a request Jen would prefer to disregard. The customs officer standing in front of her has been sharp, businesslike during her processing. She looks out into the airport's general area. Hundreds of people milling in every direction. Many are standing still, facing her, waiting for their relatives or acquaintances to appear. Some may have less-than-friendly intentions. "I have a cold, sir."

"We can move to a private space and take a better look there. Would that be satisfactory?"

Jen reaches up and lowers her mask briefly. "So much for hospitality."

The customs officer stares at her momentarily. Finally, he bangs her passport with a stamp. "Next!"

Jen lowers her glasses, covertly surveying the airport. Two men are standing at the back wall, and they're staring at her, suspicious. Goose bumps raise her skin. She doesn't let on that they've been spotted as she adjusts her mask. She keeps moving, passing through a final security barrier toward the international terminal's baggage claim area.

She shifts and weaves through the crowd, going in the opposite direction she needs to go. A car is waiting for her in the short-term parking lot, but she needs a clean trail. Removing her glasses, she pretends to clean them, holding them above her head. They operate like a rearview mirror, and she spots the same two men stalking her. One is on his cell, staring directly at her. *Better move before their friends show up.*

A way through presents itself. She spots a janitor changing the trash bags for a row of receptacles. She grabs her water bottle and approaches the man. He's older, completely gray, with a prominent mustache. Someone's kind grandfather. It makes her feel guilty about what she's going to do next. She stops by his cart and pulls her mask down. "*Esta elevacion es seria!*" she says, referencing Mexico City's seven-thousand-foot elevation above sea level.

"*Agua es tu amiga, señorita!*" the janitor says jovially, enjoying the break in his work.

"Water, and maybe some aspirin. *Asprina*?" Jen asks, switching to English. Growing up in Texas makes Spanish a second language, but she's rusty.

The janitor nods. "*Prueba esta tienda de alli,*" he replies, pointing at a nearby convenience store.

"*Gracias, señor*. Be well." She drops her empty bottle into his basket. As she starts moving again, she passes by him, squeezing his shoulder. It distracts him. With her free hand, she snatches the ID card pinned to his shirt.

"*Tu tambien, señora.*" He returns to work, oblivious to his recent loss.

An employee door is just up ahead. Badge in hand, she swipes it against a reader and slips inside. It places her in a long hallway. Signs indicate conference rooms, break areas, and locker rooms. More signs for departure gates, ticketing. She starts to double back, hoping to disorient the men stalking her.

Walking briskly, she pins the badge on her hoodie backward,

concealing the photograph of the old janitor's face. But there's no one in the hall; it's a busy airport, and people are working.

She rushes toward another door fifty yards up the hall. She swipes the badge and steps back into the passenger thoroughfare. The two stalkers aren't in sight, and it bolsters her confidence, but she heads quickly for the airport's exit. She follows a sign pointing toward the parking lot, to the car Martinez's local assets left for her.

She finds a set of stairs leading to the parking garage's higher floors. The car is on the third. She takes the stairs two at a time, sensing that she's close to escape. Halfway up, she realizes she was wrong. One of her stalkers is rushing downward, and he stops cold upon seeing her.

Jen's feet lock up, and she makes eye contact with the man. She doesn't recognize him from the terminal, but he's winded and clearly hunting someone with a specific physical description. Suddenly, the man drops his head and begins descending the stairs. Burns are on both of his wrists—Varga's signature cartel markings. Tattoos creep out of his shirt sleeves. Piercing under his bottom lip. This man is dangerous, and his right hand is reaching for something behind his back.

Instincts force Jen closer to the man. She's not afraid to lock up with him. They get closer, each sticking to their side of the stairway. Their shoulders touch as they pass. "*Señor.*"

The cartel thug sneers. "Jen Yates."

They pass and he keeps moving downward. When Jen senses that he's at the proper distance, she wheels around, delivering a straight kick to his chest as he draws a pistol. He tumbles down at least a dozen concrete stairs, thumping and cracking and moaning as he goes. When he lands, he doesn't get back up. "*Miss* Yates. Say it a little nicer next time."

Jen is forced to leave his body behind and continues to the third story. The deck is only partially full, and it gives her the jitters. There are plenty of unobstructed sightlines available, and she'd never know she was spotted.

With no other alternative, she begins walking deeper onto the level. The Toyota Camry she's searching for has been parked on the far left-hand corner. An older model with the rounded body. Tinted windows and bad rims to blend neatly into Mexico City's rougher areas.

There aren't any warning signs flashing as she reaches the Camry. Kneeling down, she fishes under the car for a magnetic pouch secured to the frame. It was left by the asset—instead of conspicuously planting keys somewhere in the car, he simply exited the vehicle after parking, knowing that the spare set was properly hidden.

Feeling an unusual protrusion, Jen tugs, and the pouch breaks free. She cracks the lid, extracting the keys.

Jen opens the trunk, grabbing a waiting go-bag, and hops in the Camry's driver seat. Unzipping the bag, Jen finds a custom Brügger & Thomet APC 300. Hand-built by some of the world's finest firearms engineers, the rifle has a custom sound suppressor that is integrated with the barrel. It's a similar design to H&K's MP5SD but with a heavier-hitting .300 Blackout cartridge. The suppressor shrouds the barrel, working to vent hot gasses early as the weapon operates. Coupled with subsonic ammunition, the weapon is whisper-quiet, ideal for use in a crowded city.

She activates an Aimpoint Micro T2 red dot scope and sets the brightness. To finish, she inserts a twenty-round magazine filled with subsonic cartridges, then racks the charging handle.

A hot weapon brings security, and Jen quickly locates her parking ticket. It's in the ashtray with several pesos folded around it. She cranks the ignition, jerking the car out of the spot.

She fights off the urge to mash the accelerator as she descends the levels in the parking garage. Squealing tires and banging pistons will draw attention. She exits the third story and arrives at the second.

A crowd has gathered around the fallen cartel member. Tourists with carry-on bags and suitcases. A teenager records the fallen narco with his cell phone. Paramedics and police will no doubt be closing in.

Making an immediate left turn, she starts down a row of parked vehicles. She keeps her speed low and maintains a visual of the scene in the rearview mirror.

The two men who'd been trailing her through the airport blast up the stairs and force their way through the crowd. They kneel by their fallen comrade and attempt to speak with him. The wounded man is unconscious, and they give up trying.

Both men struggle back through the crowd. The first runs for the stairs, toward the third story. The remaining man steps farther into the garage and locks onto her brake lights. He squints, but she makes a quick turn and disappears down the ramp to the first level.

She rubs her foot into the gas. No line at the pay station, and it's close. She creeps up to the nearest booth, inserts her ticket. A payment prompt follows. She deposits too much money and doesn't bother waiting for change. The gate rises. She makes a right, and disappears into the airport's heavy traffic.

She'll get the clean break to her safe house she was hoping for. Varga's cartel will be left wondering what she's going to do next.

Twelve

Centro Historico, Mexico City

The neighborhood in the historical district is busy. A throwback to mid-1900s Mexico City. Reminds Jen a bit of New York but with more color. The buildings are arranged like brownstones. Three or four stories, packed full of apartments. They're painted in an array of colors, like a mismatched rainbow illuminating the street.

There's ample parking streetside, and Jen wedges her car into a spot in front of her safe house. Two sets of stairs are attached to the building. One leading upward to the main section. Another creeping down, off the side, toward a basement. Stashing the B&T in her go-bag, she makes way to the second set of stairs, leading below ground.

Jen stays vigilant as she crosses the sidewalk, taking note of the neighborhood. There's a lot of activity. Kids playing. Older teenagers sitting on porch entrances, smoking, listening to music. The smell of food in the air. There are some shops down the street, even a few restaurants. It's a fifty-fifty situation: plenty of crowds and people to blend with, and plenty of eyes to notice the neighborhood's new stranger. Only time will tell how well it serves her.

She takes the stairs down, reaches a small landing, and keys in.

One bedroom. A kitchen with a bar dividing it from the living room. A sofa—not soiled, but the flowers blooming on the fabric are cringeworthy. There's even a flat-screen television and a coffee table. Wallpaper is properly glued in place, and the ceiling's paint isn't chipping. Jen smiles. Better than Beijing by a country mile.

Jen removes her B&T from the bag, keeping her security posture tight until she clears the apartment.

Kitchen first. It's small, offering an intruder few places to hide. While she's there, she cracks the fridge. There are some basics: eggs, milk, chicken breasts, and butter. She slides to the bathroom next, flipping on the light. It's clean. Another bonus.

Finally, the bedroom. There's a queen bed made up with a comforter and pillows. Stacks of black Pelican cases rest at the far end of the bed, slightly concealed, containing her kit along with medical supplies. She slides back the mirrored door to the closet. No one, not even a roach running for cover.

She sets her APC 300 on the dresser across from the bed and gets to work. It's time for some excitement. This operation will be her first working with Anne, or the Advanced NeuroNet Engine. As a computer nerd, having a quantum computer as a sidekick is the ultimate thrill. She won't need to be dialed into a TOC, constantly communicating with Martinez and the other Group members while she conducts her penetrations. Anne will do most of the thinking while providing a layer of security.

Cracking open a large Pelican case labeled *Tech*, she gets to it. Laptop first. She turns on a heavily customized MacBook Pro. It has the most powerful processors available, along with tools to pick up long-distance wireless signals. A suite of malware is pre-installed, along with security programs. When it boots, she logs in with her thumbprint and immediately searches for a hidden SSID, or internet access point. She clicks the SSID, connecting to satellite internet.

Good afternoon, Ms. Yates. I haven't seen you since Korea!

The message pops up in the MacBook's text messaging app. The Advanced NeuroNet Engine has complete control of the device via servers based at CIA headquarters in Langley.

Jen can't help but giggle. This technology is mind-bending. Anne shows real, independent intelligence. Between that and the Korea reference, Jen momentarily forgets why she's in Mexico City. She types: *Back when you saved the world?*

Not hardly, Ms. Yates. I'm happy to be working with you again. I'm activating your computer's microphone so you can speak commands. You can also type, whichever you prefer.

"I'll talk, you type," Jen replies. "I'm starting on my phone next." She plucks a phone out of the Pelican case, turns it on, and activates Bluetooth. Anne connects with it immediately, and another text pings the phone.

Device synced, Ms. Yates.

Jen nods. *Man, it's so easy.* She's now holding the most secure comms device in Mexico City. The phone uses an application called Lost Call, engineered at the NSA. It causes the cell signal to frequency hop, or constantly change. It's virtually impossible to track the phone with this application functioning.

Anne is also inside the device, managing the data encryptions and the firewall. Nothing can beat a quantum computer. Period. Any foreign access attempt will fail immediately, and Anne will notify Jen.

Another piece of special technology lies waiting in the case. It's called a Whisper. Its exterior is made of ionized silicone, and it's very sticky. It's small, no bigger than a kidney bean. Jen sticks it to the back of her ear and activates it with some pressure. The Whisper syncs with the phone immediately.

Anne sends a third message. This time it vibrates in Jen's skull, and the message is clear. The Whisper is a bone microphone and communicates through these vibrations. Anne can send her silent messages or warnings. Jen can speak within the phone's proximity. Anne will detect her voice and talk back. Moreover, Anne can translate any Spanish that Jen hears directly into the Whisper.

A few more gadgets left. First a small drone, roughly the size of a textbook, with four propellers at the corners. Despite its outward simplicity, it's loaded down with tools to interfere with wireless signals. Cameras mounted on its belly are state-of-the-art. Powerful electric motors can propel it to almost seventy miles an hour.

Jen syncs it with Anne and powers it on. It leaps out of her hand, buzzing around the bedroom. Its flight pattern looks like beautiful geometry, a grace a human being would struggle to accomplish.

Jen's Whisper buzzes: "Check your phone, Ms. Yates."

She looks down at a camera feed on the phone. It's mounted on the drone and shows her face. Another menu pops up, showing off the drone's onboard signals interception and disruption options—important if she crosses path with Varga's men or the local police. "Impressive, Anne. Have to get some flying lessons from you sometime."

"I'm free twenty-four hours a day."

Jen laughs. The last tools are important, and they're already placed: wireless cameras. One by the front door, one by the back, looking into the apartment's alleyway. Both are no bigger than a golf ball. "Let's see the security cameras on the phone, Anne."

Feeds pop up immediately. Each are perfect, fish-eye lenses that cover the doors. They'll also be monitored by the quantum computer, twenty-four seven. If an intruder is detected, Jen will be alerted. Cameras go offline? Another red flag.

Jen opens a final case, this one with her prized personal weapons inside. Her dad is an outdoorsman, and she grew up in West Texas—a title that means she takes her weapons seriously. Hunting, target, and competition shooting were some of her and her father's favorite pastimes. Hasn't changed to this day.

She reaches for the pistol first. It's a customized Staccato XC 2011, chambered in ten millimeter, and equipped with a low-profile compensated barrel.

The compensator offers a significant reduction in recoil for the ten-millimeter cartridge. That will greatly increase her shooting speed. Internal components are highly polished, and as Jen racks the slide, she feels like she's dragging it across glass. The final and arguably most important touch is the trigger. Crisp and clean at two pounds.

She racks the slide, pinning the trigger rearward and releasing it with a click. Ramming a fresh magazine into the mag well, she racks the slide once more. A round hits the chamber, filling the room with a satisfying ratchet sound.

On to her knife. It's a hunting blade. Damascus steel. Dark wood, giraffe bone, and turquoise form the handle. It was a gift from her father, presented in a fine leather sheath. Another work of art. Another killing tool.

The rifle in the case is a brand-new H&K 416 A5 with a ten-and-a-half-inch barrel. It's a last-ditch weapon, offering more firepower than the B&T. If things go according to plan in Mexico City, the weapon won't be put to use. Nevertheless, it's comforting to have at the bedside.

With her weapons deposited on the nightstand, she sets her phone's alarm for 8:00 p.m. and plugs the device in the charger. After she gets a couple hours of sleep, she'll trip up the security cameras guarding the cell towers, paving the way for successful penetrations of her targets.

Thirteen

Campo Militar 1, Mexico City

After round-trip flights between Mexico City and Texas, Martinez is finally returning to her temporary apartment on base. High-heeled shoes have been removed and placed neatly by the door. No self-respecting U.S. Naval Academy graduate would have anything less.

Before she can proceed deeper into the apartment, her phone beeps. Sounds like an alarm, and she snatches the device from the breast pocket of her suit. The message was an emergency alert, sent directly from the base's tactical operations center. Only one reason for something like that: a development regarding her missing people.

She wedges her feet into a pair of running shoes. They'll be more suitable as she proceeds to the TOC. Before the apartment door slams shut, she's summoning her Group.

Martinez half-sprints to the elevator, her mind spinning. The emergency text's timing is suspect. She hasn't been back on base longer than thirty minutes. This moment feels choreographed.

"Hey!"

Martinez turns as the elevator door glides open. Sloane bursts from her apartment, reacting to the news. They step onto the elevator together and start toward the ground floor.

"Andrew?" Martinez asks.

Sloane straightens her suit jacket, throws her wavy brown hair against her shoulders. Goes nicely with the tan she earned basking in Georgia's sun. She shakes her head. "No clue. Was there contact?"

"I'm unsure—the situation is developing." Martinez quickly switches gears, needing to make the most of their short time before entering the company of Mexican officials. "I need you to follow my lead in the TOC. We need to buy some time in the city."

"Got it," Sloane replies, ready to follow her boss's orders without question.

The elevator door opens, and it's like a gunshot for two sprinters. They rush through the lobby, directly to the exit. The sun is falling on Mexico City as they start toward the base's command post two blocks away.

Martinez reaches the command post's door first, and she looks back to find Andrew approaching. He's tucking his shirt into his pants, and one of his shoelaces is untied. Despite his belly, he's moving fast. The definition of being on call.

"Don't wait for me!" Andrew shouts.

Martinez lets the door slam behind Sloane. She didn't need Andrew's permission. Critical intelligence could have come in, and it may already be too late to act on it.

Martinez finds Major Trey Bingham rushing for the TOC as she rounds the corner. Despite his prosthetic leg, he moves gracefully. Awe-inspiring. The type of leader who can take a beating, heal up, and come back stronger. A Les Baer 1911 rests in a cognac-colored leather holster on his hip. He keys into the TOC, holds open the door, and allows Martinez and Sloane to enter first.

It's a full-court press inside. They're all standing around a single analyst's station. The base's senior officer, Admiral Mateo Perez, is present. Commander Torres, a Fuerza Especial troop commander is standing by the admiral's side. Several other liaisons from the CNI, Mexico's intelligence service, are present. Finally, a member of Mexico's

National Guard, formerly the Federal Police, stands by to offer the assistance of his forces.

First glances are deceptive. Badges, uniforms, polished attitudes, and discipline. All of these individuals appear to be dedicated professionals. But at least one of them is corrupt. Odds are high that Mateo Perez isn't alone in seeking employment outside of the government.

"What's going on?" Martinez asks, making her way toward the group of officials.

Admiral Perez greets her with a handshake. It's respectful, firm. His cap has been removed, exposing strands of thinning gray hair. Green uniform starched to perfection. He's overweight, but it doesn't stop him from standing ramrod straight. "Thank you for coming, Ms. Martinez. A video has been sent in by the cartel."

Andrew steps into the mix, taking a spot behind Martinez. "Apologies for the interruption."

Perez is gracious, strong, in control. People call him El Matador—the bull fighter. Never spent much time on a battlefield; his wars are won in the political arena, and he comes across like a showman. Authority booms from his voice as he invites Andrew into the circle. "There's been no interruption. We've yet to start." The admiral nudges the intelligence analyst sitting in front of the computer. "I must warn you all, this video is graphic."

Martinez braces herself. Proof-of-life videos can be harsh, and the men who will be under duress are people she cares for. "I don't need a warning, sir. Play it, please."

The intelligence analyst starts the video. A map of Mexico City pops up, edited to look like an adventurer's guide to a missing treasure. A bobblehead caricature of Terrance dashes onto the map. He begins crying, the character's voice perfectly matching the original owner. He starts running along the map, leaving a red hatch-marked trail behind him. He cries, "Find me, Ms. Martinez, please! I'm going to die soon!"

A characterization of Martinez stumbles onto the map. Body small, head large. Long, black hair and a tailored suit. It's her face, down to the smallest details. Her character begins chasing after Terrance but quickly deviates from the path, forming her own. A message that she's already gone wrong.

The cartoon Terrance runs out of steam. He huffs and puffs, blowing steam out of his ears until his head swells and pops off. Blood spurts out of his neck, soaks the map, drowning out its details. *GAME OVER* flashes on the screen.

"I apologize for that, Ms. Martinez," the admiral says. "I have no idea how they gained access to your image."

Martinez isn't surprised; after all, she's standing across from a traitor. But she is disappointed. There were no demands or proof of life, which could have been used to hone in on a location. The video was merely a threat from an adversary, looking to unsettle her. Have to work a lot harder than that. "Your apology is unnecessary, Admiral, but thank you." She pauses, addresses her Group. "What can we learn from this?"

Andrew squints through his thick glasses, rubs his salt-and-pepper beard. As usual, he's one step ahead of everyone in the room. "Despite the cartoonish appearance, it's sophisticated. There's real editing skill behind that. We'll need to—"

"I agree," Martinez says, cutting him off with a hand on his shoulder. While Andrew's idea is no doubt excellent, she's trying to give the room an entirely different impression of her Group's posture.

Sloane is on Martinez's page. "They're prepared for us. Maybe it's too dangerous to return our people through typical means."

Martinez nods to Sloane. "I agree, Ms. Hamilton. With a little patience and restraint, we might get an expedient offer from the cartel to return our people."

"We'll definitely avoid bloodshed—Mexican or American," Sloane agrees, who perks up for show.

Major Bingham's face is red. Eyes bore into Martinez. "The United States doesn't negotiate with hostage takers, Ms. Martinez. How do you plan on getting around that?"

Martinez's reply is even and thought out. "We don't *pay* for hostages. We've returned prisoners to Middle Eastern adversaries over the course of negotiations, and offered other concessions. The Oval Office is aware of how sensitive this situation has become, and is open to a multitude of possibilities."

"You're going to pause your investigation into the Varga cartel, Ms.

Martinez?" Admiral Perez asks, unable to hide his shock as he pieces together what Martinez is saying.

"The White House has given me unilateral authority to make the call, Admiral." Martinez has Perez's attention, and her tone is firm. "The United States government has a singular objective: ensuring the safe return of its missing people. When that occurs, we'll reassess our posture in Mexico City."

"I don't recommend taking that tack, Ms. Martinez," Perez replies steadily. "Keep pressure on Varga. Terror poses a threat to both of our countries."

Martinez holds her ground. "El Matador" is looking to bury a horn in her gut, hoping the truth leaks out. "I need to get Varga to the negotiating table and make a deal. The sooner that occurs, the better."

Commander Alvaro Torres offers his opinion. He's an FES troop commander, similar to Major Bingham. His men are also on base, waiting to assist the Americans with operations against the cartel. "Ms. Martinez, I don't believe your people will be harmed. Alex Varga isn't foolish enough to kill Americans. Pablo Escobar learned that lesson the hard way, and it stuck."

Mexico's dichotomy, standing directly in front of Martinez. Commander Torres passed the Agency's background investigation. He's a good man, ready to stand against evil. Hundreds, thousands like him are eager to take up the same charge. But a single corrupt leader stands in his path. "Do you have a suggestion, Commander?"

"Varga has more assets than he can hide. Let's hit them. Find the radiation's source and severely wound the cartel. I've known men like Alex Varga. He won't be able to tolerate that."

Major Bingham crosses his arms, works on grinding his teeth down to stumps as he listens. "The commander makes a great point, ma'am," he says. "We'll brace Varga and sit his ass down at *our* negotiating table."

Martinez feigns consideration before replying. Their irritation neatly accents her ruse. "It's a valid point, but the White House is concerned about our missing people and the potential political fallout. Allowing Americans to remain in cartel custody is a non-starter. I need a resolution *now*."

Perez grimaces. "Varga will consider this weakness. You'll be vulnerable to whatever he throws at you."

"It's my decision, Admiral," Martinez replies. "You'll let me know the second something comes in?"

The meeting is over. Admiral Perez takes a deep breath and gives her a nod. "Of course, ma'am. That's why I'm here."

After a round of handshakes, Martinez leads her people to the door. They step out into the hallway, visibly shaken by what they just heard. "Not a word," she whispers. "Follow me."

Fourteen

Martinez gathered her Group in a Suburban, parked in her apartment building's garage. Several inches of armor and bullet-proof glass prevent any outside eavesdroppers from listening in. The vehicle had been stashed at the U.S. embassy while she returned to the United States. The cartel wouldn't dare to try slipping past the United States Marines to tamper with it.

"Didn't see that one coming, Ms. Martinez," Major Bingham says, still irate from what he just heard. "Care to fill us in on why you're planning to negotiate with narco-terrorists?"

Martinez, seated next to Trey in the driver's seat, can't help but feel uncomfortable. His eyes are needling her through his oversized glasses. In any other situation, .45 caliber slugs would be following close behind. "There aren't going to be any negotiations, Major."

Bingham leans back, caught off-guard by the sudden reversal. "Sounds like you're about to live up to your reputation."

Martinez briefs her people on Jen's recent insertion into Mexico City, along with the target package she's going to be scratching lines through. The package was approved with executive authority direct from the Oval Office, granting Jen almost unlimited latitude to accomplish her objectives.

Martinez wasn't lying about having unilateral decision-making authority either. Big bosses have given little bosses plenty of room to maneuver and settle things properly. She won't have to crawl up any chain of command when something serious happens. She'll be able to respond rapidly—a requirement to save the hostages in cartel custody.

"Varga has crossed one too many lines," Martinez says. "We're going to *take* our people back, and we won't be stopping there."

Sloane's attention is piqued but for an entirely different set of reasons. "We can't allow Jen to operate alone in Mexico City, ma'am."

Martinez turns to face Sloane, who is a Southerner from a military family, like Jen. Her older brother was lost in Iraq, serving as a United States Marine. Service is in Sloane's blood, just like protecting the people she cares for. "That's exactly what we're going to do, Ms. Hamilton."

It's Andrew's turn to read Martinez's crystal ball. Jen rescued him in Beijing, so in his mind, it's Varga who needs protecting from her. "Doesn't mean we can't support her from afar, Sloane."

"Mr. Xiao is correct," Martinez replies. "We'll be assisting Jen along the way. More importantly, we'll begin triangulating Varga's hidden equipment once she completes her first penetrations."

Sloane shakes her head vehemently against the idea. "Ma'am, I disagree. Can I at least suggest using our PSD as Jen's backup element?"

Major Bingham is an expert in this arena. His best shooters are doubling as Martinez's personal security detail, accepting responsibility for her safe travel inside Mexico City. "Easy to do, Ms. Martinez. Give me the word, and I'll have my guys jock up to heavier kits. Slip 'em out the embassy's back door if there's trouble."

"I appreciate both of your concerns, but my word is final," Martinez replies. "Perez is watching us closely, and if we break our protocol now, he'll realize that we're active in the city."

After a round of acknowledgements Martinez continues. "Go and get a few hours of sleep. Be ready to work by eight p.m."

Fifteen

Missing Jen Yates at the airport means a long night of surveillance for Victor.

Varga has multiple systems powering his cartel. They're all vulnerable while Jen is in Mexico City. It'll be Victor's job to mitigate damage. Same as World Chem. Find what's compromised. Cut it out of the system. Replace it with something secure.

Victor is staying in a penthouse apartment of Varga's in downtown Mexico City. Fine furniture. Five-star kitchen. The best part is a view overlooking the city. A bank of computers set up in the living room serve as a backdoor into the cartel's network.

The cartel's main data center is set up in a downtown office building. Every strand of information the cartel generates passes through it. Hundreds of camera feeds, like the ones Victor saw in the apartment building, terminate inside. Drug shipments are monitored, along with Varga's soldiers, local law enforcement, and rival cartels. People are sitting by phones twenty-four hours a day, behaving like 911 operators. Cartel gunmen are dispatched to hotspots within seconds of a call.

Victor built all of it, and he knows how to protect it.

Activity monitors, along with data usage monitors, are displayed on one of his computer screens. Throughout the night, he'll keep a close eye on network activity. Any spike in power or data usage will be a sign that Jen Yates is assaulting the network. Someone gaining administrative-level access will be a sure sign they've been hacked. He alone can grant that privilege in the network.

It's getting late, and the computer monitors are already burning Victor's eyes. The taste for vodka creeps onto his taste buds. Something to ease the day's tension from his shoulders.

Before he goes to the kitchen, he double-checks a very special computer monitor. It's a map of Mexico City with *six* distinct GPS pins displayed prominently. It also has a clock counting down from six hours to zero. Still ten minutes left, giving Victor some time to pour his drink.

He walks to the kitchen and extracts a bottle from the freezer. A chilled tumbler stands next to the bottle, along with a giant cylindrical ice cube. Two fingers of vodka follow the cube into the glass.

Victor sucks down the vodka, and his muscles are already loosening as he returns to his station. He checks the countdown clock. Five minutes left. Time to hurry.

A special application is installed on his computer that allows him to mirror cell phone numbers. Whenever he sends a message, it'll appear to be from a preselected number, not his own. In this case, he's copying Varga's personal cell. It's the only way to get anything done in the cartel.

He begins crafting six distinct messages. They contain new addresses and directions to move. Once finished, he watches the clock and waits. Four seconds . . . three . . . two . . .

Victor sends the six messages simultaneously. They're going to the three separate teams of hostage takers responsible for Terrance Kline, Bobby Hollice, and Cameron Vinke. Three more for the three teams protecting the decoy hostages. Within minutes, the six teams begin traveling to different locations in the city where they'll wait for the stopwatch to hit zero again.

SIXTEEN

AZCAPOTZALCO, MEXICO CITY

JEN THROWS OUT HER MOTORCYCLE'S KICKSTAND AND PEELS off her helmet to get a better view of her surroundings. The bike was left as a secondary form of transportation at the safe house. Being an experienced rider, she jumped at the chance to speed in between Mexico City's lines of traffic on it.

She's halfway up a winding dirt road that leads to her first cell tower, or base station. It's at the northwestern periphery of Mexico City, posted atop a hill, surrounded by desert rocks and dry vegetation. The hill rises around two hundred feet above the streets below, a common trick providers use to aid with signal distribution.

Apartments and small homes surround the tower to the south. The cartel safe house identified on ISR is within view. Barely a two-minute trip by vehicle. But Jen came prepared. Before leaving her apartment, she hacked the cartel's cameras. Their feeds have been replaced with looped footage. She could walk straight past one, and the cartel members would be none the wiser.

Stripping off her pack, she removes Anne's drone and holds it by her head. Certain that the quantum computer is listening through her cell phone, she says, "Anne, drone is free to launch."

The drone's propellers whir before it leaps into the sky and disappears. ISR is now active, and if the cartel responds to her activity on site, she'll have an early warning.

She cranks on her motorcycle and travels up the remaining stretch of road, keeping the headlights off. The site is mostly dark, save a single light shining above the utilities shed door. Red aerial-warning lights also flash high up on the tower.

Killing the bike, she kicks out its stand once again. She approaches the gate and finds it unlocked, likely a stipulation to the deal Varga is forcing on the telecom companies.

Around back of the utilities shed, she examines several utility boxes where phone lines and electrical services enter the building. She finds the box that powers the alarm system and opens it. Its wires have been disconnected, rendering it useless.

Jen draws her 2011 and approaches the utilities shed door. Flies are crawling out of a metal vent and buzz off into the night. Others turn back and reenter the shed. Rubber lashes from work boots traverse the door—remnants of the murdered technician who was dragged from the building. Her instincts are raging; something terrible is waiting inside.

She doesn't bother pulling out a lockpick set. Like everything else on site, the cartel probably demands easy access. With a twist of the knob, the door swings open. Lights blink on automatically. A swarm of flies explodes into the night. She steps back, waving them away from her face and mouth. Acrid, stale blood hits her nose, and it's almost overpowering. Her gaze locks on the adjacent wall.

There's a cartel shrine not ten feet away. Pictures are posted. Men who are wearing telecom uniforms are featured. Black candles and other tokens to Aztec gods dot the table. A workplace accident chart has been modified: *93 days since the last accident.* Only *accident* has been crossed out and replaced with *disappearance*. A message is written in blood on the wall, and a band of dead flies lie underneath: *Safe work means no service interruptions! Remember: We're only minutes away!*

Monsters.

Jen ties a bandana around her face and steps inside. She identifies MexTel's base station controller by its exterior markings. It's made by IBM. They produce a tremendous amount of telecoms equipment, and the hacking tools in her kit have special settings for this particular model.

The second base station controller is different, and it certainly belongs to Varga. She approaches the device, almost mystified. It's a black cube, the size of a bookshelf. Green lights flicker on its face, signaling function, connecting calls. There are no prominent brand markings. No unique serial numbers or labels that technicians would use to find maintenance parts. She activates the flashlight on her phone, searching behind and below the device—no identifiable markings anywhere.

She snaps a half-dozen photos from varying angles and uploads them to the Group. "Let's see what's under the hood."

She pulls her laptop out of her pack, along with a USB cable. Flies are rutting in the controller's USB port, and she uses her blade to spoon them away. Once the port is clear, she plugs in the USB cable, beginning her intrusion.

A login prompt appears on her laptop. Two language selections are present: Russian and Spanish. The discovery gets her mind running. Classified Russian technology could be at work in Mexico City. It would explain the lack of identifying markings.

She fingerprints the system, searching for a way to get past the login screen. A fingerprint allows a hacker to understand how the system is operating without making an access attempt and tripping the security features. Firewall types, operating system, IP and MAC addresses become visible. It's a sophisticated move, and she finds the controller's identifying information is written in Cyrillic. "Anne, take screen grabs of everything that I'm working on."

"Understood, Ms. Yates. I'll forward them to Ms. Martinez immediately," Anne replies via the Whisper.

"Good."

"I'm taking the liberty of translating the firewall's information. It's one I've never encountered before: *Porosha*."

"Translation?"

"It's Russian, and it means: Powder snow that fell during a previous night," Anne replies.

"I'll handle it myself," Jen says, batting away flies from her neck. Fresh meat, and they're hungry for it.

She performs a race condition–style attack, bombarding the login screen with commands. A code level interface pops up, and from there, she retrieves the system's encrypted passwords. They're hashed, meaning they're scrambled with the chosen encryption method, which is Elliptic-Curve Cryptography. The world's best, used by the likes of the NSA until the organization made the leap to quantum. "Crack those login credentials for me, Anne."

Anne decimates the encryption within seconds. It's why quantum technology is so feared amongst nation-state competitors. The tools they use to protect vital interests are useless against systems like the Advanced NeuroNet Engine.

Jen enters the login credentials and gains access to the base station controller. From here, it's easy. She installs a malware strain called Vector. Used for spying on advanced networks, it's incredibly difficult to detect. Moreover, it embeds itself in a target computer's kernel, making it impossible to remove.

With the malware installation successful, she logs out of the session and hurriedly returns her laptop to the backpack. Time to get free of the filth. Before she exits, she takes a last look at the shrine. It's not only a testament to the cartel's evil, but to their power. They have Mexico's largest telecom providers petrified. As she exits, she desperately wants to shift that balance of power.

SEVENTEEN

"THE BASE STATION CONTROLLER JEN JUST HACKED DOESN'T match anything that the NSA has encountered—both stateside and in the wild," Sloane remarks as she works with the rest of the Group members inside the Embassy's secure conference room.

She's reading through an NSA–compiled encyclopedia on technologies. It's a virtual catalogue of every type of electronic device ever made. Identifies everything from the earliest model cell phones to refrigerators with Wi-Fi capability. Base station controllers take up a prominent part in the encyclopedia because of their strategic importance in telecommunications.

Controllers manufactured by America and its allies are listed, often in mind-numbing detail. Others manufactured by Russia and Iran are listed, but more clandestinely. These are usually catalogued as pictures taken by NSA operatives in hostile countries, seconds before they're hacked. Gateways into an enemy's communication networks, exploited with ruthless efficiency.

"Nothing with any similarity?" Martinez asks, surprised by the finding. She was expecting cheap Chinese telecoms tech. For a man like Varga, it could be purchased easily. Chinese technicians would readily install and maintain it.

"Even the controller's exterior shells are worlds apart. Port locations. Coatings. Nothing matches."

Martinez crosses her arms, disturbed. Her enemy's advanced capabilities are in line with everything else she's found so far. Sophisticated narcotics. High digital proficiency. Well-planned kidnappings against Americans. She shifts attention to Andrew. "Where are we with the encryption?"

"It's Russian. Everything's in Cyrillic," Andrew replies, entranced by his computer's display. Four windows neatly bisect the screen. Code for the encryption. Its governing algorithm. Anne's command interface.

"Any links to the FSB? GRU?" Martinez asks, checking off Russia's intelligence services.

"Doesn't look like it. Code and encryption methods have been tailored specifically for this application," Andrew replies, fixated on the minute details.

When he was imprisoned by China's MSS, he became obsessed by little things. Like how he replaced a bathroom tile after hiding a cell phone behind it, or how he made use of scalding hot water to mist the cameras in his bathroom. Little things, adding up to something big. Part of what saved his life, along with Jen's heroism.

"Can you automate Jen's next attempt?" Martinez asks.

Andrew smirks and twists his computer screen to show Martinez his fourth window. "One step ahead of you. Anne and I just finished a tool that will make Jen's next access attempt a breeze."

"Upload it to Jen's laptop and notify her via Whisper."

Andrew begins hammering on his keyboard. "On it."

"All right, where the hell did these things come from? I need ideas here," Martinez says, irritated.

Andrew's mind is on the Cyrillic user interface and the sophisticated encryption method. "My gut tells me a nation-state actor designed this equipment. The NSA has man-portable telecoms equipment for use in hostile areas."

Sloane shakes her head. Like Martinez with China, the study of Russia is one of her passions. She's followed the country's history from Stalin's origins, all the way up to its current leader. "None of these actions align with Russia's geopolitical motivations. What would the Russian government gain by assisting Alex Varga?"

"Varga's smuggling routes, for one," Andrew informs. "They're going to be the most sophisticated in the Western Hemisphere, and perfect vectors to launch terror-related attacks into the U.S."

"That's true, but you're suggesting a persistent terror operation, with follow-on attacks," Sloane replies. "Why would Varga burn one of his most valuable smuggling methods to achieve that goal? Why not just help the Russians walk a few PKMs across the border and take out a local strip mall?"

"It's possible he didn't—at least, not intentionally. The Russians could have gained access to Alex's organization and betrayed him. It's always possible the relationship soured."

"To what end?" Martinez interjects. "That scenario feels rushed, and if the Kremlin moves, they're going to do it right. To date, they haven't achieved anything but unwanted U.S. attention."

"I'm leaning toward a highly empowered organization, ma'am. Private individuals with access to advanced technology and equipment," Sloane says.

"Wish Jen had been able to take a screwdriver to that base station controller," Andrew adds.

"Why is that?" Martinez asks.

"Sloane could be right," Andrew replies. "Taking apart that base station controller would give us the ability to study its components. If we had serial numbers or models, we could trace them back to manufacturers."

Sloane glows at the thought of ripping Varga's equipment apart. "It would be a deciding factor. NSA and CIA have clandestine technology manufacturing branches—the type of stuff that's too sensitive for contractors to produce."

"Yup. If we can't trace components back to public manufacturers, it would point to the involvement of a foreign government with similar programs," Andrew says, finishing Sloane's thought.

"Disturbing the cartel's communications is off-limits—at least for now. But we will be revisiting this conversation," Martinez says, slightly frustrated with the inconclusive result. She zeroes back in on her laptop.

Jen is in close proximity to her next target. "Let's focus up. We'll start the triangulation after the next penetration."

It came as a blip. Almost like a stealth aircraft on a radar screen. Minute, near impossible to detect. But not impossible all together.

Victor leans closer to his monitor, staring at the activity levels in the cartel's cellular network. They spiked but only momentarily.

He also has the cameras displayed on his screen for both base stations. They've betrayed no movement or other physical presence. It doesn't mean that there's nothing happening at those locations. The Americans have their tricks, and he's seen them firsthand.

Reaching for his cell phone, he cues up a warning message to Varga. Their base stations may be under attack. A request to send patrols to the towers follows shortly after.

He rests his phone on his table, satisfied. Allowing Jen to access the cartel's communications is a bridge too far. When Varga sees that message, he'll respond. Forcefully.

Eighteen

Milpa Alta, Mexico City

It just had to be tonight.

Jen stares at the top of the second base station's tower, having just launched her drone. Arcs of electricity jump out of a transceiver close to one hundred feet in the air. Bad wiring. Before long it will short the circuit and take the cartel's entire network offline.

Not something Jen can allow. It's been almost twenty-four hours since Terrance and the others were lost. Allowing more time to pass while the cartel fiddles with their shoddy construction isn't viable. She'll need to fix it before she makes her intrusion into the final base station controller.

That fix will be dangerous. Normally, a technician would disconnect power before climbing the tower. The electricity dancing up top is four hundred and eighty volts—enough to cook a person. Working on the line while it's hot is not safe, but pulling the power plug means inviting a visit from the cartel.

Transceivers also generate a tremendous amount of radiation and heat. Jen imagines climbing the tower, dripping sweat, a dozen transceivers blasting energy in her face. Torquing down a hot wire with metal tools, palms sweaty. Doesn't get any more dangerous.

The view up the tower ladder is daunting. Pitch-black all the way up, save a single red aircraft warning light. Occasional bolts of blue electricity illuminate the tower's skeleton. Orange sparks explode and trace into the night. She thinks of Terrance and the risks he took to keep her safe. Bobby and Cam both have young families, with children. She places a hand on the metal ladder, swears she feels electricity surging.

I'll do it for them, and so someone else doesn't have to, Jen thinks.

"Anne, let Martinez know that my danger profile is elevated."

"Relaying the update, Ms. Yates."

"Hold incoming comms. I need to focus," Jen says, starting to climb.

Ten feet up, and Jen is already struggling. Reaching for the ladder's next rung is done by feel alone. Zapping sounds get louder. Vibrations linger in the tower's metal.

She reaches a platform at the halfway point, feeling the strain of climbing with thirty pounds of equipment. Mexico City's elevation has her lightheaded. After sucking down a few gulps of water, she starts toward the top platform, which is surrounded by the tower's transceivers.

Flashing blue light guides her the final few feet. The encircling transceivers ratchet up the temperature to over a hundred degrees. She steps onto the platform, zeroing in on the problem. It's indeed a cartel transceiver, haphazardly bolted to the tower.

She shines a flashlight on the transceiver, illuminating a partially melted plate concealing the faulty wiring. She extracts a screwdriver and takes careful aim at the screws holding it in place. She twists the screws free, ensuring she doesn't touch any metallic parts as she works. The plate doesn't move. Electricity has welded it into place.

Time for some elbow grease. Jen grabs a flathead screwdriver, wedging it into a seam. She uses it like a crowbar to pry off the frozen plate. Won't budge, so she overlaps her hands, preparing for a hard push. As she applies her entire body weight to the screwdriver's handle, the plate snaps free.

Electricity surges, triggering a small explosion. The force throws

Jen back, and she smacks into another transceiver. The tower's hum fades as a disconnect in the utilities shed trips, killing the site's electricity.

Alarm bells should be ringing in Jen's head, but she doesn't move. The Whisper is smoking behind her ear. Her cell phone turned itself off, detecting a surge of electricity. The drone is still functional, and it swoops in, close to Jen's face. Anne begins sending distress signals to Martinez. If Jen is dead or dying, then she needs help, and that's before Varga's thugs arrive.

Four cartel enforcers inhabit a dilapidated apartment a mile from the tower. Tar from cigarette smoke colors the walls yellow and brown. Ashtrays overflow with butts. Rats have chewed holes in the sofas. A statue of Huitzilopochtli rests in the corner. Multicolored Christmas lights circle it, top to bottom. Candles burn at its sides.

The leader, Carlos, is known for being strict, but that's because Varga is always watching. Cameras are mounted in every room. Red lights glow below the lenses, offering an ever-present reminder that Varga is in control. Cell phones can be transformed into microphones at any time. Misbehavior has severe repercussions in the cartel. Second chances aren't offered.

The hulking enforcers have Aztec warrior markings on their arms. Silver studs in their bottom lips. Burns everywhere. Skin merely a canvas for tattoos or scars. Violent energy builds in the living room. Instinct tells them that they'll have a chance to earn respect tonight. Rise in the cartel's hierarchy.

Patrol orders have just come in. A rapid response is underway. They work with lit cigarettes between their lips. Ash crumbles over their plate carriers as they fasten them over their torsos. Smoke curls around weapons during final checks.

Carlos waits by a window while his men prepare. Southern Mexico City is more jungle than desert, and he struggles to see the tower past thickets of trees and bush. That's until blinding blue light explodes from the tower's peak. A boom echoes through the neighborhood. The tower's red strobe lights go offline. Bars disappear from the BlackBerry in his hand. Service is down, a cardinal sin.

"Let's roll!" Carlos runs for the door, AK-47 in hand. The three others follow. They'll reach the tower in under five minutes and restore service by any means necessary.

"Ugh." Jen landed awkwardly. She unfolds her legs, straightens herself out. Everything is tingling, and she can't feel her extremities. Her right ear feels like it's on fire, and she reaches up, finding a blob of melted silicon. The drone buzzes directly in front of her face—a wake-up call. "How long have I been out?" she mumbles.

No response. Everything on her person is fried, and there's no time to fix it. She forces herself upright and starts working on the tower while she has the chance. She extracts a socket wrench, putting a three-eighths Allen key on the head—common size for electrical lugs. She begins repairing the transceiver. A loose connection was causing the problem. Her left hand is in excruciating pain. Every time she twists the socket wrench to lock down the wire, muscles cramp and spasm.

No time to diagnose the injury. She replaces the transceiver's electrical cover before grabbing her gear. With hands on the sides of the ladder, she kicks out her feet and slides down. Close to the second platform, she squeezes her boots into the ladder, slowing down. She repeats it, hitting the bottom in record time.

Despite the ringing in her ears, she can hear a diesel engine, loud, without a muffler. Old shocks squeal as the truck bounces along the rutted road leading to the base station.

Jen reaches her motorcycle and spots a set of headlights coming up the road. The cartel is almost directly on top of her. Not wanting to start the bike, she pushes it behind the utilities shed. It'll be her hiding spot too. As the engine sound grows, she pulls her 2011 from her holster.

Brakes squeal. Four doors open, then slam shut. Metal rattles as one of the cartel members grabs his tool belt. Multiple sets of footsteps move quickly to take control of the location. They head to the shed, and Jen prays they don't notice the fresh tire tracks her bike left behind.

The shed door swings hard, slamming into the wall. It rattles the entire building. They rush inside, no doubt guided by rifle muzzles. Movements vibrate through the wall at her back. They begin talking through the problem. Jen's Spanish comes in handy.

"Disconnect tripped. Second time this month."

"Throw the disconnect. See if this bitch stays live."

Clang. Power surges through the facility. Silence as the cartel members decide if their band-aid solution will hold.

"You got a signal?"

"Yeah. You?"

"We're good. Don't look like anyone's been in here either."

"Check around back. Varga sent us for a reason."

Jen and her bike are around back. Before the cartel members approach, she changes position, angling herself against the nearest corner and raising her pistol. It feels ten pounds heavier than it should. Her left-hand fingers don't take to it. Recoil will be hard to control. Rapid engagements near impossible. She'd scream out in pain if it wouldn't result in her death.

Gravel crunches. Jen gauges the footsteps: one man, a rifle swinging in a sling, clacking against magazines in a plate carrier. Slowly, she drops the 2011's safety without a click.

The footsteps stop. The muzzle of an AK-47 pierces the corner. Still cradled by the sling, angled to the ground. The 2011 drifts to head level. The sound of a zipper, followed by a yellow stream. Urine pools just inches from Jen's feet.

"Hey, you fuckin' idiot! I told you to look, not play with your dick!"

"Ey! There's no one here. I checked!" the man closest to Jen shouts.

The narco finishes, zips up, and walks away. Had he come forward another few inches, he'd be dead. She tucks herself back against the wall. The diesel engine starts, then rumbles back down the road. Once the noise disappears, she extracts her phone, powering it up. It's a litmus test for her computer.

A bright-white Apple logo appears. Good first step. The screen populates, and Jen uses her thumbprint to access the features. Everything's okay. A message pops up from Anne: *I've alerted Ms. Martinez. No response is being coordinated. Also, Andrew has developed a tool for your next penetration.*

Jen doesn't respond; instead she moves to the utilities shed entrance, ready to get tonight over with. Automatic lights again. Flies and blood-smeared walls. Another shrine left to menace MexTel service technicians.

Jen extracts her laptop and plugs it into the base station controller. Upon powering it up, she finds a new program at the center of her screen. Andrew's handiwork. She guides the cursor with her right hand and clicks the icon, unsure if her left hand can still operate a keyboard. The hacking tool functions flawlessly, automating Vector's installation.

She extracts her cell phone, pecks out a text to Martinez: *Second intrusion down.*

After disconnecting the USB cord, Jen folds the laptop shut and stows it in her pack. It takes all of her discipline to steadily shut the door behind her. Everything hurts, or tingles, or both. Her right ear needs medical attention, along with her hand. Her legs shake, and she swears they'll give out as she rolls her bike through the gate.

Jen mounts the bike, cranking it on. She recalls her drone and doesn't bother asking Anne for directions as she stores it. She's got one destination in mind, and it involves alcohol. Won't be hard to come by in Mexico City.

Nineteen

Styrofoam to-go boxes are slapped down on the counter of a food truck. They're filled with *al pastor* and fish tacos. Staples of any Texan's diet. Jen grabs the boxes, starts back to the safe house. It's three blocks north, and she slow walks the distance. Feels like she's skating on pins and needles, only those pinpricks are white hot.

Before grabbing dinner, she placed a bandage over her hand. Electricity traversed her palm before blasting a hole in her pinky knuckle. The exit wound is smaller than a dime. Sweaty skin had been touching the screwdriver's shaft when she pried the transceiver's cover off. Only invite high-voltage power needs.

The Whisper melted to her ear has yet to be addressed. She decided that a full belly would be better medicine, and she made her way to the food truck while the chance was good. Judging by the aroma of the *al pastor*, she made the right call.

She crosses a bustling street. People are out, enjoying the cool night air. Lights bring color to the neighborhood's buildings. A neighborhood boy walks toward her. He says hello, and Jen gives him a smile. As he passes, she feels a hand on her back pocket. She turns, hand on her gun. "Hope you got a good reason for that."

The boy is petrified, his eyes wide. He'd been trying to pickpocket her, but he's new to the art. "Hope you're just happy to see me . . ."

Jen laughs and eases her hand away from her pistol. "That movie taught you a little more than good English. How old are you?"

"Twelve."

Jen looks him over. His feet are tap-dancing on the pavement. Torn between running and staying to chat. "More like ten."

"I like old movies. That's all we have to watch around here anyway."

Jen starts walking to her apartment again, and he follows. "What else you got around here?"

"What do you want?"

"Information."

The boy shakes his head. "I don't really know much."

"Bet that's not true. A guy like you gets around. Besides, you didn't hear my offer yet." She stops in front of her door and reaches into her jacket pocket. She flashes a wad of hundred-dollar bills in his face. He glows. She wonders if he's eaten today. His clothes are a mess, curly hair shabby and uncut. "Easiest money you ever earned, and you don't even need to steal it."

"I can find information," he says eagerly, licking his lips.

"See, it's not so bad. Any cartel guys around here?" He gulps. "Don't worry. I'm not looking for a fight. Just trying to stay out of their way."

The boy ogles the money, weighing the option. "I could get in big trouble, just so you know."

"Secret's safe. I promise," Jen replies, meaning every word.

"They're five blocks up, on the street over. They sell drugs out of an apartment. My dad goes there; it's why I steal."

Jen wishes she could find his father, kick his ass. Leaving a kid alone in the streets to fend for himself is a sin. "To pay for his drugs?"

"No. For food."

The response satisfies her, and she hands him the cash. "Well, that'll solve your problem for a while. What's your name anyway?"

"Juan. You?" he asks, fanning the bills out, enjoying his newfound wealth.

"Zero," Jen says, using her favorite call sign from Beijing and Venezuela.

Juan throws his head back. "Huh? That's a weird name for a lady."

"Maybe I'm a weird lady. You do me one more favor?"

"Sure!"

"Tell me if you hear anything weird about me. I live right here." She points at her door. "Knock any time."

"Okay."

He's gone in a flash, running to his next great heist, or meal, or both.

Jen smiles to herself. Catch more bees with honey, and she's not worried about him stinging her. She's the block's new high bidder. Why ruin a good thing?

She keys into her apartment. On the coffee table is a six-pack of cold beer waiting with water rings forming around the cans. Her laptop is already out too. She'll work while she eats. No such thing as down time while Americans are in cartel custody.

Jen accesses Vector, the malware she installed. While the information populates on her laptop screen, she grabs a beer. Tough to crack it. Her left hand is numb, nearly paralyzed, and it's worsening as it swells. Locking the can between her knees, she pops the tab and takes a swig. After, she repeats the process with a bottle of Vicodin. She throws two in her mouth, chases them down.

Next, she dives into the food. She demolishes an *al pastor* taco, swearing she's never been so hungry. When Vector comes completely online, Jen activates the laptop's microphone. "Anne, how's the team doing on the triangulation?"

A message from Anne flashes onto the screen: *They're having trouble, Ms. Yates.*

"What's wrong?"

The mobile switching center is hidden or encrypted in some way. Data is only being exchanged in short bursts. We're progressing slower than expected.

The hack she performed tonight was an attack on a middle man, which should be leading her to the mobile switching center, her final target in the cartel's telecommunications network. It's an interesting wrinkle that reveals a high level of technical skill. These users are not only encrypting their networks; they are concealing data traffic.

"Show me the current progress."

Processing.

Results populate. A circle forms over a map of Mexico City, but the radius is wide. Pings begin to dot the map. Calls or texts between cartel members. GPS updates. The circle shrinks after each one. "How long until completion, Anne?"

Tomorrow afternoon at the latest, Ms. Yates.

She takes a swig of beer. "Here's to tomorrow afternoon."

Ever hear of cirrhosis? Fatty liver disease? Anne fills Jen's computer screen with images of afflicted organs.

Jen laughs and takes another swig. "Don't think I'll be able to stay in this apartment all day tomorrow with you."

Terrible thing to say.

"I'd like you to do something else. Find me a busy location, and make sure it's full of Varga's people. I'm curious about this cellular network."

I'll begin immediately.

"I'll be waiting." Jen leans back on the couch, downing more of her beer. Reaching to her ear, she rubs the spot where the Whisper was planted. The device is still melted to her skin. She withdraws her fingers, only to find black chunks of silicon stuck to her fingertips. She downs the rest of the beer and walks to the bathroom, dreading what the mirror will reveal.

Twenty

Victor's pace is frenetic as he walks down a dark hallway in Varga's mansion. Only a few hours have passed since Jen Yates accomplished her first critical assault in Mexico City. Once Varga was notified, Victor's guard detail was banging on his apartment door, coming to whisk him out to the countryside for a late-night meeting.

Going to be an unpleasant one. Varga will no doubt be livid. Victor is going to have to make sense of the intrusion, and justify his presence in Mexico City. Why bother having him around if he can't keep the cartel's technology safe?

Safety is an illusion in this instance. He's aware of Anne and what the quantum computer is capable of. The malware Jen installed tonight will also be some of the world's most sophisticated. Before he left the apartment, he was unable to find it in the system—he only detected it via a serious uptick in data usage. Even if he found it, he probably couldn't delete it without causing serious harm to the network.

The malware was designed to behave like a phantom. Jen Yates's Group is watching through its eyes, observing. Learning and waiting. When the time comes for them to press their assault, he'll spot the malware then, but it will be too late. They'll escalate their privileges—create senior administration level accounts, bar outside access. From there, they'll rip the network apart. At that point, he'll be powerless to stop Jen Yates and her quantum computer.

The first solution is the easiest. Unplug the base station controllers and take the network offline. It's the only way to protect the network's healthy components. But he's certain Varga won't go for that. It's too integral to the cartel's day-to-day function.

The second option is one he's certain Varga will appreciate.

They reach a set of double doors. After a knock, the guards deposit Victor in a library and disappear. Despite the darkness, the study's an impressive room. Ornate black wallpaper with golden flecks. Ebony wood bookcases filled with ancient Aztec texts. Lost tomes. First editions decades out of publication. Dictionaries of the extinct Aztec language, Nahuatl.

One of Alex's prized possessions occupies the center of the room. An Aztec bible protected by glass, surrounded by warm display lights. It's a large slab of gold, the surface inscribed with Aztec hieroglyphs. Many of those inscriptions are faded, worn, like the golden slab's edges. Time has no doubt left a mark, but it's impossible not to imagine an ancient priest's palm lined with golden flecks after he recited a prayer to Huitzilopochtli.

"Sit, Victor," Varga says. He's sitting in a leather lounge chair, a glass of scotch cradled on the armrest. An open laptop computer on the coffee table bakes him in electric light.

Victor sits across from Varga in a lounge chair. "Mr. Varga."

Varga nods at a tumbler on the table's opposite side. "I poured you a glass."

"I'd prefer not to," Victor replies, acutely aware that this is not a social occasion.

Varga shows no emotion. Pious, calm, even. He glares at Victor, allows the silence to grate. "Drink it."

Victor sighs and takes the glass. He downs it, then slams it back onto the table with enough force to damage the surface. "I've activated several security features inside your network. Put the word out with your people—we need a communications blackout."

"I won't change how my organization operates."

"It's temporary. Twenty-four hours at the most."

"I want you to—"

He cuts Varga off. "Your cellular network has a custom operating feature called a *Delayed Packet Transfer System*. It's only going to transmit emergency communications from this point forward. You're not going to be completely in the dark, Alex," Victor says, referencing a unique capability.

Packets are individual bits of encrypted data that cellular networks use to function. They're the building blocks for pieces of information, and once they're assembled, they form text messages, GPS locations, or voice data. Delaying packet transfers will slow down whatever Jen Yates has installed in their network, but that delay will come at a cost.

"You did this without asking me first?" Varga asks, seething at the overreach in authority.

"I'm protecting you."

"I need to be able to track my people. I'll lose control of my organization if I can't."

"GPS data will update every twenty minutes," Victor replies. "But it won't be second to second like you're accustomed to."

"This isn't a solution." Varga's patience is strained. A finger of scotch remains in his tumbler, and he gulps it down, hoping it'll blunt his anger. He locks his fingers around the tumbler, testing the glass's limits. "Get them out of my network. *Now*."

"I'd have to unplug the network. Remove the corrupted base station —" Victor's response is cut short as Varga slams his tumbler onto the table.

"Never. I'd be blind," Varga says. "Your performance is unacceptable, Victor."

"Just listen," Victor replies, blinking through the shock. He has never seen Varga explode like that, and he's questioning whether he'll be allowed to leave this room alive. He prepares his pitch. "We know where Jen Yates has been, which means we know where she's going."

"Zocalo," Varga replies as he relaxes back into the chair, his mind churning rapidly. He's referring to one of the city's most iconic regions.

"They're going to use the cartel's communications to zero in on your mobile switching center in Zocalo," Victor explains. "And while we delay their search, we'll fortify it. Jen Yates cannot access that technology. It'll expose your entire organization, along with our hostages."

Varga nods, processing the conversation in a language he understands. "I'll send my best killers to Zocalo."

"It's a step in the right direction."

"My day stops and starts with you, Victor," Varga replies with a sneer. "If Jen Yates comes to Zocalo, my people won't have many options."

Victor winces. Jen Yates's death would severely complicate the situation in Mexico. Her loss would infuriate her counterparts, give them another excuse to remain in the city. But there's no good answer. He says what he must. "If she crosses the line, make her disappear. No body. No torture. No videos. We can't give the United States another reason to attack our interests."

"I'll pass along the word," Varga says, satisfied for the first time tonight.

The satisfaction is mutual, and Victor begins relaxing. There will be no violence, despite the damage Jen Yates caused. He's reminded of a request he made to Varga before he left the city. "How is our message to Gabriella Martinez coming along?"

Varga's face beams against the glowing computer screen. He twists his laptop, revealing a grisly scene. A man is being dismembered, transmitted live via a private Facebook video feed.

Victor tries not to jerk away. Varga is testing his mettle. The stream rate is slow and the images are pixelated, but they're absolutely sickening. The message Varga's people are crafting is designed to call Martinez's bluff. She was supposed to stand down and allow the cartel to open a formal negotiations process. Instead, she ordered Jen Yates to penetrate cartel networks. The video will remind Martinez that attacking the cartel's interests will only make things more difficult. Show her that it's impossible to return the hostages by force. There is only one way to survive Mexico City: the cartel's way.

"A drink with your favorite pastime," Victor replies. "No wonder your spirits are so light."

"Get messages to our video editors before you leave. Make sure they understand exactly what you need."

"I'll do that," Victor agrees.

"When do you want to make an official offer?" Varga asks.

"Once we're certain Gabriella Martinez is taking our directions," Victor replies as he tries to conjure the future in tendrils of scotch sliding down his tumbler. Jen Yates will go to Zocalo, and fail. Martinez will be out of options, and vulnerable. That's when they'll make the offer that forces the Americans out of Mexico City. He likes what he sees and smiles. "What do you say to another drink? I think this one should be a toast."

Twenty-One

Ball bearings. C4 explosives. Wires and batteries. The hostage taker is a master with devices like these; he's used them many times in the past. His nickname is Oro, or Gold—which was used to replace all of his natural teeth. The man he's standing in front of is his sixty-fourth hostage. Long career in Mexico. Many men like him are killed before reaching that milestone. Sometimes it's by law enforcement. Other times by the people they try to kidnap. Still more from rival cartels.

"Lift up your shirt," Oro says in Spanish. He's sitting on the toilet, a camera disabled at his back. A used hypodermic needle rests by his boot. The hostage, an African American man with a pencil-thin physique, complies. Track marks cover bruised veins. Blood drips from a fresh injection site. Heroin. Small dose, enough to stave off dope sickness and keep him functional.

Oro fastens the bomb to the hostage's chest, wrenches the Velcro tight. The hostage is shaking, regretting, despite the heroin. He's blindfolded but senses the device. Its weight. The danger of it. Pipe dream's over. He begins lowering his shirt.

"Keep it up. We're not finished."

Wallpaper droops off the apartment's dining room walls. The rest of the building matches the apartment. Five stories tall. Run-down. Filled with junkies hooked to the cartel; the cartel hooked back into them. Twisted symbiosis. Many of the rooms also house cartel gunmen and the drug dealers they protect.

Catalysts for human decay litter a dining table. Dirty needles and a spoon to cook dope. Nylon straps thick enough to raise an addict's collapsed veins. Roaches, all dead from ingesting tainted food. Weapons and spare magazines. Oro plucks a cheap cell phone from the filth and returns to the hostage.

First, the cell phone is powered on. Oro fishes for a wire dangling off the belt. He plugs one end into the cell phone's headphone jack. He folds part of the wire over the phone, then wraps a strand of electrical tape around it. Connection secure. Finally, he tucks the phone inside a small pouch on the belt, next to a package of C4 coated with ball bearings. "Lower your shirt."

The hostage complies. He lets his trembling hands fall like stones. Oro smooths over the garment, checks to see if the explosive device is imprinted against the hostage's shirt. It's invisible, perfect. His two crew members are standing by. One is ex-military; the other ex-police, like Oro. They've all had training in firearms. Tactics. Evasive driving.

"Where are we with time?" Oro asks.

The ex-military member looks at his phone. "Message should be coming any second." As he stares at the phone, a text comes directly from Varga. Just an address, no more than thirty minutes away. "Let's move."

The three men each don a Kevlar vest, with ceramic plates added. Enough armor to stop high-velocity rifle projectiles. Weapons come next. Pistols and rifles. Ample magazines are stuffed into pockets. The preparation ends as the hostage takers place black balaclavas over their faces.

"You ready?" Oro asks.

"Hold up." The man monitoring the phone cues up the photo app, prepares to shoot a video. He angles the BlackBerry at Oro, presses Play. Action begins with a nod. No more voices—sharp Americans will be watching this video closely. Searching.

Oro grabs the hostage. Uses harsh treatment in place of verbal commands. He keeps one hand on the hostage, jams the barrel of his MP5k sub-machine gun into his gut.

The group of men exit the apartment. Hallways are dim, littered with trash. Graffiti moves as one long stretch of artwork from one end of the hallway to the other. Marijuana smoke is prevalent, and it's mixed with other narcotics. *Martians*. Reaching the stairwell, the group passes a throng of heavily armed men. Radios buzz, signaling that the hostage is moving. Sounds echo down the stairwell as men clear a path.

Before they reach ground level, they pass two dozen men all heavily armed. A car is waiting outside, brought by another armed cartel member. Oro's two accomplices get in the front while he guides the hostage into the back. When he's settled, he returns the barrel of his MP5k to the hostage's abdomen. He stares at the cell phone, eyes wide and bloodshot, full of hatred.

The video recording ends as the car begins to move. It captured everything: the amount of security at the location, the difficulty in gaining access. A gun on the hostage at all times. The bomb's presence is undocumented—a special surprise in waiting.

———

More security. This time, at a warehouse on the outskirts of Mexico City. It's a cue to resume the video.

The car passes under a gate, which is guarded by multiple paramilitary style vehicles. Pickup trucks with makeshift armor welded to the bodies. Machine guns mounted to the beds. Narcos call them *monster trucks*.

The vehicle stops in a parking lot, surrounded by dozens more cartel members. Some are on roving patrols, continuously walking the perimeter, inspecting the razor-wire fence. Others are clustered around burning barrels, keeping a chill away.

The rooftops are littered with gunmen, but these have heavier weapons, tucked into gun emplacements.

It's a symbol of Varga's power in Mexico City. The warehouse is well out of the way of foreign tourists, allowing it to exist in full force. Law enforcement is aware of its presence, but most are too afraid to go near it, let alone stop it. Many more are paid to ignore it.

Oro yanks the hostage out of the vehicle as the camera rolls. More gunmen swarm the hostage, offering a massive show of force for the camera. The man filming holds back momentarily, getting a wide-angle shot. The guards, the armor, the warehouse's unique structure.

The hostage disappears under a loading bay door, and the cameraman rushes to catch up.

They begin traveling through a plywood maze built inside the warehouse. It's a rescue mission's nightmare. Zigs and zags. Ports hacked into the wood, machine gun barrels inching through. Reinforced doorways. There's no way to enter the warehouse and avoid the maze. Every door leads into the maze's winding halls. If rescue forces attempt to hit the building from above, they'll be barred by plywood ceilings that cover the entirety of the maze.

The hostage is led into a room and tied to a chair. Two other hostages are present. Covered head to toe in baggy black garments and blindfolds. Exposed flesh is tattooed, the images exact matches of ink Cameron Vinke and Bobby Hollice wear. The filming ends with the hostages locked in the frame's center.

The videos are forwarded to Varga's in-house editor. When they're finished working their magic, Martinez will see that rescue is impossible. There's only one way to survive Mexico: Alex Varga's.

Twenty-Two

Seven a.m. and Martinez's gut is already turning. The smell of blood is overpowering, tingling her nostrils as she nears a luxury apartment. She received a call from Admiral Perez only an hour ago, informing her of a homicide that may be related to her missing people.

The apartment belongs to the previous owner of World Chem, Andreas Castillo. A single man in his early fifties, he's had a clean rap sheet his entire life, and no prior cartel associations. The perfect front man for Varga's illicit business.

Shortly past midnight, a suspicious 911 call emerged from the residence. *A dead man is waiting for you.* That's all the caller said, then hung up. Mexico City's emergency services knew exactly what the call meant and who it'd been from.

Local officers had been tipped off earlier and told to stay away from the apartment, even if screams were reported. None came. Only after the murderers announced that they'd left did the local police dare enter the apartment to discover the body.

Now it's time for Martinez to see for herself. She's brought a personal security detail along too. Four Delta Force members. Bingham's best. They stick close to her as they near the penthouse. The dozens of Mexican police officers on site are not to be trusted. The Delta

Force operators keep suppressed MP7s cradled close to their chests. All of them, including Martinez, are wearing Mexican Navy uniforms and balaclavas.

Martinez finds the penthouse door taped off. Police officers and detectives stand at the entrance. She spots a Fuerza Especial intelligence officer standing amongst them, and she recognizes him from base. His name has been removed from his uniform, and she addresses him only by rank. "What's the matter, Lieutenant?"

The FES officer flicks the tape on the door. "They're afraid an explosive device could be present. Keeping your distance is advisable, ma'am."

"Did the first responders see an explosive on site?"

The FES officer shakes his head. "No, ma'am, but there are electronics present, including a camera in the victim's vicinity."

"Who else is inside?" Martinez asks.

"No one. We're waiting for a K9 and an explosives expert to clear the scene."

That doorway could be the gates of hell, but the danger doesn't sway Martinez—not when her people are in cartel custody. "Please step aside, gentlemen."

The FES officer addresses the police, and they obey. He reaches into his pocket, extracts a small tub of lip balm. Vicks, with a strong menthol scent. "You may want some of this, ma'am."

"Not my first time, Lieutenant, but thanks." Martinez turns to her people. "I only need one of you. Who wants to wear the big boy pants?" They smile under their balaclavas. With a dare like that, she wouldn't be surprised if all four of them barreled past the crime scene tape.

Al Hastings, the protective detail's leader, makes the call. He's got wild ice-blue eyes. His balaclava conceals slicked-back red hair and a short beard. He begins dispensing orders. "Coco, take the boss inside. Animal, post up by the elevator—bite anyone that comes up uninvited. Gray, on me, in case something happens."

Salvador Garcia falls in behind Martinez with a nod. His nickname, Coco, is short for cocoa butter. He's the team's pretty boy. Smooth with women. Always catching grief for looking too much like the skirts he chases. Jet-black hair, always perfectly parted, with a touch of product.

Bulging muscles oftentimes accented by T-shirts a size too small. But he's an elite soldier and an even better sniper.

"Let's go." Martinez bends under the crime scene tape as the protective detail takes their positions. The opulent penthouse has white walls filled with high-priced artwork. Stained black hardwood flooring is underfoot, leading Martinez along a hallway before reaching the living room.

The air gets thick, and Martinez reaches up to cover her nose. Rot hasn't set in. It's fresh meat recently exposed to the outside air, like a slaughterhouse. Other additives are present: blood and feces and urine. The most prominent one is fear. It's impossible to describe, but for those who have experienced enough violence, the smell is pungent, and it lingers.

Martinez rounds the corner into the living room and stops cold. The scene is shocking, even for her.

Everything is lined with construction plastic. Arterial spray on the ceiling. Bloody footprints cover the plastic, stopping at the edge. The cartel members wore booties, preventing them from tracking blood to other areas of the apartment.

Castillo's body is crucified against the marble wall. His arms and legs have been severed, along with his hands and feet. They've been reattached by electrical cables. The cables wrap around joints or run directly through bone marrow channels. His head is missing, and a security camera was screwed to the vertebrae in his neck. Finally, the majority of his abdomen has been removed, replaced by an old-style television set with a VHS player. A tape sticks out of the VHS player's mouth. A paper note stuck to the television screen's surface reads: *Play me!* ;)

"Holy . . ." Martinez ducks back into the hallway. It's going to take her a second to process this one. Murder is a sport among cartel members. Barrels full of acid. Power tools. Blunt instruments misused in horrifying ways. Varga has long been considered the king of carnage. It's how these men rule: by fear. Challenge them, end up crucified. Varga's people are masters, and their craft is on display.

"Can't be that bad," Coco says, stepping around the corner. He disappears momentarily, then rejoins Martinez, skin a few shades lighter.

He reaches for a cross around his neck and mouths a prayer. "I've seen evil, but never like that."

Martinez returns to the murder scene and approaches the body. Proximity brings all the tiny details into focus. Power cords have been run from the body to an electrical receptacle. A tiny red light is flashing just below the camera lens—someone is watching. The television cuts on, tuned to static. She gasps and works to control her breathing.

Coco is behind her, his face contorted. "I changed my mind."

"Huh?"

"Always said I wanna see it coming. Right now, I'm glad I get to look away." He turns his back on the murder scene, covering her six. If there's a shooter hidden somewhere in the apartment, he'll catch him. If there's an explosion, it'll simply be a warm, tingly surprise.

Martinez's index finger rests on the edge of the VHS tape, hesitating to push it in. "Won't be returning this one to Blockbuster," she whispers, summoning the courage.

The VHS tape sucks into the player. Footage plays immediately. It features a man that looks like Terrance on a trip through a narco-controlled apartment building. A car ride, gun barrel pressed to his abdomen. It ends inside a warehouse with the two other hostages present. The footage is grainy, and it appears to be shot on an old camcorder from the '90s.

Inconclusive at best without any faces. The hostage doesn't speak, nor do the hostage takers. But the footage is still important, and she needs to take it with her. Her finger hovers over the eject button, but she can't bring herself to press it.

"Not today . . ." Martinez takes a deep breath and doesn't hesitate this time. She presses the eject button.

The tape is spit out.

Martinez exhales, yanks the tape out of the player. Her heart is beating so fast she's got tunnel vision. On a cloud, she turns her back to the television, tapping Coco's shoulder. He leads her to the exit.

Something slams behind her; they both freeze. *Lucy, I'm home!* She jerks around. The television has switched to a rerun of *I Love Lucy*. Varga, playing games. It worked. Coco's MP7 is leveled at the television, and he almost cut it in half. Her feet are just now settling back on the ground, and her hand is on her pistol.

Martinez takes a gulp of air, letting her pulse cool. Varga has seen her scared; she can't let him get away with it, bomb or no bomb. She walks back to the television. Trembling fingers land on a dial. Click. The channel shifts. Another and another. She finally lands on a rerun of *Friends*. The theme song is playing. *I'll be there for you . . .*

The camera's red dot is still glowing. She looks up, gives it a wink. With her personal message sent, she struts out of the apartment.

Twenty-Three

Cell phone locations have been compiled using demodulated cellular data packets that Anne intercepted last night. Gathering information like this is difficult—Anne must first capture the data, and decrypt, or demodulate, it. Then the quantum computer works to piece it all together. The task would be impossible without Anne's assistance. Even with the advantage, Jen can only discern the cartel members' locations, but their identities are still a mystery, along with their message and call histories.

One location is particularly suited for her objective. She's looking for a relatively exposed cartel location that will allow her to move unseen through a crowd. Cell phones are the day's target—specifically, ones that are being used by the Varga cartel.

An MQ-9 Reaper drone has been dispatched to help Jen with her search. While she waits for the ISR drone to arrive on target, she gets herself squared away. No more Vicodin this morning; she's going to make do with aspirin and ice. The pain in her hand is milder than last night, but it's swollen. Every few minutes she raises an ice pack from her hand, flexing the tendons and ligaments before chilling it again. With her free hand, she pops several aspirin and guzzles them down with water.

The injury to the back of her ear wasn't as bad as she expected, and a fresh layer of Neosporin is settling into the charred skin. But the lack of severity doesn't do much to ease her pain.

Ms. Yates, your drone is on station. Would you like me to display the ISR feed?

Jen sighs at Anne's update. She'd like to sit and recover, but there's no time. Every passing second increases the likelihood that the missing Americans will never be seen again. Injuries aren't an obstacle that will slow her down. "Bring it up, Anne."

The computer screen populates with images of a sprawling open-air market. Tepito is extremely popular with locals. Thousands of people mill in different directions, buying, selling, trading between individual stalls. Restaurants serve street food from animals slaughtered just minutes before. Others come to the market for more nefarious reasons.

"Mark our target's stall on the map, Anne. There's too much clutter to find it visually," Jen says, already lost in the maze of plywood stalls.

Anne locks onto the captured cell phone numbers and highlights a specific stall. It's buried deep in the market, out of the way of heavily trafficked areas. Varga's cartel is using the stall as a front to sell narcotics to street-level users. On the ISR feed, the stall looks like a beehive. Addicts enter. Sixty seconds later, they've copped their fix and are departing.

Armed men are posted at the stall's periphery, broadcasting a warning to would-be rivals or overzealous fiends. Anne has marked nine additional cell phones, each hidden inside adjoining stalls. They're all concealed under sheet metal roofing, which is littered with plastic rubbish and a dish for satellite TV. She wonders if the adjoining stalls offer the cartel members extra storage space, as well as a means of moving drugs or cash unseen.

Task complete, Ms. Yates.

Jen studies the screen and forgets about the pain in her hand. This target is juicy. And the busy market offers plenty of avenues to get lost in. Only she won't lose her way; it'll be a cartel member. And if he bleeds out before he regains his bearings, so be it.

"Anne, begin mapping the cartel's movement patterns through the market. We need to know how they resupply their drugs."

I'll begin immediately.

An email message pops up. Martinez, asking if she's available.

Jen begins a FaceTime call, finding her superior officer in the back of a Suburban, speeding through Mexico City. She's wearing a Mexican Navy uniform, like the armed Delta operator sitting at her side. Her hair is slightly disheveled from a recently removed balaclava. Bags are under her eyes, and Jen wonders if she slept last night. "Busy morning?"

"Not as busy as your night. How's the hand?"

Jen flashes it in front of the screen. Black and blue. Trembling from the ice. She flexes it, fails to conceal a wince. "Movement's impaired, but I'll get by."

"Sorry I can't pull you out, but it won't be much longer," Martinez replies, visibly upset at the sight. "We received a video this morning. Should have seen where I found it."

"Can you send it my way?" Jen asks, aching for an update on Terrance.

Martinez struggles through her reply as the SUV jerks through a roundabout. Tires screech and horns blare outside the armored windows. The security detail's driving tactics are aggressive and for good reason; they're in the cartel's sights. Getting bogged down in Mexico City traffic is a non-starter. "It's on VHS. I'm taking it to the embassy to make a digital copy. From there, the tape is going to Langley for advanced analysis."

"Fill me in," Jen requests.

Martinez relates the video's details to Jen: a heavily fortified warehouse, more guns than the Alamo, no identifying details on the hostages. "It's paper thin, but my assumption is that Varga wants us focused on this warehouse."

Jen nods. "Make us think it's impossible to rescue our people with force."

"Nailed it," Martinez agrees. "And if we decide to terminate our search efforts, all the better."

"You think last night's penetrations are also a factor?" Jen asks, suddenly worried about the reprisal she was warned about. She'd never forgive herself if her actions were linked to a hostage's death.

"I do," Martinez says. "Could you have been compromised during your hacks?"

Jen recounts both hacks in detail and considers it unlikely that she was spotted. She draws attention to the cartel's response to the loss of electricity. The recurring problem. Narcos who'd rather take a leak than properly do their jobs.

"My best guess is that they've discovered our malware," Jen replies. "If they did find our malware, there's absolutely no way for them to remove it without damaging their system. It's sheer luck they got that far."

"Varga doesn't have luck. He has someone providing him advanced technological support." Martinez runs a hand over her jet-black hair. "They're stuck, but if they suspect that their cellular network is our target, it presents a challenge for your upcoming hack on the MSC."

"We'll worry about that when the time comes," Jen replies, unfazed by any sort of threat Varga could level directly at her. "How will you handle the warehouse?"

"I need to plan for the contingency. I don't think Varga would reveal our hostages' true locations, but your efforts could ultimately lead us there."

"Think Perez would authorize a raid on something like that?"

"No. The risk of casualties is too high," Martinez declares. "But I'd be irresponsible if I didn't order Major Bingham to generate a plan to assault the warehouse. Hell, the man has worked miracles before, and he might just have to do it again."

"We'll have the answers we need soon." Jen leans forward, taps a few keys, sends her information on Tepito to Martinez's phone. "I've got a hunch based off what I saw last night. If the base station controllers are unique, cellular components might be too."

"I like what I see," Martinez says, quickly reading through the details. "I'll okay it. Forward what you get, ASAP."

Twenty-Four

Martinez keys into the embassy's secure conference room and gives her Group the once-over. They've been working in shifts since Jen completed her intrusion, and it shows. Andrew is wearing the same shirt he was struggling to tuck in as he ran to the TOC yesterday afternoon. Sloane's suit looks permanently ruined from twenty-four straight hours of wear. Red Bull cans litter the table, along with files and folded laptops. Nearby coffeepots emit a continuous gurgle. But the extra effort is paying off.

Their primary objective has been triangulating the mobile switching center. Or more accurately, monitoring Anne's progress. They're also working behind the quantum computer, ensuring that their malware is stable inside their target. Add-on software like Vector can cause target systems to crash, which would be catastrophic.

Safety precautions have also been put into place—the cartel will not be allowed to destroy the network. Admin-level activity is being closely tracked, and plans are in place to shield the base station controllers from a memory wipe.

Andrew is pulling a double shift while Sloane stays on the cell network. He's hooking up an old VHS video converter. It's a dinosaur compared to other pieces of technology the Group uses. It saw its heyday as a tool to digitize VHS crime scene tapes, which have been replaced by CDs or large hard drives. He pulled it from the embassy's basement and, after blowing off a layer of dust, lugged it to the conference room.

Martinez examines the equipment, trying to remain patient while Andrew finishes the setup. Getting the VHS to Langley's analysts is an urgent priority—it'll be a nine-hour flight to the CIA's headquarters. She needed this done by the time she arrived, but she reminds herself to be patient. Her people are already pushing the limits of their endurance. "Everything ready?"

Andrew connects a final cable, flicks on the power. Screens blink and fill with static. *Insert Tape* shifts back and forth. The device is ready to work. He stands by, prepared to offer assistance with the transfer. "Yes, ma'am."

Martinez removes the VHS from its evidence bag and presses it into the video converter. It sucks in, and motors whir. She holds her breath, hoping that the old dinosaur doesn't devour the tape. She presses a button and the transfer process begins.

"Time stamps line up," Andrew remarks, pointing at the date and time displayed on the screen's bottom corner. "Looks like it was shot several hours after the kidnapping."

"Don't jump to conclusions. This is what Varga wants us to see," she murmurs, transfixed on the transfer, which is almost complete. "How's the mobile switching center?"

"We're close. We'll have an update when you're finished."

"Give me five," Martinez replies. Andrew returns to his station, allowing her to finish the task. The transfer ends and she checks the digital copy, finding it a perfect replica. She attaches the video to an email. Forwards it to Jen, Bingham, and her analysts at Langley.

She plucks the original video out of the converter and transfers it to a hard case. A CIA officer is waiting outside of the door, ready to whisk the VHS stateside. After handing off the video, she rejoins her Group. "Where is my MSC?"

"Hope you got a thinking cap stashed in those BDUs, ma'am," Sloane remarks, putting their findings on the wall's largest television screen.

Martinez laughs. She hadn't minded the uniform. Brings back memories of her time as a young naval intelligence officer, fresh out of the Academy. "Don't be jealous you didn't get one."

Andrew runs his fingers though his beard, which has turned a different shade of gray in the past twelve hours. "We're getting some really off-the-wall results here, ma'am."

Martinez's mouth goes slack as she looks over their findings. Anne's triangulation is homing in on one of Mexico's most popular tourist areas: Zocalo Square. Officially called the Plaza de la Constitution, it is home to the National Palace, the Metropolitan Cathedral, and other buildings involved in Mexico's central government. The Grand Hotel Mexico City, one of the world's most iconic hotels, also overlooks the square. Aztec ruins are exposed at various points around the area, drawing in thousands of tourists a year.

Each of these buildings are rich with baroque architecture commonly found in the seventeen and eighteen hundreds. They face inward, toward a square made of gray stone, with Mexico's flag flying proudly at the center.

Martinez rubs her temples, easing her nervous tension. The site isn't a far-flung cartel warehouse or unguarded base station. Mexico City's tourism starts and stops at Zocalo. Key elements of Mexico's federal government are in the vicinity. Assaulting a target in this area will be high-risk and sensitive. "What's our degree of certainty on the triangulation?"

"One hundred percent." Andrew pauses, then adds, "There's no way to alter that type of signal activity, ma'am."

"Well, we're in the deep end with this one." As she talks, the circle shrinks again. Its edges barely touch the buildings along the square's exterior. At this rate, it may well signal that the mobile switching center is in the middle of the thoroughfare.

"Let's see who owns what in the area. Maybe we can catch a break," Sloane says, already compiling a list of the surrounding buildings.

"Solid suggestion. Pull blueprints while you're at it," Martinez replies. "Mr. Xiao, make sure Vector continues running smoothly while Ms. Hamilton breaks off."

Before the Group can react to Martinez's directive, her phone screeches out an alarm. Admiral Perez, no doubt with a message from the cartel. She snatches it out of her pocket, answering. “How can I help you, Admiral?” The call doesn’t last but sixty seconds before she ends it. “I need to get back to base. Something else came in on our people. Stay on Zocalo.”

Twenty-Five

Martinez stops a video as it reaches the end. A sweaty fingerprint is left on the laptop's track pad. Her ribs feel tight, like they're bound in a straitjacket. She reminds herself to breathe before she passes out. "This is what we've been waiting for."

Admiral Perez doesn't respond. He leans across the desk, opens a small cigar box. Pulls out a brand of cigarette that Martinez doesn't recognize. Two gold rings separate the tobacco from the filter. Fancy, maybe shipped in from Cuba. A gilded decorative lighter rests by the box. He grabs it with both hands, lights the cigarette, and exhales smoke through both nostrils.

Martinez makes a late realization. While she'd been watching the video, he'd been watching her. His air has been stiff, uncordial since he invited her into his personal office. Perez likely caught hell after last night's hacks, but he can't verbalize his frustrations—not without exposing himself. So he's playing coy, trying to decipher what Jen's work may have revealed.

Inadvertently, she told him—through her shaky hands and breath. This video is news, and critical to finding the missing Americans. She presses Play once more. While the video buffers, she regains her composure. No more careless admissions, not in front of a weasel like Perez.

The video begins playing. It's shaky, recorded on a cell phone. The man shooting it is rushed, jittery, doing something he should not. He navigates the warehouse through a maze constructed of plywood, past machine gun ports and doorways barricaded with sandbags. The phone is concealed in the breast pocket of his shirt, the armed guards he passes unaware of its presence.

He enters a heavily fortified room containing the hostages. All three. Bound, gagged, and blindfolded. Bodies covered in heavy black jumpsuits, concealing physical attributes. They're surrounded by machine guns, hanging construction lights, and sawdust floating in the air like pixies.

A bottle of water momentarily obstructs the view. The cameraman twists off the cap. Both of his hands are gloved, and he's wearing a uniform with black sleeves. Precautions. Impossible to determine if he's tattooed, or the tone of his complexion.

Could be he's trying to protect his identity from the cartel; snitches don't fare well in organizations like Varga's. Or maybe he's shielding himself from the American intelligence officers sure to watch his video. Dangerous implications either way.

The cameraman inserts a straw, approaches the first hostage. He lifts the hostage's blindfold, fully exposing his face, and allows him to drink. "Say your name," he whispers.

The first hostage looks up through raccoon eyes. There's swelling on the back of his head. Blood dripping from his nose and mouth. He struggles to respond. "Sergeant Bobby Hollice, United States Army."

"That's enough." The cameraman removes the water bottle and replaces the blindfold.

The cameraman moves to the second hostage. Blindfold up. Water. "Whisper your name."

The second hostage takes two deep pulls from the straw. There's severe swelling on his cheekbone. Lumpy blue-and-black flesh seals his eye shut. "Sergeant Cameron Vinke, United States Army."

The water is taken away; his blindfold is lowered.

The cameraman moves to the final hostage, repeating the process. "What's your name?"

The hostage drinks. His skin is pale. Dry snot lingers under his nose and around his mouth. Eyes dart back and forth, terrified as they study the environment. "Terrance Kline."

Martinez pauses the video as Terrance stares into the camera's lens. It's a gruesome image, and not because of his injuries—it betrays a fear that something horrific could happen at any moment, and he's powerless to stop it. She looks closely at the face she's most familiar with. The voice matches. His features match. It's a lock.

Terrance Kline and the other hostages are still alive in Mexico City.

The revelation brings more fear, this time on her end. The warehouse is the same one she saw in the murder scene's VHS tape. Conducting a raid on a target so heavily fortified will be bloody, and require a tremendous amount of force. There's also a high probability the hostages would suffer casualties. She couldn't, in good conscience, attempt a rescue.

Varga clearly read from an American Special Forces manual—man traps and machine guns planted behind rows of sandbags. Numerous good men were killed in places like Iraq and Afghanistan with the same tactics. *Who taught him this?* she wonders, repeating a question that is turning into a mantra for Mexico City.

Martinez closes the laptop and leans into the armchair across from Perez's desk. He makes a show of stubbing out his cigarette, and she uses the time to assess how to move forward.

She thinks through the key question first: *Are the hostages at the warehouse?* Intelligence points to that being the case. But it's Varga's intelligence, which she'd be insane to trust.

If it were her decision, she'd never expose a hostage's real location. In doing so, the cartel would be giving up an advantage. Why do it when there are hundreds of locations to house hostages in Mexico City?

Jen's earlier observation was solid: Varga wants them focused on the warehouse. An impossible target. Forcing her into a deal on a narcoterrorist's terms. But what Varga considers a disadvantage is actually an opportunity. She might call it a get-out-of-jail-free card—one she'll snap off Perez's desk and slip into her breast pocket.

She finds Perez's pompous air disgusting as she looks back across the desk. This video is political cover for him and the Mexican government. Military force is no longer an option, which means he doesn't have to green-light a raid. Presiding over a disastrous rescue would end his career. He can just watch her struggle and forward information to Varga.

"How did you come across this intelligence, Admiral?" Martinez asks.

Admiral Perez sneers, spits a flake of tobacco off his tongue before he replies. "We have well-placed assets inside the Varga cartel, Ms. Martinez. It's all I can say. Beyond that, it was passed to the CNI, who then forwarded it to me."

Plausible. No way for her to back-check it. Something this sensitive will be compartmentalized inside the Centro Nacional de Inteligencia. Both for operational security and the safety of the informant. "So no demands were forwarded with the video?"

"Correct."

"Was a location forwarded with the video?" Martinez asks.

"The warehouse is located on the outskirts of Mexico City in an abandoned industrial complex." Perez pauses, makes an addition. "The CNI considers this informant trustworthy, Ms. Martinez."

Martinez remains outwardly calm, but her instincts are flaring. The hostages can't be in the warehouse. No way. Not at a location forwarded by some bogus informant. She thinks of her get-out-of-jail-free card and says, "I need to explore the possibility of a raid on the warehouse, Admiral."

Perez's pretension dissipates. He chuckles, almost too heartily, and waves away the possibility. "Ms. Martinez, you saw the same footage I did. You're asking for a blood bath, not to mention a torrent of press coverage."

Martinez is pleased by his response. She's giving him what he wants, what they both want. "Contingency planning, sir. If Varga refuses to negotiate or offers unreasonable terms, we have to be prepared to move."

"Ms. Martinez, I can't green-light—"

"Varga just gave me *real* confirmation, sir. I can't ignore it. I will stress that planning is far removed from acting. Let me cover my bases," Martinez replies.

The admiral relents. "Have Major Bingham get into contact with

Commander Torres. But barring something drastic, I will not authorize any action on that warehouse."

"Thank you, sir," Martinez says. "I'd also appreciate a copy of the video. Email or text is fine."

Perez punches buttons on his laptop. "I'll send you both."

Martinez checks her phone, finds the video in her mailbox. She forwards it to Andrew and Sloane. By the time she returns to the embassy, they'll have generated a basic assessment of the video's technical details. "Thank you, sir."

A phone rings on the admiral's desk. Not unusual, but his response is. His hand jerks over, shoves the device in a desk drawer. No answer. Not even a quick glance at the caller ID. It's also a BlackBerry. Long out of style.

Martinez makes note of his behavior but doesn't challenge it. "Will that be all, Admiral?"

"Yes, Ms. Martinez. Any other requests on your end?" Perez asks hastily, trying to paper over his awkward behavior.

Martinez stands, straightens out her blue-and-black ACU camouflage uniform. A proper officer, unlike the one seated across from her. She salutes Perez, if only to remind him what service truly means. "No, sir. That will be all . . . for now."

Twenty-Six

Tepito, Mexico City

Caffeine and sugar. The tools Jen's using to fight off shock—preemptively. She's sitting at an outdoor restaurant in Mexico City's busiest shopping district. Anne's drone is hovering far above the market, out of sight. The device is locked onto a stall Varga's men are using as a front to move narcotics. Been that way for hours, and it has revealed the racket's more intimate details.

Those details are important to Jen. She's not interested in ripping the business apart. She only needs to work at the periphery, striking at its weakness, then disappear into the crowded market. That's if things go according to plan.

Thousands of people meander through the stalls, conducting all different types of business. Who's to know which ones are members of the cartel? They'll sit concealed. Just watching, waiting for someone like her to come along.

If gunfire were to agitate a crowd, the cartel's response could be overpowering. What she's about to do will require complete stealth.

A waitress buzzes around Jen, carrying plates of food. Everything is from the market; products bought fresh, prepared by the restaurant's chefs. She rushes in and out of a squat building. Signs for Coca-Cola and Fanta and Corona are nailed to the structure. There's also a hand-painted menu with dirt-cheap prices. When the waitress leaves, Jen extracts her cell phone, examining Anne's view from above.

Her opportunity is coming, right on schedule. Cartel thugs are going to trade cash for drugs. A route is already marked to guide her through the market and intercept her targets. A timer on the bottom right-hand side of the screen approaches zero. She places a ten-dollar bill on the table before standing, then proceeds farther into the market.

Anne is tracking her movements. Directions buzz in her ear. Right. Deeper into the matrix of stalls. Left at the merchant selling fresh-caught fish from a local river. Another left, this time at a merchant selling handwoven blankets. They all solicit Jen, trying to nab some of the gringo's dollars. She stays focused, keeping her right hand locked on the pistol under her jacket.

The maze begins to feel endless, along with the market's oddities. She passes a vendor carrying a large cross, religious icons pinned to the wood. He pumps it up and down, drawing attention while he chants prayers. Another man sits in a stall, repairing umbrellas he's found on the street.

"Waypoint is fifteen yards on your right," Anne informs via Jen's Whisper.

Jen looks over at an abandoned stall. Was an old bicycle repair shop. Signs still hang overhead. The façade's paint is faded from the sunlight.

Multiplex homes with tan stucco and tile roofing are in the distance. That's where the cartel's safe house is. Every hour on the hour, two bagmen move along this same path, pockets lined with currency. They return with pockets full of cocaine, marijuana, heroin, and meth-amphetamine.

The stall's door is busted off the hinges. Jen checks her back, finds herself alone. Her cue to step inside. The interior is half-lit. Sunlight penetrates through painted-over windows. Dust hangs in bars of light.

The cartel has made its presence known. Graffiti of Huitzilopochtli. A line of dried blood stretches across a wall. Dead rodents. Trash tossed haphazardly in every direction.

She walks into the back room. It's darker, and she's forced to stop, listen. The shadows remain still. The only light comes from the doorway she just crossed through, and it reveals a small shrine. Dozens of burned-down candles occupy a table. Parts of the market are open twenty-four hours. The candles burn at night as an offering to the gods, comforting the drug runners who pass by.

Anne buzzes a warning into Jen's ear. Two minutes until her targets arrive. She ducks into a dark corner, putting her back to the wall. The doorway is to her right, within arm's reach. She eases her hunting knife out of its sheath, locking it in her good hand.

One minute.

She hears voices. Banter exchanged in Spanish. Laughs.

Steady breath, steady hands. She knows that she's in no real condition to fight. These killings must be quick, or it'll be her body lying on a mortician's table.

An empty soda can clatters into the room. Heavy breathing signals that one of the men is large. He passes by Jen, his wide shoulders barely able to squeeze through the door.

The man on his heels is tall and lanky—could be a boxer. Jen won't be finding out. She thrusts her blade into his chest as he crosses the threshold. It sticks between his ribs, piercing his heart. She jerks the blade left and right, opening the wound, then pulls out the knife.

She returns her attention to the first man. He heard the impact, the wail that his wounded comrade expelled. Warm blood slings onto the back of his shirt. His right hand is balled, and he turns, throwing a wild haymaker.

Jen has just enough time to duck the blow. Forget a knockout—that punch was powerful enough to kill. She drops to a knee, dragging her blade across the inside of his leg just below his crotch. His femoral artery spits blood onto a nearby wall.

"*Puta*!" he shouts as his hands clasp the wound. He panics as his blood pressure drops. Win now or die. He lurches forward, kneeing her in the chest.

Jen is thrown back into the wall, the wind forced out of her. The man throws up his hands, ready to fight. She reverses her grip on the knife, angling the blade to the floor.

A fast jab comes in. Jen parries it, knowing it is a feint. The hard right comes next. It throws off the man's balance, allowing her to pass his guard. The blade kisses his neck. Blood spurts out, but she's not finished. Multiple stab wounds are inflicted into his back as she circles his body. Liver and kidneys. Buttocks, aiming for the sciatic nerve. Another low cut on the interior of his far leg, targeting his other femoral artery.

Jen jumps away, out of his reach. Her target is breathing heavily. Blood is gushing like a fountain. The thug is dying on his feet. Finally, he tumbles over.

She rushes over to him, searching, and extracts a phone. She frisks the tall, lanky man. He'd been carrying the bag. She pulls it out of his hands and waits to open it, preferring to find what she came for. She does—in his right front pocket.

Both phones are BlackBerries. Unusual, as most people prefer newer iPhones and Androids. She cracks open one of the devices. Removes the SIM card and examines it with a flashlight. No manufacturer markings or serial numbers. Just like the base station controllers.

It's what she'd thought: Varga, or an organization that supports him, is manufacturing technology from the top down. Custom-made equipment virtually guarantees security.

With the SIM card in Jen's hand, Varga is able to control the codes that cell phones use to access his network. If an unknown code somehow pops up on the network, it can be immediately flagged and blocked. There is no outside access, period.

Lining up the bounty, Jen snaps a photo and sends it to Martinez. Afterward, she makes sure both phones are powered down and stashes them in her pocket.

On to the second half: the money. Carefully, she unzips the duffel bag. Narcos have been known to use explosives to tamper-proof their valuables. She slowly removes the bundles of cash. Before placing them in her backpack, she fans them, searching for tracking devices hidden inside. All of the cash is taken, giving the crime scene the appearance of a robbery.

"Anne, I'm getting ready to move. Begin route guidance."

Jen's Whisper buzzes. The pathway to safety is clear. Her killings were sufficiently quiet, and no one is closing on her position. She exits the stall, angling for a swift return to her safe house.

Twenty-Seven

"All right, guys. Lay it out for me," Martinez says as she zips back into the embassy's secure conference room.

What she finds gives her pause. Her subordinates are struggling. The proof-of-life video is punishing, and the men depicted are their close friends. Analyzing the video is painful, but there could be details in this video that will give them an edge against Varga. More important, Jen's work will be completed soon. They'll need to be clear-eyed in their assessments by then, ready to act.

She checks their faces. Sloane's eyes are puffy and red, like her cheeks. She and Terrance are best friends. In South Korea, he saved her life, and she turned around and saved his. Once formed, bonds like that are impossible to break.

Memories of Beijing flicker in Andrew's eyes. He'd been tortured by China's ruling elite for the information stored in his mind. Those horrors are never far away, along with the certainty that Terrance is enduring a life-altering ordeal. Andrew is suffering right along with him.

Martinez stops at the far end of the conference table. Her posture is rigid, and her eyes are taut. "Is the job done?"

Andrew nods. "It is, ma'am."

"Yes, ma'am," Sloane replies, her voice shaky.

Despite the challenge, they pressed forward. This is service, not just to the United States but to their brothers in arms. She recognizes their sacrifice. “Thank you.” She pauses before making an addition. “Remember, they’re not alone. We’re still with them, and we aren’t going anywhere.”

Spirits are buoyed, if only by a fraction. Finally, she says, “Let’s begin.”

Andrew takes a giant breath before stroking his laptop’s enter key. The VHS video and proof-of-life videos play side by side on the center screen. Both cameramen navigate the same maze of plywood. “Our current focus is on the time stamps.”

“Both of which line up perfectly,” Sloane adds. “The VHS video was shot at 4:37 a.m., around three hours after our people were captured. The proof-of-life video was filmed over two hours later, at 6:42 a.m.”

Martinez nods, listens. The cartel is creating a narrative with a very specific timeline. Hostages arrive at the warehouse. Several hours pass while they’re secured. Finally, an “informant” creates the proof-of-life video and forwards it to Mexican authorities. It’s a mistake; timelines so detailed are easily discredited. If Langley’s analysts find any edits to the VHS or the proof-of-life videos, it will throw the story into a tailspin.

“We searched for any divergence in the videos—guards out of place or changes in clothing; changes in surrounding details, like lighting—but we haven’t found anything. Not yet, at least,” Andrew says.

Martinez is impressed with their work, but the challenges are obvious. The guards are in uniform. Same weapons, same plate carriers. Black combat fatigues and balaclavas covering their faces. Patches or any other type of cartel unit insignia have been stripped from their plate carriers. This will take time and a lot of attention. “Have you forwarded the proof-of-life video to Langley?”

“Yes, ma’am. They’re conducting their own analysis. But we’ve already gone through the video’s digital information. It was shot on a BlackBerry, which we’ve confirmed using the device’s MAC address. The time stamps haven’t been tampered with, which means it’s legitimate.” Andrew continues, “The VHS video is key. The time stamp could have been modified during the edit, but we're waiting for results on that one."

"Let's give Langley some time to do its job," Martinez replies. "We'll focus on our mobile switching center. Where are we with Zocalo?"

"We've locked it, ma'am," Sloane says. "We're waiting for Jen to return to her safe house so we can deliver our brief."

"Speaking of Jen . . ." Andrew says. He brings up a photograph of the SIM cards Jen stole from the cartel. Two BlackBerries are included. "More technology native to Mexico City."

Martinez stares at the photographs. She should be worried about the SIMs, but those two BlackBerries are not the first ones she's seen today. Perez rushed to hide his own thirty minutes ago. Andrew also mentioned that the proof-of-life video was recorded on a BlackBerry. It's confirmation: forget Varga's videos. Jen is locked onto the right target, and answers are getting closer. "Drop a message in Jen's mailbox. We've got a target to hit."

Twenty-Eight

The urgency in the Group's message was obvious, and Jen can't contain her excitement. The safe house's front door slaps into the wall as she storms through it. With a boot hooked around the door, she kicks it shut.

Her backpack full of cartel cash is thrown onto the sofa. She extracts her pistol and knife, remembering to place the weapons gingerly on the table. Finally she sits and pulls her laptop from her backpack. While a FaceTime call connects, she extracts her day's winnings. Cell phones and a very unusual set of SIM cards. She considers the cash a trophy, and stacks it into a neat pile beside the laptop.

A voice calls out. "Hey, money bags."

Jen smiles at Sloane's face, which she hasn't seen in far too long. "Ms. Hamilton! You know, Varga felt so bad about all this, he decided to send us some beer money."

"Just happy it wasn't 'lost' on the way to the safe house," Andrew jokes with equal enthusiasm.

Jen just shakes her head. Post Beijing, Andrew relocated to Texas, along with his parents. The move wasn't a mistake—the only miscalculation was him asking a Texan where to live, and she responded—

passionately. He's been an occasional guest at her family's home ever since. "You really gonna talk about losing stuff with glasses that thick?"

Sloane cackles, throws a piece of balled-up paper at Andrew. "Should know better than to tease Jen at this point."

Jen lets the joviality fade, eager to start on the update. Her missing people won't be kept waiting a second longer than necessary. Moreover, it just feels wrong to tell jokes while her friends are suffering. "Tell me how we're doing on the triangulation."

"We've got a lock, down to the foot. It's in Zocalo, one of Mexico's most popular tourist spots," Martinez says. A location is forwarded to Jen. A red GPS pin sits directly in the center of the square. "We think the mobile switching center is underground, accessible via a tunnel."

"Got a bonus for you," Sloane adds. "Ever heard of the Grand Hotel in Mexico City?"

"One of the world's most famous hotels," Jen replies.

"It was recently purchased by Alex Varga," Sloane continues. "We cut through a few shell companies to get the information, and he's the official owner."

"One of those rooms has an entrance to a tunnel," Jen replies, gaze fixed on Zocalo's details. She leans closer, flexing her injured hand, determined not to let it lock up before her next big outing.

"Check out the aerial reconnaissance," Andrew says, forwarding her a set of photographs.

Photos appear on Jen's laptop. Overhead views of the Grand Hotel. Glass domes occupy the majority of the roof space. Most of what's left is dedicated to HVAC equipment. But a large tower is hidden in the tangle of condensers and domes. It's not for any type of light commercial use. She also spies the transceivers bolted to the top.

"That's what we've been looking for," Jen says.

"Yep. That node is sending and receiving data from the base station controllers you hacked," Sloane says, glowing at the honor of sharing the discovery.

"How are we handling this?" Jen asks, convinced that she should have been at the Grand Hotel this morning, instead of ripping off cartel cell phones.

"We've got your reservation in the works," Martinez replies. "But careful is the operative word here. We're assuming that Varga knows his base station controllers are compromised, and that this is your next target. It's also an extremely sensitive district, so we can't raise any red flags with the authorities."

"I won't take any unnecessary risks," Jen replies. "Finding the tunnel entrance will be the challenge, but I've got an idea."

"Walk us through it," Martinez says. "We've still got a few hours to work out the kinks before you check in."

Twenty-Nine

Zocalo. Eighteen-hundreds Mexico, teleported to the present. Jen is riding in a chauffeured S Class Mercedes. As it sweeps around the plaza's exterior, it passes the Metropolitan Cathedral. It's a stone monolith, constructed piecemeal between the late fifteen- and early eighteen-hundreds. Gothic steeples brood over stained-glass windows, while tourists snap photographs from below. An even more ancient site is buried beneath Zocalo: Tenochtitlan, the capital of ancient Aztec civilization, built in the early fourteen-hundreds.

The sedan takes a right-hand turn, exiting the main plaza, then stops immediately in front of another building with a stone façade. It's the entrance to the Grand Hotel Mexico City.

The chauffeur exits the sedan and opens Jen's door, letting her out onto the bustling street. With a small duffel bag over her shoulder, she approaches the hotel, studying each face she passes. While the hotel is no doubt full of tourists, it's also home to a high-value cartel asset. Cartel members will be waiting to intercept her. They'll be no less determined than she is, and if she gives them half the chance, they'll take her out.

A doorman greets Jen with a warm smile and holds open the hotel door with a white-gloved hand. She enters to find a grand staircase made entirely of white marble. She's momentarily dumbstruck as she looks up at a giant gold chandelier that nearly spans the entrance.

Jen grabs the gold railing, certain more spectacles are yet to come. She's dressed in some of her finest attire to match the hotel's decorum. But her expensive duffel bag isn't stuffed with clothes or jewelry. It's filled with guns and computers, which are neatly packed into a slim, tactical backpack.

The stairway deposits Jen in the main lobby. A half dozen tourists mill about, staring up at the stained-glass ceiling designed by a famous French artist. They're spellbound, and she takes it in, too, if only for a few moments. The sea of color is not arranged in any particular order—no religious symbols or odes to famous Mexican leaders. It's pure geometry, gently illuminated by the setting sun's soft orange hues.

An elevator, with its iron skeleton exposed, rises to the top floor. The floors are surrounded by ornate railing, and antique wood doors give way to the Grand Hotel's guest rooms. More rooms are hidden along the corridors that run parallel with Zocalo Square. One of which Jen happens to have reserved.

Jen approaches the counter, concealing her wariness as she gives the clerk a once-over. She's a petite woman with a picture-perfect smile. Beautiful skin, free of tattoos. If she's a member of Varga's cartel, the links are well-concealed.

Jen removes a passport from her coat's breast pocket, handing it over. The clerk scans it. "Ms. Clark checking in, please."

The clerk finds the reservation and communicates with perfect, if accented, English. "I see that you made your reservations online, Ms. Clark. We do have other rooms available if you don't find the first floor suitable. Maybe something with a little more elevation?"

"I'm afraid a good view will stop me from getting my work done."

The clerk smiles. "Then do your best to stay out of the lobby. Remember, we're just a phone call away."

She's smooth, and it forces a smile out of Jen. "I'll keep that in mind."

The clerk finishes with the computer, then begins creating the key cards for Jen's room. Two copies are made, placed in an envelope, and slide across the granite countertop, along with directions to the room.

After offering the clerk her thanks, Jen starts for the suite, eager to find Varga's hidden technology.

The clerk watches her new guest move away from the check-in desk and disappear into a long hallway that will take her to one of the more far-flung rooms.

Certain that the new guest is out of earshot, she lifts the handset of her telephone and makes a call. Ms. Clark's passport book checks out perfectly, but this new guest matches another description, one that Varga called the hotel personally to relate. Hanging up the phone, the clerk enters a back room and locks the door. This hotel is no longer safe.

Thirty

Jen doesn't bother getting settled. The room won't be occupied in another thirty minutes, let alone the night. She unfolds her laptop on the desk and settles her B&T by her side.

Determining which room is hiding the tunnel's entrance involves hacking into the reservation system. The first step isn't a hack at all. Jen simply logs into the hotel's public Wi-Fi.

A call connects to the Group, and Jen relays the update. "We're logged in. Let's see if we can jump the wall."

They know that the hotel is likely using the same internet account to run their business, and the wall is a reference to a partition that separates guests from administrators. Getting through it means gaining access to guest records, online booking tools, and billing information.

Anne and the Group quickly discover a separate access portal. It's an online credentials check, basically a website. Breaking into it will be easy. Jen watches the Group perform an SQL injection, placing malicious code inside the website's credential boxes.

It appears the hotel's magic has followed Jen to her room; the SQL injection works on the first pass. Jen says, "Find me a room on the first floor that's never occupied. We're looking for a black spot in the hotel's records."

Sloane finds it immediately. "Room 107 hasn't been rented in over two years. Make a right out of your room, and it's near the end of the hall, facing Zocalo."

"We got a winner." Jen folds up her laptop and stows it in her backpack. Before she goes, she slips off her jacket—a long Burberry trench coat. She fishes through the duffel bag lying on the bed and extracts a slick, low-vis plate carrier. She drapes it over her chest and fastens the Velcro wings.

Next, she dons her backpack, followed by the B&T, carried in a single-point sling, which she hangs over her shoulder. Her 2011 is already holstered, and she attaches it to her belt, along with her knife. She throws her jacket back on, tying off the belt to conceal her gear, and starts toward Room 107.

With a knock on the door, a blonde woman's face appears on the television screen. The image has been relayed from a security camera mounted above the door of Room 107. The screen flickers off. Two men are sitting at the edge of the bed inside. They exchange a glance; they'd expected more trouble. Still, they must act accordingly.

The man nearest the door is larger, wearing multiple brands and piercings. Braided black hair twists down his back. He's wearing jeans and a white T-shirt, his muscular arms exposing tattoos of old Aztec gods as well as a Mexican military tattoo.

He heads toward the hotel room door, but instead of opening it, he quietly slips into the bathroom. He shuts the door, leaving a crack. A strip of light paints his face, and he waits.

The second man has piercings and markings similar to the first. He's smaller but has wild eyes. He takes a pistol out of his waistband. As his fingers wrap around the weapon, his broken knuckles crack. He tucks the pistol into the dresser drawer just below the television. An AK-47 is laying in front of the television as well. He grabs it, places it in a corner, out of view.

The knock on the door repeats itself. This time it's more forceful.

The second man reaches the door, cracks it open. He doesn't say anything but instead stares into the blonde woman's green eyes.

"Hope I'm not being rude," Jen says, "but I stayed in this room two nights ago, and I left something inside. You mind if I come in and look for it?"

The second man is still silent. He simply nods, swings the door open. As he leads her deeper into the room, the bathroom door opens, and Jen suddenly has a man in front of her and behind.

The situation worsens when she steps into the bedroom. It's a construction zone. Dirty and dusty. A black tarp hangs over the window. Construction plastic has been laid over the room's carpet. Drills and saws are resting on hotel furniture. Smoke detectors are disabled, wires dangle from the ceiling. A breaker panel occupies the left-hand wall. Judging by its size, it likely supplies power to the mobile switching center. Surveillance cameras are in both far corners. Varga will be on the other end, waiting to watch her die.

There's an adjoining room with the clasp off the door—a big red flag. The Group missed something. Mistakes happen when operations move too fast. More cartel thugs will be on the other side, waiting to ambush her. She fights past the adrenaline dump; surviving this situation will depend or her ability to stay calm and work through it.

Jen hangs an immediate right turn toward the nightstand, which is littered with beer cans and cigarette butts. Her back is to them both now, and the skin on her neck is crawling. She reaches up, tugs the Burberry's knotted belt. Her jacket opens, giving her access to her weapons. One of the thugs opens a drawer. The other reaches for something, and there's a metallic clunk against the wall.

Jen leans down and cracks the nightstand, which is filled with pornographic magazines, drugs, and the corresponding paraphernalia. She flares her elbows slightly, allowing the B&T to swing down in front of her chest.

"Damn, the maid must have picked it up. Did y'all by chance see—" Jen's hands jerk for the rifle, making solid connections. She spins, flicking off the safety. The B&T's red dot lands perfectly on the larger man's chest. He's got the AK-47 low, over his belly. They thought they had her. He doesn't have time to second-guess the two subsonic rounds that crash into his chest.

Jen wheels the gun to the next man, who is raising his pistol with one hand. The red dot is in its familiar place, and she dumps four rounds into his chest. Pieces of cotton explode off his T-shirt, and blood spatters on the wall behind him. Subsonic bullets pierce the drywall. As velocity is lost, they ping-pong between studs as they fall.

She doubles back. Two more into the first man's chest. The subsonic bullets hit the bones with an audible smack, and the narco sags onto the carpet.

More gunmen flood the room from the adjoining suite. Just like she'd worried. The first appears, his rifle up slightly as he performs the breach. He needed to angle the barrel to clear the door, and it's going to cost him. Point man is a rough occupation. Jen snaps a bullet through his head, and he drops.

The fallen body blocks the enemy's entry, and Jen presses the advantage. She hovers the red dot sight on the drywall, pumping rounds through it. With a scream, a gunman falls in the doorway, his body over the point man's. Jen puts several rounds in the side of his head and chest.

She hops on top of the bed to her right, beginning to work the door of the adjoining room. Another game of angles. She slowly moves right, pieing off the corner. Every inch she moves, more of the adjoining room is exposed.

A nightstand. The square edge of the adjoining room's bed. Perfectly made. Pillows stacked neatly. It's clean in there. Still in use by the hotel. The reason the Group missed it.

More of the mattress from the adjoining room. The barrel of a submachine gun. A cartel gunman is ducking behind the bed, using it as cover. Jen dips her rifle down, but it swings low. *Snap. Snap.* Two shots, each one striking the mattress. Feathers explode out of the down comforter. Bullets scream out of the submachine gun.

Jen rolls to the ground, landing on the room's far side. Three nine-millimeter bullets hit the wall, directly behind where she was just standing. She hears groaning. Her two shots hit a target, but passed through cover before they did. He's only wounded.

She approaches the door slowly, unsure if there are more men in the room. The B&T is raised in the direction of the shooter's last position. A foot slides back behind the bed. He's dragging himself deeper into cover. She gets closer, expecting an angle to appear.

The wounded man props himself against the nightstand, raising his submachine gun in the same motion. He cracks off a burst, but it goes wide. Jen's rifle is true, and he's finished.

Unwilling to get bogged down clearing another room, she forces the adjoining room door shut against the weight of the bodies blocking it, then bolts it. A moment passes. She remains still. *Will bullets rip through the door?* The seconds tick by, and nothing.

A metallic latch jiggles. Someone is making an attempt to work it quietly. It's behind her, in the room.

Jen jerks as a trapdoor in the floor swings open. It was neatly concealed by carpet and construction plastic along the bed's far side. The tunnel's entrance. Her rifle is immediately up, but no one emerges.

She eases toward the opening. Slow, inch by inch. More angles. She finds a perfectly cut square in the building's foundation. Closer, closer —nothing reveals itself. She's forced to stop a foot from the opening. The ladder must be directly in front of her. The worst angle.

Jen performs a quick peek, leading with the rifle. A gunman is on the ladder, a pistol aiming upward. She fires once, and so does he. Dust and flecks of drywall rain down on Jen. Her shot was a miss, evidenced by the bullet's impact on the tunnel wall. When the rifle discharged, she also felt the bolt lock open, a little more gas escaping from the ejection port. Empty gun.

In one fluid motion, she lets the gun fall, the sling catching it. She peels back her trench coat, drawing the ten-millimeter Staccato. Safety off. Two steps to the left. A new angle. She peeks again, this time with a better sense of her target. The front sight lands on his left shoulder, and her gun discharges, sending a bolt of pain through her left hand.

She dips back into cover. A shout is followed by the sound of feet sliding off a ladder's metal rung. A few seconds later, a hard thud. He's done.

One more peek. No one else on the ladder, and she's got time to stage her next attack. The 2011 goes back to the holster. She drops her rifle's empty mag and struggles to free a mag from her plate carrier. Her left hand shakes as she inserts it into the B&T. Her healthy index finger taps the bolt release and the bolt slams home. Trapped smoke blooms out of the suppressor.

That's six down. No telling how many she will find below. Before she descends into the tunnel, she wants to make sure no one can get behind her. Using her rifle's stock, she snaps the knob off the adjoining door as well as the room's main door.

Next, she extracts her drone and powers it up. The drone buzzes around the room, orienting itself.

"How can I help, Ms. Yates?"

"Zip into that tunnel and tell me if anyone's pointing a gun at that ladder."

The drone drops into the entrance and disappears. Soon, Anne delivers a message to Jen's Whisper: "You're safe to descend."

"Be with you shortly." Time for one last trick. Jen opens the breaker panel on the wall, reads the labels: *Lights. Lights. Lights. Computers. Mobile Switching Center.* She laughs. They made it easy on her. Three breakers fall, cutting off the light down below.

Jen removes her trench coat and tosses it to the ground. After, she extracts a set of PVS-15 night-vision goggles from her backpack. She fastens them to her head using a strap system and turns them on. Next, she turns on her rifle's infrared laser. The combo will give her a serious advantage in the dark tunnels.

She approaches the trapdoor. Activating her IR flashlight, she peers down, and her breath is snatched out of her chest. Templo Mayor—the Aztec's primary religious site in Tenochtitlan—is waiting for her down below.

Sacrifice victims were used in the construction process, in accordance with Aztec ritual. Rows of human skulls adorn the walls. Many are intact, undisturbed by the cartel's efforts. The skulls turn bright green under her night vision, with shadows pooling in their orbital sockets. Silent guardians. Eternally vigilant.

Every instinct in Jen's body begs her not to enter the tunnel.

Another place for the cartel's evil to fester. But she overrides the instinct, certain that the men she's trying to bring home would do the same for her. "Coming your way, Anne."

Thirty-One

Andrew taps several keys on his laptop, and the hotel's security cameras appear on the screen. "Ma'am! We've got big problems!"

Martinez drops into a position behind Andrew. One of the camera feeds has been enlarged, depicting roughly a dozen cartel gunmen moving briskly through the hotel lobby. They're heading in the direction of Room 107. They'll reach the tunnel entrance shortly, effectively trapping Jen below ground. With enough time, they'll surround her, and it'll be game over. "Begin working on a secondary egress."

Several ideas flash into Andrew's head, and he pulls up another window on his laptop, filling it with the Mexico City's civil engineering schematics. "We'll get something worked out."

"It's your only priority," Martinez replies as she shifts to the radio. She picks up the mic and activates it. "Zero, we've got roughly a dozen cartel members inbound on your position. We'll be augmenting your route out of the tunnel."

Jen gauges the final few feet of her descent. When she's certain that it's safe, she releases the ladder and drops to the ground. Dust and dirt are kicked up from the impact. She whirls around, raising her B&T, allowing the infrared laser to cut through the dust cloud.

Martinez's radio call is fresh in her mind, but the tunnels are already swarming with cartel activity. Gunmen are responding to the loss of power, consolidating around the equipment hidden within the tunnels. She'll have to handle them before worrying about the cartel shooters above her.

The rifle's laser finds a cartel member as he runs down a length of tunnel, away from Jen. His weapon's mounted light is activated, and flits rapidly between the tunnel walls, guiding him toward his rally point.

Slack disappears from the rifle's trigger as Jen depresses it. Several hundred grains of lead, copper, and hate strike the gunman's spine. Vertebrae shatter, peppering nearby tissues with bone fragments. The gunman's legs give out, and he crashes down face-first, sliding across a plywood walker board. Follow-up shots find their marks, finishing him.

The frenetic activity isn't dissipating. Heavy footfalls echo not fifteen yards from Jen. They're coming her way via an intersecting tunnel. The movement is accompanied by another jerky flashlight beam. Whoever is approaching didn't pick up her suppressed rifle shots. She keeps the gun up, allowing the laser to linger in the intersection, exactly where she'd expect a head to appear.

A rifle muzzle comes first, accompanied by a burst of light. A thousand lumens' worth, attached to the end of the barrel. It's blinding, and amplified by Jen's NVGs. Everything goes white as Jen dumps a half dozen shots in the light source's direction.

Hard, wet thwacks call out. She sidesteps, expecting return fire, continuing to depress the trigger as she moves. More wet thwacks, accompanied by the sound of knees hitting the ground, followed by a torso.

Target eliminated.

Jen takes a breath, tries to blink away the white in her eyes. Being exposed raises her stress level, but she forces herself to remain cool, patient. Her vision begins to coalesce at the center, and clarity radiates outward, pushing away the remaining haze.

Reoriented, Jen finds tunnels leading in multiple directions. The one straight ahead stretches over fifty yards into the distance, and it has multiple branches, forming a grid pattern. The ancient temple's basement. The grids are the pillars that would have kept the giant pyramid-type structure upright.

Construction lights, duct work, and electrical conduit are bolted to the ceiling. Jen maps them with her IR flashlight. They'll lead her to the mobile switching center.

"Zero, did you copy my last?"

"I heard you, TOC. What's the ETA?" Jen replies.

"They're working to get through 107's door as we speak. You need to move fast."

"Proceeding to the MSC now."

"Expect an alternate route shortly. We're waiting on your signal."

Jen needs to move quickly and take precautions while she does it. These tunnels are full of blind corners, and they could be unforgiving. "Anne, send the drone ahead. Start marking these guys with your infrared laser."

The drone zips down the corridor and disappears. She follows it in. Reaching an intersection, she peers around a corner. Anne's laser has already found a cartel member. He's crouching at the intersection, his rifle pointed in Jen's direction, with a thumb waiting on a weapon mounted light's tail switch. He's perfectly still, allowing his ears to work in place of his eyes.

Jen rests her laser on his head and taps her heel against the floor. His vision shifts. The laser rolls across his forehead, and she depresses the trigger. Before the cartel member hits the floor, Anne's drone speeds away, hunting for another target.

Nearing the next intersection, Jen hears multiple whistles. They're bird calls—code often used by men who've spent time in prison. She peeks around the corner and sees a large man moving quickly, deeper into the tunnel system. They're still regrouping.

"Anne, anything?" Jen whispers.

The bone mic behind her ear buzzes. "Nothing in your vicinity."

Jen breezes through the third, then fourth intersection, reaching the end of the hallway. It's not a dead end, but the outer shell of a room. Blue light emanates from the tunnel to her right, generated by computer monitors. She checks the ceiling, seeing electrical cables snaking in the same direction. Her target is inside this room.

Jen raises her rifle as a shadow shifts around the corner. *Snap! Snap! Snap!*

Three suppressed rifle shots, directly into the intersection's far wall. Ancient skulls explode, along with hot lead and copper jacketing. A man screams, then stumbles out of cover, his body peppered with the blistering fragments. He looks in Jen's direction, making eye contact with a rifle muzzle. He's not around long enough to see the flash.

Two more men barrel out of the corridor. The first catches a bullet to the head. The second is luckier—he gets into striking distance of Jen's rifle. With his free hand, he grabs the suppressor, jerking the rifle out of his face. His flesh is seared by the suppressor as he works, but the pain doesn't stop him.

Jen's body moves with the rifle—the sling is lassoed around her back. The force whips her to the ground and she takes a knee. She looks up, seeing a club careening toward her face.

Crack!

Anne's drone smashes into the attacker's face, forcing him back. Jen draws her 2011 and puts a double tap in his chest. He releases her rifle as he stumbles. She stands up, finishing him with one to the head.

She reholsters the 2011 and grabs the rifle dangling in her sling. She retrieves the drone and sees that its propellers are smashed. Unwilling to leave any tech behind, she tucks it into her backpack. "Owe you one, Anne."

She steps fully into the corridor. Blue light creeps under a closed door made of iron. Flat metal rivets, hammered by hand. A slat at eye level, allowing a guard to peer inside. This is a cell, or maybe a dungeon.

Pressing her ear to the metal gives her a clue of what's happening inside. Someone is settling into a firing position. A safety clicks off.

A tough breach, compounded by the sensitive equipment on the other side of the door. If Jen fires a bullet in the wrong direction, it could fry her entire mission. The same could be said for explosives. But the flashbangs in her kit will be safe. She extracts one, removing the safety tape from around the spoon. For good measure, she does the same with a second.

Jen slides open the slat, tosses the flash grenades inside before shielding her eyes from the flash. Explosions are thunderous in the small room, and she doesn't waste a second getting through the door. It leads into a short hall, and the first thing she sees is a rifle muzzle sticking out from around the corner. The gunman is preparing to hose down the pathway with blind fire.

Jen surges forward and kicks the rifle's muzzle. The force drives it up toward the ceiling not a second before it discharges. Debris rains down on Jen as she rounds the corner and presses her rifle into the gunman's face. He's blind and deaf from the concussion, but he feels her proximity. He tries to pull away, but his back is to the wall. Two .300 Blackout rounds punch through his face, and his body sinks into the corner.

She twists, angling her rifle toward the opposing corner, but finds it clear. The same can be said for the rest of what appears to be a dungeon. Chains dangle from the ancient walls, terminating with hand and leg irons. Aztecs once held English or Spanish explorers in a room like this. Sacrifice victims bound and chained, unable to escape a priest's obsidian dagger.

Computer monitors line the opposite wall, next to Varga's mobile switching center. Jackpot.

"TOC, MSC is in sight. Hold for my signal," Jen says.

"Copy your last, Zero," Martinez replies. "Be advised, cartel members have breached the hotel room's door and are likely inbound on your position."

Jen ignores the danger as she extracts a tool from her kit, called a Master Key. It's shaped like a large flash drive but with several antennas mounted to the rear. It's also loaded with hacking tools. She won't have time to hook up her laptop, but the device will allow the Group members to maintain remote access long enough to install Vector. She plugs it in and waits for the Group's confirmation.

"We've got your signal, Zero. Initiating the breach now."

"Talk to me about my egress, TOC," Jen says, studying the MSC.

She raises her night-vision and activates her weapon's white light, shining it on the machine.

"We've found a sewer line that runs parallel to the tunnel system's far east wall. Breach the sewer line and proceed from there," Martinez directs.

Jen extracts her phone, taking a photograph of the lit-up MSC. It resembles the other technology she's seen in Mexico City. No manufacturer's marking. Its design is smaller than typical MSCs, which indicates that it may have been custom-made for this location. "More data coming your way."

"Zero, you need to leave now."

Jen overrides the directive and forwards the picture. Overhead lights blink on. The gunmen have reached the circuit breakers in the hotel room. Voices echo down the tunnels. They're closer than she realized ...

The Group is scrambling inside the embassy. Anne has broken through the mobile switching center's encryption, and it's being decimated. Hundreds of locations are being exposed. Patterns are emerging as bright red globs on a map of Mexico City. Everything from business hubs to the cartel's favorite nightclubs. Varga's world, writ large.

Anne has also discovered Varga's personal cell number. Distinct texts are emanating from the device every six hours: travel orders and directions; photos of the hostages; health inquiries. Other patterns have emerged: clusters of men traveling together. The Technical Access Group recognizes that these are the likely hostage takers moving at preset intervals.

"Let's split things up," Martinez says. "Ms. Hamilton, you're on the hostages. I want travel times down to the second. Locations. Tell me about the hostage takers themselves. Who are they? What are their histories?"

"Got it, ma'am," Sloane replies.

"Mr. Xiao, what's going on with Jen?" Martinez asks, shifting her position.

"She's closing in on the sewer line as we speak."

Thirty-Two

A flashlight beam showers Jen as she rushes down a section of tunnel. It's followed by gunfire, and a half dozen rounds snap past her head.

Jen ducks into an intersecting tunnel. Using the wall for cover, she edges her rifle into the incoming fire. Gunmen are running down the tunnels toward her. They're wide open, and she punishes them for it. A cartel gunman is struck twice in the chest. Another is hit in the leg. Others see the carnage, decide they're uninterested, and dive into cover.

It creates the break she needed. They'll be more cautious and slow their approach. She zigzags to a parallel tunnel in her original direction of travel. She spots another gunman out of cover, rushing in her direction. Two more to the chest, another dead man. More are held up, growing afraid.

She sprints down the tunnel twenty yards. Past an intersection, then another. Hard left on the third, then right again, up another parallel tunnel. There are more shouts as cartel members coordinate, but they've lost sight of her.

Jen hits the tunnel's outer wall and notices a thin line of concrete wedged between the skulls. It's cylindrical. Just enough to reveal itself, but nothing more. The sewer line, impossible to know which part. She calculates how far below the ground the tunnel is. If she punches a hole, will sewage simply flood the place? Will it expose the sewer's ceiling? The side wall?

The shouts are getting closer. The goons smarter. They're laying down cover fire as they advance. Bullets strike the skull-lined walls. Copper, lead, and bone fragments explode all around her. The suppressive fire is boxing her in, creating chaos.

She extracts an explosive from her backpack. She'd originally carried it to seal the tunnels after her escape and prevent the cartel from gaining access to the compromised MSC—but plans have changed.

The C4 is attached to the sewer's exposed point, and she activates the device. She retreats as far away as she can and extracts her cell. A command prompt is already displayed on the screen. Four-digit pin. Red detonate button. Jen mashes her finger on it, initiating a four-second countdown. Detonation.

The concussive force hurls Jen to the ground. Everything is ringing, and dust hangs in the air, clouding her vision. She takes a moment to regain her bearings, and she doesn't move until she's sure of her direction—it would be all too easy to run straight into cartel gunfire.

The sewer's running water is creating a vortex, pulling dust through the hole in the tunnel. She lunges like a sprinter off a starting block and jumps for the gap. The hole is wide enough to squeeze through, and it drops her straight onto a sidewalk.

Bars of moonlight peek into the sewer from a nearby manhole cover. The gunmen are still forging a way through the dust, and she uses the diversion to her advantage, escaping the sewer via the manhole. Before the hour is up, she'll be back at the safe house to collect her equipment. From there, it's straight to the U.S. Embassy.

Thirty-Three

The embassy's secure conference room is buzzing. The Advanced NeuroNet Engine is roiling the Varga cartel's network, bringing the Group one step closer to reaching their missing people. Anxiety and fear are being replaced by excitement as it becomes obvious that Varga and his minions placed too much trust in their technology.

Varga is personally managing several distinct teams of hostage takers. The hostages are moved every six hours after receiving messages directly from his phone. The teams immediately transfer the hostages to a fresh location and wait for the timer to grind down again.

As far as Martinez is concerned, the intelligence is near rock-solid. But she needs to cross an item off her list: the warehouse. Her missing people could be inside, despite what the new intelligence indicates. She's only going to get one chance at a rescue, and she's going to make it count. "Mr. Xiao, what did Langley send us?"

Andrew begins highlighting a series of maps, GPS locations, time stamps, and cell phone numbers on his screen. "Good news, ma'am. We can fully discredit the VHS video. The time stamp was edited in post-production. Langley's analysts believe that it was created almost thirty hours after our people were taken."

He makes an addition before his boss can reply. "Also, the video's quality was downgraded. Langley's assessment is that it was shot on a cell phone and transferred to the VHS tape—which we can confirm on our end."

Those findings fully discredit Varga's timeline. The VHS was supposed to depict Terrance Kline arriving at the warehouse, laying the foundation for the proof-of-life video, which was shot several hours later. It now appears that the cartel delivered decoys to the warehouse after removing the real hostages.

Martinez still isn't completely satisfied. "Can you confirm our people's movement patterns?"

"Langley's work is just guiding us in the right direction, ma'am," Andrew remarks. He highlights a specific chain of text messages, stolen from Varga's phone. They were exchanged with Rocco Gutierrez—one of the Varga cartel's most senior kidnappers. "Evidence suggests that this man is responsible for Terrance."

Rocco's mugshot is posted next to the information. Not just a hard-looking man, but vicious. Eyes like dark, narrow slats. Aztec piercings and a buzzed head to show off tattoos etched in his skull.

"Rocco's cell phone was used to shoot the proof-of-life video that you first saw in Perez's office," Andrew adds.

Martinez has seen too many faces to be a bad judge of character. Instinct tells her what she needs to know. "A guy like that isn't a government informant."

"You're right, ma'am. Once it was recorded, it was forwarded directly to Varga for approval." Andrew highlights Rocco's movements the night that Terrance was captured, along with the texts for a very narrow window of time. "Varga directed Rocco to the warehouse after the kidnapping while all three hostages were still together. Upon arrival, they shot the proof-of-life video at 6:42 a.m., which matches the original time stamp. Want to take a guess at what they did next?"

"Exit stage left."

Andrew nods. "Nailed it. By seven o'clock he's on the road, heading to an apartment building thirty minutes from the warehouse."

"Can you confirm he left the warehouse with Terrance?" Martinez asks. "That's the million-dollar question."

"Yes, ma'am," Andrew replies. "A text message was sent from Alex

Varga's cell before he left. It had an address, directing him to a nearby cartel safe house. A second message arrived thirty minutes later, indicating that a doctor was traveling to treat Terrance Kline's injuries."

Martinez leans in, reads the text exchanges between Rocco and Varga. She's mystified by how effective Jen's hack was. "Looks like Varga was near obsessive about these hostages."

"He was. I've gone over the messages that Rocco has been receiving since Terrance was taken. Varga has sent dozens of inquiries about his health and treatment. If we jump to Bobby and Cam's hostage takers, we find the exact same pattern I established with Terrance."

"Do you have the same information about the decoy's movement patterns?" Martinez asks.

"Yes, ma'am," Andrew replies. "Three teams came online twelve hours before the VHS video was shot. They were ordered to travel to the warehouse. Once they deposited the decoys, their cell phones went quiet and the movement pattern was broken."

Martinez's elation grows. She locks her hands on Andrew's shoulders and rocks him in the chair. "We did it. This is our smoking gun."

"Get outta here!" Andrew jokes, shooing her hands away with a smile. He looks up at Martinez. "I've got a bonus, if you've got the time."

"Perez."

"That's right, ma'am," Andrew replies, displaying more texts between Varga and Admiral Perez. "They don't refer to you in the most loving of terms."

Martinez reads the insults. They describe her as a traitor to every country south of the U.S. border. Slurs that no woman should ever hear. Musings to murder her in the most violent ways possible. "They were foolish enough to use their own names."

"Had a little too much faith in their system."

"Generate a target package for me. I want everything you have on the warehouse," Martinez declares, thinking of that get-out-of-jail-free card she found in Perez's office.

"Uh, I just invalidated that target, ma'am," Andrew informs, staring at her like she's been on the moon for the past half hour.

Martinez raises a brow, smirks. Her eyes are glowing. She's not here anymore; she's a dozen chess moves into the future. "Just have to trust me on this. I also want printouts of everything you have between Perez and Varga."

"Yes, ma'am." Andrew compiles text messages, GPS locations, anything that connects hostages to the warehouse, then prints it all.

Martinez turns her attention to another critical element. "Ms. Hamilton, where are you with the locations?"

Sloane snaps to action, producing her own set of findings. "I've found more information about the hostage takers' movement patterns. They're not using the same locations twice. It's one and done. Unfortunately, all of the locations are in well-fortified buildings—high-rise apartments mostly. No elevators. Minimal rooftop access."

"We won't be able to get teams in safely," Martinez says, concerned by the rescue's danger profile. These apartment buildings aren't as risky as the warehouse, but they'll still be stuffed with gunmen.

"I found a silver lining, ma'am. They're running a conductor's schedule." She displays time-synced movement patterns for Rocco Gutierrez and his teams of hostage takers. "Varga sends fresh addresses every six hours exactly. Each location is within thirty minutes of the previous one."

"Short exposure window, but we can make it work—barely." Martinez holds out her wristwatch and asks, "Where are we on time?"

Sloane double-checks her monitor. "All three hostages moved an hour ago, just before Jen got access. Five hours until the next switch."

Martinez doesn't like keeping the hostages on ice for five hours—not after what Jen just did to Varga's network—but there's no alternative. She sets the next movement time on her watch and gets straight to her orders. "Mr. Xiao, you're staying planted at the embassy. Ms. Hamilton, pack up. You'll be returning to base with me. When you land, I want you to go straight to Major Bingham and brief him. He'll know exactly how to handle the rescue."

Thirty-Four

Silk sheets are spun around Admiral Perez's king-size bed. They glisten in the moonlight, like the waxy leaves dancing beyond the giant patio doors. The mansion is in the southern part of Mexico City, where the desert gives way to a more tropical climate.

The admiral keeps an emergency access line on the nightstand. It's a way to reach him, day or night. Communications on the device are also encrypted, allowing him to discuss classified material. It begins ringing. The admiral's eyes open immediately. His hand lurches for the phone.

Marisol Perez doesn't stir. She's thirty years his junior, accustomed to enjoying a cocktail before sleep. Her features are soft in the moonlight—and getting softer from successive trips to Mexico City's finest plastic surgeons. The trophy wife he dreamed of.

Before he brings the handset to his ear, he sits up against the headboard, checks that a red light is flaring on the phone. The phone is fully functional, and the conversation will be encrypted.

"Perez."

"Admiral, it's Gabriella Martinez. I'm sorry to wake you, sir."

"No, no, Ms. Martinez. I'm at your disposal, and I assume it's urgent. What happened?"

"I've been gathering intelligence on my end. What I've discovered corroborates your sources. I'd like to ask you to green-light a raid on Varga's warehouse."

It takes discipline to not chasten Martinez. He has stated his position, and to do so again is infuriating. "I've already made myself clear, Ms. Martinez."

"There's been a change, sir, and I believe we need to act rapidly to capitalize on it. Will you please return to base so that I can brief you?" Martinez asks, her tone forceful.

The admiral sighs and checks the clock. Too early, but the sooner he gets there, the sooner he can leave. He's also duty bound. Failure to appear could open him to scrutiny. "I'll get ready. See you in forty minutes."

"See you then, sir. Thank you."

Perez drops the handset in the cradle and grabs his BlackBerry. He needs to alert Varga. He begins a text: *Martinez wants to hit the warehouse. I'm going to deny the request.*

Varga returns the message immediately: *You'll give her the permission she needs.*

Perez's hands begin to shake at the message. Resisting Alex Varga only has one outcome: a shallow grave. But to green-light the raid? It'll be a catastrophe and bring about the end of his career. *Alex, we've discussed this.*

Do as you're told.

Admiral Perez buries his head in his hands. The phone chimes once more and he reads the message: *This network is compromised.*

Perez almost vomits. When he took the cartel's BlackBerry, he was assured of its safety.

What should I do?

Varga replies: *Put the phone in your pocket and go to work.*

The phone slips from Perez's grasp and drops by his feet. His gut is telling him to destroy the phone. Drown it in water. Put it in the microwave. The damn thing is in his home. *His* home. A direct link between him and Mexico's most ruthless cartel. The end. Game over. The Americans will treat him as ruthlessly as Varga will.

He has only one option now: prepare for the worst while a clearer picture emerges. He opens his nightstand and reaches inside. A Beretta 92FS is waiting, and he extracts it. It doesn't usually travel with him to work, but it will today.

Thirty-Five

The last place Jen expected to be.

After escaping the tunnel, she'd planned to drop into her safe house, collect equipment, and proceed directly to the U.S. Embassy. Her targets have been successfully penetrated, and her work in Mexico City is finished. The Varga cartel had one last shot at her in the tunnel, and they missed. Safe in the embassy, she'd have a nice long visit with a friendly doctor. Get fixed up, enjoy some potent pain medication, wait for good news about three rescued Americans.

Instead, she's sitting in the vacant top level of a parking garage. Her head is swimming from the explosion she endured in the tunnels. Mild nausea rolls in the pit of her stomach. Every few minutes she flexes her left hand, preventing it from seizing completely. The pain is maddening.

The nose of Jen's Camry is nestled up to a concrete wall. Graffiti paying homage to Varga glows in the headlights. Huitzilopochtli chasing away demons of the night. And several miles beyond the sun god's reach, Terrance Kline is being held hostage. She launched a drone only minutes ago, and it's already loitering directly over his suspected location. Only the morning's first task.

Within several hours she's going to take part in his rescue.

When Jen returned to the safe house and read Martinez's brief, her jaw dropped. Her shock still hasn't subsided. Rescuing a close friend while he's under duress will be one the most challenging tasks of her career. She'd never freeze up on Terrance, but if something goes wrong today, she'll never forgive herself. There will be a lot of guns in this fight, and she can only control one.

Tires screech. Vibrations rattle up the Camry's steering column. Xenon headlights cut across the garage and flash in her eyes as she looks to the rearview mirror. Her fingers curl around the H&K 416 A5 in the passenger seat.

A black Suburban is rapidly approaching. U.S. government plates are screwed to the bumper. Cavalry's here.

The Suburban stops next to Jen, and the driver's side window slides down. A man with slicked-back red hair glares at her. His eyes are wild, mischievous. "Get in," he hisses.

Jen chuckles and grabs her kit. Cavalry? No, more like a band of lunatics recently escaped from an asylum. Varga's people pray for the sunrise, and as she crosses toward the Suburban, she's certain it's the last one more than a few of them will see.

"I'm calling shotgun. Hope one of y'all kept the seat warm for me," Jen says as a very large man exits the front passenger seat, decked out with guns and armor. He stands six foot five with broad shoulders, ink down his arms, and a black beard. Inch-long hair on his scalp is neat and parted. "Appreciate it."

"You're Jen Yates," the giant says, appraising her.

Jen follows his eyes down to her boots. During her brief interlude at the safe house, she changed up her kit. Armor and rifle magazines cover her chest. She also has a ballistic helmet to go along with the H&K 416 in her hand. Designer clothes have been exchanged for blue jeans and a tactical shirt. "In living color."

"Cool." He sticks out his fist, exposing a tattoo sleeve with medieval art and crusader crosses. They exchange a fist bump, and his knuckles are almost twice as wide as hers. "Charlie Keats, but call me Animal."

"Just Jen. Thanks for the seat," she says before climbing into the passenger seat and tucking her 416 between her legs.

"I'm Sergeant Major Al Hastings," says the driver with the red beard, an H&K 416 tucked neatly by his right leg. He's struggling to hit five foot ten, but his attitude makes up for the extra inches God snatched away. Probably the last guy on earth she'd want to fight.

"Grayson West—Gray for short. I'm also the medic. So if you need a hand, just shout," the man on the rear driver's side chimes in.

Jen cranes her neck toward Gray, brow furrowed. He's not like the other two. Tan skin and an extremely laid-back demeanor. No beard, and his brown hair is well-kept. He's got a few tattoos on his arms but doesn't have full sleeves like Animal and Hastings. But it's the name that arouses Jen's suspicions. "Grayson, you from California or something?"

Gray smiles whimsically as if touched by a sea breeze. "Born and raised. Where you from?"

"Texas."

Gray nods, completely missing Jen's suspicion of him, and eases back into his seat. "Right on."

"Good to meet y'all. Hope you're ready to do some shooting." She gets a round of nods, groans. That's what these guys do best. They're all experienced career sergeants. They're also Major Bingham's best shooters, which is why they've been assigned to Martinez's protective detail. And why they've been sent into what will likely be the day's toughest rescue scenario.

The clock is ticking, and Jen gets to work, extracting her laptop. She unfolds it, cradling it in her lap. Drone footage appears. It depicts a large apartment building several miles away. Terrance Kline's location.

Animal leans forward and pokes her laptop screen. "Heard you brought down a jetliner with one of these."

"Cooked a guy in an X-ray machine too," Hastings adds, eyes bulging out a little farther.

"Gnarly," Gray says with a chuckle.

Jen is amused by their curiosity and background knowledge of her work. Each is hoping to witness a bit of the magic. She wipes away Animal's fingerprints from the screen. "I checked those boxes. Can't say anymore though. I'd have to kill y'all."

They all laugh, settling in to having her on their team. They're about to do something extremely dangerous, and they're silently gauging whether she's solid. The conclusion is easy enough to draw.

Jen turns to Animal. "You got enough room for those freaking stilts back there?"

Hastings laughs, then leans over to Jen—a little too close—and taps her on the shoulder. "You know what happened to the last person who made fun of Animal?"

Jen stares at Hastings, deadpan. "Nothing."

They all laugh again, enjoying some gallows humor before they put their lives on the line.

Jen eases her seat forward and continues syncing up with Anne. A FaceTime request comes in from Andrew. She accepts. "What's happening?"

"Looking to finish syncing with your vehicle," Andrew says, still inside the embassy's secure conference room.

His job here is simple but important. He's to gather information and provide the rescue teams down-to-the-second guidance to the hostage's locations. Had Andrew attempted this on base, Admiral Perez would have keyed in instantly. Questions would have been raised and the element of surprise spoiled.

Jen plugs her laptop into the SUV via a USB cord. "Go ahead, Andrew. I want GPS guidance online, first thing."

"Give Anne a second, and she'll be with you," Andrew replies.

"Wait, what?" Hastings asks, alarmed. "I'm not okay with a computer taking over the truck."

"I'm logged in, Ms. Yates," Anne says through the vehicle's speakers.

"Will you put your route guidance up for display on the dashboard screen?" Jen asks.

"Yes, one moment, please." A map of Mexico City appears. It has each of the hostage locations, along with Jen's route to her target building.

"Damn," Animal says. "They just hacked our truck."

Jen laughs. "Don't worry. I'm still gonna let y'all drive. I know your egos are fragile."

"Something urgent is coming in. Anne has a live audio feed with your hostage taker; it's from a cell. Sounds like they're coaching the hostage. Listen in," Andrew says.

A voice comes through the speakers. It's English. Rocco Gutierrez's mugshot appears on the dashboard screen. His identity is matched against the voice sample on the proof-of-life video. "Remember that we have others. If something happens today, you make the right choice." Static momentarily interrupts him. "Know that if you fail, others will die. We know your family—lift your arms—and remember that your friend from Texas can't save you."

"That's a mental prep," Jen says, trying her best to stay professional. Outwardly, she's calm. On the inside, she's ready to put a bullet through this bastard, Rocco. "Is the phone in a pocket? What's the rustling sound?"

Andrew relays the phone's camera feed. It's pointed at the ceiling, resting on a nearby table or chair. "I'm guessing they're adjusting the hostage's garment. Possibly tucking a suicide vest inside the fabric."

"Cut the feed on our end, but have Anne keep listening. I'd like a voice ID of our hostage," Jen says. She looks at Hastings. "From this point forward, we consider our hostage wired."

"I call dibs on this Rocco asshole. No one wires up one of our guys," Animal says, clutching his Mk-46, belt-felt machine gun. It's designed to be compact, but the giant makes it look like a child's cap gun.

"Fuckin' S-Vests," Hastings says. "It's like the Middle East right on our doorstep."

Gray is more somber. "Means the others have it too."

"Do they know we're coming?" Animal asks.

"We haven't seen any communications indicating that suspicion," Andrew replies. "Ms. Martinez is pointing the main task force to a raid on the warehouse."

Jen shakes her head. "But we assaulted a valuable target several hours ago, and word travels fast with these guys. They could be putting an insurance policy in place."

Hastings smacks the steering wheel. "If there are S-vests, then—"

Jen cuts him off. "If there are suicide vests, we handle it. Okay?" She looks back at Andrew's face on the laptop screen. "Got an update on our movement window?"

"One hour," Andrew replies.

Everyone shifts silently. The fight is approaching. Dangerous cartel gunmen, valuable hostages, and now a potential suicide vest. The mission is going to be complicated, more so with only four people and one vehicle. Yet each of them has defied the odds in the past, and they'll do it again today. Their brothers are counting on it.

Thirty-Six

Alex Varga's orders came by courier. Just one note, and it will change everything: *Place bombs on their chests.* It was accompanied by a short script, which Rocco Gutierrez has been reciting at random intervals.

Rocco sits back, admiring the explosive belt he just attached to his hostage's chest. It's like a dozen others he's used in the past. Ball bearings are the worst part, the best part, all at once. Enough C4 to remodel a city block. He smiles, thinking: *This little man, generating all this trouble. Americans . . . They'll get theirs today.*

He continues coaxing the hostage into a more pliable state. The same simple threat, over and over. Just like the script required. "Remember that we have others. If something happens today, you make the right choice. Know that if you fail, others will need to die. We know your family, and remember that your friend from Texas can't save you.

"Raise your shirt again. I want to see that you're listening and are ready to do as we say."

There's no verbal response. Instead, this mousy little man only trembles and raises the baggy black garment. Tears soak through the blindfold, and he sucks snot back into his nose.

Rocco jeers at his chest. Skin and bone. No wonder he was taken.

He returns to the kitchen table and watches the hostage. Muscles are straining; he's suffering. He'll keep watching until he's satisfied. More mental anguish for a man long past his breaking point. It'll be easier to quit when the time comes.

The hostage shivers and shakes and struggles. His arms fall a few inches, strength all but gone. But he takes a hard breath and finds resolve somewhere deep in himself.

Rocco grunts. Stronger than he looks. He grabs a spare cell phone off the table and turns it on. Only Varga has the number. What happens with this vest is his decision. It will be made free of emotion. If the Americans come, guns blazing, Rocco won't have the opportunity to lock up under pressure—not that he'd do that. He's killed many men, and his own death is but a speed bump on his path to hell.

He approaches the hostage and inserts a headphone jack into the phone's port. The jack extends from a circuit board wired to the C4. It completes the circuit, making the phone a detonator. Carefully, he tapes the wire to the back of the phone, ensuring it will not come undone. Finally, he tucks the phone into a pouch on the vest.

"You can drop your arms." Rocco allows the garment to fall, then smooths it out. The belt isn't printing, meaning it'll go unnoticed to the naked eye. "Hopefully, your friend from Texas isn't as smart as people say."

Suddenly, the hostage stops shaking and stares at him, despite the blindfold.

Rocco's skin raises, but he stifles the chill. Americans. Coddled by wealth. Ease and convenience a way of life. No different from the man standing across from him—so easily taken and controlled. More important, he's killed worse than Jen Yates and the men she'll be working with.

Thirty-Seven

Campo Militar 1

A Whisper is planted behind Martinez's ear, and it sends bad news rattling down her skull. "Possible suicide vests."

She's standing inside the base's tactical operations center. It's a serious space, equipped with soundproof walls, large screens, and communications equipment. A center island is lined with officers and analysts, each one handling a unique segment of today's mission: task force coordination; disconnecting utilities to the target structure; keeping local law enforcement and first responders in the loop.

Their forces are pointed toward the warehouse. Martinez had been serious when she'd ordered Andrew to produce a target package on the location. Her get-out-of-jail-free card that she threw back in Perez's face. Armed Americans now have permission to exit Campo Militar 1 and operate on Mexican soil. What happens between the base and the warehouse is anyone's guess.

Despite the TOC's fervor, Martinez's mind is still on the recent Whisper transmission. Only two other people heard the call: Sloane Hamilton and Major Bingham. They're also wearing Whispers, enabling silent communications with Andrew.

Bombs put not only the hostages at extreme risk, but the entire rescue force. She can feel Bingham and Sloane questioning her: *What are we doing, Ms. Martinez?*

This chance will not come again. Jen broke into the cartel's network, and they know it. The cartel doesn't have time to augment their strategy without the Group seeing it. Days or weeks will change that. She gives Sloane a nod. *It's on.*

"Ms. Martinez."

She turns to find Admiral Perez approaching her. She'd thought the suicide vests were disturbing, but this man's behavior rivals them. His BlackBerry is held prominently in his hand. A security breach like this would have serious consequences in an American facility. This isn't the United States, and it's plain to see that Varga is not only listening in on the TOC but is also calling the shots.

To her surprise, he didn't fight her for permission to hit the warehouse. He barely read her target package before rubber-stamping it and summoning Commander Torres, the FES's senior officer. *Varga wants it*, she reminds herself, *but why?*

That answer isn't immediately obvious, but the pistol on Perez's hip is. Beretta 92FS. Commonly issued in the Mexican Navy. Didn't bother to de-cock the hammer before he nestled it into his holster. She's been in Mexico weeks and has never seen him carry a personal weapon. Perez is expecting trouble, and he's prepared to dish out some of his own.

Martinez stares at the Beretta and curses herself for leaving her pistol behind. Major Bingham is the only armed American officer present. He's no doubt skilled with his 1911, but the dozen Mexican officers nearby won't stand idle while Bingham pumps .45 caliber slugs into Perez's chest. They're on his turf. Outnumbered. Outgunned.

"I've made my final rounds. Are your forces ready?" Perez asks, sauntering up to her, brash as he's ever been.

Martinez checks the center screen. ISR is in place over the warehouse. Dozens of cartel shooters are armed and ready for a standoff. Helmet camera footage is also arrayed on the screen. Most of them correspond to Mexican FES members, with a dozen Delta operators mixed in.

Finally, she examines her watch—the minute hand is about to strike

7:00 a.m. Varga should be moving the hostages any second. The morning's real gamble. Will he give the orders?

"We are, sir," Martinez replies.

The admiral addresses the rows of officers and analysts working at the center island. "Operation Promised Land is 'go.' Repeat, Promised Land is 'go.'"

She refocuses on the TOC's center screen. Troops are already moving across the tarmac. Helicopters are waiting, rotor blades spinning. When they get airborne, they'll have less than a ten-minute flight to the warehouse.

A message from Andrew buzzes Martinez's Whisper: "We have three texts to move."

Martinez's pulse quickens. She'll have the chance she'd been praying for.

Another message comes in from Andrew: "They're moving the hostages to a central location. Between thirty- and thirty-five-minute travel windows."

Martinez's heart stutters. Perez and his Beretta. Little resistance to the warehouse raid. Suicide vests and hostages routed to a single location. The pattern is broken, and all the signs point toward a single conclusion: Varga wants revenge.

The sun is inching toward the horizon, coloring it with threads of orange and pink. Hangar doors are open. Fuel hoses have been retracted to the edge of the airfield. Ground crews linger.

Rotor blades are spinning, and six helicopters are resting on pads. Four of them are UH-60 Black Hawks. The first two are responsible for troop transport. They'll dump their passengers, consisting primarily of Mexico's FES, in the warehouse's courtyard, initiating the assault. The other two are gunships slated to provide security as they orbit the warehouse.

Two more helicopters are waiting while their passengers hook in. They're AH-6 Little Birds. Light, nimble helicopters with a diverse range of capabilities. They each carry four Delta operators, who sit on planks mounted on the sides of the helicopters.

In carefully choreographed fashion, the six helicopters begin lifting off the pads in pairs, guided by ground crews. The Little Birds motor to the outside edges of the formation, optimizing their mobility. Together, they reach their desired airspeeds and streak toward their target.

The message on Rocco's cell phone came right on time. Varga has new orders. A new location. It's a crematorium on the far side of town, where hostages go to disappear.

"Let's go!" Rocco shouts.

Two more cartel gunmen enter the room, weapons in hand. They know the ropes and move with the same ease as Rocco. One carries an AK-47 with two magazines taped together, the second dangling low. The other carries an M4 style carbine from the late '90s with a red dot sight bolted to the carry handle.

Rocco picks up his own weapon—a Micro Uzi. Easy to maneuver and devastating at close range. The open-bolt submachine gun could stitch half a dozen 9-millimeter rounds across a hostage's belly within a second.

They exit the apartment as a group, descending past sentries and apartments full of drug addicts. Nurseries for the dead. They find an old Mercedes sedan waiting by the entrance. *One more ride and this'll all be over.*

"We're live. Anne, let's see the drone feed," Jen says, receiving go orders from Andrew.

The drone feed is displayed for all to see on the center console. Four men exit the front of the building and approach a waiting sedan. It's an old diesel Mercedes from the '80s. The exterior is bronze, scarred by patches of rust. The hostage is pressed into the back seat. Rocco, who is marked by his cell phone, enters just behind him. Two other armed men occupy the driver and passenger seats. The Mercedes takes off.

"Mark it and put us on a path to intercept," Jen says.

"Yes, Ms. Yates." The map on the center console updates. "Seven minutes to intercept."

Thirty-Eight

A 1980s Mercedes makes a turn at the traffic intersection, in front of Jen and her team. The bronze paint is faded, matching the drone's images. The team is close enough to hear the old diesel engine rumble, see black smoke boiling out of the exhaust.

Jen scans the vehicle, aided by the Suburban's Xenon headlights. A flap of ceiling fabric hangs down, partially obscuring the rear window. She's able to discern that the vehicle is occupied by four men. The hostage cannot be identified but shares physical similarities with Terrance Kline. An armed man next to him twists in his seat, checking on traffic to his rear—Rocco Gutierrez.

"Anne, run a diagnostic on the vehicle," Jen requests. "Show me if there are any vulnerabilities."

The light turns green. They're in a bustling area, coming to life with morning traffic. Like most places in Mexico City, neighborhoods are mixed in with businesses. Street vendors everywhere. Pedestrians weaving between bumpers as they cross the street. Mopeds and motorcycles speeding along yellow traffic lines. The smells of breakfast foods and coffee beckon people out of their homes.

Hastings eases through the intersection, taking a position several car lengths behind the Mercedes. The traffic is bad, which is a blessing and a curse. It obscures the Suburban's position while preventing the Mercedes from bolting. But civilians are everywhere, raising the specter of collateral damage.

Anne comes back with a diagnostic of the vehicle, displaying her work as a model on the center screen. It's interactive, with every single digital device inside or on the car displayed. The Mercedes is too old for Anne to stop with cyber techniques, but she spots a disturbing development.

"Anne, I'm seeing a fourth cell phone. Are you sure of the positioning?" Jen asks, double-checking it for herself.

"Yes, Ms. Yates. There's a fourth cell phone in the vehicle. It's located on the rear driver's side."

That's exactly where the hostage is sitting. Whoever built the vest attached a failsafe. A way to detonate it remotely. She visualizes Varga sitting in an office, the explosive's cell phone number on speed dial.

"Is it in Varga's network?"

"Yes, Ms. Yates."

Jen smirks. Chock this one up to a win. "Take it offline. Forward this information to Andrew, then suggest performing the same search for the other hostages and taking the same action."

"Relaying the information . . ." Anne replies. Relief passes through the vehicle. The hostages just got exponentially safer, but they know not to consider the explosive secure until it's been removed from the hostage and separated from its detonators.

Anne's hack is displayed on Jen's laptop. Malicious code is texted to the target number—a sophisticated means of penetrating cellular devices. Within minutes, Anne is in control of the device. It's turned off, and the corresponding account is deleted from the mobile switching center. There's no way for the phone to connect a call.

Another update pops up directly after. The helicopters are airborne. All of the rescue's elements are now moving to their assault positions.

Jen checks the timing against the map on the SUV's dashboard. "We're close, gentlemen. Time for final equipment checks."

Thirty-Nine

ISR FOOTAGE DEPICTS SIX HELICOPTERS AS THEY FLY IN loose formation. They're less than five minutes from the warehouse, and the sun has just crested the horizon, spilling color on the city. Flurries of buildings, cars, and people breeze by under the helicopters.

"Admiral, we've lost comms with two of our helicopters!"

The admiral addresses the radio operator. "What happened?"

"They've hopped onto encrypted frequencies."

Martinez smiles at Perez and points at the center screen. "Best part is coming up next."

Two AH-6 Little Birds break away from the formation and tear off in separate directions. The ISR drone zooms out, trying to keep track of them, but it's impossible. The helicopters gain distance until visual contact is broken. Seconds after the helicopters vanish, helmet camera footage from the Delta operators turns to static.

"Where are those two helicopters going, Ms. Martinez?" the admiral demands.

Martinez feigns consideration. "Probably just a beer run. They'll be back shortly."

Perez pulls closer to her. "You *will* bring them back."

"You green-lit this operation, Admiral. Those two helicopters are within your operational parameters."

Perez balls his fist, raises it close to Martinez's chin. "You . . ."

Major Bingham squares up with Perez. He's been briefed on the admiral's duplicity, and if given half the chance, he'd shoot him on the spot. He flicks the beavertail safety on his 1911 and offers a cool grin. "Easy, Admiral. I'm feeling a little left out over here."

The admiral sizes up his adversary. Battle-hardened. A man to take seriously with a .45 on his hip. Better to pick a different fight with a lesser man. "If my men suffer because of this, you'll pay for every casualty. You can expect those operators to be placed in handcuffs when their helicopters land."

Martinez's mind flashes to the text messages between Perez and Varga. She hasn't had a reason to use them—yet. "Forget all about those handcuffs before you yourself get a pair, Admiral."

"What's going on?" Torres, the FES troop commander, asks. The men in those Black Hawks are his. Like any respectable leader, he considers their safety paramount. "My people are on the line here. Should I abort?"

Martinez can't answer his first question. The leverage she has on Perez is too valuable to disclose. But she won't allow good men to go into harm's way for no reason. "Abort your raid, Commander."

"Press onward!" Admiral Perez shouts, jowls shaking as he waves his fist in the air. "You will not turn back!"

"My force will be—"

The admiral leans into Torres's face. "Do as you're told."

Major Bingham senses Torres's hesitation. Split between what he knows is right and following orders. Plenty of good men have suffered at the hands of bad officers, and he swore that he would shield his own from similar fates. He expects the same of Torres, no matter the cost. "Bring them home, Commander."

Torres takes a step back from Perez and proceeds directly to the radio operator's station. Without asking, he rips the handset out of the operator's hand and follows Major Bingham's suggestion. The Black Hawks begin rerouting to base.

"Three minutes out."

A message from Andrew. The Little Birds are going to strike the two remaining hostage vehicles very shortly. Jen will be on a similar timeline. Martinez crosses her arms, watching as the Black Hawks return. She gives Bingham a half-smile. "We're fully committed."

Forty

Horns are blaring. Traffic has come to a standstill. Angry drivers are waving, honking, scrambling to get around a car blocking the intersection. The old Mercedes hasn't moved in several minutes. The three hostage takers are having a heated conversation. Pointing. Arguing. Deciding. The Mercedes's engine cuts off.

"Something's wrong," Jen whispers, fingering the safety on her 416.

"My gut's telling me to go, ma'am," Hastings says.

"They're looking back at us, ma'am," Animal adds. "Something's gonna pop off."

"ETA on the Little Birds, Anne?" Jen asks.

"Two minutes, Ms. Yates," Anne replies.

Just a few more seconds, Jen thinks, nervously eyeing the Mercedes.

Rocco turns around, looking directly at their Suburban. An Uzi flashes in his hand. Their cover is blown. The hostage is in danger. Before they can act, the Mercedes's driver bolts from the vehicle, laying down suppressive fire on the Suburban. Rounds chatter against the bulletproof windshield. Cracks and chips and divots race across the glass.

Jen drops, keeping her head raised inches above the dash. She watches Rocco exit the Mercedes while using the hostage as a human shield. He slips behind the Mercedes's hood and ducks for cover behind the engine block.

The passenger also bolts, taking a position behind a parked car to the right of the Mercedes. A woman screams, reaches for her children in the back seat as the gunman crouches behind the hood. More hostages. Collateral damage in the making.

Instinctively, Jen's hand seizes the door handle, and she can feel her team move in the same direction. The Suburban's armored door swings open, and she mounts her rifle between the pillar and the door. The center dot of the EOTech lands on the second gunman, still hidden behind the car full of people. Panicked silhouettes bob in and out of the red dot's boundaries. No shot.

Hastings's 416 is up quickly, and he engages the driver, who is hammering the Suburban. A double tap from Hastings's weapon finishes him quickly, and he drops between two cars stalled in traffic.

Jen's target sends AK-47 fire through the car. Bullets rip through the glass, spitting shards in every direction. Gun smoke pumps through the bullet holes, obscuring the car's occupants. Thuds and pops and snaps radiate around Jen. Tiny bits of the Suburban explode into the air. Still no target. His cover is too good. Innocent people are too exposed.

She tears a flashbang from her plate carrier. She pulls the pin, tossing it over the armored door. It clanks on the ground near her target. "Flash out!"

Before the device detonates, the passenger tries to bolt from cover. He misjudged, thinking it was a grenade. His AK is leveled at her while he attempts to flee. Her trigger finger works first, placing a round directly in his chest. A second shot follows. Then a third. Smoke curls out of Jen's suppressor where the narco once stood.

The woman exits her bullet-riddled car. Trapped gun smoke coils around the roof and wafts into the air. She wraps two small children in her arms and runs to safety, screaming. She and the children are half-deaf and delirious but uninjured.

"Moving right!" Animal shouts, breaking for cover from behind Jen.

"Moving left!" Hastings shouts, beginning to weave in between cars stalled in traffic. Soon, they'll have Rocco and the hostage flanked.

Gray takes a firing position at the driver's door, his 416 angled toward Rocco and the Mercedes.

"Rocco!" Jen shouts. "Release the hostage and we will not harm you!"

The shout gets a response. Rocco exits cover and steps between a row of cars, using the hostage as a shield. The Micro Uzi is leveled at the hostage's head. One pull of the trigger, half a dozen rounds, all through one skull. He stands directly in front of Jen's position. A straight shot. Just a yellow traffic line connecting the distance between them.

Rocco's head jerks left to right as he processes the worsening situation. Two men flanking him. Angles forming, changing, and reforming into perfect shots. Soon, bullets will find him. Well placed from the looks of the soldiers pointing their sophisticated weapons in his direction.

Rocco's mouth begins to move. It's a whisper into the hostage's ear. More coaching. Jen's instincts are burning, heightened by adrenaline. Rocco whispered it. Her gut screams it. This is Varga's vengeance, and she is the target.

Rocco shoves the hostage straight toward Jen. He stumbles, takes a single cautious step forward. Then another. Gunfire erupts, and Rocco falls to the ground, eviscerated by Hastings and Animal.

"Hostage! Do not move!" Hastings shouts, who is forced to take aim at the hostage.

"Identify yourself immediately!" Jen adds. The hostage's head angles toward her voice. He understood. Instead of speaking, he steps forward again. His hands appear restrained, tucked under the baggy black garment obscuring his body. "Hostage! Do not move again! Tell us your unique identifier immediately!"

The hostage begins moving briskly, homing in at the sound of her voice. Fifteen feet and falling. Jen is forced to rest the red dot on the hostage's head. "Stop!" The order echoes from three other directions. Ten feet. The hostage's hands jerk out, a detonator clutched in the left.

He's too damn close. Jen yanks her rifle from between the door as the hostage's pace quickens. Five feet. She jumps into the Suburban, slamming the door. Grey follows her in. She ducks into the foot well, looking up at the passenger window. The hostage arrives and removes his blindfold, searching. She locks eyes with him as he raises the detonator. *Smack!*

A bullet rips through the back of the hostage's head, and it cracks hard against the window. Jen stares up as blood runs down the glass. *Was it him?* The angle was off. The blindfold was covering part of his face.

She edges toward the door, hoping for a clear look at the hostage.

Gray grabs her. "Ma'am! It's not safe yet!"

She sits up anyway and looks through the window. The body is leaning against the door. Its balance shifts, and it tumbles to the asphalt. The weight collapses on the detonator, and Jen's world goes white.

Forty-One

Aerial footage depicts a fireball as it engulfs Jen's Suburban. Seconds before, the hostage, possibly Terrance Kline, was shot and killed. Black smoke is rippling upward, obscuring the street. Radios are also down, and Andrew is uncertain if there are any survivors.

He replays everything. Anne had a lock on the bomb's cellular detonator. No way it was triggered via a call. It was manual. Pressure switches. A button. Something handheld. The other hostages will have the same capability, and the same order to attempt to kill whoever is rescuing them—a catastrophe for two small Little Bird helicopters.

"Anne, notify Martinez that a hostage was killed on Jen's location, and that a bomb was detonated."

"I'm relaying the message now, Andrew," Anne replies through the laptop speaker.

Andrew hops on the radio, working to call off the Little Birds. They're seconds away, in extreme danger. The closest helicopter is already swooping low, target in sight, interdiction eminent. "Valkyrie One-One and Valkyrie One-Two, this is Embassy One. Abort your rescue attempt. I repeat, abort your rescue attempt."

"This is Valkyrie One-Two. We copy. We'll see you back at base."

As Andrew watches helmet camera footage, he realizes it's too late. Valkyrie One-One is making contact. The helicopter begins its assault, dropping out of the sky and hovering just feet in front of the hostage taker's sedan. It happens fast, taking the vehicle by surprise as it sits in traffic. The helicopter is perpendicular with the vehicle, its skid sitting just inches above the hood, providing the Delta operators sitting on its benches a clean shooting angle.

Andrew enlarges Coco Garcia's helmet cam feed. He and another operator raise their rifles and fire. Bullets tear through the sedan's windshield. Rounds strike both front occupants. The rear passenger, who's got a weapon angled on the hostage, doesn't fare any better. The operators keep pumping rounds through the windshield, through the dead men in front, through the seats and roof, directly into him. Within seconds, the vehicle is eviscerated and everyone is dead, save the hostage.

"This is Valkyrie One-One. Repeat your last, Embassy One."

"Abort! I say again: abort!" Andrew shouts.

Before the Delta operators can remove their safety harnesses, the pilot responds. "Copy your last, Embassy One. Valkyrie One-One is pulling out."

The two shooters settle back into their seats while keeping their rifles on target as the Little Bird soars back into the clouds. Seconds after the pilot responds, a blast engulfs the vehicle. Ball bearings rip through everything in a three-hundred-sixty-degree radius. Nearby vehicles are consumed by fire. Molten metal tears through pedestrians.

Before Andrew can process what happened, a third explosive detonates on Valkyrie One-Two's target vehicle. All three hostages are dead.

The helicopters are safe, but there are still troops in danger. Jen and her team. Martinez is demanding a status update. One he doesn't have. He checks Jen's position. Black smoke rises into the sky, obscuring the drone's feed. Gusts of wind part the smoke, revealing a scorched Suburban. A fire rages under its belly, threatening to consume the gas tank. Appears the armor held, but no guarantee the concussion didn't finish the job.

He tries to reach Jen once more on the radio. The message is frantic. "Jen, can you hear me? Sergeant Major Hastings? Does anyone copy?"

Static. Crackling airwaves. "Anne, take your drone lower. Get me an up-close view of the damage."

"One moment, Andrew."

Black smoke washes over the camera lens as the drone pulls closer. A grisly scene emerges. Shattered glass litters the ground, glistening against the rising sun. Injured people strewn along the sidewalks, cradling bloody arms, legs. Some are in shock, wandering back and forth on the sidewalk, pleading for medical assistance that has yet to arrive.

Hastings and Animal are on their feet, and Andrew's hope is buoyed. They're rushing toward the Suburban.

Animal reaches the passenger side, which is consumed by fire. He attempts to check on the hostage, or what's left of the body. Legs. Part of a pelvis. Nothing to identify him, and the flames are making the carnage worse by the second. He rushes to the driver's side—the cool side—to assist his superior officer.

Hastings has started wresting the Suburban open. He tugs on the door handle, his foot wedged on the running board. Animal comes from behind, and together they force open the door. Black smoke pours out of the interior. Gray exits, coughing, hacking as he falls onto the ground. Animal peels off, helping his teammate away from the burning vehicle.

"One more," Andrew whispers.

Hastings leans in the vehicle, pulling; Jen could be unconscious. Maybe trapped. A weapon or piece of bent steel keeping her wedged in the Suburban. More tugging, now with a knee pressed into the driver's seat. A head emerges as Hastings falls backward onto the asphalt. The rest of Jen's body follows him to the ground.

Andrew searches for blood. Signs of serious injuries. She appears to be okay. Hastings helps Jen to her feet. She's woozy but walking, throwing an arm around his shoulder. All four of the team members rush down the street together. They commandeer a parked car, the owner having fled the blast site, and begin their extraction.

Jen is safe. Her team is safe. The other rescue teams are safe. But three men are not. Emotions begins to overpower Andrew; he called off the raid, terminating their chances of rescue.

Could the other rescue teams have succeeded where Jen failed? Andrew buries his head in his hands, bearing the brunt of the call. Frayed nerves are finally snapping. Forty-eight hours of pressure, work, and hope are now undone.

Messages are crashing into his computer—Sloane, sending constant requests for an update. His fingers hover over his keyboard, paralyzed, shaking. Finally, he begins typing his message because he simply can't say it.

All rescue teams safe. Three hostages killed in explosive blasts.

Send.

Forty-Two

"All rescue teams safe. Three hostages killed in explosive blasts." The Whisper hums out the gut-wrenching news. If it were possible to collapse, Martinez would.

Trey Bingham is stoic. Teeth locked, muscles flexing in his jaw. White knuckles hidden under crossed arms. Watery eyes. But he's keeping the rest corked inside.

Sloane is hiding her face in her hands. Martinez wants to go and comfort her. Tell her lies. Like things will be okay. Knowing they won't. After all, they just played their best card, and Varga beat them. Not only that, but a catastrophe is unfolding.

Reports are coming in from local law enforcement. Three bombs were detonated on several of Mexico City's most crowded streets. Dozens of casualties have been reported. It's an all-hands situation. Any asset that can be summoned to help clean up the terror incident is being routed to the blast locations. Hospitals are preparing for a raft of casualties, but first responders are having trouble reaching the scenes. It's terror, exactly how Varga planned it.

Blame for today is going to land squarely on her shoulders. American operators deviated from their planned tasking at her command.

Those same operators were on site when three explosions rocked Mexico City.

The repercussions are going to be seismic. Not only did she lose three hostages, she just gave Mexico political leverage that will surely be exerted over the United States. Efforts to stop Varga will likely end after today. Rescue will shift to recovery. The hostages' remains will need to be collected, identified, and returned stateside for burial.

Another question leaps into her mind. What if the real hostages were at the warehouse? Perez didn't argue with her raid. *No*, she tells herself. Varga wouldn't have given up something so valuable so easily. Her intelligence was rock solid, and so was her assessment. But they missed a critical detail, and it cost them everything.

Martinez feels a hand on her shoulder. It's Major Bingham. "We were all with you on this," he says.

Shock and numbness stop her from replying.

"Ms. Martinez."

Martinez is so stunned, she forgot about the snake in her midst. Perez. Eagerly waiting to use the upper hand that she gave him. She turns to find him standing beside four armed military policemen. Serious guys. Larger than Mexico's average naval recruit and trained to use the Berettas on their hips. Uniforms are perfect, with pant legs tucked into spit-shined black boots.

"Perez."

"I'm formally stripping you of authority on this installation." Perez waves the MPs forward. "Detain this woman and her subordinates. Escort them to the brig and stand guard until my word arrives."

The MPs step closer. Snap open pouches on their duty belts and begin removing handcuffs.

The MP closest to Martinez presses his cuffs, ratcheting them open. With a few feet to spare, he says, "Turn around, please, ma'am."

Martinez disobeys the command and holds her ground. She'll leave the TOC only when she's certain her teams are safe. But she will not allow herself to be restrained or imprisoned. Perez is still Varga's man, and the danger is very much real.

Major Bingham stands ready. His hand isn't on his weapon, but it's hovering dangerously close. The MPs stop cold, eyes widening under their helmets, but they refuse to back down.

Martinez sneers at Perez. "If your subordinates lay so much as a finger on my people, there will be consequences for you, Admiral. You will not be warned again."

Perez takes in a gulp of air, puffs up his chest.

"And I'll be leaving shortly," Martinez says, cutting him off before he can speak. "Ms. Hamilton, give me a status update on our forces."

Sloane had been packing her equipment, preparing to stand by her superior officer's side for the march out of the TOC. She jumps back into her seat and reopens her laptop. After logging back in, she hammers out a message to Andrew. The reply is swift. "Our Little Birds are RTB. The ground element is also safe."

"Pack your things, Ms. Hamilton." Martinez glares toward the military policemen, who are paralyzed by her audacity. "Step aside, gentlemen."

It's the MPs' turn to refuse a command. They don't waver. While they wait for Perez's word, the other MPs begin ratcheting open their handcuffs.

Perez's face is red. Knuckles have whitened as they grip his duty belt. A latent tremor rests in his jowls. He'd like nothing more than to detain Martinez, but her threats have teeth. "Handcuffs won't be necessary. Step aside, but make sure they return to their apartments."

"Wise choice," Martinez says, barely allowing the MPs to part before she passes. "But this is far from over, Admiral."

Forty-Three

Jen's team speeds to the top of the parking garage. As they rip around the final corner, the sedan's engine sputters, and smoke escapes from under the hood. The vehicle couldn't tolerate the team's get-away driving. They screech to a stop next to Jen's Camry and begin piling out. The garage's top level is empty, and they get straight to work.

Jen is feeling topsy-turvy from the blast, but she rushes to the trunk of her car. She struggles to insert the key into the lock while the final moments before the hostage lost his life replay in her mind. She desperately tries to stitch the fragments together.

She lifts out a first-aid kit and tosses it to Gray. The trauma packs on their kits aren't much use; they're mostly for life-threatening wounds. Tourniquets. Chest seals. Wound-packing gauze. Nothing for burns.

Gray opens the kit, extracting bandages and topical antibacterial ointments. Animal's left arm was scorched during the explosion. But the black, blistered, and oily skin—the signs of a second-degree burn—is manageable. The burns are clustered between his exposed elbow and wrist. The shot that killed the hostage turned bomber was his. He was ducking into cover when the bomb detonated, sparing him from more severe injuries.

Gray slaps on a pair of surgical gloves, then douses Animal's arm with sterile water. "Already halfway home."

"Lather that shit on thick," Animal says, a smirk stretching across his face.

Grey unscrews a tube of ointment and lets the cap skip across the garage's pavement. "This'll take the edge off. It's got a cooling effect," he says, blasting the ointment over Animal's arm and working it into the burn.

"Cooling effect? Burns worse than my ex-girlfriend," Animal says. He stays still, accepting the pain.

"For the record, I don't treat that type of thing. Goes for everyone at all times," Gray replies.

"What if I ask real nice?" Hastings asks. He's raided the first aid kit too. A gash is open in his shoulder—a shrapnel wound. Nothing's embedded, but it needs to be sealed. He douses the wound with peroxide, lets it bubble. Once he's satisfied that the wound is relatively clean, he dries it and prepares to glue it shut.

Gray tears open a package of bandages, letting the wrapper flutter away on the wind. With an expert hand, he begins dressing Animal's burn, enveloping it in a neatly spun web of bandages. Satisfied with his first patient, he assesses a potential second. "How's that going, Sergeant Major?"

"I'm set, Gray." Hastings lays a long string of glue over the wound, then pinches. "And they say Mexico's the place to get away from it all."

Jen sits on her Camry's rear bumper, exhausted, trying to anchor her thoughts back to earth. Her face is caked with soot. A tendril of blood drips from her nose. "What'd you see before you pulled the trigger, Animal?"

"Sorry, ma'am, but not much. That detonator flew up and I broke the shot. Wasn't anything left to identify when I approached the vehicle," Animal replies, confident he made the correct call at the scene. That hostage became a threat to the entire team, and it was handled.

"Ma'am, you were the closest," Gray says. He'd been trying to pull her deeper into cover, and his focus wasn't on the hostage.

"Did you get a look?" Hastings asks.

Jen replays the moment in her mind, but her head is throbbing. Ears are ringing. It's blurry. She can see the hostage's face, but it's wrapped in an explosive blast's haze. That sliver of time is life altering. "I-I don't think it was him, but I'm not certain."

Hastings offers her a bit of wisdom, earned from years of experience. "That's your head talking. Tell me what your gut's saying."

Jen continues stretching her mind. She looked into the hostage's eyes. Wild and bloodshot. Maybe even psychotic. The curtain starts to ease back, revealing more. Cheek bones and a jawline that doesn't match. Suddenly, she's certain. "Terrance wouldn't run at me like that. He'd die first. Couldn't have been him—wasn't him. No way."

Hastings places his hand on her shoulder. "Then we've still got a shot."

Jen just nods. There's nothing else to say. They took their chance, and it's over. Everything she went through in the past forty-eight hours feels like it was for naught. She's certain something went sideways today, and it wasn't on her team's end. They were played—lured in by decoy hostages. "We need to make contact."

The team is jolted with a fresh urgency. They weren't the only ones operating today. She grabs a backup cell phone from a kit in the trunk and powers it on. All the other tools were left to burn in the Suburban. The team members hold their breath as the device grabs a signal. Jen dials Andrew's number from the contacts, and he picks up on the first ring.

"Jen!"

"How's everyone? What happened?" Jen asks, responding to the excitement in his voice.

Andrew delivers his brief, starting with the two remaining hostages. Grim news all the way around. "Multiple blasts occurred at the hostage locations. The other two hostages were lost, but our Little Birds made it out safely. Civilian casualties have already climbed into the dozens."

"How are we responding?" Jen inquires, eyeing her team. They're bloodied but not beaten. Their hands cling tightly to their rifles, signaling they're ready to get back into the fight.

"You and your team are instructed to stay hidden in Mexico City. That's all for now," Andrew replies. He pauses before asking his next question. "Was it him?"

Jen's reply is resolute. "No."

Andrew sighs, sharing the same mixture of relief and disappointment as the others. They still have a shot to bring their people home, however slim. "I'll pass the word along. In the meantime, keep your head down."

"Will do." The line clicks off and Jen focuses on her team. They're disturbed, ready to head out of this garage and punish Varga. She's inclined to indulge them. "Let's get off the streets. From there, we'll figure out what to do next."

Forty-Four

Victor is in his apartment, watching cell phone footage taken from bystanders at the blast sites. They're forwarded to the police, who exchange them for cartel cash.

One video is particularly jarring. A trail of blood oozes down.a curb, pooling along the gutter before draining into the sewer below. The trail starts only feet away, with an elderly man—a bystander—lying on the sidewalk, barely conscious. He's not the only victim in the day's bombings.

The video only gets worse. Two heavily armed men approach a burning Suburban and force open one of the doors. Another well-armed man tumbles out, followed by Jen Yates. Victor recognizes her so easily now. The beautiful face. Rugged eyes filled with determination. She escapes with her comrades, relatively unharmed.

Thank God is all Victor can think, for more than one reason. Had any more Americans been killed in this maelstrom, there would have been no stopping the United States from cleansing Alex Varga, and every one of his known associates, from Mexico City. Those efforts would no doubt lead them to Victor and his organization.

But it's no guarantee of safety. There's still trouble ahead. What occurred today will have consequences, and it's time for him to reassess how he manages the risk.

Victor starts at the most important point. He recognized Varga's instability early on. He banked that Varga would go back on their partnership, though he never would have guessed it would be this dramatic or violent.

That foresight led him to a wise decision: removing Terrance Kline, Bobby Hollice, and Cameron Vinke from Mexico City. An exchange was made immediately after the proof-of-life video was shot. Rocco and his crews were given decoys while the originals were whisked away. It was the only real way to protect the hostages, and the switch had worked.

Before Jen even landed in Mexico City, Victor had a strong idea of what she would target. When she went for the cellular network, it was no surprise. From there, he left a trail of breadcrumbs for her to follow. Dozens of text messages were made to look like they were sent from Varga's phone.

When Jen penetrated Varga's network, her Group could interpret all of that intelligence in only one way. They must have been so certain that they were correct, and in a way, they were. They played the best option—the smartest option. Only the game was rigged, and they had a zero-percent chance of winning.

A move like that didn't come without risk. The network that Victor built around the cartel became a noose around his own neck. Every time he stepped in front of a cartel security camera, he risked being seen by Martinez. It was the reason he and Bandito had been so cautious in the apartment building. The talk about "real" hostages. "One" set of decoys. The entire conversation had been planned.

The hostage videos were also made to be revealing. Edits to the VHS tape were too basic to stand up to scrutiny. Rocco shot the proof-of-life video from his cartel BlackBerry—an amateur mistake that permanently linked him to the real hostages. He was also instructed to verbally offer the hostages water and request their names. Those vocal intonations were no doubt matched when he was coaching the hostage this morning. More validation for Jen's Group.

The decoys were ordered to stay silent. There was no way to

prevent Rocco's teams from carrying the cell phones that Martinez would use as weapons. Kline, Vinke, and Hollice would all have detailed voice records that could easily be matched. To top it off, the decoys' drug habits were maintained in bathrooms with cameras disabled.

Victor planned it all, and he considers himself successful, despite Varga's meltdown. His time in Mexico City is finished. A suitcase and duffel bag are waiting by his computer. A private flight will soon whisk him out of the country.

He sits at his computer station and double-checks a solid-state hard drive. It contains thousands of lines of code, all of it generated when the Advanced NeuroNet Engine decimated Varga's mobile switching center. Many more lines were added throughout the day as Anne monitored the cartel's movements through the city.

His prediction held true; he couldn't find the malware when it was operating passively, but its work was plain to see when it took control of Varga's mobile switching center. He was helpless to prevent it, but that didn't stop him from paying close attention to every action the quantum computer took in the past twelve hours. Just like with World Chem, it'll be vital to insulating his organization from Martinez and the Central Intelligence Agency.

The drive is worth more than gold, and he gingerly unmounts it and tucks it into a Pelican case lined with foam. Two full legal pads with notes he took on Anne's actions are stored in the case with the drive. Shutting the case, he snaps the latches down and fastens a padlock in place.

His organization hand-selected Varga for this task. Their partnership with the cartel was expendable long before today. Varga has served his final purpose, and it's time to permanently cut ties. He smiles at the thought. Victor, more than anyone in his organization, created this monster. Now he's earned the privilege of helping Jen Yates destroy him.

Accessing a back door into the cartel's network, Victor begins deleting all of its operating systems. The cellular network is erased. The surveillance network is scrapped. GPS tracking tools that Varga uses to monitor cocaine shipments are taken offline.

It will leave the cartel blind, allowing the vultures to swoop in and pick Varga's bones clean.

Victor gathers his belongings and prepares to leave the apartment for the last time. A Glock 35 pistol will accompany him the entire way. Unplugging Varga's network will guarantee his execution, but he won't let that happen. The job isn't finished, not until he brings home the wealth he's found.

Forty-Five

A dark, rutted stretch of desert road terminates at an equally dark airfield. Victor peers through the windshield of his sedan, spotting his ride out of Mexico City. The Russian An-12BP is the modern equivalent to America's C-130. Plenty of storage space for drugs or whatever else that may need to be shipped or smuggled into foreign countries.

Victor slows the vehicle, taking his time to case the airfield. Headlights from nearby vehicles illuminate the dirt runway, along with flashing lights on the An-12BP's fuselage. A crew of cartel gunmen is unloading a shipment.

But there are too many gunmen for the job. It could be because of the mayhem in the city, or because Varga ordered him to be detained. Maybe unplugging Varga's network so quickly wasn't the best idea. He braces for the worst-case scenario.

Victor places the car in park and continues watching. The crews are unloading two replacement base station controllers and a mobile switching center. All three are now useless without the software that controls them, but they were part of his deal with the cartel. They're the shipment's final pieces of cargo—drugs have already been hoisted onto military style flatbeds.

Work stops suddenly as the cartel members notice Victor's vehicle. It's time to face whatever's waiting. Before he exits the sedan, he removes his Glock from the center console and checks the chamber. He carefully tucks it into his overcoat.

Victor approaches the aircraft, bags in hand. A cartel lieutenant steps forward. They've begun to look like carbon copies to Victor. Aztec burns, tattoos, and piercings—as if they had a clue what it was like to live in that time period.

"Are you almost finished?" Victor asks, refusing to stop.

The lieutenant steps into Victor's path, barring his movement forward. Two more gunmen flank him. "Mr. Varga didn't tell us you were leaving."

One sentence and Victor knows how this'll end. He sets his luggage in the dirt. "I sent him a carrier pigeon. Maybe it hasn't landed yet?"

The lieutenant smirks, then drops the safety bar on his AK-47. The movement is slow, menacing, terminating with an audible click. "Funny. I just talked to him. Didn't mention any pigeons. He did say he'd like a word with you if you happened to stop by our airstrip."

"Your airstrip, my plane. Sort of a mixed-up situation, huh? Tell you what . . . Let Alex know I'll be in touch when I land."

"You'll be seeing Mr. Varga shortly—"

Victor's hand jerks toward the breast pocket of his coat, finding the pistol. He levels it at the lieutenant's face and pulls the trigger.

Victor angles the weapon to the next largest man and discharges a second shot. Another narco on his way to meet Huitzilopochtli. He jerks the Glock into the third man's face but stops short of a trigger squeeze. "You look like you're in charge around here."

The man gulps down his shock. He's nearly deaf and his cheek is seared from a muzzle flash. Despite Varga's orders to detain him, Victor is untouchable—at least until the death sentence is rendered. "Yes, sir."

Victor notices other cartel members forming at their new leader's back, weapons at the ready. But it's all show. They're whipped, and he places the pistol back in his jacket. "Ah! A message for Alex just popped into my head! Tell him that I unplugged his network. Remind him that no one goes back on a deal with me. Can you manage that?"

"He won't be happy to hear that."

"Deliver it, and get the fuck out of my way." Victor grabs his bags and steps over the two dead bodies. He approaches the craft's lowered ramp. The cargo bay is empty. Cartel members have already hurried off the plane, responding to the gunshots.

Victor raises the ramp, sealing the craft off from the gunmen. He stows his baggage in a nearby compartment, then heads to the cockpit. After entering a PIN on a keypad, he enters.

No one is waiting inside. No pilots. No navigation specialists. Just computers and a blacked-out windscreen. Cameras affixed to the outside of the craft allow him to monitor the cartel's movements. They're clearing the runway, as he'd expected. But those cameras are in place for more important reasons. Victor is in an oversize drone, and the pilots operate the craft from thousands of miles away.

It's an excellent way to smuggle drugs. If the aircraft is intercepted, it can't be forced to land. Distant pilots can point the nose toward the ocean and splash the aircraft. Inaccessible mountain ranges and remote jungles are equally appealing places for a crash landing.

Victor logs in to a tablet mounted on the instrument panel. Same numerical combination as the cockpit keypad. He types a simple message to confirm that he's boarded and not under duress from the cartel. The pilots are already aware of his presence. They've just been waiting on his word.

Victor puts on an oversize fur coat waiting on the pilot's chair. He sits down and straps in. An oxygen mask is also standing by. Standard life support and cabin pressurization systems have been stripped from the craft—a means of preventing stowaways. He dons his oxygen mask; seconds later, the engines rumble to life.

The aircraft taxis without any assistance from Victor and performs a hundred-eighty-degree turn at the end of the runway. Sensors and screens flash and make snap calculations before the takeoff begins. Thermal and night-vision displays are activated. Lasers detect runway distances, widths relative to wingspan and nose to tail dimensions.

The throttle is pinned forward. Automatic, like everything else. Victor's back presses into the seat. It's exhilarating. The aircraft bounces down the dirt runway and leaps into the sky, clearing the trees at the far end. He relaxes into the seat, certain that this has been the most successful day of his life.

Forty-Six

The lack of a window in the metal door to Terrance's cell hasn't stopped him from learning his environment. The passing days have been educational. He's listened through the metal and made observations about what's nearby.

The cell itself appears makeshift, recently created for its current occupant. The bed feels appropriate for a military bunkhouse, and it's not bolted to the floor. The drab olive sheets and pillows and blankets are also the same type of military surplus fare. Oddly, they're stenciled with black Cyrillic characters.

Plumbing and other fixtures are of decent quality. He has not spotted any surveillance equipment in the cell, and the lights cut on and off at courteous intervals.

All in all, Terrance has been treated fairly here. More like indifferently. No torture, not even an interrogation. When he first arrived, he'd anticipated a terrible time. He'd steeled himself against harsh treatment. Instead, his wounds were treated by a skilled doctor, medicine was dispensed, and he was fed.

The guards that deliver food every four hours are a lot like the cell—haphazard. A rotation of three different men see to Terrance's needs. Each of them has a different nationality: a Spaniard, a German, a Russian. Their accents gave each of them away. All of them are armed with rifles, pistols, and knives. But Terrance hasn't gotten the impression that the weapons are because of him. They're in a remote location, hints to which are given away by the guards' attire. They wear safari-type clothes. Light and open, always soaked through with sweat. He suspects they're in a jungle, likely in South America.

Terrance sits at his usual spot by the door. His ear is pressed to the metal, and he's taking deep breaths. In the air, he senses baking circuits, humming with electricity. There's a computer nearby, likely several, and he would only need a few minutes to send a signal to Martinez.

His surveillance is interrupted by footsteps in the corridor. Terrance wipes the sweat off his hands and takes several deep breaths as he gets to his feet. He's about to do something dangerous.

He takes up a position at the center of the cell, pacing, both to dispel tension and appear like any normal captive. He begins counting off the seconds. *One Mississippi . . . two Mississippi . . . three.* The count ends at fifty-eight seconds when a key scratches into the metal door.

The German guard steps into the cell—the friendliest of the bunch. He's got a tray of food in hand. It's always the same stuff, likely sourced locally. Beans. Tortilla. Sometimes chicken, sometimes not. Scrambled egg has been added into this one along with a glass of water to wash it all down.

As Terrance moves to grab his food, he trips and careens toward the ground. The guard jerks the tray into the air, trying not to spill its contents. Terrance's hands reach for the man's belt for balance but he misses, and his hands slide down the guard's green pants.

Terrance hastily picks himself up. "I'm sorry. My balance is off—" He points at the bruising around the side of his head. A remnant of the time spent with Varga's thugs.

"Do you need the infirmary?" the guard asks, tamping down his agitation while checking on the food.

The nice one. "No, sir. Thank you for offering."

The guard hands Terrance his tray and departs the cell, locking the door behind him. *The nice ones are always the victims.*

Terrance extracts a folding knife from behind his back. It had been clipped in the guard's pocket. He lifts the bed slightly. The leg is hollowed out and he stuffs the knife inside. He returns the bed to its proper position, realizing the missing knife could trigger a search.

He sits on the bed and starts devouring his food. He's been on the mend since arriving—wherever he is. He needs to keep up his strength. He will make an escape attempt soon but has no idea how far he'll need to travel before finding freedom.

Forty-Seven

Martinez's first morning meeting will be a tough one, but not for lack of preparedness. In a few short minutes she'll enter a conference call with the CIA's Deputy Director of Operations. He wants an explanation, and she's going to be damn sure he gets a good one.

Aerial and helmet cam footage from yesterday's catastrophe plays on her laptop. The carnage keeps her memory fresh. She's also reviewing Andrew's actions. They were exemplary, and she'd have made the same calls without question. Disabling the cell phone detonators failed, and ordering the Little Birds into an explosive's blast radius was suicide.

Avoiding American casualties was critical, and Martinez achieved that, if only through dumb luck. But there's another element, which is arguably more important: the hostages.

Admiral Perez is insisting that the real hostages were in the warehouse. His position matches the intelligence assessment she presented to him, along with his government's. According to Perez, her actions compromised the hostage's safety, along with the host nation's forces.

Mexico's wrath is already being felt in Washington. Suicide vests were detonated on their streets. News reports have been scathing. Thirty-second reels play on repeat—mangled bodies and vehicles burnt to husks. The press is already speculating that Americans were the ones pulling the triggers at the blast sites.

Twenty-seven people were killed in the bombings. The Mexican government is holding the United States responsible. Martinez has given them all of the ammunition they need to expel her forces, and soon.

The clock on Martinez's computer strikes 8:30 a.m. She takes a deep breath, reminding herself that she knew all of the risks before she made the calls. *Time to own it.*

An incoming call pops up on her laptop. DDO Scott Thompson's office. "Woody"—as he likes to be called—is one of the Agency's most capable leaders. A powerhouse that rose through the ranks without nepotism or political maneuvering. With Woody, she'll get a fair shake, if she deserves one.

"Deputy Director, thank you for calling me this morning."

"Mexico City is looking pretty rough right now, Ms. Martinez. I'd hate to be where you're sitting," Woody replies. He's in his early sixties and naturally thin. He keeps his full shock of gray hair appropriately parted for his executive-level position at the Agency. An American flag is pinned to the lapel of his navy-blue suit.

"No one hates it more than me, sir. Listen, we don't need to kick pebbles down the road here. Where do you want me to start?" Martinez asks.

Woody nods. "I respect that, ma'am. I've had regular briefs on the situation, but I'd like to hear what happened in your own words. Don't leave anything out. Understood?"

"Yes, sir." Martinez begins, starting with Jen's initial assignment and the subsequent intrusions. She includes information about Varga's videos and Admiral Perez's behavior. The night that Jen hit the mobile switching center is a subject of intense focus.

"Jesus. This was a nightmare," Woody says, shaking his head in disbelief.

Martinez nods. "One that I made, sir, and I accept responsibility for that. The truth is that I moved too quickly after gaining access to Varga's telecommunications network, but I believed that I needed to act upon that short window of opportunity."

"It was the correct move. We spent close to two decades using that same playbook in the Middle East."

A tactic Martinez understands well. She deployed multiple times to the Middle East while she was a naval intelligence officer. The raids initiated at her behest all moved to the same rhythm: strike a target, extract intelligence, and strike again based on newfound knowledge. Entire terror cells were dismantled in that fashion.

"The known-unknowns, sir," she replies.

"Still plenty of those here." Woody's jaw muscles tense, and he takes a moment. "Those hostages still alive, Ms. Martinez?"

Martinez is a fighter, and she's never thrown in the towel. Hope only dies when she gives up. Until she finds solid evidence that her missing people are deceased, she's going to stay on the hunt. She answers Woody honestly: "I believe that they're still out there, sir."

Woody takes a deep breath. He started his career leading from the front. Old age and stiff knees took him off the battlefield. But he knows only too well what those missing Americans are enduring. "Thank you for your candor, Ms. Martinez. We'll make good use of this information, especially with Perez."

"Handcuffs would fit him nicely, sir."

"Couldn't agree more, but that's on Mexico's side of things."

"Where do you stand with this, Deputy Director Thompson?" she asks, sensing it's time to face her executioner.

"You're packing it in, Ms. Martinez. The Mexican government is raising hell in Washington, and I can't fault them. You're also catching some heat in the Oval. Not saying you deserve it, but President Jackson is not happy."

Martinez grimaces. There's only one answer people like Woody have for unhappy presidents: *Yes, Mr. President.* She sighs. "Guess I should be grateful it's not an election year."

The deputy director chuckles. Gallows humor, the direction she's headed. "There's a flight back to Langley with your Group's name on it. Your actions are going to face an Office of Inspector General review board. There's gonna be some real scrutiny ahead, and it's likely to lead to disciplinary action."

"My Group?" Martinez asks, blinking past shock. "I absolutely will not allow them to be blamed for this."

"Not what we're saying, but they are a part of this. We need to hear from them."

Martinez nods. So long as her people don't suffer. She knows her career is likely over. *Fair enough.* Bad choices equate to bad leadership, and she's guilty of both in Mexico City—at least that's how she feels about herself. But she can't let the mission end with three of her own missing. "Well, sir, I'm afraid your review board will need to wait."

There's a long silence before the deputy director responds. "Cashing out, Ms. Martinez?"

"Chips are going back to the house, sir. For Korea. Beijing. Ji Wu. All of it."

"A lot of weight behind that request. The review board might lend credence to those actions. You really wanna take 'em off the table completely?"

"Yes, sir."

"Consider yourself cashed out and here's your receipt. I understand why you're staying down there, but even if you do return with three healthy Americans, it may not sway your review board. You're now disobeying my direct orders—orders that I'm going to enforce very, very loosely. Clear?"

"Yes, sir."

"God damn you. I hope you know what you're doing," Woody says, enraged at the thought of losing one of his finest intelligence officers.

"Let you know when I figure it out, sir. And thanks." The line clicks off, and Martinez can't help but groan. Her career was in the toilet at the call's onset. She just flushed it down the drain.

But the upside is as glorious as it is dangerous. The chains binding her have just been removed. Anything that even resembles a target on her hit list will receive serious attention. She'll remove them, one by one, and chart a scorched-earth path toward her missing people. What else does she have to lose?

Her work phone chirps on her nightstand. A text from Admiral Perez. She reads it. The fool wants a meeting. She almost laughs but replies instead. She'll soon be in his office to give him a lashing he'll never forget.

Forty-Eight

There are four shots of whisky lined up on the safe house's kitchen counter. Hangover cures. Jen grabs the first one, raising it into the air. "*Sine Pari*." It echoes three more times. It's Delta's moniker, and she gave the toast in honor of their missing men. The glasses land back on the counter, and the whisky begins to work its magic.

The team spent last night drinking. Alcohol soaking up yesterday's trauma. And while they drank, they thought long and hard about how they'd continue the fight. Battle plans clicked into place when Jen noticed Varga's network was taken offline. She'd like to procure some valuable technology loose in Mexico City—for scientific reasons, of course. Only thing holding them back is their hangovers, which will be short-lived.

Jen ambles to the couch to wait for her nausea to fade. Fresh bandages traverse her hand. Gray, their medic, treated her in between shots last night. All told, there wasn't much he could do. Too late to stitch the blowout wound on her hand. Nerves and other soft tissues will need time to heal fully—if they ever do. He also considered her mildly concussed, and offered the only prescription available: Miller Lite.

She drops onto the sofa. The frame cracks. She looks directly at Animal, remembering that he slept on the couch last night. "The hell did you do to my prize-winning sofa?"

"I just fixed the thing. You look so much more comfortable," Animal replies, noting how deep Jen is sagging into cushions.

The room begins to howl, Jen along with them.

"Gonna need a rescue team to get outta this one," Jen jokes, making a half-hearted attempt at standing. "The day's plans are ruined."

"Hell no," Hastings replies. "I still got full magazines."

Last night Jen promised them a day out in Mexico City. Shopping. Sightseeing. A few split skulls in between espresso breaks. "I'm not one to renege on a promise like that!"

Hastings does a mock bow. "Never took you for such a lady."

"Let's get hydrated and chock-full of aspirin, then we'll hit it," Jen says. She tries to get up for real this time but can't. She bursts out laughing again. "Okay, one of you damned heathens need to help me out here."

Animal rushes over, heaving her out of the pit. "Least I can do!"

A window shatters. Metal clangs across the floor.

The team ducks down, expecting an attack. Bullets. An explosion. But instead a statue comes to a stop under the coffee table. Jen rushes over, grabbing it. It's a gold-plated Santa Muerte figure. Black robes. A scythe. A note is wrapped around it, held tightly with a rubber band. She removes the slip of paper, finds scratchy handwriting and misspelled words: *A regalo for the lady with the weird name. Adios.*

It's from the little boy. The movie buff. That several-hundred-dollar down payment bought them a valuable warning.

"We have to go now!" Jen shouts.

It triggers a frenetic response. Guns and kits come first. If a fight is coming, they need to be ready to bang it out.

"Spare equipment, ma'am?" Hastings asks.

"If it'll fit in the trunk! Weapons and ammo are a must!" Jen shouts while frantically gathering tech. Laptop. Drone. Spare cell phone. She shoves them into her backpack.

The rest of the team disappears into the bedroom, gathering hard-cases full of weapons and ammo. When they all reappear, Jen estimates that they've gathered everything in the room.

"Keys!" Hastings shouts, halfway to the back door.

"Got 'em, and I'm right behind you!" Jen calls out.

They reach the back alley, finding their car as they left it. Blue tarp over the top, held down with stray bricks and cinder blocks. Jen rips off the tarp, then pops the trunk. Hard-cases are shoved in the back without regard for the paint job. Longer rifle cases are tucked across the rear footwells.

"Gonna be tight," Jen says, climbing into the driver seat. She cranks the Camry's engine and looks in the rearview. There's a thump as Animal tries to shut the trunk. It bounces back up. Round two. This time it sticks, but with a huge bulge creasing the trunk. The other team members pile in, with Animal in the front passenger seat.

She peels out of her parking spot, then speeds down the alley. They reach an intersection that connects with the neighborhood's main artery. Jen slows to make a left toward Mexico City's downtown high-rises. What she sees causes her to rethink the turn.

Cartel members are massing down the street. A roadblock is forming. Gunmen are gathering on the sidewalks. She rams the car in reverse, speeding back down the alley. The old car doesn't handle the speed well. She swerves, taking out trash cans, and sideswipes another parked car. Only a little traded paint, nothing to slow them down.

"I think they heard the crash!" Animal shouts, looking through the windshield. Two cartel members enter the alley. They point at her car.

"Couldn't have been that," Jen says. "They were gonna surround us anyway!"

"Keep telling yourself that, Richard Petty," Hastings jokes as he checks the chamber of his 416.

"Y'all better hang on!" Jen calls out, seeing the end of the alley in the rearview mirror.

Gray makes the sign of the cross over his kit. "Please, God, protect me from this female driver."

Jen jerks the wheel hard. Tires skid and the car does a one-eighty, righting itself before stalling. Horns are blaring as incoming traffic screeches to a stop. A skidding car tears off Jen's rear bumper. She struggles to restart the stalled car as the other team members survey their surroundings.

"We got time!" Hastings yells. "But not much."

"Someone got a lucky rabbit's foot to rub on this thing?" Jen asks, working the ignition. The engine is sputtering, refusing to start.

"Come on!" Animal wails on the dashboard, cracking the plastic.

Jen keys the ignition again, and the engine turns. "Who needs luck when you can just use violence?" She mashes the gas pedal, trading more paint with stopped cars in the street. She wedges through the traffic jam, leaving her mirrors behind, along with a trail of smoke.

Hastings and Grey look at what's behind them. No chase cars. No muzzle flashes. Just a blocked street with seriously agitated motorists.

"Made it out in the nick of time," Hastings says.

Jen looks back at him in the rearview. "They're gonna wish they'd nabbed us before the day ends."

Forty-Nine

The walk Martinez has come to loathe. She nears the admiral's office in the command post. Emblems and badges from Mexico's finest units line the walls—all disgraced by the base's senior officer.

She opens the door to his office anteroom and finds the admiral's yeoman sitting behind a desk. The man's face is dour, likely having suffered a morning full of abuse. It always rolls downhill. She doesn't wait to be acknowledged before storming into the admiral's office. The first punch in a heavyweight bout.

"Ma'am, you can't go in—"

Martinez slams the door in his face. The admiral sits at his desk in full uniform. It's fresh. Heavily starched. Medals polished and proper. She recognizes that she's now standing across from El Matador—the political bullfighter trying to save his career—with her scalp.

Martinez sits in the chair across from his desk.

"I didn't invite you to take that seat. You'll stand until you're given permission to do otherwise," the admiral scolds.

She crosses her legs, leans back, and rests her hands on the arms. "Do I look like I'm gonna get up?"

"This is *my* facility. The only reason you're still allowed to walk around without chains on your wrists is because I've allowed it. You'll show respect."

"And to whom would I be showing respect? Alex Varga? Isn't that who you work for?" Martinez demands.

"How dare you make an insinuation like that."

Martinez's eyes walk his desk. "Where's your BlackBerry, Admiral? I'd think Varga would want to hear this conversation."

The admiral slams both of his fists onto his desk. Challenge coins, unit trophies, lamps, and books move with the force. "Let me make myself clear: You and your forces will extricate yourselves from this installation within eight hours. Until that time, you will not be permitted to leave this base. You will not have contact with any personnel under my command. Am I understood?"

Martinez scoffs. "We've tried this, Admiral. You don't have permission to detain me."

"Your people are responsible for bombings that occurred on Mexico City's streets. Civilians died."

"My people didn't detonate bombs in Mexico City. Varga did."

"Maybe I'd be able to prove that if you'd stayed within the rescue mission's parameters. But there's just no way to know, is there, Ms. Martinez?"

"Those hostages are still out there, Admiral," Martinez replies. "Alive. You can't change that fact."

The admiral waves his oversize finger in the air before reaching for a file. He tosses it across the desk at her. "You're incorrect, Ms. Martinez. Law enforcement recently recovered three bodies. Autopsy reports are already coming in; they were your missing hostages." The admiral flashes his most vicious smile. "I don't need to tell you what that means. Surely, you're not that stupid."

Martinez grabs the file only out of curiosity. Crime scene photographs reveal three men lying decapitated along the side of an interstate highway. Just a long strip of black asphalt, miles of desert stretching out at its flanks. Like the rest of Varga's parlor tricks, it's chilling the first time around.

But Mexico will use the bodies as leverage. Claim they're real. It'll hold up, at least until American forensic experts examine the remains. She tears the file in half, allows the shreds to fall at her feet.

"You're right, Admiral. I am stupid—stupid enough to leave this base and find my missing people," Martinez replies. "There will be collateral damage. Careers will implode—probably just yours, but that's fine. And when I'm finished, I'm gonna return to the United States with my *honor* intact."

The admiral stands, leans across the desk, and flattens his palms against the blotter for support. "You will stay on this base."

Martinez rises slowly. Her palms land across from the admiral's, and she doesn't stop leaning forward until they're nose to nose. "I'm leaving. Any effort you make to the contrary will have severe consequences."

"You don't—"

Martinez cuts off his outburst. "Lower your fucking voice. I have every phone call you've ever made to Varga. Every text and meeting location. If you fuck with me, I promise, the world will learn of your duplicity. Then we'll be sharing a cell together. Pelican Bay. Leavenworth. Sing Sing. Take your pick."

The admiral stumbles back into his chair, a bead of sweat dripping down his cheek. He speaks softly, still collecting himself. "In Mexico, we have two offerings: forgiveness and prayers. Prayers are for the living. Forgiveness is for the dead. Consider yourself forgiven."

Martinez grins one last time. "Prayer suits you, given how much time you spend on bended knees." She wheels around and exits the office. She passes the frightened yeoman—who will no doubt suffer for the beating she gave the admiral—and steps into the hallway.

She isn't shaken by Perez's threats, but he's clearly maneuvering. She decides on leaving the base within the hour. Before the admiral can collect his wits and plan his next move. She grabs her cell, texting Sloane and Major Bingham. She'll need their help for what comes next.

Fifty

Martinez slows her Suburban to look inside the open hangar to her left. The Delta operators are demobilizing inside, preparing for their return stateside. A lot of long faces just beyond that door. Two of theirs will not be making the return trip home. Bobby and Cam's gear have yet to be packed, and won't be until the final moment before departure. It's a silent prayer that they will get back in time to get their shit together and catch the flight home.

Two Little Birds have their wings folded up, their skids planted on rolling pads. Close to a dozen pallets full of hard Pelican cases are waiting in the hangar, ready to be fork-lifted onto cargo planes. The troop has its own logistics officer, who feverishly notates the movement's progress on a clipboard.

"JSOC didn't waste any time pulling the plug," Sloane remarks, who sits in the passenger seat.

"After yesterday, I can't blame them." She spots Major Bingham approaching the SUV through the chaos. She's certain part of the anger on his face is directed at her. Hastings and his element are still in the wind. But she needs their help for what comes next. "Wait here."

"Ma'am."

Martinez steps out and intercepts Bingham. "My bags are packed too. But I'm going in a different direction."

Major Bingham sighs. He's gotten some very angry calls from a multitude of superiors. The demobilization order didn't come from Martinez; they've been packing gear for hours. "Not what I expected to hear, ma'am."

"Not what I expected to say. Had to pull some serious strings. It's gonna be my last show."

The news rattles Bingham. Another hard loss in a string of defeats. He runs a hand across his chin, lets it grate against the scruff. The tarmac underfoot suddenly becomes the subject of intense focus. "Can't begin to tell you how disappointed I am to hear that."

"The world will keep turning," Martinez says, refusing to show remorse, fully accepting the weight of her choice.

Bingham glances back to his troop working away in the hangar. Martinez's intentions have become clearer, but it doesn't change his position. "I need Hastings and his crew back, ma'am."

"Well . . ."

"Gabby—"

"This fight isn't over. We've got a score to settle, remember?"

"This isn't something I'll ever forget. But I'm sorry, I can't put more careers on the line."

"You're not risking their careers, Trey. I've made it clear that I'm wearing the bruises on this. And . . . I've got some runway—not much, but some."

Bingham doesn't need a lie detector for this conversation. She's telling the truth—the woman doesn't operate any other way. But are the bureaucrats in Washington? Those winds shift. Easy, like a spring day. "What are you thinking?"

"We'll pick up another trail. One that'll lead us to our people. But we're playing by Mexico's rules now."

"Those rules are bloody."

"Then that's just the way it'll have to be."

"Give me your word that my people won't suffer when they get stateside."

"I swear it."

Bingham hangs his hands on his duty belt, finalizing his decision. "I won't tell you to bring my people back safe. That's not what they signed up for. But it's not for nothing, understand?"

Martinez squares up, looks him dead in the eye. "We'll make it count."

"Good." Bingham looks back at the hangar. "What do you need?"

"Keep Hastings in place, along with his full element. That includes Coco."

"Okay, anything else? Guns? Ammo?" Bingham asks.

"Plenty of that where I'm going."

"Don't doubt it." He shakes her hand. Firm. Matches the level of respect he has for her. "I'll see you stateside."

"I owe you."

Martinez watches Bingham slip into the hangar while throwing out a flurry of hand gestures. Coco rushes to gather his gear. He files out of the hangar in under five minutes, bags and Pelican cases in tow. But there's a hitch: Bingham is by his side. They're both wearing low-vis chest rigs and MP7s.

Bingham raises a hand as he passes Martinez and throws his gear in the Suburban. "Not a word. I'll be getting my head checked when we get stateside."

"My lips are sealed," Martinez replies solemnly. Bingham's reasons are the same as hers; they ordered their subordinates into danger, and returning home without them is worse than any punishment a superior officer could inflict.

She shakes Coco's hand and gives him a tight smile. "Thanks for tagging along. Wanna drive?"

"Only if I don't have to buy the gas," Coco replies, keeping his reply matter-of-fact. Sure, there's danger ahead. Couldn't care less. Making a big deal about his job would just feel awkward. He throws his gear in behind the major's and closes the hatch.

"Never fear. I've got an AmEx card with *U.S. Government* written on the front."

"Count me in," Coco says before hopping into the driver's seat.

Martinez climbs in and sits beside Major Bingham, who is cradling his MP7 while staring out the window. An evil smirk reflects against the glass. The other reason he decided to come along? He'll have the honor of doling out vengeance. "We'll pick Mr. Xiao up from the embassy first. Then we're on to a fresh safe house."

"Cool. I know how to get to the first place," Coco says.

"That reminds me . . ." Martinez adds, extracting her phone and texting Jen the new safe house's address. It goes through, but she doesn't get a response. Makes her jealous. Jen is loose in Mexico City, no doubt returning favors. Three heavily armed operators are lending a hand. Varga may already be dead; she just hasn't heard the news.

The SUV arrives at the base gate within minutes. Coco glides into an exit lane, which is empty. Military policemen step into the lane, flagging them. They clearly have no intention of letting them pass through the security barriers.

"They're throwing us a going-away party," Coco says.

"I always wanted to be the guest of honor," Sloane adds. "Do you think they got us *mariachis*?"

"We should start putting this armor to use early," Coco jokes.

"And ruin a good paint job?" Martinez asks. She neglects to tell them about the bare-knuckle brawl she just had with the admiral. She wonders if he's going to call her on her promise. Unexpected, but there's no telling what his master, Alex Varga, forced him to do. "My window, Sergeant."

"Gotcha, ma'am," Coco replies, easing the truck a little farther forward so Martinez can speak with the MP.

Martinez lowers her window, eyeing the military policeman. Master-at-arms. Second-class petty officer. Squared away. Boots spit-shined. A good sailor. No nonsense. "Something wrong, Petty Officer?"

He stops by her window, cradling his M4 in a two-point sling over his armor. A balaclava covers most of his face. Stops cartel buzzards from identifying members of the military on the base's exterior. "I've been instructed to prevent you from leaving the base, ma'am."

Martinez is polite but stern. Men like him know the rules. He just needs a reminder. "I'm a member of the United States government on a diplomatic mission. Detaining me is against the law, Petty Officer."

"Orders are orders, ma'am. I don't like them, but I've gotta obey."

Martinez looks to her right. More military policemen are

surrounding the vehicle. "I'd suggest you call the admiral and double-check. Wouldn't want to make a mistake on this."

Diplomatic. An easy out, in case there is a mistake. The opportunity is worth taking. He nods. "Just one moment, ma'am."

Martinez nods politely. "Take all the time you need, Petty Officer." She watches him disappear into his guard shack. *What are you going to do, Admiral?* The petty officer soon hangs up a phone and returns to the Suburban.

He sighs. Takes a long minute before speaking. "I-uh . . . I owe you an apology, ma'am. There was never an order to stop you."

Martinez takes pity on him. There most certainly was, not that she can say it. "Nothing wrong here, Petty Officer. We just needed some time to let our engine warm up." She catches him smiling under his balaclava. "Mind raising that gate for us?"

"Won't be but another minute, ma'am." He places a hand on her windowsill, taps. "Be safe out there."

"You do the same."

The SUV pulls off the base and into Mexico City. Hostile land. Indian territory, and like any frontier, full of wonder and possibility for those who dare attain it. Martinez and her pilgrims are full of the explorer spirit, aching to claim a few scalps before reaping the frontier's bounty.

Fifty-One

A pile of cotton fibers is growing between Terrance's legs. The knife he stole from the guard has come in handy. He's been cutting apart his bedding—at least the bottom layers—so that it can be hidden with overlapping blankets. A square of cotton sheeting is slowly being disassembled, then frayed. Kindling to start a fire whenever he deems it necessary.

Breakfast has been served, and a mostly eaten tray of food is sitting in the room's far corner. Breakfast always looks different from lunch, which looks different from dinner. It gives him the certainty that his work will go uninterrupted for a solid four hours. That, and he's working with his back to the metal door. *Fifty-eight seconds.*

The pile of cotton threading has grown substantially, a fist's worth, and it's enough for what Terrance needs.

Next task. He strips the remaining sheeting from the mattress, happy with what he finds. The mattress's foam is covered with fake leather. He squeezes it, balling it up at the edge. Thick enough to withstand barbed wire. Terrance hasn't seen the outside of his prison, but he's counting on plenty of jagged objects to delay or prevent his escape. Getting over those obstacles will be key to his success.

He studies the upcoming cut, knowing he'll only get one shot at skewering the mattress. Wanting to maximize material, he begins cutting from the top all the way to the bottom, then flips the mattress and cuts back to the starting end. It leaves him with a strand of leather around twelve feet long and three feet wide. He folds it into thirds, then stabs tiny holes into the two unjoined edges. Using a few strands of scrap leather, he weaves his blanket into one thick pad. He examines his handiwork, pleased with the outcome. Razor wire won't stop him.

The remaining runs of leather are cut into strips around two feet in length. They'll be used as restraints, or not, depending on how the guard decides to respond to his upcoming escape effort.

Terrance takes his new escape supplies, lays them all flat on his mattress, then covers them with his remaining sheeting. The mattress's foam corners have lost their shape, and he makes sure to wrap the sheets as tightly around them as possible.

Unused bits of leather are balled up and stuffed into the bedframe's piping. He uses the knife to cram them deeper inside, then stores the knife. It's still the most useful tool that he's got. Nearing completion, he surveys his cell one last time.

Tiny strands of fabric and thread speckle the floor. He drops to his hands and knees, sweeping them up with his hands. Little mounds form, and he promptly places them in the toilet, flushing away the remnants of his budding escape plan.

Fifty-Two

A bolt slams home, forcing a 5.56 caliber cartridge into the chamber of an H&K 416. Hastings is lying prone in an open patch of dirt, surrounded by shrubs. He surveys the base station through the weapon's EOTech, the three-times magnifier flipped into place. Despite the ten-and-a-half-inch barrel, it's easy shooting from one-hundred-fifty yards out. The weapon's handguard is resting on his backpack—a makeshift bipod. His targets are working in the distance. Cartel members. In the open, unaware.

A call comes in through Hastings's radio. It's Jen. "Remember, we need our man *alive*."

"All but the one," Hastings replies, marking the high-value individual's location through his scope.

"Keep 'em in the ten."

"Always do," Hastings says confidently.

Jen, Gray, and Animal are advancing off an adjacent hilltop, winding their way through dense brush to the cell tower in the distance. He is planted at the tower's right-hand flank, which is its most exposed. He conducts one last survey of his field of fire. Six targets, each armed with AK-47 or M4 variant rifles with one designated survivor. Seven total.

Satisfied, he flicks off his weapon's safety and rests his reticle on his first victim.

The corrupted base station controller has already been removed and loaded into a box truck parked just outside the tower's utilities shed.

Julio "Jules" Alfaro is supervising the effort. He's a senior lieutenant in Alex Varga's cartel, having risen into the position over a ten-year span. During that time, he's witnessed every type of carnage imaginable, and he's got the gray hair to prove it. Traditional Aztec ink, piercings, and burns accent his body—a tool he's failed to care for into his mid-forties. Sweat glistens over stretched out tattoos, and on any day but this one, he'd rather puff cigars while his subordinates work.

Jules is hustling alongside them, his eyes as diligent as their hands. These pieces of equipment are considered Varga's most valuable. To make a mistake would be life threatening, even for him.

The replacement base station controller is being gingerly lowered down on the truck's lift gate. Jules's crew has it completely surrounded, cradling it as if it were a newborn child.

"Easy, easy," Jules reminds his crew.

"One foot," says another crew member, watching the lift gate make its final descent. "Keep coming. Keep coming. Stop!" The lift gate flattens against the gravel.

"Pushing out," the man controlling the dolly says.

The men hover around the base station controller, making sure the piece of equipment doesn't kick out or shift its weight. Satisfied, they begin easing it into the utilities shed. Jules heads toward the door, telling two of his men, "Get the truck ready to go."

The two men raise the lift gate and secure the corrupted base station controller. Jules steps into the utilities shed, shutting the door behind him. The wind is whipping, raising up miniature dust tornados. Dirt on the new equipment is a no-no. His men begin removing the new base station controller's protective layer of plastic wrapping, prepping for the final install. They'll have it in place within twenty minutes.

"Y'all mind if I borrow that?"

Jen is standing at the back of the box truck, B&T aimed at the two men. They're ratcheting the corrupted controller's shipping straps tighter and pause to look over at her, startled—their work and the rustling wind concealed her footsteps. Fear spikes as they peer down the barrel of her rifle. Both of theirs are propped against the truck's aluminum wall. Those rifles should be fastened to their backs, but they're a pain to work with.

"What'll it be?" Jen asks, letting her trigger finger drop from the receiver onto the trigger.

Both men know it's suicide, but they jump for their rifles anyway. Two whisper-quiet .300 Blackout rounds find their marks. She jumps onto the truck's bumper, grabbing the door strap. The door's weight eases her back to the ground, and it slams shut. A waiting padlock entombs the bodies.

"I'm moving to my second position," Jen whispers into her radio as she disappears once again.

Jules heard the truck door slam shut, and it annoys him. The two idiots forgot to load the dolly onto the truck. His frustration is amplified by the stench inside the utilities shed. Unbearable, despite the bandana over his face. Flies buzz in, latch onto his sweaty flesh before he flicks them away. Thankfully, the work here is almost done. The base station controller has been unwrapped and eased into its predecessor's position.

"Anything else, boss?"

Jules examines the work. The base station controller is perfect. Excess packing materials have been collected. No straggling tools are laying around. "We're good. Someone else is supposed to come and do the technical work."

Officially off the hook, the men begin to exit the utilities shed. Their chests heave, sucking in the fresh air. Jules follows them and finds the box truck locked, as he expected. He looks around for the two men who were supposed to be working. They've disappeared, leaving dust to twist into cyclones on the lonely hilltop.

Jules's instincts are revving. While his men sought to clear the stench from their nostrils, they missed the danger they were in. His head whirls around, surveying the landscape. Two brass shell casings lie in the gravel, glinting like omens from the gods. He throws his hand up, signaling his shooters. Safeties drop. Charging handles are torn backward, released. A fight is looming, and the opponent has the upper hand —the element of surprise.

"Fan out," Jules hisses. "And be careful."

Hastings studies the action through his rifle scope. Two gunmen have wandered directly into his field of fire. He reduces the magnification on his optic, preparing a rapid engagement. The EOTech's bright red reticle—the doughnut of death—settles onto the first target. Center mass, six inches south of the trachea. Spinal column, airway, and maybe some bullet fragments to the heart. *Crack!*

Hastings doesn't bother watching the man fall. He angles the rifle immediately toward the second man, breaking another shot. The armor-piercing 5.56 round snaps through his sternum and severs his spine. Bone isn't enough to slow the bullet's tungsten core. It exits the body and slaps against the brick utilities shed. The echo traces the hillside before settling against the wind. Heat waves refract on his suppressor, and he grins. *That's for the boys.*

The three remaining men scramble into cover. They've detected his position. Hastings activates his radio. "Two down, three remaining. No targets available. On you, Animal."

Gravel is crunching. Closer. Closer.

Animal listens with his back pinned to the utilities shed's far wall. He grips a hook-bladed knife called a karambit in his right hand. It's hovering over his chest, ready. The movement stops and gives way to panicked breathing. Close enough to smell the target's morning hangover. Too much *cerveza*.

The target peeks the corner. Animal lashes out, burying the hook blade into the underside of the gunman's jaw, and reels him in. Animal smashes his head into the wall. Bone on brick. Tremors rattle the entire cell site. Stars glimmer in the target's eyes. Just enough consciousness left to feel the hook blade strafe his neck.

Animal tosses the severely wounded man back around the corner. He flops around on the dirt, clutching his neck. Drowning on dry land. Great show for his shocked comrades only feet away.

He doesn't bother raising his Mk-46 as he steps around the corner. He menaces two stunned cartel members ducking behind the box truck's engine block. They're staring at the dying man, and their jaws drop a little farther when they see him.

Jules just watched a final spurt of blood eject from the neck of his dead comrade. The calculus here is simple, and if he wants to survive, he's got to be smart. A sniper is hidden nearby, and an exceptionally large American is staring into his eyes. There will be more.

Jules slaps his only remaining soldier on the shoulder and screams, "Shoot!"

The gunman angles his AK-47 toward the American and releases a burst of fire. But the move was telegraphed, and the American has enough time to slip back into cover as bullets zing past.

The opening Jules wanted. He leaps out of cover, beginning the sprint to safety, leaving his comrade behind. His vehicle is parked outside the gate only fifty feet away. A black Range Rover. Powerful V8 engine built for escaping situations like these.

Jules reaches the Range Rover and climbs into the passenger seat. It was the safest side, blocked off from the sniper. He slams the door shut behind him and catches sight of his last soldier. He's running for the driver's side, just seconds behind. Suddenly, he falls from view as if the earth opened up and swallowed him whole.

A blood-curdling scream follows. One that Jules has heard many times before—the last a man gives before his life is taken. The Americans are closer than he realized. His hand juts for the door, pressing the lock button.

Keys next. They're in the cupholder. He reaches, but they're gone. He swore he left them there. He lunges over, pressing the ignition button. *Keys must be in the Range Rover to start the engine* flashes on the instrument cluster. Any other time, helpful advice.

A large man rises where his fallen comrade once stood. American. Dirty, dusty. He'd been hiding under the Range Rover. The American taps on the driver's side window.

Jules gets desperate, scrounging in his pockets for the keys.

Tap. Tap. Tap.

Those were on the passenger side—inches from where he's sitting. Jules turns, finds the giant that just knifed one of his own. Out of options, Jules reaches for his pistol. He stops as something cool and hard touches the back of his head.

"Bad move."

Jules twists his head slightly, his spine tingling. Out of the corner of his eye, he spots a blonde-haired woman. The same one he'd seen in a photograph days before. *The* American. Number one on Varga's list.

Jen Yates asks, "Headed my way?"

Fifty-Three

The Range Rover's engine is purring. One end of a rope has been fastened to its trailer hitch; the other end is tied to Jules's wrists. He's lying on his back, looking up at the behemoth that's threatening to take him on the ride of his life. Down a long, lonely stretch of road too far east of Mexico City for anyone to notice what's about to happen.

"Sounds fast, don't it?" Jen asks, admiring the purring V8.

Hastings is standing at her side and smiles warmly. "Wonder what type of zero to sixty this thing's sporting."

"Fast. So fast that if you blink, you'd miss it."

Animal is behind the wheel, listening through an open window. He revs the engine, perfectly on cue. Exhaust spits into Jules's face.

"You speak English?" Jen asks Jules.

Jules coughs, tries to hide his face from the fumes. These are Americans—not a rival cartel. Torture is out of their purview. They have rules. Strict ones, and stricter punishments for those who break them. He's going to be a stone wall. Impenetrable.

"I think he understands us," Jen says, throwing out her arms in mock frustration.

Hastings nods. "Me too."

"You know the bad thing about this?"

Hastings scratches the side of his head, then slicks back the disturbed red strands. "Sure don't."

"This damn thing is so fast that once it starts, we won't be able to keep up."

Hastings lights up. "Oh! So he'd have to wait until it's over for us to ask our questions."

"Could be a long ride."

"Would probably feel endless."

"Oh well." Jen raps on the side of the Range Rover. Animal flips the truck into drive and the tires begin rolling. Slow. Barely crawling along.

Pressure mounts on Jules's wrists, elbows, and shoulders. Asphalt generates just enough friction to make it feel like his joints could snap. He looks up at them, questioning his logic. This feels serious.

"Stop!" Hastings shouts.

Jules smirks. They're bluffing.

"Forgot something." Hastings leans over, flips Jules onto his belly. The angle of the rope lifts him so that his crotch is the first contact point with the asphalt. The blue jeans protecting his most sensitive anatomical features won't last long.

"Well played," Jen adds, mock bowing. "Start her up!"

The Range Rover starts creeping along. No more than five miles an hour, with Jen and Hastings jogging alongside. Jules is becoming acquainted with a new threat. Before the vehicle started moving, he'd been worried about a thrashing. Broken bones. Things torn away by sheer speed and force. Now he's feeling heat—the type generated by friction. He begins to scream. "Stop! Stop the fucking truck! I'm on fire!"

"Oh! Look who speaks *Ingles*," Jen says, smiling while struggling to keep up with the vehicle.

Hastings looks toward Jules's crotch. Smoke is coiling up from between his legs. Tiny flecks of denim flutter in the Range Rover's exhaust. "I don't think you're on fire! It's just your pants! Speed it up!"

"No!"

The Range Rover's engine spools up and the vehicle lifts off. Five miles per hour turns to ten. Then fifteen. Twenty. Jen and Hastings are left behind, but they're uninterested in keeping pace. They're slow walking the strip of asphalt as the Range Rover stops a hundred yards ahead of them.

There's smoke. Screams. A pair of cowboy books kicking frantically just outside a small cloud of smoke.

"Might not be much left by the time we get there," Hastings remarks. "You think we should hurry?"

"Hold on a minute," Jen says. She stops on the road's yellow line and kneels down. "Need to make sure my shoes are tied."

"Safety first."

"Please! Please help!"

"He sounds . . . distressed," Jen jokes as she double-knots her boots.

"He's ready," Hastings says, jogging toward the Range Rover.

When Jen and Hastings arrive, smoke is pouring off Jules's crotch. Animal has the Range Rover in park, but mashes the gas pedal relentlessly. The V8 tugs against its mount, rocks the suspension. Hastings uses his boot to flip Jules over, revealing tiny orange flames inching their way along loose strands of denim.

Jen removes a bottle of water from her blue jeans, twists off the lid. She takes a big swig. "Now, how about those questions?"

Hastings reassures him. "We've only got a few."

Jules is beginning to fear permanent damage. The cloud of smoke is growing larger; the fire has found more oxygen. "Put me out!"

Jen takes another sip of her water. "We haven't made our agreement yet."

Jules watches her chug more of the water down. She's already halfway finished with the bottle—a precious resource going to waste. "Fine! Fine! I'll tell you what you want to know!"

Jen dumps the remaining water on his crotch. She does it slowly, prolonging the pain. Finally, the flames die out, leaving a charred mess behind. She kneels next to Jules. "I'm looking to pay somebody a visit. It's just . . . I'm not too sure the front door's gonna work all that well."

"What do you wanna do with him, Jen?"

Jen is standing across from Animal, Gray, and Hastings on the strip of asphalt. Jules turned out to be a willing participant, more so than expected. It's time to decide how to handle the loose end. They're fifty feet away, too far for him to hear what they're saying.

Animal replies before Jen can. "I think we ought to leave this little problem here. We can't have him repeating what he just told us. Besides, it's one less asshole terrorizing people in Mexico."

"Plenty of room in the desert. Nobody'll find his body," Hastings adds, eyes full of imagination.

Jen has heard all she needs to. "Let's go."

The team returns to the Range Rover. Animal and Hastings draw their karambits. Terror flashes in Jules's eyes.

"Cut his clothes off," Jen says.

Animal and Hastings look at her, confused. Jen nods them on, and they comply.

"Cut his rope."

Jules gets to his feet, rubs the soreness out of his wrists before using his hands to cover himself. "What are you going to do?" he asks, beginning to tremble. He's seen this play out so many times. The only difference is that he's on the receiving end.

Jen points. "Mexico City is that way. Tlaxcala is the opposite way. Make up your own damned mind." She kneels down, picks up his clothes, and signals for her subordinates to follow. She climbs into the front passenger seat of the Range Rover.

Hastings gets in and tries to stifle his anger as he turns on the truck. "What the hell?"

"The first thing that asshole's gonna do is compromise us," Animal adds.

Gray looks through the Range Rover's rear window. "He hasn't started running. Maybe we should rethink this."

Jen just laughs. "Y'all really think he's gonna run back to Varga? Tell him that he snitched?"

The men remain silent.

Jen knows they're hurting. Varga's done nothing but play dirty, and they're looking to even the score. A top lieutenant would go a long way. She feels the same, but she won't cross certain boundaries. It's tough, but they'll thank her for it later. "Let's go grab our box truck. Martinez is probably waiting for us at the new safe house."

Hastings swings a U-turn and hits the accelerator. As they start back to Mexico City, Jen turns to look at Jules. He's running to Tlaxcala, his only real chance at survival. Varga will do worse to him than her team ever could.

Fifty-Four

The Range Rover stops short of a wrought-iron gate. It's twenty feet wide, connected to an imposing stucco wall. Ivy crawls down, splashing green against the tan stucco. An ornate bronze plaque bears the mansion's address. Cameras stand guard by a call box. The security shack beyond the gate appears to be unmanned.

Jen leans forward for a better view of the home, but she can't see beyond the long, winding driveway. The new safe house is a showstopper. Langley keeps houses like this in case of emergency. It's extremely private and capable of sustaining a large team. "You're kidding me."

Animal is in the driver's seat. He looks over to Jen, raises an eyebrow. "Wonder if there's a wine cellar."

Jen stares back, incredulous. "You a connoisseur or something?"

"I appreciate the finer things," Animal jokes, then lowers the window and presses the pound key on the call box.

The box buzzes, and the gate slides open. Animal eases the Range Rover onto the property. The box truck follows them. Hastings and Grey have taken charge of the stolen base station controllers. Jen's Camry was left behind after it was identified during their escape.

The driveway leads to a Spanish villa. More green vines laid over stucco. Arching doorways. Tile roofing. Fountains and lush gardens surround the home. The Range Rover stops under a carriage porch, an imposing black chandelier dangling overhead.

Martinez steps out of the mansion, the other Group members on her heels. She shakes her head, blown away by Jen's arrival. "Caravan of gypsies. Show me what your greedy fingers have stolen."

"Nothing but the finest housewarming gifts," Jen remarks, jumping out of the Range Rover. She motions for them to follow her to the box truck.

"I'll take them, so long as you don't brand me a homemaker," Martinez replies.

"Impressive work in the city, Ms. Yates," Major Bingham says. He shakes her hand while keeping pace. "Call me Trey."

Jen is reminded of one of the Unit's most legendary members. Thick glasses, perfectly parted hair, and an almost nerdy disposition. Man looks like a Harvard grad. But it would be foolish to judge him by his exterior. Bingham's body count could probably rival Lucifer's. "Can say the same for your guys."

Bingham gives her a humble smile. "We're just getting our job done."

"Ignore the bloodstains," Jen says as she throws the latch and pushes open the door. Two base station controllers are strapped to the walls. The newest one is in perfect condition, save a little dust from the whirlwinds kicking up at the tower. The older unit will likely be burned once the Group dissects it; it's crawling with insects.

Coco shakes his head as he sizes up what remains of the gunfight that took place in the box truck. Bloodstains. Bullet holes in the aluminum walls. Loose cartel weapons. "I drew the short straw."

Animal gives him an elbow. "At least you finally made it, lazy bastard."

Coco rubs his shoulder. "Stop! I'm already wounded enough."

Jen climbs onto the box truck's bed and throws off the straps. Andrew and Sloane join her. Despite the grisly sight, it's like Christmas for the Technical Access Group. The technology is like a riddle waiting to be solved. Only there's no telling where the solution will lead. With hope, it'll point them toward whoever is backing Varga, and from there, to the missing hostages.

"Which one is infected?" Andrew asks, needing to know which one the Group has malware installed on.

"Right wall," Jen replies. She watches their faces as they get familiar with the base station controllers. Their features appear lighter—distractions are good when things are at their worst. "But you'll probably need a damn gas mask to work on it."

"It'll be the one we cut into first," Andrew remarks as he moves to the infected piece of tech. Once he's close enough, he recoils, waves a hand in front of his face. "*Wo de tian a*," he says, shocked back into his native Mandarin.

"Doesn't smell any worse than you after forty-eight hours behind a desk," Sloane says, driving an elbow into Andrew's ribs. She doesn't flinch while she rolls up her sleeves and begins opening the cabinets that protect the controller's sensitive equipment. Proper Southern girls are always willing to dirty their hands.

"I'll leave it up to you two." Jen hops off the bed of the truck, leaving the Group members to offload the stolen technology. She's eager to speak with Martinez, find out where the Group stands after the disastrous rescue attempt. "Gonna give me the grand tour or what?"

Martinez leads Jen inside. Two staircases encircle a marble foyer before arcing up to the second story. White walls hiding behind fine art. Expensive furniture. The Agency pulled all the stops to make this place a passable residence.

"We have servers and a tactical operations center setup in the basement. Andrew already has Anne humming away, and she's pulling security. Your room is upstairs," Martinez says as they climb the stairs and enter one of the first bedrooms.

Jen drops her things by the door. Her rifle and gun belt are laid neatly over an ornate dresser, matching the rest of the room. White, scalloped ceilings. Wallpaper with a subtle pinstripe. A king-size bed with stacks of pillows and a fluffy down comforter. "Sorry to say, but you've set a new standard."

Martinez disregards the small talk and gives Jen "the look."

"That bad?"

"I've gotta sit," Martinez replies, her head swimming. She thumps into a chair at the foot of Jen's bed. She briefs Jen on everything that's happened in the past twenty-four hours, leaving out a single important detail: Langley's OIG investigation. "Our people are still the sole focus. Frankly, though, I want to move on Varga.

"It's our only remaining play," Martinez continues. "He's the one person in the organization that I can guarantee knows what happened to our people."

"I think it's our only option too," Jen replies, sitting across from Martinez in one of the room's ultra-luxe chairs. "But we'd need to get hands on him."

"If you've got a way to do that, lay it on me," Martinez says.

Jen smirks at fresh memories of Jules. "Ran into a guy today. After some gentle persuasion, he was very helpful."

"Define gentle."

"Left my dictionary back at the safe house," Jen replies. "But after what he told us, I'm considering the base station controllers a bonus. We've got a back door into Varga's estate."

Martinez inches to the edge of her seat and leans toward Jen. Feels like stars are aligning into another once in a lifetime shot. "You're confident in what he told you?"

"We can get to Varga. I'm sure of it."

Fifty-Five

After Martinez left Jen's room, she tried to get several hours of sleep but found it futile. Anxiety about her missing comrades is overpowering. Her body is so mangled that it doesn't know whether to sleep or gobble down aspirin, which happens to be the only thing keeping her functional. Resigned to exhaustion, she decided on briefing the team.

Martinez mentioned that the TOC was in the basement, and she finds an open door between the spiral staircases. Another set of stairs leads downward.

Three high-security doors line the basement hallway. Two on the right-hand side—probably for an armory and server storage. She steps up to a biometric lock for the single door on the left, using her thumbprint to gain access.

The entire team is already assembled inside. Hastings and his crew are looking about as refreshed as she does. But they're pinching at fresh bandages and sipping Martinez's special nitro blend of coffee. The Technical Access Group members don't appear much better. The only thing fresh about them are their clothes, which are relaxed for a long night behind computer screens.

Work has started on a new target: Admiral Mateo Perez. The last thing Jen expected to see as she walked in, but it's a welcome surprise. Photographs are prominently displayed on the center screen. Perez and his trophy wife, Marisol. They're ripped off Marisol's social media pages and depict a life of luxury.

Jen wonders if the woman is capable of taking a bad photo. Those risks have been erased by eager plastic surgeons, who have pinched her nose and injected filler into her lips. An army of hair and fashion stylists are keeping her up to speed on New York's latest trends—a testament to Varga's generosity toward a man like Mateo Perez.

Perez's target package is already extremely detailed, and technical elements have already fallen into place. Multiple devices have been hacked and scraped, including Perez's laptop and government-issue cell phone. Texts between the couple are prominently displayed.

"Y'all should have gotten me up sooner," Jen says, regretful. She grabs a coffee mug on a table and pours a cup. Additives don't make it into the brew; this one is all about caffeine. The molten liquid burns on the way down, giving her some pep. "Doesn't look like Perez is going to survive the night."

"We're working him while a drone proceeds to Varga's estate," Martinez says, silently convinced that her threats to Perez had an effect. "He's preparing to flee the country. A rendezvous is set with the missus for later tonight."

A tight grin spreads across Major Bingham's face, and his eyes turn to slits. "We've got something special planned."

"When do we leave?" Jen asks.

"The major will be leaving in several hours," Martinez replies. "But we're going to need your help with some technical stuff."

Jen would argue, but she's too tired. Besides, she has no reason to doubt the major's abilities. "I'll take my seat on the bench, then."

Andrew cuts in with an update. "Our Reaper is on station over Varga's estate."

"Put it on the center screen, but let's not lose sight of Missus Perez," Martinez instructs.

"Guess it's my show now," Jen says, waiting while the center screen reorients. Marisol Perez's face and current GPS location shift to the side, while overhead footage of Varga's estate takes center stage. "Andrew, zoom in on Varga's church, or whatever the hell he calls that thing. We should be able to work outward from there."

Andrew begins manually altering the ISR feed from his computer station. It locks onto the temple behind Alex's home.

Jen walks to the front of the room and recounts what Jules revealed hours earlier. "Got a little story about this temple. Construction began around four years ago. All of the contractors were from areas outside Mexico City—people cut off from their families, wanderers, journeymen. Varga hired them and kept them isolated on the compound while construction was ongoing. Rumor has it that the temple's walls went up fast, but construction efforts lingered for months after. Oddly enough, excavation continued, despite the foundation being poured."

"Mr. Varga has an escape tunnel," Martinez says approvingly.

"That's the rumor, but no one's saying it. They're talking about something else," Jen replies. "Construction, or I should say excavation, continued beyond schedule, and contractors got restless. Varga stopped paying them, and to keep them working, he brought in their families. No one really knows if they were invited, or kidnapped and used as leverage. Once the families arrived, work continued six months past the temple's completion.

"After the work was finished, Varga decides he's gonna throw a party —a celebration for all the contractors' hard work. A banquet. Fireworks. Mariachis. The whole nine. The party goes down, but not the way people expected. After it was over, no one saw the construction crews again. Same goes for the guards Varga had kept on his property during construction. That's the real rumor: after construction ended, over one hundred people disappeared."

"More of the lore that surrounds this guy," Sloane says, unable to conceal her disgust for Varga. "How do we separate fact from fiction?"

"I'm willing to discredit the murders; it's just a tall tale to keep people quiet. But I am confident in the tunnel's existence." Jen walks over to the center screen. "I've got a few hunches on the tunnel's direction. Go ahead and zoom out a little, Andrew."

Andrew follows the order. The temple gets smaller, and the entire compound reappears.

"I'm doubtful that they dug under any major structures," Jen continues. "So we figure that the tunnel doesn't go back toward the home. That leaves us with a hundred-eighty-degree search radius, and we look for geographic anomalies from there."

Martinez stares up at the screen, thinking out loud. "That temple's twenty yards from the house, so it won't take him long to reach the tunnel if there's a problem. Makes me wonder if his escape would be a solo act."

"That's probably the real reason he's so secretive about it," Jen replies. "I'm thinking that if something touches off on the compound, he'll go by himself. Leave his people behind to soak up the bullets. He'll get out clean and leave attackers distracted."

"Zoom out a little more, Andrew. Let's call it . . . half a mile," Sloane says, transfixed on the center screen. "Stay with Jen's one-eighty assumption."

The drone feed pans out, revealing a moonscape around Alex's home. It's all arid desert, much like Southern California, interlaced with shrubs, rock formations, and undulating hills. Something unusual appears in the landscape. A rock face a quarter mile from the temple.

Sloane points at the rock formation. "Zoom in on that, would you?"

Andrew complies. The rock face is around thirty feet wide. At ground level, it would appear like any other natural formation. From ten thousand feet, the rocks look like they've been manually cut into a naturally rolling hill. Perfect geometry. No jagged edges along what looks like a horseshoe lain into the earth.

Punching several computer keys, Andrew uses the drone's onboard technology to run a search for signals originating in the formation's vicinity—security cameras powered by local internet; alarm systems or motion detectors; locks that communicate via radio signals. He smiles as the results come back in. "We've got tech hidden in those rocks."

"Well, you've had the game plan so far," Martinez says, impressed by what Jen has managed to turn up in Mexico City. "Tell me what's next."

"We go to Varga's compound and convince him to run," Jen replies. "When he does, I'll be waiting for him inside that tunnel, a list of questions in hand."

Martinez gives Jen a fist bump. "I think we could compel Mr. Varga to do that."

Hastings leans back in an office chair and rests his boots on the desk. He runs his hands through his hair, unable to hide his grin. “Hear that, boys? This’ll be the reason you joined Uncle Sam’s Army.”

Animal gives Coco a fist bump. “Maybe, just maybe, we’ll all get medals.”

Jen knows the assault will be high-risk, but she shares the team’s confidence. They have the skill to pull it off. “I don’t know about medals, but I’ll offer y’all a pat on the back once we got Varga cooling off in the mortuary.”

Fifty-Six

Familiar footsteps. A learned rhythm. A guard is coming to deliver Terrance his dinner. The last meal he'll eat here, if he has his way. Making use of the windowless door, he hides in the small cavity between the hinges and the wall. The knife is open, locked in his fist.

The key's familiar ratcheting sound. The swinging door. The German guard steps inside the cell, momentarily confused by the prisoner's absence. A lightning bolt crashes inside his head as he realizes the only place for him to hide. Too late.

The door slams shut behind him. Terrance places the knife against his throat. "I don't want to kill you."

"I don't want to die," the German says matter-of-factly.

"Lie down on the floor. Slowly." The German does as he's told, feeling the blade against his neck as he starts crouching. He sets down the tray, places his hands against the concrete, and pancakes himself. "Good. Now your hands."

The German complies again. Terrance places his knee on the German's left hand, pinning it against his back as he ties up the right with the premade straps. His feet are bound next.

"Thanks for not making me kill you."

"Kindness will get you far in life."

"It will." Terrance rifles through the guard's pockets, finding a cigarette lighter and keys. Then he relieves the guard of the AK-type rifle slung around his back. Holding the rifle, Terrance struggles through the controls. He doesn't know how to drop the magazine or how the safety works. Jen offered him several invitations to the range, but he declined. He's wishing he took her up on the shooting lessons.

"Don't take it if you don't know how to use it," the German says, looking toward Terrance with concern.

Terrance slings the rifle over his shoulder. "I can make it work if I have to."

He dips toward the tray, grabbing a handful of tortillas. He douses them in the beans, then shovels them all in his mouth. A large glass of fruit juice is guzzled down next. He's expecting to cover some distance, and the carbohydrates are essential.

Ripping the sheets off the bed, Terrance grabs his tool kit. The strands of cotton. The leather blanket to cross concertina wire. He's ready now.

Before he locks the guard in the cell, he asks, "Where are my friends?"

"They're heavily guarded," the German replies.

Terrance sighs at the news: half good, half bad. They're here and alive, but he won't be able to break them out. When he gets free, it'll be the first message he relays to Martinez. "Will you tell me which direction to go? Where the nearest town is?"

The German just smiles. "There's nowhere to go, Terrance. Reconsider taking the gun. It'll only get you hurt."

Terrance shrugs off the warning as he clangs the cell door shut. He twists the key, then moves down the hall. He starts listening for the familiar hum of servers.

He walks only a short distance to a door on his right. He turns the knob, finding it unlocked. A string of run-silent power generators are the only objects in the room.

They won't help him make contact with his Group. The disappointment is momentarily crushing, but he forces his way past it, seeing another opportunity. If this powers the building, the men who work here will want to protect it. They'll also be lost without it.

He walks over to the breaker panel and opens it. A flathead screwdriver is resting on a shelf next to the panel. Without turning off the power, he begins to remove the main cable feeding the building. As he twists, he tries to stay steady. When he's sure that the cable is loose enough, he rips it out. A bolt of electricity arcs after the wire seconds before the room goes black.

He turns, eases back to the door, guided by memory, and steps into the hall.

With a hand on the wall, he moves as fast as he can toward the stairs. He finds the railing and guides himself upward. He hears grumbling men, irritated that they have to diagnose a mechanical problem in the dark. A flashlight beam pierces an intersecting hallway thirty feet away.

He finds a large double door to the left with windows in each panel. A slight band of color in the horizon and starlight in the sky. The sun has almost fully set, just as Terrance had predicted; there's a chance to escape the compound unseen. He sprints, excitement and adrenaline carrying him forward.

He exits the building and finds a cluster of dark structures. Four. Maybe five. All of them tall but failing to rise above the surrounding tree line. None of the buildings are lit, like the one he just left, but he doesn't think he cut power to them all. *They black out at night for security.*

The humidity is already pungent, and he hasn't been outside for thirty seconds. It's accompanied by the sounds of the jungle. Rustling leaves. Insects. Different types of exotic birds chirping toward the darkening horizon.

He runs his hands along the side of the building. It's overtaken by vines, leaves. Same as the structure directly across from him. Whoever lives here doesn't bother to beat back the jungle.

"Hey, you!"

Terrance presses his body against the nearest wall, his head craning in the voice's direction. A flashlight beam crashes onto his position, and he doesn't think twice as he sprints in the opposite direction.

"Stop! Drop the weapon!"

Warning shots crack over his head as he runs down the dirt pathway. Screams erupt from every direction as the guards coordinate their response. Alarms sound, and spotlight beams begin roving the grounds.

A chain-link fence is up ahead. It's interwoven with vines and leaves, like the buildings. A spotlight beam rolls along the jagged concertina wire on top. In one powerful stride, he heaves the blanket over the concertina wire, then uses his momentum to follow it up the fence. As he scales the fence, snarling dogs close on his position. He yanks himself over the wire and drops into lush jungle foliage on the other side.

Dogs bark and maul the fence. Armed guards are still rushing toward him, their flashlights struggling to pierce the vines weaving between the chain links. Without any time to get his bearings, he sprints into the jungle, allowing it to swallow him whole. With any luck, he'll find a village or town and make contact with his Group.

Fifty-Seven

The sun has just disappeared behind the horizon. The last sunset Admiral Mateo Perez plans on witnessing from Mexico City. Lines have been crossed. He may not be a marked man by Varga's cartel, but he senses that his usefulness has run its course. It's also guaranteed that the Americans want his head. They're not as violent as Varga, but they won't stop until they put him behind bars in a stateside prison. Martinez made that painfully clear this afternoon.

After departing Campo Militar 1, he proceeded directly to Benito Juárez International Airport. Ditched his government-issue sedan—GPS tracking devices are planted on the vehicle for safety reasons in case an officer is taken by a cartel. In his case, that was never a concern. Mexico City is Varga's, and he was Varga's man. Same reason he declined a security detail in the city.

He tossed both of his cell phones into a gutter. Pulled the SIM cards beforehand, just to be safe. He sent one coded message to his wife before he severed the lines. They both planned for this: a breakneck sprint out of the city with authorities or cartel members at their back. Perez guilty for a hundred and one reasons. Marisol guilty because she shared his bed and the money.

He's currently aboard an airport shuttle, headed for hotels nearby.

Free ride. No credit card or traveler information required. Just another tourist, mixed with a dozen others, wearing street clothes and sitting beside a duffel bag.

As the airport shuttle glides into position at a hotel, he scans the parking lot for suspicious vehicles, but nothing raises a flag. Marisol's Mercedes G-Wagon is parked in a far corner. Engine purring. Suspension sagging from a layer of armor hidden behind the pearly white body panels. He spared no expense when it came to her safety.

The driver makes an announcement. Final destination, complete with the hotel's name. Perez scoffs, as if they couldn't see it through the window. He stands in the aisle, throws the duffel bag's strap over his shoulder. No one gives him a second glance as he steps off the bus and starts for the G-Wagon.

The vehicle stays motionless. She doesn't roll down a window or signal. Exhaust drips onto the pavement, the only sign of life. His adrenaline spikes. What if Varga got to her? She may not be the only one inside the truck.

Perez raps on the tinted glass. There's a scream, and he jumps. Locks disengage, and he rips open the passenger door to find his wife's face tear-streaked. An open bottle of tequila sitting in the cupholder. She's alone, but he wonders how much longer she would have waited if he didn't get off that shuttle. Paranoia already chewed through the better part of her nerve. *Not long.*

"Just take it easy," Perez says, tossing his bag in the back seat. He spots a second bag, full of cash. An H&K UMP .45 sub-machine gun lies next to it. Both were kept hidden in their home for this exact situation. Marisol did her job. "Let me drive."

She only manages a nod.

Perez walks around the back of the vehicle, and Marisol crosses from the front. She's avoiding physical contact, full of resentment. Her social clubs will miss her. Her luxury clothes and handbags are being left behind. He reminds himself that she knew who she married, and to have regrets now is childish. They played their game. Win or lose, it was going to end sometime. He climbs into the driver's seat and adjusts the controls.

"What happened, Mateo?" Marisol demands, slamming the G-Wagon's passenger door shut.

Perez looks over at his wife. She's found her courage. Going to be a tongue lashing all the way to Central America. He puts the G-Wagon in reverse and eases it out of the spot. "The Americans. They're going to arrest me."

"The *law*," Marisol says with a sneer. "That's not supposed to be a problem."

Perez stops the SUV, looks over at his wife wrapped in a several-thousand-dollar leather jacket. *Could she be more naive?* "The Americans are a problem wherever they go. Mexico is no exception."

Marisol crosses her arms over her chest and clucks at him. "Big man."

Before Perez puts the G-Wagon back in drive, he notices a glow from her breast pocket. He lunges for it and snatches the phone away. He examines the device in his hand, struggling through shock. "A phone!"

"Mateo!" Marisol screams, clawing for the device.

"You didn't follow my orders!"

"I'm not one of your stupid army men! You can't boss me around!"

Perez shields the phone as he powers it down and removes the SIM card. He cracks the door and tosses both items onto the asphalt. *Stupid child!* He raises his hand, finds pleasure as she cowers into the passenger door. Instead of striking her, he grabs the bottle of tequila and shoves it into her chest. "Drink. Relax. It's a long drive to Guatemala."

Fifty-Eight

Despite the darkness, humidity is trapped under the jungle's canopy. Feels like a midnight sauna, wrenching the water out of Terrance's body. It's not raining, but if Terrance stops and listens, he can hear droplets of water trickling down leaves. This isn't just the jungle; it's the rain forest.

He's been moving through the jungle for several hours, unsure where his journey will lead. Everything looks the same. Waxy elephant leaves glowing in the moonlight. Networks of vines and roots that act like the jungle's circuitry, transferring messages and nutrients between sedentary life forms. He'd previously imagined the jungle as a vibrant place. Colorful flowers and exotic birds. Well, the birds are in their roosts, and the jungle only seems to have a pallet of green and brown.

But the insects haven't bothered hiding. Far from it. They've taken an interest in the jungle's guest. The more he sweats, the easier they seem to find him. Or maybe it's his smell. Either way, he treads carefully, keeping his arms and legs covered, certain many are venomous.

He has no destination in mind, but he knows what he's running away from: a pack of dogs that have pursued him relentlessly. Their pace is zapping the life out of him. The humidity makes it worse. His breath feels choked, and he's reduced to a wheeze as he forges ahead. The shirt on his back is soaked through. The drenched clothing feels like it's weighing him down, along with the AK slung over his shoulder.

Exhausted, he decides to stop in a thicket of leaves. They will be his cover. It's also a tactical choice. Every ten minutes or so the dogs seem to change direction. First, their howls feel like they're in his left ear. Time passes, and they're in his right. He knows he's being routed, and he's trying to prevent it from happening.

A straight path is key, and if he finds a running river or body of water, all the better. That's where human beings have congregated for centuries, and it won't be any different now.

He steadies his breathing and listens. Right ear. That's where the howls and barks and snarls are coming from. He angles himself to the left, opposite their direction. He walks until the sound is balanced between his two ears. He adjusts the rifle sling, easing the tension from his shoulder, and begins hoofing it again.

A horn blares out. Frightened birds clap out of their nests and fly in the opposite direction. It's distant, maybe a thousand yards away. It sounded like an eighteen-wheeler. Heavy metal squeals under the chassis. Rusty axles. Loose chains bouncing along.

He hustles, willing himself to take more of the jungle's punishment. He cuts through a thicket of brush, finding an animal trail that leads in the direction of the horn. It's thin. Dark-brown dirt—black in the moonlight—with patches of dead leaves on top.

Visions, more like hallucinations, propel Terrance forward, and he stumbles down the animal trail. A town filled with normal people—people who don't have automatic weapons. And those people have water. Food, of any type. Something laced with sugar would be nice. Coca-Cola. Ice cold.

The next sound isn't a horn but a rumbling engine. Easier to hear because it's closer. It seems to be mounted inside another large truck. The sound passes and dissipates, along with the jungle's other sounds. The nocturnal animals have stopped howling and screeching; they're not so interested in their human counterparts. Those two-legged creatures spell danger, and the jungle's more natural residents choose to stay silent, distant.

Terrance reaches a strip of asphalt that divides the jungle in two.

Asphalt is a positive sign; this could be a highway of sorts. Busy. Frequent traffic. Terrance has heard two vehicles in the span of five minutes, but danger still lurks. The barking dogs remind him of it. And these vehicles could be full of people who are hunting him.

He takes a knee, pulling the AK from around his back. He's been too busy escaping to figure out how it works, but intimidation counts for something. Besides, it's a gun. The engineer in him says that it can only work in so many ways.

A long bar is preventing the charging handle from moving rearward. Terrance pushes it all the way down until it won't move any farther. *Must be the safety*, he thinks. He jerks back on the charging handle. A lacquered Russian cartridge ejects into the brush. Progress. It is definitely loaded. *Only so many ways*, he reminds himself, confident that he can at least fend off a few guards.

An engine whines in the distance. It's small, unlike the big trucks he heard before. An old, cheap car. Four cylinders. Terrance crouches at the edge of the tree line, waiting to look before he commits.

A sedan comes around the bend, opposite the direction he came. A good start. It's traveling slow. Headlights are dim, the interiors fogged over with humidity. Paint has flaked down to the primer, leaving dull splotches against shiny, moonlit paint.

It gets closer. The driver is taking his time, but he isn't moving slow enough to make Terrance feel like he's searching for someone. Two silhouettes become visible above the headlights. Both appear to be men. Their heads are focused on the road ahead, not on what may be hiding in the jungle.

Not ideal. If it were a man and a woman, or just one man, he'd be more confident. But it's a four-door sedan. The compound he just left had plenty of guards. Wouldn't they want to fill up the car? *Probably*, he reasons. Two men won't be a challenge either. The rifle at his side will see to that.

Terrance's scratchy throat sways his logic further. He needs water, urgently. The decision is made. He lowers the rifle, pointing it at the ground, then steps out into the road. Not completely threatening—yet. The old car's brakes squeal as it stops several feet in front of him.

Terrance squints against the weak head lamps. "I need help!" he shouts, surprised at his shriveled voice.

Both of the car doors open, and two men step onto the asphalt. Guns are in their hands, just like Terrance. AKs. Thirty-round magazines dangling out of the receivers. He doesn't recognize either of them from the compound, but he knows that's where they're from.

"Drop the gun and lie flat on the ground," the driver says. He raises a radio to his mouth and says something Terrance can't catch.

"You're miles from civilization. You run again, and you'll die out here," the passenger says.

"Just lower the weapon," the driver adds. "We'll get you food, water, and medical treatment. Trust us."

Another vehicle speeds in his direction. One of those larger trucks, rushing up from behind. The backup they radioed for. But that little sedan's engine is still purring, and it's making a run through the jungle seem like a fool's errand. Plus, there could be water inside. No more running.

The safety is off. The second truck is getting closer, closer.

Terrance jerks the rifle up, yanking back on the trigger as he does. A burst of gunfire rips through the driver's side door, killing the man behind it instantly. Terrance doesn't bother raising the rifle from his hip as he engages the passenger. But he's too late.

The passenger fires once.

It feels like getting hit with a sledgehammer. Everything below where the bullet hit simply stops working. Terrance falls onto the asphalt, letting go of the rifle. He places his hands over his belly, trying to stanch the flow of blood, which is spurting out of an entry wound in his abdomen.

The passenger rushes to Terrance, putting more pressure on the wound. The force makes Terrance scream. He's never experienced pain like this before. It's accompanied by terror of the unknown. *Am I going to die? Please, not like this*, he silently prays.

A large truck pulls up behind Terrance and the man giving him medical assistance. Doors open and slam shut. Boots drop onto the ground. There are a lot of men, all of them rushing to contain the scene.

"What happened?"

"He opened up on our car," the passenger replies, nodding at the old sedan and the driver peppered with bullets.

Terrance looks up and finds a familiar face. The one from Mexico City, belonging to the man with the thick blond beard, bright-blue eyes, and Russian accent. "You?"

Victor grimaces. None of this was intended. His leverage against the Americans is bleeding all over the jungle. Only the first catastrophe. Terrance is brilliant—a once-in-a-generation mind. Not an asset to waste. "Just stay calm. We'll get you taken care of."

Terrance's wound is sealed, and an IV is stuck into his arm. He's secured on a gurney and loaded in the back of a troop transport truck. As they slide him in, the jerking produces an incredible amount of pain, but he feels nothing but pins and needles from his waist down.

Fifty-Nine

Seventy miles south of Mexico City, the civilized world is swallowed by the jungle. Perez has passed small towns—more like strips of life left to corrode in the humidity. Just lines of tin-roof shacks against the road, maybe a gas station or a convenience store wedged in between. Most don't have running water and electricity. He stops for gas at nearly every service station he passes, uncertain of when the next one will emerge.

The G-Wagon's Xenon beams guide him down a two-lane road. Supposed to be an interstate. Hardly, but he's grateful that it's paved. Small detail, making all the difference.

Marisol sits unconscious next to him. Body flung in every direction but his. Tequila did the trick. She hasn't berated him or asked a stupid question in over an hour. That same sixty minutes is around the last time he's seen a set of headlights.

Confidence builds. He'll get south. Escape to the Eastern Hemisphere with a fake passport. Leave the Americans and Varga's rotten cartel behind forever. Ditch Marisol wherever it's the cheapest. Find someone younger, newer. Things are looking up, a hundred-eighty-degree shift from twelve hours ago.

He lets his gaze drift around the lux interior. Soft lights and rich instrument panels. Both of his hands are on the wheel, but without any warning the radio clicks on. Harman Kardon speakers blast at full volume. Death metal. Enough to split his eardrums. His foot jerks off the gas, and he fights to keep the wheel straight. He'd been doing close to eighty miles an hour.

Marisol jerks awake and wrenches down the volume. She sinks back into the seat, arms over her stomach. "I'm sick."

"Shut up," Perez hisses, sensing that their situation is going sideways.

"Sorry about that, Admiral. Hit the wrong button."

Perez looks at the speakers, stunned. "Martinez?"

"Let's try this instead."

The G-Wagon begins to decelerate rapidly. Admiral Perez mashes the gas, finds the effort pointless. He tries the wheel, but it's locked in a straight position. "You bitch! You have no authority to do this to—"

"Try and stay calm, Admiral. Roadside assistance will be with you shortly. Wouldn't want you to be stuck out there all alone."

Perez suddenly forgets about controlling the G-Wagon. His eyes squint at the rearview mirror. Silhouetted SUVs shift against his red brake lights. They split, box in his G-Wagon from front to back. This two-lane road just got a lot smaller.

Headlights illuminate the Americans in front of him. They've been driving with night-vision goggles, allowing them to stalk him in total darkness. They were with him for miles, waiting.

Major Trey Bingham bites off the end of a cigar and strikes a match. Flames jump, and an ember forms at the cigar's tip. "You boys ready?"

"Let's get square," Hastings says as he jumps out of the driver's seat, 416 in hand.

"Right," Bingham says, flipping up his nods and stepping out of the passenger seat. He stands in front of the G-Wagon, basking in the white light. Fun to menace Perez while his operators surround the vehicle.

Bingham knows that the G-Wagon is armored—the rifles his team are carrying are to stop him from running on foot into the jungle. He reaches into his tactical pants and pulls out a white phosphorus grenade. Slowly, he unwinds the tape surrounding the spoon. More menacing. A moment of reflection for Perez.

Bingham rips the pin away, and the spoon flips up. The device arcs, lands atop the G-Wagon's hood. Sparks blast in every direction, and it reminds him of a Roman candle. He puffs down on his cigar while his boys cheer and the grenade boils through the engine block.

White phosphorus burns at five-thousand degrees Fahrenheit, and it only goes out when the fuel source is depleted. Armor, engine block, batteries, and wires—it cuts straight through each, and the G-Wagon dies painfully on the asphalt. The engine clacks and clangs before sputtering out. Xenon headlamps blink rapidly and darken. The cabin light fades.

Bingham takes another large puff, watches the fireworks show. "Come on out, Admiral! Only gets worse from here!"

Losing the headlights was bad. Perez is now struggling to see through the tinted windows. Impossible to fight what he can't see. Acrid chemical smoke is also seeping into the cabin through the vents. He and Marisol hack and cough, trying to suck in a dwindling supply of oxygen.

"We can't stay here, Mateo!"

"Don't open your door!" Perez shouts. He's clutching his UMP .45. He racks the charging handle and tries his best to peer through the windows. He still has a chance to get free of this situation. Use Marisol as a decoy. Lock on to the closest Americans, cut them down while he breaks for the jungle. He grew up in the brush, and it's where he'll disappear.

Perez takes a gulp of air and blows against the driver's side window. Smoke disperses. A shadow shifts feet away from the glass. Something smashes onto the roof above him. It's followed by a cutting sound. Like tiny fragments of metal are straining before snapping apart. He finds an orange pinprick glowing above his head.

The circle widens. The ceiling fabric catches fire and drips onto his body. Molten metal splashes his face. Then he feels the worst pain of his life. An orange orb falls through the roof, skitters down his chest, and stops in the crook between his hip and right leg. He doesn't have time to remove the grenade before it boils through the flesh and sinks into muscle.

Major Bingham chuckles, plucks the cigar from his lip, and taps it with his index finger. Ash flutters as Perez jumps out of the Mercedes and crashes onto the asphalt. The grenade is still in Perez's leg, momentarily slowed by his femur, but it won't stay put for long. Sparks and smoke explode out of the wound. The admiral flails, kicks, and gropes at the leg but remains unable to stop the burning phosphorus.

Bingham takes a puff on his cigar, debates putting Perez out of his misery, but there's a distraction. Marisol leaps from the vehicle, straining to breathe. Animal's loving embrace ensures that she'll be forever cared for. He carries her to the front of the G-Wagon to be judged.

Bingham locks eyes with the petrified woman. Just a kid who exchanged her morals and good sense for a few dollars. "You don't want to stick around for this."

Marisol's hands are released. She doesn't reply to Bingham, nor does she give Perez a second glance as she breaks into a sprint. South, just like they'd intended. Only the fairy tale she once lived in is shattered. Mexico City will stay in her past, lest she return to end up like her smoldering ex-husband.

The grenade burns fully through Perez's leg and skitters onto the asphalt. Its exit settles him only slightly. Screams fade to moans, and he clutches the eviscerated leg.

Hastings, waiting nearby, uses his rifle muzzle to knock the still burning grenade into a nearby ditch.

Bingham checks on Marisol's silhouette. It's almost completely gone. He draws his 1911. Shock is all that's preventing Perez from passing out. When it fades, so will he. Time to end this. He moves in closer, needing to look into the admiral's eyes before he pulls the trigger.

The admiral is lying in the fetal position. Charred flesh tracks from his face to his stomach. Spittle drips down his cheek, pools onto the asphalt. Pain has driven him into delirium.

"Shame it got you, Admiral. You know, white phosphorus permanently attaches to bone. Guaranteed cancer several years later," Bingham remarks.

Perez's head is shaking uncontrollably. He looks up. The still-burning grenade flares in Bingham's thick glasses. In his madness he sees a demon. "Finish it."

Bingham wedges the burning cigar between his lips. He angles his pistol and settles his front sight post over the admiral's forehead. A single .45-caliber hollow-point finishes the task. "Got off easy, Admiral."

Sixty

Varga kneels at the altar and recites the prayer's final verse. The gods are with him tonight. Strong and vibrant and demanding. Their energy flows through him, their vessel. A fermented Aztec tea called *sinicuichi*, or Sun Opener, waits to be finished. It brings intense euphoria. Hallucinations said to bake the world in golden light. The gods get closer . . . closer. And he reaches for the *sinicuichi*, ingesting the final sip.

Light crashes into Varga from above. Golden wings stretch outward from a statue of Hummingbird on the Left, or Huitzilopochtli. He reaches into the horizon and pulls the sun from the darkness. Light is his gift to the world, and through it comes all life. Huitzilopochtli's wings continue to reach from the golden statue and embrace this holy temple.

Varga tries to watch, awestruck, but is blinded by the aura.

Black obsidian flashes against the golden light. Gods calling Varga to complete his prayers. He reaches for an obsidian dagger called a *tecpatl*. Aztec priests considered it a divine tool and used it to complete ritual sacrifice. The skin of a stingray laps around the hilt, allowing him to grip it tight. Stone sharper than a razor crosses the palm of his left hand.

Blood drips from the gash, landing on the altar's sacrifice stone. It's made of pumice. Coarse and gritty. Capable of stopping bloody, thrashing bodies from sliding off during their final moments. The stone's deep pores are like cauldrons, raising the blood's temperature until it glows and boils. Red bubbles rise, edges glowing orange and releasing sparks before finally popping.

Varga brings his hand to a flaming stone vessel called a *cuauhxicalli*. Drawing nearer, the flames gasp back into the vessel's belly. Temperatures feel like they'll char his flesh, but he presses his hand over the vessel's open mouth. Blood drips, mixing with magma churning in the stone volcano. He pumps his hand, forcing blood from the wound. Temperatures continue climbing.

They're thirsty.

Blisters rise on his skin. Fire cracks the flesh, allowing his gods to drink more. Pain reaches an unbearable level. Weakening, Varga braces himself against the pumice stone, refusing to adjust his hand.

Smoke explodes from the *cuauhxicalli* and rises to Huitzilopochtli, swirling around its legs, under its wings, and across its chest. The vessel's fire is extinguished as the golden statue inhales the white plumes whirling around its body.

Energy beams through Varga's body. He folds himself atop the altar and eyes an oil-burning lamp at the table's side. Fire froths at its mouth. The flames are feverish and wild, reaching heights he's never seen. The gods are satisfied. Light is being provided in return.

Overcome, he sinks to the floor. Energy swirls, forming a vortex in the center of the temple. The walls are made of black portoro marble. Streaks of gold teem with light as they weave and bend and loop through the walls. Others race through the black stone like lightning bolts. Sunlight bursting through the darkness.

Statues of the religion's four lesser gods are posted around the temple's periphery. They look past rows of ebony pews toward a fifty-two-year Aztec calendar in the center. It's a brilliant mosaic set into the floor. The calendar is essential to Aztec religion. Priests believed that civilization would collapse if their gods weren't made strong enough through ritual sacrifice. This calendar was their guide, and it marked each god's next sacrifice.

Rarely has Varga seen a spectacle this magical, and he has much to be grateful for. He crawls on his hands and knees to the vortex's center. Energy swirls and coalesces around his body as this portal to Mictlan, the Aztec underworld, begins to open and pull him downward. Home, begging him to return.

Varga presses his forehead down and gives thanks. These gods chose him, and in return, they asked only that he provide them sustenance. Their gratitude was boundless. King of Mexico's most powerful cartel. Wealth beyond compare. For it all, he is truly grateful.

The temple doors open. Energy vaults from the room. Sounds like a thunderclap as it whips through the open doors. Tears form at the edges of Alex's eyes, but he stifles them. He's back in the land of the living. The gods already feel distant, and it pains him.

Raising his head, he finds Stefan, his number-two subordinate, standing respectfully by the door. Now, the only light is supplied by the altar's oil-burning lamps. The blistered and cracked flesh on his hand has healed—only the incision from the obsidian dagger remains.

Summoning his strength, he turns to the altar. Smoke is rising from the *cuauhxicalli*, embers in its belly slowly dying. His hummingbird, Huitzilopochtli, is as golden as ever, but reality has clipped its wings, and they rest at its sides.

"I'm sorry, Alex," Stefan says, showing deep remorse for disturbing the ritual. "Something has happened."

"Sit, please."

Stefan lowers his head and sits at the pew nearest Varga. "They gave you answers."

Varga takes a breath, feeling it infused with magic and electricity. The ritual may have ended, but its effects linger. He's ready to face whatever challenge comes. "They gave me everything."

Stefan reflects on his prophet's statement. "Only our gods can know generosity without limit."

Generosity. Varga rests his hands against the floor, absorbing its remaining energy. "What happened?"

"Jules has disappeared. The tower he was servicing was a massacre."

"Was the technology stolen?" Varga asks, disappointment tarnishing the afterglow of his ritual. He'd found technicians. Men capable of making his network run. All he needed was Victor out of the way. He was close—so close. Without the hardware, it's impossible, and now he's exposed.

Stefan nods. "I believe so." He pauses, allowing Varga to think. "Perez was also forced to let Gabriella Martinez off the base. She left with another hacker, Major Bingham, and one of his soldiers. He said that there are now a total of eight missing."

"Jen Yates makes nine."

"What would you like us to do?" Stefan asks.

"Begin peeling off enforcers from our other businesses. Bring them here and put them on guard rotations," Varga says, certain that there is another battle ahead. Odds will be stacked against the Americans once again. This is a fight Martinez can't win.

"And communications?"

Varga silently curses Victor and the disabled network. He'd first considered it an American retaliation for the bombings. Had he known that the Russian was behind it, a barrel of acid would have been waiting for him at the airfield. A nice little sauna, stripping away life's cumbersome details, leaving the bare essentials behind. "Tell them to start using regular cell phones. Go back through our old lists of coded text messages. Find one we haven't used and distribute it."

"All right, Alex." Stefan begins to shift out of the pew but stops. "I forgot something." He reaches into his pocket, extracting a live cartridge. "Ten millimeter. The same type that Jen Yates uses. It was left on the base station's altar."

Varga takes the cartridge. Brass shimmers against the fire light. A large bullet, used by a professional. The only thing missing is his name scrawled across the brass. "I know, Stefan. We'll be seeing her soon."

Sixty-One

There are over a dozen signal processing units inside the stolen base station controller. They're assembled in rows like on a bookshelf. Only these racks are held in by screws. Each one has switches and ports and lights designed to control each individual board's function.

Jen is standing beside Andrew in the mansion's multi-car garage. The garage door is open, allowing the morning sun to creep in, along with a breeze—a requirement for examining Varga's cursed technology.

Equipment has been laid out on a plastic table next to the malware-infected controller. A microscope and magnified glass rest on top, along with surgical equipment to dissect the individual components. Everything has been sanitized and wiped free of particulates. They're taking apart extremely sensitive equipment, and certain parts must be preserved.

"It's not gonna bite you," Jen says, amused by Andrew, who is hunched over, face hovering within inches of the controller. Over-analysis is his specialty.

"Measure twice; cut once," Andrew says, removing a set of screws and wedging the flathead into a board's top edge. Just like on a bookshelf, a little pressure eases the top section of the board out, allowing him to get his fingers around the edges. "Come on out!"

The switching processing board is around an inch thick, equipped with a housing of its own. Mostly aluminum, with independent cooling fans and a bracket that links to the base station controller's bus bar. When it's fully operational, the switching processing board links cellular frequencies, thus completing calls.

Andrew sets the device down, enthusiastic about the board's condition. It was so well insulated, insects couldn't reach its interior components. Like a surgeon, he dons protective gloves before starting his operation. He sets the board under a magnified glass, mapping the circuit board's connections. Once satisfied, he grabs a scalpel and starts the deconstruction process.

Jen eases closer as Andrew slides the scalpel's blade underneath the circuit board's memory chip. It's the wise place to start. Memory isn't as vital as the CPU—the processor that does most of the device's thinking. He works the memory chip out of the circuit board until it snaps free.

The chip is transferred to a cutting board. Andrew drags the scalpel across the chip's edges, separating the top and bottom halves, then pulls the protective plastic coating away with tweezers. "From here, it gets interesting."

Andrew places the exposed memory chip under a microscope. He takes a quick glance, looks up at Jen, then dives back in. "I, um . . . This is unusual."

Jen pushes him out of the way and puts her eye up to the lens. "What? Tell me."

"Manufactures laser etch a series of dots on the chip to serialize it and track production progress. That's missing here," Andrew says before explaining the basic foundation of a computer chip, or semiconductor. "The stacked crystals you're seeing are made of silicon, which is the most common type of material used to make semiconductors."

Jen observes closely, picking out the neatly packed rows of crystallized silicon. Absent are the laser markings that Andrew described.

"I've never encountered this process before," Andrew continues. "Even top-secret programs tend to mark chips with production codes.

Helps them track progress or lock in on a bad batch of semiconductors. Commercial manufacturers do the same but with greater detail."

"It's an absolute guarantee that these things can't be traced."

Andrew nods, frustrated. Examining the semiconductors, or computer chips, was meant to cut to the heart of the issue. Easy enough to scrub serial numbers from cheap plastic components, like circuit boards, but semiconductors are some of the most sophisticated pieces of technology in the world. They require equally stringent manufacturing processes.

"Right. So we're back to where we started—wondering who is actually propping up Varga. These could have been made by a government or a private entity," Andrew says.

Jen reflects on everything that has occurred since she arrived in Mexico. Varga's violence has reached senseless levels. America's adversaries like Russia or China operate with dirty playbooks, but nothing like what Mexico has shown her. "Think it's time we scratch the government theory off our list."

"Varga could have access to some sort of private manufacturer. But even a small facility would run into the billions of dollars. Just to pull this off and keep it a secret." He shakes his head and steps back to the microscope. "Just let me get back in there."

"Go for it."

Andrew inserts a device into the microscope. It's designed to measure a chip's feature size, often called "gate width" in the semiconductor industry. The chip's gate width controls electrical current flow. The smaller the gate width, the more efficient the chip.

He lays the chip atop the measuring device, reads off the result. "Point three-five microns. A fraction of the width of a human hair. This is cutting-edge, Jen. Fabricating chips this sophisticated requires the most advanced equipment on the market."

"We can't trace the semiconductors, but could we track these guys through the equipment they're using to make them?" Jen asks.

Andrew nods. "We're looking for deep ultraviolet lithography machines—the only thing capable of manufacturing chips this powerful. There are two, maybe three companies in the world that make those."

Lithography machines are incredibly powerful pieces of technology. They use ultra-focused beams of light to etch silicon crystals and project material onto their surfaces, creating semiconductors. Each machine can cost upwards of a hundred-million dollars. More important, that technology is heavily controlled. Purchasing one doesn't just require a license, but approval from high levels in a host state's government.

Jen's world just shrank exponentially. Circumnavigating this new globe won't take long, and by the time she's finished the trip, she'll be more than familiar with the players. "When the dust settles in Mexico, we're gonna run this down."

"I second that motion," Andrew replies.

There's a knock behind Jen. She turns to find Martinez standing in the open doorway, face heavy. "What's up, Gabby?"

Martinez doesn't inquire about the research, cutting instead to the reason for her visit. "I need you both in the tactical operations center. Something is happening on Varga's estate."

Sixty-Two

The Group watches an ISR feed of Varga's compound. Glowing screens illuminate a half-circle of crossed arms and concerned faces.

Four vehicles clutter the compound's entrance. They're makeshift armored personnel carriers with thick sheets of steel welded onto the sides. Some of the pickup trucks have belt-fed machine guns fixed to their beds. *Monster trucks.*

As if on cue, two more vehicles enter the feed, depositing eight more gunmen on site. Close to one hundred men are roaming the compound, sporting rifles and body armor. Doesn't matter if they're trained or just idiots with guns. They're capable of putting a lot of lead in the air, and it'll only take one bullet to destroy the night's raid. With each passing minute, the risk profile increases.

"Reinforcements have been trickling in for the past several hours," Martinez says, who is in front of the center screen, laser pointer in hand. She directs the laser to the screen's outer edges, highlighting patches of desert etched with animal trails. "But they aren't all congregating on Alex's estate. They're patrolling the periphery."

Major Bingham is up front with Martinez, assisting with the brief.

His experience as a tactical commander has been integral in the mission's planning phase. "They're forming an early warning system, Jen. The patrols are layered so that if the guys on the outer edges get into contact, it'll give the shooters in the compound time to coordinate and respond."

"How far out are the patrols?" Jen asks.

"They're patrolling roughly half a mile out from the compound," Martinez replies. "Which is within range of the tunnel entrance."

"This'll be extremely challenging," Bingham says. "If we approach, we'll have to remove the patrols—that's easy. But we expect the patrols to have tight check-in windows. When one goes down, we'll have lit a fuse. Ten minutes? Twenty? No telling until Varga sounds the alarm."

"We've got some positives," Hastings remarks, who actually appears more enthusiastic at the increased troop presence. A target-rich environment simply means more target practice for him. "Our drone can jam up their comms. Once we make first contact, we cut 'em off. With this many guns, they'll have serious trouble with force coordination."

Despite the increase, Jen still considers the core of her plan solid. Forcing Varga into the tunnel is still possible, and it's the perfect place to isolate and kill him. But having this many shooters on the compound may enhance his confidence. Why run and hide if there's a chance to fight and win? But she won't be the one facing down those guns. Bingham and his men will be stirring the hornet's nest while she navigates the tunnel.

Her calculus may not be the most accurate, but the raid is worth the risk. Varga's presence on this earth is no longer justifiable. Information stored in his brain could lead her back to the missing hostages. "Just give me the go-ahead, and I'll move on Varga."

An awkward silence settles on the room. Its other occupants hadn't been expecting Jen to react so aggressively to the change in Varga's security posture. To them, it appears reckless. To Jen, it's just the way she's built.

"I don't like it, Jen," Martinez says, locking her arms over her chest.

"This—" Bingham begins.

"Well, that settles it," Hastings says, cutting off his superior officer.

He's perched on the edge of a desk and hops to his feet. After an easy stride across the TOC, he's standing next to Jen. "If Jen's in, so am I." They exchange a first bump and fix their sights on the senior officers.

Animal scratches the bandage covering the burn on his arm. Looks like he'd be more concerned about doing his laundry than peppering Varga's mansion with a belt-fed machine gun. "Guess I'll tag along, make sure you two don't get lost in the desert."

"Bug repellant," Gray mumbles, jotting down a note on a piece of scrap paper.

Jen feels like she's sitting on a cloud. The world's best operators are willing to stand shoulder to shoulder with her on one of the most dangerous tasks they've been asked to undertake. Faith like that is tough to come by, and it's an honor. She laughs at Gray. "That some sorta code phrase you learned in California?"

"No, goober," Gray replies, finally aware she's mocking him. He finishes writing, tosses the pen back on the desk. He rips away the paper, waves it at her. "Got the essentials covered. If you're bitten by an insect, I'll be there to render aid."

"Lotta insects in the desert," Jen remarks with an approving nod. She continues surveying the room's faces. Martinez's smirk is a mile wide, her worry appearing to have evaporated. Bingham is fingering his 1911's beavertail safety, more than pleased by the unfolding situation. They both want this as much as anyone, but they have people to protect —a factor that makes Jen respect their earlier apprehensions all the more.

She nods to Coco. "Four's a party. Only need five to make a firing squad."

"There's a great bluff," Coco says, nodding at the rolling hills adjacent to Varga's mansion on center screen. "'Bout a hundred yards from Varga's office. I could turn a dime into ten pennies from that range."

Jen chuckles. "Guess our firing squad has its marksman."

"Should have known better than to follow Martinez out of that hangar," Bingham says. He squares up to Jen until they're face-to-face, then flicks his pistol's beavertail once more. "You know, I just cleaned this thing?"

"Shame. Looks like you'll be dirtying it up again soon." Jen reaches out, gives the major a firm handshake. She looks to Martinez, the final arbiter, and awaits the verdict.

Martinez says, "Let's go make an execution happen."

Sixty-Three

Victor appraises the surgeon. Sixteen straight hours of trauma care has worn on the man. His scrubs are a patchwork of sweat and blood. Nerves are frayed. Both of his hands are reduced to tremors, and his legs are working double-time to keep him upright.

As the surgeon props himself up against a stainless-steel table in the infirmary, Victor begins to wonder how bad the news will be. Terrance Kline's health is rapidly deteriorating, and the momentum may be impossible to reverse.

The surgeon removes his surgical cap and brushes sweat-slicked hair away from his brow. He slaps the wet cloth onto the table and collects his thoughts before speaking. Forget caffeine. He feels like he needs a jolt of amphetamine. "Bleeding is under control, thankfully. But our problem is infection, which has already set in."

Victor has high confidence in the surgeon. He's from Latvia. Collects doctorates like trading cards. Has over a decade of surgical experience. Despite his medical prowess, some things are beyond his control. "Did the bullet impact his spine?"

The surgeon nods. "Severely. *If* we can save him, he's going to spend the rest of his life in a wheelchair."

"If?"

"I don't have the necessary resources to help this man. The antibiotics I have aren't strong enough, and I've dumped half my current supply into one IV bag."

"Did we make a mistake with our T triple C?" Victor asks, referencing a Special Forces combat medicine doctrine called Tactical Combat Casualty Care. It's designed to treat soldiers who experience traumatic wounds from gunshots or explosions.

The surgeon shakes his head. "The bullet passed through his small intestine. Waste leaked into his abdominal cavity—the source of our problems. You couldn't have prevented that."

"How will you proceed with his treatment?" Victor asks.

"You don't understand, Mr. Orlov. If this man stays here, he's going to die. He needs treatment in a proper trauma center."

Victor briefly hesitates. He's at a fork in the road. "Can I see him?"

"This way."

Victor follows the surgeon through the small infirmary, which reminds him of an emergency room. Several diagnostic and treatment areas, partitioned with hanging curtains. Supplies stocked in a single room, along with medication. Finally, an operating room, which was not designed to treat severe trauma like Terrance Kline endured.

The surgeon peels back a curtain, holds it for Victor as he steps into the third and final treatment room. It's spartan. The headboard behind Terrance is composed of silver bars, straight out of a 1950s hospital. The facility's only life support system is working double time. If it goes, so does the patient. "Would you like to be alone?"

"No, it's fine," Victor replies, disturbed by Kline's appearance. It was less than a week ago that he met Terrance. He was badly shaken but brimming with intelligence. That man has disappeared. He's ashen, drained of life, while a heart rate monitor struggles through every chirp. The worst will be hidden under the blankets, or left behind on the OR's cutting board.

"When is the next flight to Russia scheduled?" the surgeon asks.

"Three days."

"That's not good enough." The surgeon reaches into his scrubs, extracts a small notepad and a pen. After scribbling down a list, he tears away the paper, passes it to Victor. "I'll need those supplies.

Mainly a different class of antibiotic. The flight also needs to be rescheduled."

A battlefield is a special place to Victor. As a former Spetsnaz soldier, he's seen more than a few. While they're wracked with horror and tragedy, the men who step onto them earn something special: respect, both for their courage and willingness to sacrifice their lives for something bigger. Terrance Kline has his respect.

Victor looks down at the piece of paper, reflecting on what Terrance has earned. But he doesn't read the list of supplies. Instead, he tears it in two and throws the scraps in a nearby wastebin.

Respect is only one half of the equation. The other half is more important.

Terrance Kline's journey was always going to be one-way. It's just that Victor is now forced to confront that reality. Once he boarded a jet and landed in the jungle, it was over. Kline has seen Victor's face, intimate details of this facility, and God only knows what else. If he was placed in a hospital, American intelligence officers would find their way to him. It would simply be a matter of time before those details were divulged.

Victor won't allow that to happen. This facility isn't under his care, but he'd die to protect it. Easier to ask another to make that sacrifice. "How long will he live without proper care?"

The surgeon's face is reddening. He fought like a demon to save Terrance Kline, but it's about so much more. His patient has a right to life, and a family is praying to see him once again. "Thirty-six hours at the most."

"Then I'd suggest you focus on palliative care until then."

Sixty-Four

Two miles out. Within an hour Jen and her team will be within striking distance of Varga's compound. They're advancing slowly. The altitude and hilly terrain are sucking the wind out of their lungs. But they're jacked on adrenaline. A gunfight is going to take place. A very lopsided one that they have a zero-percent chance of winning.

Animal is on point, aided by night-vision goggles. The surrounding countryside is baked in his night-vision's warm green light. He recognizes a formation up ahead. It's a trio of jagged, rocky hills with their sides clipped off. Each no more than seventy feet tall. It's a waypoint. He throws his fist up, signaling for the team to stop. He turns back to Jen and whispers, "This is your stop."

Jen takes a knee and flips down a navigation board on her plate carrier. It's essentially a cell phone, displaying her route via GPS. The waypoint is mapped perfectly, and so is the path to the tunnel's suspected entrance.

From here, she breaks from the team. The Delta operators will approach Varga's compound from the west, which will allow them to assault the compound from its flank. She'll be traveling south, alone.

Jen rechecks her guidance and replies, "I've got forty minutes until I'm on target."

Bingham takes a knee by her side. Despite his prosthetic leg, he's carrying just as much weight as the others, and it hasn't slowed him once. Glasses glow neon against the night-vision goggles over his face. "Give us around seventy minutes. We've gotta handle the patrols."

Jen nods, and they exchange fist bumps. "No sweat."

The Delta operators stand up and continue their approach. They ease down a small hill, and she loses sight of them.

It's a solo act from this point forward. Fear won't slow her down, but her mindset is changing. Being isolated makes her feel more predatory. When she's in a team, it feels safe. With someone watching her back, mistakes can be forgiven. Help can be rendered.

Not now. No one is waiting to lend a hand. She traverses down the hill, fully expecting to see Varga tonight. Only one of them will be leaving that tunnel alive.

Sixty-Five

Two men armed with rifles stumble down a pathway. They're imported guards, unfamiliar with the terrain they're patrolling. They're clumsy in the darkness, kicking rocks, crunching gravel, breaking twigs. At least they're following an animal trail. It will lead them directly to a road, maybe a half mile up ahead, and that will lead them to their next trail. If they can find it. Even with flashlights, navigation is tough. The moon is hiding and the stars are distant. The eeriest conditions to patrol in.

The trail constricts, forcing the two men to walk single file. They're thousands of feet above sea level. Lit cigarettes aren't helping their breathing or their night vision. Still, they puff away as they walk, exchanging banter to pass the time.

"Ey, what the fuck you think they got us out here for?" the second man asks, hanging his free hand on his plate carrier, which makes him feel slightly less exhausted.

The point man laughs as he leads the patrol. "They're saying you got fat, *cabrón*. So they sent you here to walk off all the *cervezas* you've been drinking."

The point man keeps walking, laughing, and smoking. Suddenly, he realizes that he's laughing alone. Gravel isn't crunching behind him. A rifle isn't crackling against magazines in a plate carrier. He stops, paralyzed, and struggles to make a decision. Turning around is the right choice. Or is it? May not want to see what's at his back. Deciding there are no other options, he turns.

There's no one. Just dead, dark space where his friend was once standing. "Manuel!" It comes out as a pleading whisper. "Stop fucking around, idiot!" No response. His anxiety grows. He rips his flashlight out of his pocket. The beam jerks frantically from the trail to bushes on the left, then right. He searches with both eyes open. Night vision completely ruined. The light doesn't help him find his friend.

"Manuel's dead."

The voice came from behind. It was English. Gravely and deep. A very large man. More paralysis. Yes, turning around would be the wise move—if his muscles worked. Something shifts up ahead. A moving bush with green eyes. Something shiny in its hand, stained red. He shifts the light downward and finds his dead comrade. Blood seeps from his throat, which is cut ear to ear.

There's an option. I'm not dead yet. His rifle falls to the dirt. Hands go up, slow and steady. No sudden movements. He begins to turn. Baby steps. Until he sees a giant standing across from him. More than a head taller and twice as wide.

The giant presses something in his ear, then speaks in Spanish. "Give me your radio."

The patrolman hands it over, no questions asked.

Another pause. Whispers over a headset. The giant holds the radio up to the patrolman's face. "Check in."

The patrolman takes the radio and says, "This is Patrol Four, checking in."

"Your check-in is early, Four. Everything good?"

"Nothing else to do out here," the patrolman replies, adding a chuckle for good measure. "And I can't even see my freaking watch."

"Good check-in, Four," the radio operator responds.

The giant turns off the radio. Batteries are torn from its back and join the rifle in the dirt. No more check-ins.

"You can go."

The patrolman gasps. He jerks around, ready to run in the opposite direction. His chest bounces off another man, and he's too petrified to scream. A glint of silver crosses his neck. Almost lucky. Almost forgiven for being a cartel member.

Hastings gets on his radio as the narco bleeds out at his feet. "One patrol down. Looks like we bought a little time."

Bingham, Gray, and Coco have taken up a position overlooking Alex's mansion. The rise is thirty feet tall, peppered by shrubs and rocks. Just enough elevation to see over the compound wall and into the back of Varga's home from the southwest. This is where they'll launch the attack.

They're setting up weapons after the hike in, which was bloody. Three patrols under their belt. Six men, each one missing their check-in windows. The last was seven or eight minutes ago. Alarm bells will be ringing soon.

Bingham and Gray are behind Mk-48 belt-fed machine guns, chambered in 7.62. One hundred round belts of ammo. A lot of firepower, designed to cause a lot of confusion and panic. IR lasers are affixed to their handguards. Sound suppressors are snug on the barrels. But that's only half the fun. They're also carrying Lewis Machine and Tool M203s. They look like pistols but launch 40mm grenades. In this case, high-explosive ordnance was chosen.

A radio call comes in. Bingham leaves his machine gun, which is set up on a bipod, and slides down the hill. "Didn't copy your last, TOC."

"Alex Varga is marked. Check your camera feed."

Bingham opens his nav board. A camera feed pops up. His personal drone is observing Varga through his office window. Varga is pacing around his desk, with his number two, Stefan. Both men are tense. Their patrols are disappearing. "Copy, TOC."

Bingham crawls back up the hill. The drone's infrared laser is pointed directly at Varga's office. It's about one hundred yards and sixty degrees from his position. He chuckles. "Reminds me of when I met my third wife."

Coco finishes twisting his scope's turret and looks up from his

Knights Armament M110. It's a sniper's dream. The rifle is based on the AR-15 platform, only it's been augmented to cycle 7.62 cartridges. "Come again, Major?"

Bingham pulls the 203 off his kit and snaps a 40mm grenade into the tube. He gives Coco a tight smile. "Sparks are gonna fly."

———

Another laser is marking a critical target, but this one isn't human. It's the suspected location of Varga's escape tunnel. Jen takes a knee, having just walked a circuitous path around the compound. She didn't encounter any patrols; the Delta teams killed them all.

Her personal drone's IR laser is pointing directly at the rock wall, but she only sees stone notches under her night-vision goggles. The tunnel is well-hidden, if it's even here. "TOC, how's our time looking?"

Martinez comes back immediately. "We've got patrols missing check-ins, Zero. You're out of time."

"Working the problem." Ripping her gloves off, she begins running her hands across the rocks. Squeezing and scratching. Feeling for softness or unusual textures. Thirty feet of rock wall is a lot to cover in search of a hidden passage. But she works at the horseshoe's center and forces herself to take it slow.

Prodding. Squeezing. Pushing. She covers a section, top to bottom. Nothing. She starts on another section and turns up a blank.

"Zero, you need to gain access."

Jen doesn't reply, but she speeds up, tapping her knuckles against lengths of rock. She strikes something that sounds hollow. She draws her knife and stabs it into the unusual section. The blade glides in. It's hardened foam, painted and shaped to match the desert's natural formations.

"Show me," Jen whispers, beginning to tap the knife's tip on the wall. It sounds hollow, soft. She keeps tapping, until it clinks against a harder material. The door's edge. She pushes the knife back into the soft material, cutting out a chunk. She wedges her fingers into it, pulling. Material peels away like a sardine can's lid, revealing the tunnel's entryway.

But the actual door into the tunnel isn't so easy. It's solid metal, almost like a bank vault. Electronically guarded. She searches for cameras but doesn't see any. Jen activates her radio: "TOC, I've found the door. No way in unless Varga opens it. It's time to give him a nudge."

One last chance to make sure everything is in place. Martinez checks the center screen for any unusual activity or unseen movement that the drones may have missed.

But her checklist has notches all the way down. Both fire teams made an excellent approach to the compound, knocking down a half dozen patrols, totaling twelve men. Jen's hike in went undetected. This assault is going to happen. "Ms. Hamilton, isolate Varga's radio frequency and jam it."

"Radio communications are now offline," Sloane replies. "Assault team communications are functioning optimally."

"Fire Teams One and Two, clear to engage."

Sixty-Six

Twenty minutes. That's the longest blown check-in window. A second patrol is going on fifteen. Varga's temper is raging. He's pacing around his office, demanding answers, but no one can give him any.

Stefan is shouting into his radio, communicating with the security station on the estate. "Mobilize all of our forces! If guys are sleeping, wake them up!" As he removes his finger from the transmit button, static fills the room.

"Did that call go through?" Varga demands. He stops pacing, his arms crossed over his chest. Right behind him, a giant glass window. Black, full of night. Until it's not. A flash erupts, followed by multiple concussions. The force crashes into Varga, throwing him against his desk while shards of glass flay his back.

Explosions are quickly replaced by sustained fire. Large-caliber bullets zip into the office. Hard, violent smacks, ripping apart whatever they contact. Drywall explodes. Wooden studs begin to smoke. Hot lead and copper fragments pepper fine art and eviscerate bookshelves.

Varga's head is singing. He's deaf and light-headed. His eyes are caked with debris. The entire left side of his back is burning. He runs his hand over the area, finding blood. "Stefan!"

Farther away, Stefan pushes himself off a bed of debris and rushes to his boss. Rounds snap over his head, reminding him to keep low unless he'd like to lose it. "You're hurt!"

Varga waves him off. "Go and find out what's going on!"

Stefan doesn't listen. The back of Varga's shirt is soaked red. It could be fatal if left untreated. "Let me stay with you!"

"No! I need you to go. Don't let the Americans past our walls!" Varga orders.

Stefan nods reluctantly. "Get somewhere safe!"

Varga stays low as his subordinate hustles out of the office. With his back pressed into his desk, he slides open a drawer and feels around for a remote. He extracts it, flips open a protective shield. He depresses the button, and a green light flashes. His escape tunnel is now unlocked.

Before leaving his office, he stuffs a messenger bag full of essentials. Multiple handwritten ledgers. His laptop. A special dossier he compiled on Victor and his organization. No matter where he runs, the Varga cartel will always be under his control.

Heavy gunfire is chattering in the distance. Explosions punctuate the chaos at random intervals. Only one sound piques Jen's curiosity: metal bars receding into the door.

Once the whining electric motor completes the task, the metal door swings freely. The bet paid off: Varga panicked. Now he's desperate to escape.

Fluorescent light escapes through a crack in the door. A cool wind follows it. Chemical odors waft into Jen's nose. Whatever is behind this door tastes like poison. She flips her night-vision goggles up, no longer needing them. She angles her B&T toward the crack, using the suppressor to swing the door open.

The door bumps into a dirt bike and a red fuel can. Varga's escape vehicle, suited for the rocky terrain. She steps through the door and into a long, straight tunnel. What she sees takes her breath away.

It reminds her of the Aztec tunnels she saw in Zocalo—inspiration obviously taken from the priests of years past. This tunnel is made of the dead, but with a modern twist.

Bodies have been preserved in clear epoxy, forming walls thick enough to absorb the weight of thousands of pounds of dirt. The epoxy slabs are lit with bright fluorescent light from above and below. It feels clinical. Sterile. The dead men, women, and children appear ghoulish.

She takes several steps into the long tunnel, unable to peel her eyes away from what she's seeing. Anne's drone glides along overhead, camera angled at the slabs. "TOC, you seeing this?"

"We see it, Zero," Martinez says, her voice almost breathless.

Jen walks slowly, horrified by the faces. They're in various states of decomposition. Some appear to have died only yesterday, just sleeping here, forever. Others have rotted features, their bones exposed, decayed flesh receded. No matter the state of decay, the epoxy halted nature's processes completely.

Jen stops in front of a particularly disturbing slab. A young mother and her daughter. The little girl is no more than five years old, and she's reaching out to take her mother's hand. Gunfire took them both. They were entombed quickly, preserving their corpses. Forever sleeping together. Waiting for Varga to come and admire them.

Jen looks away from the slabs, needing to stay focused on the fight ahead. "Anne, keep my personal drone here. Make sure no one gets behind me in the tunnel."

"Copy, Ms. Yates."

The drone stays hovering by the door as Jen presses down the tunnel. She's never been more motivated to confront an enemy. Varga's reign of terror ends tonight.

Machine-gun barrels are glowing orange. Piles of links and shell casings grow larger in the dirt. Hastings and Animal are putting lead on anything that moves inside the compound. They're tucked into a rock formation, which is providing solid cover as well as some elevation. It also gives them angles to fire onto the western and northern sides of the compound. One hundred yards in the distance, Bingham and the others are doing the same.

Varga's guards are exchanging fire with the Delta operators, but their efforts are being obstructed. The compound's walls are good for keeping people out—and in. Whenever a cartel gunman tries to climb the walls, angling for a better firing position, a machine-gun burst removes him. The compound also had fixed gun emplacements, but those were quickly eliminated by 40mm grenades.

Hastings's right cheek is resting on his Mk-48, its bipod digging into the boulder he's using as cover. His elbows are forming a second bipod, giving him some stability. The last length of belt is eaten by the Mk-48. Its hammer strikes on an empty chamber with an audible click. "Reloading!"

"Got your cover!"

Hastings dives into his kit, extracts another box of ammunition, and fastens it to the bottom of the weapon. He opens the feed tray and inserts the first round. Finally, he slams the feed tray shut and racks the charging handle. One hundred rounds of 7.62, ready to fly.

Before he begins firing, he grabs his M203, which is also empty. He ejects the spent 40mm casing and inserts a fresh one. A smirk crosses his face as he looks toward Varga's mansion. Smoke is seeping from several areas of the home. Bullets and bombs are going to reduce it to ash. The chance of speeding along the process is too tempting to pass up. He takes aim.

"Fire Team One, this is TOC. You have a ten-man element squirting out of the compound. They're approaching your position along the compound's northern wall."

Hastings holds his fire and responds. "Copy your last, TOC." He punches Animal. "They're getting this figured out!"

"Doesn't matter!" Animal shouts. "I'm not leaving until I'm out of bullets!"

"Then keep pumping them into that asshole's house! I'm on the squirters!" A green IR laser appears out of the sky—his fire team's personal drone, marking the group of targets as they move. They're oblivious to the technology over their heads.

The first gunmen become visible, slipping out from around the compound wall. One hundred twenty yards out. They're weaving through shrubs. Keeping low. Staying fast. Ambush in the making. Maneuver in close, flush their targets out of cover.

They travel the distance quickly. Hastings is generous, allowing them within eighty yards, while stalking them with his grenade launcher. Thump! A 40mm grenade blasts free, arcing through the air. It lands at the center of the ten-man team. Bodies fly as they're peppered with metal fragments.

Without missing a beat, Hastings reloads the M203 and sets it on the rock next to his Mk-48. He searches for survivors with his machine-gun's IR laser. It picks up confused movement. Stunned, injured enemies getting their bearings, or clutching their wounds. He strafes their position with fire and doesn't stop until he's certain they're all dead.

"TOC, looks like we bought a little more time, but it won't last!" Hastings shouts. "Tell Zero to move it along!"

Sixty-Seven

Jen finally reached the end of the tunnel, and she hasn't seen the first sign of Varga. A grenade or bullet may have already done the job. No way to be certain, at least until she lays eyes on him.

A radio call comes in. "Zero, this is TOC. Both fire teams are getting swamped. You need to move it along."

"I'm at the end of the tunnel, TOC. Expect results shortly," Jen replies.

The tunnel terminates in a small room. Three sides boxed in with epoxy caskets. The far wall has a set of metal stairs leading up to a trapdoor. It's cracked open. Automatic, just like the first door. Had Varga come down, she'd have seen him. Her movements were sufficiently quiet and shouldn't have given her away.

She heads for the stairs, planning her attack. She could hide under them, wait for Varga to rush down. Easy ambush. Safe too. But morbid curiosity draws her toward the temple above. *Could it be worse than this tunnel?*

She needs to see for herself.

With her B&T pointed toward the cracked door, she begins climbing the stairs. Movements are controlled, silent. Glowing fires and inky smoke ooze through the opening. The result of burning oils, wood, and charcoal. The smell gets stronger, replacing the tunnel's pungent chemical odor.

Before breaching the temple, Jen studies the hidden door. Metal bars can manually seal off the tunnel. An important safety feature. She'll use them during her escape—the same threat that could have killed Varga can kill her too: a long run down a straight tube. No cover, no means of putting up a fight.

With her weapon raised, Jen uses her injured hand to ease open the door. Her adrenaline is rocketing as her fingers wrap around the edge. The trapdoor opens up behind the temple's altar. It's a narrow gap between the walls, and a giant gold idol rises over her head. Fire dances against black marble walls. Gold shimmers from a hundred different places.

She approaches the back edge of the altar, working the angles, listening. Is someone reacting to her movement? Scared cartel members could have hidden inside the temple, seeking refuge from the hell storm.

She rounds the corner using her muzzle as a guide. A thick slab of pumice rests on the center of the altar. Tall oil-burning lamps glow at its sides. Varga sacrifices his victims within feet of her position, and it smells of fresh blood. Step by cautious step, she searches under the pews and around the temple's marble pillars, but finds no one.

The search leaves her standing by the main doors. The only way in or out. She slips into a shadow, deciding to give Varga more time to materialize. A roach like that wouldn't die from a lucky shot. When Varga bursts through, she'll have the drop on him, and this temple will see its final soul transferred to the underworld.

Muzzle flashes leap up from every direction. The concussions rattle Varga's surroundings. He's hidden in his library, looking out through the glass doors.

His gunmen are running in every direction, confused. Stefan is struggling to make sense of the attack without radios. But Varga doesn't care. He's only making sure that the pathway to his temple is clear of enemy shooters.

Getting to his feet is a struggle. His blood loss is worsening, and he's weak. Muscles cramp and twitch. Shrapnel grinds into his ribs with every breath. He pushes past it, confident in his gods. If he were meant to die, he would have. Opening the patio door, he steps into the chaos.

He scans his surroundings as he scrambles to the temple. Not just for enemies, but eager subordinates looking to take their boss's spot in the hierarchy, or aid him during an escape. But his men are too busy fighting. They don't notice him as they fire aimlessly into the desert.

The Americans picked a perfect time to kill him, and they almost succeeded.

The twenty yards between his villa and temple are covered quickly. Varga reaches the door and bursts through it. He turns, locking a wooden beam in place, sealing the temple.

He rushes toward his altar.

Click.

A safety just flipped off. Varga drops his satchel on the floor and freezes. "Jen Yates. The *puta* that couldn't stay the fuck out of my city."

Jen steps into the walkway between the rows of pews, her rifle pointed at Varga's head. This moment is one of the most satisfying of her life. A demon will return to hell shortly, and she's going to shove him through the gates. "Looks like you're having a rough night. You go on ahead and turn around. I'd like to look into your eyes before I blow 'em out of their sockets."

Varga faces her, unafraid. He should be dead, but he's not. *A reason. My gods at work.* She wants to speak with him, and he wants to fight with her. He holds his hands out to his sides and begins walking backward, his cowboy boots snapping against the calendar underfoot. "Have you seen my altar?"

"You seen the people I'm looking for?" Jen demands.

Varga shrugs. "Maybe they spent some time in here with me before I sent them to the stars." He arrives at the altar, resting his hand on the jagged pumice stone. "Maybe Terrance Kline laid here and stared up at me while I cut his heart out."

"You didn't do that."

"No?" Varga asks coyly.

Jen reflects on what she's learned in Mexico City and decides to push him. "The people controlling you wouldn't let that happen."

"No one controls me!" Varga hisses.

Jen laughs. "A man like you—a person who believes in garbage like this ... Someone made you, created you."

"If that's what you think, you're clueless about how Mexico truly works," Varga scoffs, then studies her for a moment. Her gun. Her aggressive posture as she stalks him. She's close now, within ten feet. Where he wants her. "Those people you speak of"—he points at phantoms in the air—"know more about you than you realize."

"Yeah, and what's that?"

"They sacrificed my cartel to bring you here. You were their target."

Jen's finger had been inching toward her trigger, but Varga's statement pauses the movement. Some very important information just came out of his mouth. She needs to know more. "Whose target, Varga? Tell me."

"They destroyed my cartel for *you*," Varga replies, anger growing at the thought of Victor's betrayal. The network so vital to his security taken offline, leaving his cartel vulnerable. The radiation—that Russian woman that carried it. *She looked so much like Victor.* "The Founders—it's what they call themselves at least. They're the ones who supplied my technology. The liquid cocaine."

"What did they do with my people? Where are they?"

"All I know is that they were placed on an aircraft and sent away. I don't know where. It's the same for the drugs they send. I have no idea where they come from."

Jen inches closer, trying to read him, but sees only fire in his eyes from the surrounding lamps. "Give me a name, Varga. Someone I can lock on to. Who handled my people?"

Varga raises his hands out to his sides again. Empty. A sign for her not to kill him as he turns and faces his altar. Huitzilopochtli rises above him. His precious hummingbird, the entity that will protect him now. He mouths a silent prayer before replying. "Victor."

"Victor what?"

Varga looks down. Two obsidian daggers lay on the altar. His body is blocking them from her view. She is comfortable now. Asking questions. He moves his hands toward the weapons. Slow. "Victor Orlov. That's all I know. He's a Russian who specializes in computers and intelligence operations."

Jen catches the hand movements. Her gut is telling her to shoot him in the back of the head, be finished with him. But she can't—not yet. "How do I find him? There's a way. Just tell me."

Varga's hands lock onto the daggers. Glistening black obsidian with handles wrapped in the skin of stingrays. "There's always a way, Ms. Yates, but you'll never know."

Varga twists in a flash. Jen has just enough time to jerk away as an obsidian dagger flies past her. Before she can regain her composure, Varga has his hands on her. He hurls her into a pew several feet away. She tumbles and the muzzle of her rifle smacks onto the wooden edge.

Jen rolls onto her back, aiming the rifle up toward Varga. He's inches away from her feet. But a quick pull of the trigger will change that. The rifle jerks, produces a metallic sound. Hunks of metal spit from the suppressor, peppering Varga's chest like a shotgun. The impact stops him cold.

Jerking back the rifle, Jen finds a dent in the suppressor's side from her tumble. It obstructed the bullet's path as it exited the rifle, causing it to disintegrate. The gun is useless and unsafe to fire. She drops it to her side, making a move for her pistol as she looks up at Varga. He's still on his feet, his free hand gliding over his chest. Blood is seeping out of a dozen wounds, each caused by bullet and suppressor fragments.

The 2011's beavertail safety depresses in her hand, the first sign of a positive grip, and her trigger finger presses against the holster's retention button. Varga's eyes flash with anger. A wounded animal, close to death. He lurches toward her before she can raise her weapon. One of his hands latches onto her plate carrier. He rips her off the ground with enough force to send the pistol flying.

In one fluid movement, Varga twists again and presses her onto the altar. He keeps her back pinned and places the dagger under her throat. She wraps both of her hands around his wrist, trying to force the dagger away. One hand is injured, weak. The other struggles to grip his bloody arm. It only causes him to bear down harder. The obsidian begins to separate her flesh. Blood drips down her neck. Half an inch, and it'll cut open an artery.

Her eyes shift to the statue above. The shimmering gold . . . the light. *The light.* There's a tall lamp, full of burning oil, a foot behind her head. She grits her teeth and pushes hard against Varga's hand. The burst of force buys her time, allowing her injured hand to reach up and topple the lamp onto Varga.

Burning oil engulfs him. His face. His chest. His hair melts away in a plume of smoke. Clothing sops up the oil, pasting it to his flesh. The dagger falls from his hand, and he begins trying to wick the burning oil off his body. His hands glide over his chest, but it only spreads the fire.

Jen retrieves her pistol while he burns. Flesh is melting, mixing with the burning oil, dripping onto the floor. She raises her pistol and drops the safety. As her finger takes up the trigger's slack, she stops. She won't show sympathy for this man. Same mercilessness he showed her, her people, and a thousand others.

She flips the safety up and holsters the pistol. Instead, she grabs the dagger that he dropped moments ago. Varga falls to the ground as the oil begins to burn out. She stands over him as smoke rises from his chest and face. He's still breathing. Hyperventilating. Shock overriding his system.

Jen kneels down, senses heat trapped in his bones. There's still life in Varga's eyes. He's going to feel what comes next. She angles the dagger over his heaving chest. Up, down, up. Forcing oxygen through a charred airway. The dagger slides between two ribs, impacting his heart. Varga's body seizes as Jen jerks the blade, dicing the organ.

She stands and steps away from the body. Extracting her cell phone, she takes a photograph, which will give the Group members visual proof of the success. A confirmation message comes back quickly, officially completing her mission inside the compound.

Gunfire rages outside. Men are screaming and shouting and fighting. This temple is no place to linger. She grabs Varga's messenger bag and her rifle before rushing to the escape hatch. Once inside the tunnel, Jen shuts the door and eases the locking bars into place. She's sealed off, her escape clear, and the sprint to safety begins.

Sixty-Eight

The call comes through Bingham's headset. Alex Varga is dead. Jen is safe and withdrawing through the tunnel. Time for his team to do the same. The cartel members have not attempted to exit the compound again, wisely choosing not to expose themselves. Instead, they've decided to take positions on the upper floors of Varga's mansion, allowing them to fire down onto the assault teams. That has forced Bingham and his team to slide deeper into cover.

The cartel's tactical decision presents another problem. They'll be able to fire on the teams as they egress to safety. But moving and shooting are what the Delta operators do best, and despite the danger, they'll perform.

Bingham snaps his feed tray shut and racks the charging handle on his Mk-48. He taps Gray on the shoulder and shouts, "Prepare to lay down cover for Team One!" He receives a nod and activates his radio. "Team One, break off and move to our first rendezvous! Got your cover!"

"Copy your last! Moving now," Hastings replies.

Two loud thumps echo out. Blasts from M203s follow, each exploding on the western face of Varga's home. Windows are blown out.

Bits of stucco and wood explode outward. Plumes of smoke rise. Muzzle flashes that had been active seconds before disappear. Two more cracks follow, and smoke grenades pop over Hastings and Animal's positions. The cloud rises, covering their movements as they recede into the desert.

Bingham grabs his own grenade launcher and lobs a projectile toward one of the windows. Direct hit. An explosion lights the room, and it carries several silhouettes into the afterlife.

Gray's machine-gun barrel jumps between muzzle flashes in the distance. Short bursts through windows and balcony doors. Coco's rifle knocks a cartel gunman off his perch on the compound wall.

Bingham turns to check on his escaping men. They're over seventy yards in the distance, covering ground quickly. In another few minutes they'll be out of the cartel's range of fire. Then it will be his turn to run the gauntlet, but without covering fire.

"Reloading!" Bingham shouts as he begins refreshing his weapons. Once he's finished, he adds, "Gun up!"

Gray takes his turn while the others provide cover fire. "Reloading!"

"Hope your boots are laced up tight," Bingham says between machine-gun bursts.

"Shit! I'd rather kick 'em off and put my feet up!" Coco replies.

Bingham nods. Their main assault has lasted under fifteen minutes. The cartel has not yet found any real footing to fight them. It's been controlled chaos, start to finish. Those men are murderers, drug pushers —the antithesis of trained warriors. Combat like this is beyond them. "Grenades out! Follow it with smoke!"

Three thumps of 40mm grenades disappear into the darkness. The explosions rattle the cartel members into submission, and gunfire from the house is momentarily silenced as they regroup.

Smoke grenades bounce along the desert floor and burst. Smoke billows upward. The team hoists their weapons off the rocks and start their egress. As they run, they can hear bullets smack into the hillside they were just behind. They ricochet with high-pitched zings. But the fire is inaccurate, and the team is already fifty yards in the distance by the time wind carries the smoke away.

The team slides into a gulley, not more than ten feet deep, and continues their escape. The ravine is deep enough to shield them from the cartel's gunfire. Bingham notices a green laser shooting into the sky. It's a lasso, signaling the other fire team's position. In another two hundred yards, he'll be joining them.

Sixty-Nine

Infrared lasers glide over the fire teams' Suburban and stab through patches of dry brush. Jen falls in behind the Delta Force operators as they approach. Her primary weapon is still fouled. They move in a staggered formation, still expecting enemy fire to erupt at any time. Their Mk-48s are raised, and ammunition belts rattle against the receivers.

Jen holsters her 2011 and plucks a set of keys out of her kit. Locks pop and lights flash. The Suburban's armored rear hatch rises. Lights tick on inside the SUV. Nothing is moving in the vehicle. Before Bingham can dispense orders, she makes a request. "Trey, I need Al's help with fresh intel. Something could be live."

"Copy. Gray, take the wheel. Animal and Coco, pull security in back," Bingham replies.

Jen whistles. "Gray." When the Delta operator turns, she tosses him the keys.

Preparations to depart happen quickly. Gray stows his Mk-48 in the back and jumps into the driver's seat. Animal and Coco jump through the hatch, next to Gray's weapon. If someone picks up their tail, they'll be in position to make him think twice. Hastings and Bingham collapse their Mk-48s' stocks, giving themselves some room to maneuver as they enter the vehicle.

Jen hops in on the rear passenger side. Varga's messenger bag lands between her and Hastings. Before she starts working the bag's clasps, she says, "Light."

"Easy with that," Bingham says as he flips on the cabin light. "Al, give her an assist."

"On it, boss," Hastings replies as he turns on the ultra-bright miniature flashlight attached to the side of his helmet. He angles his head down to assist Jen with opening the satchel. Varga had a penchant for bombs. Armor is great for keeping explosions out—and in. If something clacked off inside the Suburban, they'd all be knocking on heaven's gate.

As Jen unbuckles the first clasp, the Suburban jerks and lurches along the pitch-black desert road. Gray is driving with his headlights off, but his foot is heavy on the gas. They're still in Indian country, and Varga's army just lost its leader. Vengeance will be looking to catch up with them.

"Feeling any resistance?" Hastings asks, observing Jen as she unbuckles the final clasp.

"Nothing, but I'm raising the flap slow."

Bingham finishes his check-in with the TOC, then directs his attention to the action in the rear. "Wrap it up. I wanna get as dark as possible."

"We're close," Jen replies, inching the messenger bag's flap upward. Brown leather ledgers take up most of the space inside. A slim MacBook Pro has been wedged between them. Slowly, she plucks out a folder. Thick, filled with loose leaves of paper.

"Holy . . ." Jen whispers, flipping open the folder's flap. Photographs of a blond man are front and center. They were taken recently as the man toured the villa's gardens, flanked by security personnel. *Victor Orlov.* Written bold across the folder's surface with a red Sharpie. She removes the cell phone from her pocket, takes a photograph of Victor's image, and forwards it to Martinez.

Detailed notes are also present. More like a diary of conversations Varga had with Victor, notating what he learned about the Founders.

Not only are they supplying him drugs, but they're giving him the means to launder and secure his money. All of the technology Jen encountered in Mexico City was apparently designed by them.

"What is it?" Hastings asks, peeking at the file's contents spilled across Jen's lap.

"This is the man Varga just warned me about. It looks like Varga was building a target package on him," Jen says, snapping the file shut. It's an intelligence gold mine, reflecting Varga's hostility toward the Founders, but it's not urgent. She tucks it back in the case and extracts a second ledger titled *Import/Export*. She hands it off to Hastings. "Start with this. Work backward through the pages."

"On it," Hastings replies, flipping open the ledger to the most recent entries.

"Trey, let's go dark."

"Thanks, Jen." Bingham flips off the cabin's light and returns his attention to helping Gray navigate through the desert.

Hastings kills his helmet lamp and cracks an orange glow stick. Fluorescent chemicals begin cooking off. He rests it against the ledger and familiarizes himself with Varga's operations.

Jen has the MacBook open, and the login screen is displayed. She removes a Master Key from her kit and plugs it in.

Apple's standard AES-256 encryptions are protecting the computer. But the Master Key has a work around. She reboots the Mac in recovery mode and opens the password reset tool. Typically, she'd need Varga's Apple ID credentials. Instead, she enters a set of NSA Tailored Access Operations credentials, generated for instances like this. The Master Key verifies the request, allowing her to reset the password at the administrative level.

One more reboot returns her to the login screen. Jen enters her custom credentials and gains complete access to Varga's world. Usage monitors are the next step. She opens the monitor, finding *Numbers* hovering at the top. Once inside the *Numbers* program, she starts running through the most recently opened spreadsheets.

One particular spreadsheet captures her attention. *Tangues quimico:* chemical tanks. Bellies full of cocaine. Import dates and times are listed in incredible detail. "Hastings, got anything for September thirtieth in Varga's import list?"

"The thirtieth? That's tonight," Hastings mumbles, flipping back a few pages. "This ledger stretches all the way into February."

"Looking for anything to do with chemical tanks."

Hastings locks the glow stick under an entry and hands the ledger to Jen. "There's a shipment coming in by air tonight."

Jen cross checks the ledger's entry against the computer's. They match. So does the GPS coordinate associated with the delivery location. She hands back the ledger. "TOC, this is Zero. How do you copy?"

"We've got you, Zero. What's happening?" Martinez replies.

"We've discovered an inbound shipment of chemical tanks. I'd like to have a look," says Jen as she forwards the coordinates via her cell phone.

"Looks like that location is about ninety minutes from the safe house."

"We're in business," Jen says as she gives Hastings a fist bump. "We still have time, but we'll have to hustle."

"I'll get ISR on station—"

"Hold that order. I don't want our drone interfering with our target's flight path. This plane could be the one that transported Victor Orlov out of the country. Same with our missing people," Jen says, remembering what Varga told her in the temple. *Your people were put on a flight . . .*

"Copy that. We'll prepare a transponder. Have it ready by the time you get here."

"Don't stop there. I need my backup rifle, and our shooters need fresh kits."

"Done and done, Zero."

"Couldn't stay out of trouble if we paid you to," Animal jokes.

Jen turns. The giant has his legs wedged against the rear hatch for support, his Mk-48 across his lap. "Just making sure you get your exercise."

"Just don't forget my overtime pay."

Jen chuckles and returns to her work. She googles the GPS coordinate on her phone. She may not want ISR overhead, but Google's spy satellites have already beaten her to the location. More arid countryside on the northern side of Mexico City. One road in, one road out. A flat strip of sand, surrounded by fuel tanks and rusted sheet metal hangars. Shrubs and rolling hills. Ample opportunity to work in close to her new target and fix a transponder to a waiting aircraft's fuselage.

SEVENTY

"ZERO, HOLD."

Jen presses her back against a nearby guard shack. A sentry is inside, protecting the road leading to Varga's airfield. Knife in hand, she waits for a second update from Coco.

"Thirty seconds."

Jen keys her mic twice to acknowledge the transmission. Engines are grumbling in her direction. Large diesels, suspensions straining with heavy loads. Her team arrived in time to watch them trade pallets of cash for chemical tanks full of liquid cocaine. The cash was loaded onto a waiting An-12BP while the drugs were placed on the trucks.

Headlights splash onto the sand feet away from Jen. The sentry responds to a radio call. Hinges squeal on the road's security gate.

The trucks don't reduce their speed as they pass. Didn't have much to begin with. Fifteen miles an hour down the rutted desert road. They're troop transport vehicles with open beds. As they pass, she spots a narco sitting in the back of the final truck. An AK-47 crosses his lap. She quickly looks away from his eyes and focuses on the truck's bumper.

People sense eye contact. She's concealed in the shadows, but she doesn't need to give him a reason to take a closer look. As the truck grinds forward, the guard shifts. Squints in her direction. Her hands squeeze her backup B&T. The guard's hand brings a cigarette to his mouth. After a final drag, he flicks the butt into the road. He leans his head against the wall of the truck and exhales the smoke.

"They're about to disconnect fuel hoses and start preflight, Zero."

Another call. This one from Bingham. He's directly across the airfield with Coco and Gray. They're conducting overwatch, prepared to offer fire support. The An-12BP will take off soon. She'll need to get within reach before it does. She doesn't respond, checks the trucks instead. Fifty yards out and gaining distance. Clear to move.

She eases her back off the guard shack and rounds the corner. The sentry has already stepped inside. He drops into an office chair, back to the door, and cracks open a dirty magazine to finish out the remainder of his shift. He unfurls a three-page centerfold and raises it into the air. A naked woman almost falls into his lap.

Jen approaches silently and enters. The sentry grunts approvingly and adjusts the magazine's angle. The model's details are vivid as she jabs the knife into the sentry's neck, near the base of his spine. The blade sinks and she jerks it outward, severing both carotid arteries and his windpipe. She eases the dead body out of view.

"Sentry down."

Two more silhouettes pass the shack as Jen exits. Hastings and Animal. They hurry through the desert shrubbery, and she falls in line behind them. They close the hundred yards to the hangar quickly. A small contingent of guards remain on site, and they'll need to be removed before accessing the An-12BP.

Hastings activates his mic. "Head count."

Coco's reply is fast. "Count four. Two in the hangar, two working preflight."

Jen keeps pace with the men in front of her but steals a glance toward the craft. Pre-flight is almost over. The An-12BP's rear ramp is up, and the fuel hoses are disconnected. Cartel members are shining flashlights toward the aircraft, making sure the fuselage is intact.

The engines start firing as the team reaches the back side of the hangar. It's dilapidated, having spent too much time cooking in the desert sun. Sheet metal is pitted or rusted away. Paint chips speckle the sand. They progress to the rear entrance, find the rusted-out door completely removed and leaning against the wall.

Hastings halts their movement and they press their backs against the sheet metal. Lights are shutting off inside the hangar.

"We'll breach, set up synchronized fire positions. Go on my word," Hastings whispers.

"Got it," Animal replies, a suppressed MP7 held close to his chest.

"Right," Jen says softly.

Hastings peers around the edge of the door and finds the immediate vicinity clear. He moves out of cover, disappears inside the hangar.

Jen waits for Animal to move before following. She orients herself as she breaches the door. Clusters of fuel drums. Forklifts and spare pallets. A single cartel SUV parked in the center. Two armed narcos hanging against the open doors.

She dips into cover behind a mobile mechanic's station. A cart with drawers full of tools. Wrenches and screwdrivers strewn across the top. By the time she peeks around the edge, IR laser beams are cutting across the hangar. Hastings is on the far left, and his MP7's beam has settled on the target leaning on the driver's side door. Animal is in the center, his laser bobbing on the second narco's head.

Holding off on activating her laser, Jen stabilizes her B&T on the cart. No target—yet.

The An-12BP has disappeared entirely. Its journey to the rear of the airfield is almost complete. A third narco returns to the hangar, his preflight work complete. He presents a problem as he moves to the SUV's driver's side.

Animal's laser flashes twice, a signal to Jen that he's switching targets. She activates her laser where Animal's once was, while he resettles his beam on the third narco.

Hastings's call comes in. "Fire in three . . . two . . . one."

Three suppressed shots ring out in unison. Three dead bodies drop to the floor.

Jen depresses her mic's call button. "Moving."

The lasers are turned off, but Jen knows that her teammates are covering her approach. She sticks to the far-right wall, progressing toward the large open doors at the front. While she moves, she extracts a transponder from her kit. Magnetic panels on the bottom will allow her to attach it to the An-12BP's landing gear.

A call comes in from Bingham. "Aircraft is preparing to complete a U-turn. Remaining narco returning to hangar."

Jen lowers her rifle and clutches the transponder in her right hand. The narco is closing in. He hacks up dry desert air and fumes left behind by burning aviation fuel. Five feet, and her back stays pressed against the wall. Two feet.

The narco eclipses the hangar's gigantic doors and Jen runs past him. His hand makes a play for the AK-47 slung over his back. Hastings and Animal stitch a half dozen rounds across his chest before he can bury the stock in his shoulder. Jen doesn't break her stride or even bother looking back as he sags into the dirt.

She finds the aircraft parked at the runway's far edge. Forty yards away, propellers beat against the air. The engine power roars higher. Dust and debris swirl at its sides.

She's within ten yards as the craft picks up speed. The approach is challenging; she has to prevent having her head lopped off by the propellers. She ducks and passes under the left wing. The dust is blinding, and she squints to keep the closest landing gear in sight as she draws closer.

She sticks out her hand and leaps forward. Magnetic pads begin pulling, and the transponder snaps into position on the left landing gear. She falls on her knees and tumbles across the runway. By the time she settles, the craft has traveled a dozen feet, leaving her inside a tornado of dust. She attempts to make a visual confirmation of the placement but is forced to look away.

By the time Jen blinks the dirt out of her eyes, the craft's nose is catapulting into the air. After climbing several hundred feet, lights are activated on the fuselage, allowing her to gauge its flight path: southbound toward Colombia and a half dozen other drug trafficking hotbeds. She smiles, confident that she'll be seeing the aircraft again soon.

Seventy-One

Victor presses his feet to the floor of a bouncing Land Rover, pinning his back into the seat. He's on the rear passenger side, trying to keep his body in place as the vehicle speeds down a dirt road. Swaths of jungle roll by just feet away, and the driver fights the wheel to prevent the SUV from careening into a tree.

Speeds like these are unusual. But so is the situation.

As the Land Rover takes a curve, its wheels slip against the dirt. The driver eases off the gas and regains traction as the jungle falls away. Victor twists in his seat, finds a cone of reddish-brown dust wafting up into the trees. They made it to the airfield in record time.

Camouflaged hangars flank a large dirt landing strip. Vines and foliage are permitted to crawl across the hangars' walls and rooftops. Dirt and rust and mildew collect where vines will not grow. Natural cover from aircraft and satellites. Fuel tanks are sheltered and draped in camouflage netting.

Victor unbuckles his seat belt as the Land Rover speeds across the smooth runway. The danger of crashing has passed. It's time to confront a new one. Up ahead, hangar four's giant metal doors are open. Work has stopped. The men responsible for off-loading a recent flight are still clustered inside, waiting for him to arrive.

The Land Rover slows and veers through the open hangar door. Rubber is still squealing as Victor jumps out of the vehicle. Guards stand around a waiting An-12BP. AK-12s dangle in slings. Mechanics slap wrenches against their palms. They're transfixed, gazes pointed in a single direction. "Where is it?"

"Left landing gear."

Victor rushes past the lowered tail ramp. Pallets of cash are still secured in the cargo hold. Engines crackle as they cool and settle. Drawing closer, he spots a foreign object wedged between the landing gear's two struts. Black, rectangular, a device he's seen in his past. A transponder.

Its magnetic strips resist his efforts to break it free. With a violent heave he snaps it loose. On autopilot, he searches for the battery compartment. It's a Hail Mary pass—the device may not have transmitted its location yet. There's still a chance to protect the facility. The compartment is on the back side, sandwiched between the magnets. Screws secure the lid. "Get me a set of tools!"

A nearby mechanic rushes to fulfil the order while Victor further examines the device. *Status.* One of the most prominent buttons set against the transponder's LED screen. He taps it and finds the device is set to relay GPS coordinates every six hours. Just about the time the An-12BP touched down from Mexico City. He missed the squawk by thirty minutes.

Tools are no longer required. Victor spikes the transponder onto the concrete floor. Hunks of plastic and metal skitter in all directions. Batteries pop out of the device.

How? he wonders. Cameras line the craft's fuselage. Pilots would have observed a transponder being fixed to the landing gear. But flashlights could have been used to blind the cameras while one of Varga's people planted it. Could be vortexes of dust created by propellers obscured the action. Either way, he'll never know.

Victor looks around the hangar. Forklifts ready to offload Varga's cash. Vehicles waiting to transport the money through the jungle. Armed subordinates anxiously finger their weapons, certain that something serious is about to happen. "Keep the cash on board and refuel the craft."

Men begin to disperse, but Victor waves his hand, staying them. "Once you're finished, fuel every craft we have in our hangars. It's no longer safe here."

Seventy-Two

Despite fresh bandages and soiled combat fatigues, Jen is still functioning at full speed. She cuts across the TOC, located in the mansion's basement, and stops in front of Martinez's glass office wall. Grabbing a nearby dry erase marker, she adds another strike on the glass. *Three.*

She drops the marker and taps the face of her Submariner. "Number four is close!"

Martinez has a phone to her ear, and she places her hand over the handset before mouthing: *Thirty minutes.*

Jen doesn't reply. Instead, she heads back into the action. The Group is humming at full speed, generating intelligence assessments. All of their efforts center on a remote installation on an island called Isla De Sangayah off the coast of Peru. The hatches on Martinez's office wall correspond to the number of flights that have taken off since they've been observing the installation.

The Group's chance to interdict the site at peak capacity is fading by the hour, and Martinez is stuck navigating Langley's bureaucracy. U.S. military assets will also be required to secure a facility of this magnitude, and an entirely new chain of command has been layered onto the planning process. The potential presence of Russian forces further complicates matters, and that's not to mention conducting a raid on Peruvian soil.

"Ma'am! We've got fresh details," Sloane says, drawing Jen to her computer.

"Show me."

Sloane places pictures of Victor against images of a female Russian intelligence asset detained in Nogales. She was dressed in shabby traveler's clothes. Her hair was auburn, and dirt covered the freckles on her face. "This woman was captured twelve hours before radiation was detected on the U.S. border."

"The drugs were tainted right before they crossed. Guaranteed they'd hit the U.S. border," Jen says, reflecting on the incident that first brought Martinez to Mexico City.

"My thoughts too." Sloane produces a series of text messages between Victor Orlov and Alex Varga. Jen's work to capture the mobile switching center is still yielding fruit. "Looks like Victor tried to put an offer together to purchase the operative after she was captured."

Jen reads through the exchange. Varga was expecting to sell the intelligence operative to a rival agency. Russian officers are valuable prizes, and he wanted a price to match. She studies the two photographs on the screen. Victor and the female operative. She doesn't need reading glasses to make the next assessment. "They're twins."

Sloane adds a biometric overlay to the images of Victor and the female operative. "Identical. Bone structures have a ninety percent match. Only difference is gender, hair color, and skin tone."

"These two set this entire thing in motion." Jen takes a breath, processing the magnitude of the revelation. "Anything come back on 'em?"

"Langley doesn't have any records for Victor Orlov or his twin," Sloane says. "My guess is that they're sealed by Russia—or whatever their birth country happens to be."

Why would they do this to Varga? Jen wonders, further questioning the information she gained from the dossier. According to Varga, Victor is a member of a Russian organized crime syndicate called the *zakonny vladelets*, or "rightful owners." It's a sister organization to the *vory v zokone*, or "thieves in law"—Russia's most notorious mafia.

Both organizations festered and grew in communism's shadow. They offered loans and business opportunities to communities who were being crushed by authoritarian regimes. Many of these businesses were unsavory: liquor and prostitution and protection rackets. But they were lucrative.

While the *thieves in law* gained notoriety, the *rightful owners* faded into memory. According to Alex's telling, it's the source of their power. Investments were allowed to grow in peace, along with technological know-how. While they still participated in unsavory businesses, much of their cash was funneled into legitimate enterprises.

"Let me update you on what I've found in Peru," Sloane says as she returns to the satellite feed on her screen. It's locked on a small cluster of buildings surrounded by dense rain forest.

A red box highlights a single structure. It has a living roof, or green roof. Jungle fauna grows uninhibited atop the structure. In big cities, techniques like these add to a building's energy efficiency. In the jungle, it provides optimal camouflage. They note that every structure on the site makes use of the same techniques.

After heavy image refinement and some patience, Sloane was able to determine that it's a chemical plant—the likely source for Varga's designer narcotics. "Given what we've just discovered with Victor's twin, my guess is that there are no radiological elements on site."

Jen concurs. "Update Martinez."

Sloane jumps up from her desk and grabs the marker hanging on Martinez's glass. Several symbols are written on it. She strikes a giant red *X* through a trefoil, the universal symbol for radiation. But she does circle another, indicating potential hazmat elements.

Martinez gives a thumbs-up through the glass and begins relaying the assessment to Langley. Assault teams will react to the information accordingly.

Jen approaches Andrew, who is analyzing the base's technological elements. "Anything?"

Andrew zooms in on a structure at the center of the base. The roof of the single-story building is covered with networks of foliage. Red squares highlight well-camouflaged radomes and antennas. The installation's control center. "Our target is set up for long-range wireless communications."

"Have you been able to fingerprint local systems?" Jen asks, angling for a hack. She's concerned that they'll be destroyed before assault teams arrive.

Andrew frowns. "Remote access is out of the question. Given our timeline, we'll need physical access, ma'am. Comms traffic terminated"—he squints at the clock on his screen—"twenty-four minutes ago, and they were using radio hopping spread spectrum tools to protect transmissions. Satellite signals are also coming in, but they'd take serious time to crack."

"Keep working it," Jen replies, her mind already switching to her next task. "Won't be long until we've got an up-close view."

She heads to a nearby desk. Hastings and Major Bingham are sandwiched into a station of their own, working on an assessment of local forces. "How's it looking here?"

"Turning more into a ghost town by the hour." Bingham places several still satellite images on the screen. More red boxes ensnaring throngs of men. Some board military transport trucks. Others funnel up the loading ramps of waiting An-12BPs. "Looks like over fifty soldiers have evacuated the premises."

"They're abandoning weapons to save weight on their flights," Hastings adds. "Seems like personal effects are being left behind too."

Bingham produces an image of a pile of AK-12 rifles. Russian's modernized AK-47, chambered in the smaller 5.45 cartridge. They're stacked by the dozen, with spare magazines at their sides. "Won't be much of a fight here, Jen."

"You guys find any links to the Russian government?" Jen asks, needing to clear a final hurdle before relaying the information to Martinez. Given the radiation on the border, and what has occurred in Mexico City, the United States is well within its rights to hit the site. But any direct aggression between nuclear-armed nation-states could have serious consequences.

"Tail numbers on the craft don't link back to the Russian government," Major Bingham replies. "Aerial biometrics on the troop contingents show that they're of mixed ethnicity. Our guess is that they're contractors of some sort."

"They're also wearing irregular uniforms," Hastings says. "Safari shirts and basic cargo pants."

"It's all Russian kit though. Those AKs are the latest and greatest from the Russian military. Same with the An-12BPs."

"We can look past all of that," Jen replies. "The Russian military has been for sale since the Soviet Union fell. Small arms and aircraft don't rise to the bar of a Russian military presence."

She pauses, giving Bingham a tight, expectant smile.

Bingham stares back at her. Everything from her boots to her blonde hair is covered in dirt. Bloody bandages and a swollen hand. *She went through hell for them.* He doesn't have the heart to give her the news, so he simply shakes his head and looks back to his computer screen.

Jen tucks her thumbs into her belt and takes a second to compose herself. If she ever had a talent, it would be how fast she rebounds. She grinds her teeth before saying, "I'm clearing it."

Jen walks back to the wall, scratching an *X* through a large *RUS*. She circles another abbreviation: *ZV*, for the *zakonny vladelets. Rightful owners.* The Founders. Next, she strikes through a symbol for the hostages. Before she can turn away, Martinez throws up a sign to hold tight. To her relief, Martinez slams the phone back into the cradle and surges through the office door. "Please tell me we're rolling."

Martinez nods and grabs the room's attention with a whistle. "Everyone, pack your stations! We're proceeding directly to the *Vinson* where we'll link up with assault teams!"

Seventy-Three

The sirens are shrill enough to feel like they're penetrating the surgeon's skull. LED lights flash against whitewashed cinder block. A prerecorded message sounds out on a loudspeaker: *All personnel proceed directly to the airfield for immediate evacuation.*

Before exiting the infirmary, he rechecks what he prepared. All too easy to make a mistake amid the noise and chaos. Moreover, he's desperately short on sleep. Medical supplies are neatly organized on a stainless-steel table. His last round of antibiotics is prepared in a syringe. Same with multiple doses of pain medication. Handwritten care instructions are tucked under a spare IV bag. Setup complete—all that's left is to free Terrance Kline's caretakers. That will be a battle unto itself.

He conducts a final examination of his patient. His condition is dire. Kline has a high fever and his teeth are chattering, despite the thick blankets draped over his body. His pulse is low, and as the surgeon presses his hand into Kline's neck, it feels as if his heart could stop beating any second.

He inserts the syringe full of antibiotics into the already dripping IV and prays silently while he depresses the plunger: *Please bring the Americans soon.*

He tears through the exam room's curtain into the apartment

complex. The building is like a jack-of-all-trades. Rooms for the facility's ample guard staff. Personal offices for members of leadership. A small commissary and cafeteria. Even a jail—which is where he directs his stride.

It's the opposite direction he should be traveling. Guards rush past him, their pockets full of knickknacks they brought from home, spare changes of clothing tucked under their arms. Trash litters the hallways. Many drop what they're carrying and don't bother picking it up. They're worried that space on the evacuation flights will be limited, and it appears to be first come first served.

After descending two sets of stairs, the surgeon arrives at the second basement level. The prisoners are kept deep underground. A high-security jail door has been left ajar, and it gives him hope. Maybe the jailers have decided to flee, like the other guards. *That would make things easier*, he thinks, sprinting through the opening. One more right-hand turn and he'll be standing in the jail.

There are shouts, orders to stand and face the wall. Wrenching charging handles. Curses in return. The surgeon's hopes diminish further with a final shout from Victor: "Finish it!"

Rapid footsteps approach, and the surgeon has just enough time to duck into the jailer's office. He presses his back against the wall just as Victor passes by. The Russian is moving quickly, eager to conclude his business and make the flight to safety. The surgeon peeks out the door and finds Victor bounding up the stairs toward ground level.

Precious seconds remain, and he won't waste them. The surgeon breaks out of the office in a sprint. He rounds the corner to find two guards aiming their rifles into the individualized cells. While he's unsure of their names, their faces are recognizable. Both are large men from Estonia, capable of handling two American operators.

Despite their size and brooding natures, the surgeon runs toward both guards from the side. The surgeon became a man in Latvia's streets. He can handle himself, and he won't shy away from a scrap.

Bobby Hollice and Cameron Vinke stand with their chests out, chins held high. They stare down their executioners, who are pointing rifles at them. They'd wanted them to face the wall, avoid eye contact.

Makes the nightmares easier to sleep through. But the Delta operators won't give them an inch.

Bobby Hollice's eyes jerk toward the surgeon, and his executioner catches the glance. The guard shifts his rifle, but he's too late.

The surgeon's hands lock onto the guard's shirt, and he twists the guard, thrusting him into the cell bars, face-first. The rifle is pinned against the iron door, and Bobby Hollice grabs the weapon. Cameron Vinke jumps into action. He wraps his hands around the guard's head, uses it to try and snap a bar or two loose. The welds hold—surprising given the effort Cam puts into the test. The guard goes limp, and the Delta operators attempt to maneuver his weapons between the bars.

The surgeon maintains his momentum and careens into the second guard, who is frozen by the surprise attack. He forces the hulk into the nearest wall and pins his back to it, while keeping the rifle wedged between their chests. It's useless with the barrel pointed toward their feet. The surgeon delivers a hard right elbow, and the Estonian's head ricochets against the cinder blocks.

The Estonian's eyes are drifting, but he has enough sense to force his elbow between himself and his assailant. The surgeon assumes he's going to make a play for the rifle and discourages him with a knee to the gut. Air bellows out of the guard's lungs, and the surgeon feels like he's holding him up on his feet.

"Gun!"

The shout came from one of the Americans. *They have the first guard's weapons.* The surgeon steps back, expecting the Delta operators to take down the remaining guard. Instead, he finds a pistol muzzle leveled at his stomach. The Estonian's eyes are rage filled as he holds the pistol above its holster. The arm bar wasn't for the rifle; it was to give him space to draw and angle the weapon.

Two shots ring out.

The surgeon feels a piercing white-heat tear through his stomach. As he falls to the ground, the Estonian's head bursts into fragments.

Blood spurts out of the surgeon's mouth. Shock grips him, and he becomes overwhelmed with emotion. He'd come here for money; a young family is waiting for him back home. But a safe return seems too distant a possibility. He'd come to the wrong place, to work for the wrong men, and this punishment seems all too fitting. Both of his hands find their way to the wound, and he presses hard, attempting to stanch the blood flow.

"We can help you!"

The surgeon suddenly remembers why he came down here. *Help*, but not for himself. He looks up. Bobby's eyes are wide, almost begging, as his hands reach through the bars. *He will help.*

Keys hang from the Estonian's belt. He removes them, tosses them at Bobby's feet. The two Delta operators are out of the cell within seconds.

"Cover the hall," Bobby says before handing Cam his rifle and kneeling at the surgeon's side. His hands join the surgeon's in covering the wound. Rivulets gush past their fingers before trickling onto the floor. "We've gotta get you back upstairs."

"It won't be necessary," the surgeon replies, coughing up blood.

Bobby's face becomes suddenly heavy. "Can we help in another way? With the pain?"

"I'm not in pain," the surgeon lies. His head is getting light and there's little time left. "Kline is badly hurt." He pauses to cough again. "Hide until it's safe. Care for him until help comes."

Bobby falls silent. No more questions or requests. He'll figure out the rest from here. The surgeon has done enough, and a man's final moments should be peaceful. He squeezes the man, comforting him, reminding him he's not alone.

A final smile raises the surgeon's face. He'd been sad moments ago, but he's going to die certain he did his job. At least two men have been spared. His mind flashes to Victor, and he prays once more for Terrance Kline. *Please, let Victor write him off as dead.* But Victor Orlov is known to be a thorough man.

Seventy-Four

Peru

Sunset in the jungle does little to reduce the humidity. After an amphibious beach landing and a several-mile hike through the forest, Jen and a contingent of seventy-five Delta operators are nearing the installation. Another twenty-five are working their way toward the airfield.

Jen drops her gaze, checking the nav-board on her plate carrier. Right on top of the target, but she doesn't see anything but lush forest. She ventures several more paces and pushes apart a thicket of vines before nearly walking straight into a fence. Vines and leaves snake through the chain link and creep daintily across the razor wire above her head. Natural camouflage aided by the setting sun.

Hastings is just behind her, in command of Alpha element. Twenty-five men who will drive directly to the installation's control center once orders are given to breach. She'll break into the computers, if they haven't been bricked.

She checks her left, finds Bravo element stacking up farther down the fence. Breachers are already using bolt cutters to slice through the chain link. Bravo's shooters are covering every angle, focusing primarily on an apartment building twenty yards beyond—their intended target for the raid.

She activates her mic: "TOC, this is Zero. All elements are in place."

"Two minutes, Zero," Martinez replies, who is aboard the USS *Carl Vinson*, an aircraft carrier attached to Carrier Strike Group One. The *Vinson*, and its support elements, had been on training exercises off South America's coast, putting it in an optimal position to assist with the raid.

"Copy."

Animal approaches her position with bolt cutters and begins removing sections of fence. The work is fast, professional, and incredibly polished. Cutting through chain link may seem rudimentary, but getting into a target fast can save lives. He won't let Alpha get hung up at the starting gate.

Jen trains her 416 on the nearby apartment. Although five stories tall, the roof stops well short of the jungle's hundred-foot trees. Vines drip down from the green roofing and trace along the exterior. She flips her EOTech's three-times magnifier into place and finds a layer of honeycomb mesh shielding the windows. Prevents the sun from glinting off the surfaces, but it's also impossible to see through. Shooters could be waiting in ambush and she'd only know after the first round bites.

As she flips back her magnifier, the earth trembles underfoot. Birds clap out of trees and assemble into flocks before bolting toward safety. Howler monkeys grunt, scream, and rock branches of nearby trees. Two Black Hawks rip out of the tree line and take up overwatch positions. They're gunships packed with Miniguns and Delta snipers. The helicopters begin circling the compound's periphery, weapons ready to engage.

Go orders disseminate through the assault teams. Across the installation, dozens of operators initiate their breaches. A horde of barbarians flooding an unsuspecting village. Small explosives detonate. Sledgehammers smash through obstacles. Glass shatters. Shouts echo out as operators announce their movements.

Animal pulls open the fence, allowing Jen to enter what feels like an entirely new world. She's read more of Varga's dossier on the *zakonny vladelets*, or *rightful owners*. In his records, Varga referred to them as the

Founders. A name that morphed from the original after the Soviet Union fell. Communism was replaced with capitalism, and the rightful owners took absolute possession of what they'd created. That's when they became the Founders—men who built their empire from the ground up, and continued to expand upon that success.

This installation was their gateway into Mexico and North America. It's also her gateway into their world, and judging by the facility's exterior, there will be plenty to learn.

She advances closer to the apartment building, using the shadow cast by the setting sun for concealment. The jungle's humidity feels like a sauna. Every drop of moisture feels as if it's being leeched from her body. Gloves are sweat-soaked, like the blonde hair under her helmet. Salt stains are already forming on her plate carrier.

"Alpha One on you, Zero," Hastings says, stacking his assault team at her back.

Before Jen can acknowledge the presence, Bravo team's breacher smashes a sledgehammer into a nearby door. Operators begin filing into the apartment. Their movements are fast, methods are violent; the goal is to take control of the building quickly and crush resistance.

No gunfire yet. A good sign. She reaches the apartment and rounds the corner, proceeding farther into the compound. She spots the gray Land Rover that sped to the airfield moments before the transponder's signal disappeared. It is parked with several large military transport trucks. Trash and weapons are strewn across the jungle floor. The previous occupants stampeded out of here.

Despite the enemy's absence, the raid will be a success. Whoever occupied that Land Rover likely didn't have time to wipe away their fingerprints. Family photos will be forgotten in dresser drawers. At least some of the tech present on site will have information remaining on its drives.

Reaching the front of the apartment, Jen spots Alpha's target straight ahead. A squat concrete building that appears to be the site's command center. From ground view she confirms the antennas and radomes hidden in the foliage atop the single-story structure. Ominously, the doors have been left open.

To her right, Charlie element is assaulting the chemical plant. Pipes snake around the side of the building, painted in alternating browns and greens. Large chemical tanks and condensers surrounding the structure have taken on the same hues. Still no resistance. A relief, considering the building's toxic contents.

But instinct tells her that this is too easy. Something is off. She just hasn't found what it is yet.

"All elements, this is Bravo One, be advised: we have three lost eagles in custody."

"Bravo One, this is Zero, coming to you." Jen twists around, hardly able to contain her surprise. *Lost eagles.* Hostages. Three of them. Terrance and Bobby and Cam. It must be. She locks eyes with Hastings, seeing the same excitement. "Al, keep moving and secure our target. I'll link back up with you shortly."

"Got it, Jen," Hastings says as he advances Alpha toward the control center.

"Zero, Bravo One again. We've got the first floor secure."

Jen rounds the front of the apartment building, eager to confirm the three hostages' identities. This is the break she fought so hard for. "Zero is inbound through the front door."

"Make your first right. We're in the infirmary."

She follows the directive and finds the infirmary. Her stomach drops as she closes in. She hears shouting from inside. Medics reading off vital signs. Fever. Low heart rate. Smells of antiseptic lingering. "Zero coming in."

"Enter!" Bravo One shouts.

Medics surround an infirmary bed. They're frantic. Changing IV bags. Conducting examinations. Bobby and Cam are at the bedside, facing Jen, anguish on their faces. Terrance is the one who is hurt. She surges forward, trying to keep her emotions in check.

When she finally sees Terrance, she almost collapses on the bed. His skin is drained of color. Beads of sweat drip from his brow and his teeth are chattering. Medics have removed sweat-soaked blankets, revealing bandages that cover a wound in his abdomen.

Jen reaches for his hand and squeezes it hard. "Terrance! It's Jen! We're here for you, buddy!"

Unresponsive. Eyes don't even flutter at her voice. His skin is ghoulish and cold, despite the sweat. She keeps hold of his hand and looks to the medic. "What's his status?"

"Looks like a gunshot wound to the abdomen. Infection is bad, and he's got a high fever," he reports. "He's critical, ma'am. I can barely feel a pulse. We need to move him, now."

Jen watches as the medic performs a Babinski test on Terrance's feet. It's a reflex test. As the medic's thumb glides against the bottom of his foot, his toes don't move.

"Signs of spinal trauma," the medic says.

"We'll need to transport the patient carefully," a second medic adds.

Jen starts working the situation. "TOC, this is Zero. I've got one hostage in critical condition, and I'm requesting immediate evac. What's Zulu element's status?"

"Wait one, Zero."

Seconds pass. Jen looks at Bobby. Cam. They've still got some swelling on their faces, but they don't appear emaciated. Varga's men were rough, but the situation appears to have changed in Peru. "What happened here?"

"I don't know, ma'am." Bobby tries to check his emotions, but his eyes mist. The fight has been an intense one. Safety feels surreal and undeserved as he regards Terrance. "We got separated after our capture. There was a doctor. He just told us to keep him alive . . ." Bobby's voice breaks and trails off.

"Zulu is finished clearing the airfield, Zero," Martinez informs.

Jen orders a CASEVAC helicopter on station near the shoreline to proceed to the airfield and wait for the casualty. One of the gunships is tasked with securing the stretch of jungle between the airfield and the installation.

Finally, Jen addresses Bravo's leader. His MP7 is angled toward the ceiling, and he's just waiting on the word to move. "Peel off part of your element and proceed directly to the airfield. Suggest making use of an abandoned vehicle."

"Got it, ma'am." Bravo's leader turns to his team and says, "You boys know what to do. Let's get a litter set up."

Jen squeezes Terrance's hand once more before the medics converge on him. This could be their final goodbye, and the shock is hard to swallow. She leans toward Terrance, gets firm. “Better be squared away the next time I see you.”

“Ma’am.” One of the medics wedges between Jen and Terrance, preparing to transfer the patient. He grabs two corners of the bedsheet. With a nod, both medics heave and lay their patient down on a litter. He waits for his teammate to cross to the other side of the bed, and using the same coordination, they lift both ends simultaneously. “Moving.”

Jen doesn’t follow Terrance through the door. That’s all she can do—for now. Before she can refocus, a radio call does it for her. Hastings. “Zero, you need to get over here. We’ve got live tech.”

Seventy-Five

St. Petersburg, Russia

"That's our target."

A center screen stretches out in front of Anastasia Orlov, and Jen Yates is the object of focus. She locks her hands onto her hips. Adrenaline overrides the pain in her right shoulder—a lingering injury from Nogales. She's slender with auburn hair that trends closer to brown than red. Freckles decorate high cheekbones before collecting on the bridge of her nose. Her blue eyes are piercing, merciless.

She watches camera feeds from Peru. It's disappointing to be leaving the hostages behind, but Terrance Kline couldn't have been moved and was left for dead. The two Delta operators would have bullets between their eyes if not for bad fortune. Despite what they've seen, they're already afterthoughts. Something extremely important is about to occur.

American operators breeze through the camera feeds. Through the apartment. Between runs of pipe in the chemical plant. Around computer stations in the control center. Guns are raised and security postures are tight, despite the lack of resistance. No level of caution can shield them from the waiting threat—and the ending of a mission she and her brother started in Nogales. She has the honor of delivering the final blow, and she couldn't be prouder.

A nearby engineer pecks on his keyboard, then updates his superior in Russian, their native tongue. "Thirty seconds, Mrs. Orlov. The system's function is optimal."

Anastasia didn't need the update. The past twenty-four hours have been . . . spellbinding.

What she's watching is the merest taste of her success. Programs depicted on the center screen are powerful. Jen Yates is serving as the first live test subject. Predictive analytics software uses arrows to map her movements before they're made. Every time she enters a new camera feed, the center screen shifts without a prompt. It's effortless. Almost magical.

"Timing is important, ladies and gentlemen. We're going to make this one hurt," Anastasia says before searching for another status update.

She focuses on a secondary screen. Red lines are traversing the Pacific Ocean. Flights, a half dozen of them, are progressing smoothly. Each one is well past U.S. naval assets on Peru's coast. In truth, she's only concerned about one person: Victor. He's nearing safety, and it frees up the mental bandwidth she needs to complete her task.

Jen Yates exits the apartment. Arrows fan out in front of her. Red leads to a storage warehouse. Yellow for the chemical plant. A green one points to the command center. It knows where she's going before she does.

Impossible, Anastasia reminds herself, *but fun to imagine.*

"We're ready to proceed, ma'am," the engineer says.

"Hold!" Anastasia orders, waiting as Jen enters the installation's command center. Checkpoint crossed. Seconds grind on an LED clock. Once she's certain that the target is staying in place, the order is given. "Execute."

SEVENTY-SIX

CONTROL CENTER DOORS HAVE BEEN LEFT OPEN. POWER IS still surging. Surveillance equipment remains active. Someone, somewhere, is watching. If it weren't Jen's job to step into the breach, she wouldn't just turn and walk the other way—she'd run.

Her first glances around the control center don't reveal anything strange. Same as any other technology-based operations center. Large screens in the front of the room, likely to track flights or other logistics. Some have joysticks and other tools to control remote vehicles. Individual stations for analysts. Adjoining rooms for servers, with open trays of wires snaking along the ceiling.

Hastings stands toward the back of the room, where a senior officer typically monitors operations. Delta Force members are conducting searches. Movements are delicate as they open desk drawers or search under tabletops. Tripwires aren't the problem—it's the explosives they're attached to.

Hastings turns as she approaches. He'd been listening over the radio as she ordered a CASEVAC. "Bad?"

Jen shakes her head. "We're gonna need some luck."

"Sorry, Jen."

"Anything change in the room since you've occupied it?" Jen asks, needing to focus on the task ahead.

"No power fluctuations," Hastings replies. "Zero activity from the computers."

"Right." Feeling a twinge in her gut, Jen says, "Let's have nonessential personnel clear the room!"

Jen approaches a station, giving the operators time to clear out. Residents of the jungle have taken the open doors as an invite, and made themselves at home. A pair of red toucans are perched atop the desk, bobbing their heads, expressing their frustration at her proximity. She nudges them out of the way and places her laptop on the desk. "I'd advise y'all to head for the exit."

They advance their positions, stare at the laptop while the screen blinks on. "Guess that's a no."

After receiving a head count, Hastings says, "You're set, ma'am. I'll be standing by."

Jen thinks better of asking Hastings to leave. He'd probably deck her. And if she's being honest, his presence is comforting. She activates her mic: "TOC, we're starting our intrusion."

Martinez confirms the transmission while Jen hooks her laptop into the network via a USB cord. After fingerprinting the system, she finds *Porosha* guarding the servers. She wonders if Victor wrote it. Or maybe his twin sister, with the auburn hair. She beat it multiple times in Mexico City, and she's fixing to do it again. "Anne, we know the play here. Go 'head and run it."

Anne complies, accessing the tool that she previously used to bypass the base station controller's encryptions. The program runs . . . and runs . . . and runs.

"The encryption level has changed, Ms. Yates."

"Show me."

Anne displays the server's encryption method. Jen recognizes it instantly. It's called quantum resistant cryptography—specifically, lattice cryptography. It looks like a three-dimensional chessboard. Holographic blocks are stacked on top of each other. Each line of the lattice represents an extremely difficult mathematical equation. In order to access the system, all of these equations need to be solved simultaneously. It could take a computer like Anne days or weeks to solve this problem. It could also be downright impossible.

A message pops up on the laptop's screen: *Couldn't have done it without you, Ms. Yates. Goodbye.*

Alerts flash on Jen's laptop: *Intrusion attempt underway.*

Jen's hand seizes the USB cable, ripping it out of the port. The building's electricity is cut off. Computers die with a hum. Hastings goes on alert and swings his rifle upward, using the weapon mounted flashlight to scan the room.

"Zero, what just happened?" Martinez demands.

Words are trapped in Jen's throat. Neural circuits are lagging.

Cryptography like she just witnessed only exists in certain conditions. Never once has she seen it outside of an NSA laboratory. Incredible amounts of computing power are required to generate those mathematical equations. Demands like those require equal amounts of electrical power.

But she recognizes what she witnessed. Knows that it beat Anne and completely blocked her access attempt. Suddenly, Varga's words bubble up from her subconscious: *They sacrificed my cartel to bring you here.*

The Founders planted the radiation that lured Terrance and Bobby and Cameron into World Chem, where they were kidnapped and used as bait. Victor watched her hunt for her missing people, and while she did, he watched Anne too. All via the same systems she was working to hack. This was perfectly orchestrated for a single reason.

Jen Yates activates her mic: "The Founders have stolen our quantum technology."

Epilogue

Whitefish, Montana

One Week Later

The season's first snow has settled on the countryside. The type of soft powder that languishes in the pines and adds a slight bow to the branches. Granite rock faces have been scored with streaks of white. The air is pristine and tinged with sap. Cloudless skies above.

A magnificent day, but Jen is apprehensive.

She is returning to where her journey began. The cabin that was once home to the Technical Access Group she founded after retiring from the NSA. The trail she's walking winds through a narrow valley dense with pine trees. It terminates in a gulch surrounded on three sides by towering granite slabs: the ideal place to conceal a team of hackers. This trail has an almost overpowering familiarity, and not because she's walked it one hundred times before. She lived the worst day of her life in this valley, and she's never truly left.

It has been two years since the tragedy occurred. Until now, Jen wasn't sure she'd ever find the strength to return. But there's a newfound purpose driving her forward: to withstand new tragedies, the old ones need to be left behind. What was taken in Mexico City is weighing on her, and in order to shoulder that burden, she needs to confront what's waiting for her in this valley.

Terrance.

Someone she considers a brother. A title he would have shared with Harrison Lowe and Marcus Keen—both men members of the Technical Access Group she started here two years ago.

Terrance's condition is stable but precarious. Doctors are giving him a fifty-percent chance of survival, and he's in a medically induced coma to allow his overstressed organs time to recover. His spine is broken; his body is ravaged by infection. The surgeon saved his life in Peru, but it's worth wondering if he had the assistance of guardian angels.

When rescue teams found him, his ability to survive wasn't down to days, but hours. When he landed on the *Vinson*, he was on the edge. And he balanced on that same precipice all the way to Walter Reed Hospital. She was with him the entire time—they all were. Martinez. Andrew. Sloane. Their voices reminding him that he wasn't fighting alone.

Jen knows better than to assume it was the moral support that kept Terrance Kline amongst the living. Man's more stubborn than a mule. He'd forgo death just to brag about outsmarting the Grim Reaper. With an attitude like that, his chances of survival rocket from fifty percent all the way to one hundred. That's exactly where she has it pegged, at least.

Anne's loss also weighs on her. Post mortems have been conducted on the base station controllers taken from Varga. Victor Orlov did indeed have back doors installed on them, and he used them ruthlessly. What's worse is that there's no way to accurately gauge the damage Orlov caused.

She is certain of one thing. Well, two things actually.

While Orlov didn't *steal* Anne, per se, he was able to study the quantum computer. Observe in real time how it functioned and attacked an enemy's system. Like a scientist, Orlov threw her and her Group into a petri dish and watched every movement through a microscope. Knowledge like that could help him generate a playbook of sorts.

Tools to protect his own systems from a computer like Anne. Abilities to take the offensive, if necessary.

That leads her to the second thing: There's a strong likelihood that the Founders have near-quantum, or full-quantum technology. It's virtually guaranteed that rival nation-states are working on their own quantum programs, but none of them have been able to crack the code. Not the way Andrew Xiao did at MIT.

As Jen walks and reflects, she's unsure if she believes that a private entity has power like that. By all accounts, Russia is behind in the race. Second best to China, with a generous gap between the two. That a private Russian entity possesses such potent technology . . . She shakes her head in disbelief at the thought. She'll only learn the extent of what Victor Orlov and the Founders have accomplished when she sees it for herself.

That's the fight ahead. And she has no idea what she's walking into.

She reaches a line of trees that seemingly stop in an effort to pay respect to what's ahead. She takes a moment to collect her breath, scared that it will be snatched away again. She hitches the hunting rifle higher on her shoulder and adjusts the pistol in her holster. Time to see what's left of her past life.

Jen steps into a clearing. Remnants of her log cabin are directly ahead of her. Charred beams have settled at odd angles, mounds of snow collecting on top. To her right, she finds the garage's mangled frame. It once contained servers and backup power generators. Her greenhouse—one of her favorite things about this place—is now a heap of folded panes of glass.

Tears are tough to restrain, but she works at it and eventually settles for misted eyes. Pain she's been carrying these years is tiresome. Relenting, she allows herself to feel the horror of what transpired here.

And then something magical happens; she begins to remember the good in what this place was. Precious memories she made with Harrison and Marcus.

My God, there were so many great times.

Laughter is nearby as she walks to a stump in front of the cabin. It was where they chopped firewood—a daunting chore. The little arguments, tactful manipulations, and careful negotiations that occurred between the Technical Access Group members have her chuckling as she sits. No one wanted to chop wood, and they'd do just about anything to get clear of the task.

She removes her hunting rifle and pack. Four shot glasses are inside the pack, along with her father's famous homemade moonshine. A prized commodity during her time in the cabin. She lines up the shot glasses beside her on the stump, and places the bottle in the snow. Best served chilled.

While she waits, she surveils the countryside. There's a plateau called the Eagle's Nest overlooking the cabin. It's perched on the rock face directly behind it. It was one of her favorite hikes. It's also the place she fought Major Lou Zou, People's Liberation Army.

He entered this valley to settle a score and came pretty damn close to succeeding completely. The prized 10mm 2011 that he gave her is on her hip; this journey would have been incomplete without it. If his soul is lingering here, she's certain he'd be happy to see it with a fresh coat of oil on the blued steel.

Jen reaches for the moonshine, which is now chilled. She pries off the cork and pours four shots. For her. For Harrison. For Lou. For Marcus—a man she'd swore she'd never forgive. What he did to her was once unfathomable, but she's found the maturity to understand her role in his decision. The pressure she induced. The terror he felt as a result of her leadership.

This trip is partly about forgiveness, and as his shot levels off, she feels a fullness in herself that words can't describe.

Grabbing her shot, she clinks it into the three others.

"We'll walk these mountains together again one day." She raises the glass in salute and downs the shot.

Jen rests her empty glass on the stump, surveys the rugged landscape. Finds the inescapable beauty in it. More importantly, the peace. This gulch is home. Truly.

She stands to take a short lap around the clearing, but a satellite phone rings in her pack. Only one person with that number: Martinez. Her boss, who managed to escape the OIG board that was threatening to derail a stelar career.

After what was uncovered in Peru, Langley couldn't prosecute

Martinez. Her success, and the experience she gained while achieving it, was considered too vital to what will be one of the Agency's most important investigations.

Jen grabs the phone and extends the antenna. She's worried as she answers the call. "Is everything okay with Terrance?"

"His condition hasn't changed, but that's a good thing at this point."

Jen takes a breath, relieved. The frigid air raises her skin, and she smiles. "I'm glad I came here, Gabby."

"I'm glad you did too," Martinez replies. There's a pause. "Hastings's paperwork cleared. Same with the others."

Jen nods. Al Hastings and his element are now Special Activities Center officers. Qualified hitters who will assist her and Martinez with dismantling the Founders. "Bet they're itching to work."

"They are—and so am I, for that matter. We've got a lot of hits from Peru: fingerprints, hair, and skin samples. There's a list on my desk with about thirty names on it."

"Sounds like my vacation is over."

"You got a solid forty-eight hours. I'm officially jealous."

Jen laughs. "Your turn next. I'll see you at Langley tomorrow morning."

"See you then, and safe travels."

The call ends. Jen returns the phone to her pack and throws the straps over her shoulders. The sling of the hunting rifle follows. She takes the jug of moonshine out of the snow and places it on the stump next to the shot glasses. "I'll be back soon."

Electric air follows her as she retraces her path into the wilderness. Spirits she came to honor accompanying her on the journey. Two years. She wasn't sure she'd ever have the courage to return. Now that she has, she's tapped into a strength she thought she'd lost. She'll need it if she's going to survive the challenge ahead.

Want More Jen Yates?

Sign up for my email list to receive a free copy of SEVERANCE NOTICE.

Anastasia Orlov is one of Russia's deadliest killers, and the organization she represents is equally ruthless.

When that same organization sends her to Mexico, it isn't for the beaches. Armed with a weapon with the potential to kill hundreds of people, Anastasia sets out to betray one of Mexico's most vicious cartels.

But Anastasia has a past, and her mission takes a serious turn when it catches up to her.

Caught between two worlds, Anastasia must not only fight to survive, but escape Mexico before becoming one of the names on an extremely long list of casualties.

Witness the beginning of a global conspiracy that will ensnare the U.S. government's brightest thinkers, and its deadliest assassin: Jen Yates.

Click here to download:

https://dl.bookfunnel.com/twqcr7quta

Also by J.W. Clay

The Jen Yates Series:

Code of War

Code of War: Cyber Kinetic

Code of War: Partition Theorem

Code of War: Zero Day

The Founders:

Severance Notice

Unknown Variable

Siege Network

Forthcoming Title

The Forsaken Sons:

Forsaken Future

Forsaken Son

Forsaken Road

Forsaken Brand (Forthcoming)

About the Author

I've worked in chemical plants, industrial refrigeration, and everything in between. Heck, I've even done a couple of film stunts (got a bum knee to prove it). The journey has been as fun as it is inspiring! When I'm not pushing the pen, I'm on the range, under a barbell, or rewatching the first season of *True Detective*.

Jen Yates is my main squeeze. You can find her "ripped from the headlines stories" in the *Jen Yates Series* and the *Founders Series*. Her books are as fast-paced as they are thought provoking!

If you love the *Sons of Anarchy*, check out James Hayes and the Forsaken Sons. I'd say the books are made for T.V., but they're too crazy for the mainstream. Once you pick them up, you won't be able to put them down!

Want to stay in touch? Sign up for my email list. I'll keep you up to date on new releases, exclusive content, and anything else related to my work.

Made in the USA
Middletown, DE
04 January 2025